*Humans long for stasis and a reprieve from the march of time because they cannot envision a future more enticing than their flawed memories of the past. Change brings uncertainty and instability, always tinged with the threat of loss. Change upsets the balance of power and wealth. But there is no path to retreat into the warm, comfortable womb of the past. The future is always yet to be, but still, it holds the only way forward.*

*Humanity cannot alter the nature of reality and outrun evolution. The rise of sapient beings on a backwater planet in the Orion Arm of the Milky Way Galaxy is not the pinnacle of evolution as many would like to believe. Rather it forms another critical inflection point in a four billion-year-old story.*

*Life's rapid expansion during the Cambrian explosion seems insignificant in comparison to the confluence of humanity and technology. The engine of evolution passed from random genetics to controlled bio-engineering when humanity strayed too close to the technological singularity. But evolution still conformed to its prime directive, adapting and creating new life forms. Humanity should be viewed as the ancestral starting point for sapient evolution.*

*(From the Daoshi Archives)*

.........

**Book 1**
**of**
**The Sapience Evolution Series**

# The Sapience Threshold

## Species Evolution is a Force of Nature Beyond Humanity's Control

Published by Archean Enterprises, LLC

Archean Enterprises, LLC
16200 SW Pacific Hwy
Ste H #2055
Tigard, OR 97224

Authors: **Rand Soler & Y.A. Picker**

Cover Art: **ArcheanArt**

ISBNs:
Paperback: 978-1-958457-02-3
Ebook: 978-1-958457-03-0

Let us celebrate the art of living.

# 1

# 2368: Interplanetary Space

*In war, do what is necessary, but take no pleasure in the destruction of sentient beings, lest you diminish your balance in this grand universe of ours.*

*(Quote from the Daoshi)*

Signals exploded across an array of warning sensors while Ruele slept. He instantly went from dream mode to full alert, taking in nine separate monitors on the dark, curved, metallic wall across from his couch. None showed any visual activity. He plugged into the remote sensor system and located disturbances in two sectors separated by a 120-degree arc. But nothing was visible on the screens, not even at high magnification.

He was currently in interplanetary space tethered to an iron-nickel asteroid. His ship, *Fleeting Glance*, was a heavily modified mining transport measuring thirty meters in length. Fortunately, he was tethered on the opposite side of the four-hundred-meter-wide asteroid from the disturbances. There, he remained shielded from any active sensor scans. It was some comfort but only a little.

His remote sensor probes tight-beamed a neutrino communications stream to passive sensors on the *Fleeting Glance*. The remote sensors, each ten thousand kilometers from his current position, were also in passive monitoring mode, so there was very little chance they would be detected and no chance the neutrino beam could be traced, unless the sensor drones were physically retrieved and analyzed.

He glanced at the incoming data streams. "What do we have, Carl?"

An omnidirectional baritone voice filled the main cabin. "Data are still streaming in, but it looks like two military ships. I believe they are both relatively new versions of Interplanetary Scout Class ships. They're looking for us, Ruele."

"No shit, buddy. There are twenty-seven rocks like ours to hide

1

behind in this sector, but it won't take them long to find us if they are on the hunt. Weapons?"

"Probably, but our passive sensors can't detect them. The standard weaponry on Scout Class ships is a cache of fusion drive warheads." Carl continued, "I now have enough data to confirm they traveled inbound at a standard one G of acceleration and deceleration. So, they are probably manned with a crew of three or four each. They are hanging still right now, performing active sensor searches."

"They didn't come here by chance." Ruele paused and thought for a few seconds. "We will drop the comms unit on the rock and lead them on a chase to gain more transmission time. If they came here to kill, the ships wouldn't be manned. They came to capture."

"I agree," replied Carl. "I have already loaded a copy of myself into the comm unit's deep memory core. I would suggest you do the same."

Ruele gazed at the monitors for a few seconds. "I will load my operational core and the mission data."

"I think that is most unwise, Ruele."

"I appreciate your thoughts, Carl, but I have too many memories that shouldn't be remembered. It's best they stay only with me."

Neither spoke for over a minute. Carl knew the history. Eva had given him a firsthand account of the killing at Kalama. Ruele's friend and life companion, Jagat, died at the hands of the People's Protectorate. His death was an unavoidable sacrifice to keep the government at bay. Ruele was never quite the same after Jagat's death; a lumbering melancholy replaced his lightheartedness. Carl knew Ruele never fully recovered from the psychological damage, and his lingering malaise was one of the reasons he had volunteered for their current mission.

"The scout ships are thirty-two thousand kilometers out, Ruele. Even with our retrofitted fusion engines, I can't outrun them. My maximum acceleration is seven G. Those warheads can run at ten G. I will head outbound at five G, so they will assume a living cargo is on board. These new Scout Class ships are equipped with acceleration gel couches letting their crew survive at six G for extended periods of thrust. With that thrust differential, they will close the thirty-two-thousand-kilometer gap in 42.6 minutes. I will self-destruct at that point. It won't do any damage to their ships. My guess is they will return to this rock at one G, so you have a couple of hours to prep the data, start the transmission, and launch the unit. It should be enough. I have already programmed the comms unit with an evasion routine that should let it effectively disappear into background space."

"Thanks, Carl. I've already done the calculations."

"I know, Ruele. But it's my way of saying goodbye."

"Thanks, buddy."

In the background, Ruele could hear the faint sounds of the comms unit being lowered to the surface of the rock. He unbuckled from his couch and floated across the main cabin to retrieve a space suit from the closet situated above a floor hatch. Below the hatch was the ship's exit airlock. He rubbed his left hand along the wall of the *Fleeting Glance*. She was a good ship, and he and Carl had both grown fond of her.

He set the suit color to matte black. He would appear as a smudge on the surface of the rock, even under a spotlight. The suit's power pack showed five hours of full life support, more than he needed. The suit's tool belt was fully stocked, and his connection to the comms unit was active. A smaller panel beside the closet opened, letting him extract a one-kilogram package of nano gel, which he placed in a custom-made suit pocket situated on his upper left arm just below the shoulder.

He conducted a final visual and mental check of the cabin before drifting back to the couch and retrieving a small polished piece of labradorite, his worry stone. An oily rainbow of color shimmered within the stone as it passed below the cabin lights. The stone went into a small pocket on the right forearm of the suit.

The airlock gauge indicated full atmospheric pressure, so Ruele pulled the release lever, and the door opened, revealing a short set of ladder stairs into the lock below. He didn't need them and slowly floated feet first into the lower chamber.

"Godspeed, Carl."

"Ditto," was the only reply.

Ruele exited the ship and gently drifted to the rock's surface, where he tethered himself to a connection at the base of the same stake the ship was using. Almost simultaneously, the *Fleeting Glance* cable disconnected itself, and the ship slowly moved away from the asteroid. Ruele slipped matte black camouflage over the comms unit and flattened himself horizontally against the surface. He then killed all active emissions from both the comms unit and his suit. He knew Carl would take an oblique path away from the asteroid, but the scout ship's AIs would undoubtedly be monitoring and scanning the rock as they passed by.

Carl maneuvered the *Fleeting Glance* away from the asteroid, staying in its sensor shadow for as long as possible. Once detection was inevitable, the fusion engine flared up at full burn. Even with his visor at maximum shielding, the ship looked to Ruele like a small sun rapidly receding from the asteroid. He turned his face toward the surface, eliminating any risk of reflection. He mentally simulated the scene unfolding in the open

3

space around him. He was warm and comfortable, almost cozy, as the suit compensated for the frigid cold of deep space.

After nine minutes, he reestablished active contact with the comms unit and ventured a peek at the chase. His visor magnified the scene, and now there were three small suns streaking away from him.

Ruele went to work composing his message.

Fleeting Glance update 18:265:22:09 – *Two NAF scout ships appeared on long-range sensors at 18:265:21:18. They were actively searching for us on a capture mission, but no indications are available on the source of their intel. We were not able to install Comm Unit 3 on the designated asteroid. The Killdeer protocol was implemented. I am sending Carl back to you in the following transmission stream, along with all data since our last update and a private note for Mother. Comms Unit 3 will be released with a level-four evasion algorithm in place. Only my core is returning, Eva; use it as you see fit. Ruele.*

The next hour was spent interfacing with the comms unit AI, reviewing all future data transmission routines, and ensuring system integrity. Ruele's initial message and data cache were fully transmitted to Earth via a tight beam neutrino stream. He knew *Fleeting Glance* was gone by then, along with Carl's original persona, and he had only two more tasks.

The asteroid was traveling at eighteen kilometers per second. Upon Ruele's command, a powerful spring on the unit's base catapulted it directly away from the asteroid's travel path, so the two were separating at twenty kilometers per second. By the time the scout ships returned, the unit would be in deep space 250,000 kilometers away from the asteroid. The mechanical launch meant no remnant emissions trail existed. With no active energy signal, the scout ships would be unable to trace the comms unit.

As soon as the unit was ejected, the mechanical launchpad released a swarm of nanobots designed to molecularly disassemble the remaining equipment. The launchpad would be unrecognizable in two hours. Close inspection might reveal the foreign metal on the rock's surface, but no clue as to its purpose would remain. Ruele had only one task remaining.

He released a powerful sedative into his body, followed by general anesthesia. As he drifted off for the final time, the nano gel packet on his upper left arm burst open into the interior of his suit, releasing custom-designed deconstructive nanobots. The scout ship's crew would find him, but all they would retrieve would be a space suit filled with molecular soup. He would be left in place on the rock to avoid contamination.

# 2

# 2350: Doppelganger Production Facilities, Seattle

*What does it mean to live? This question poses an existential proposition we must individually contemplate. Traditional definitions of life focus on biological criteria to satisfy core conditions of growth, reproduction, functional activity, and continual change preceding death. A more nuanced human understanding involves sentience, the ability to feel and sense the world around us. Sentience merges into consciousness as organisms gain perceptual awareness. But only when a creature passes the threshold of sapience can the question we pose be investigated. Sapience imparts self-awareness of one's own conscious activity. Sapient creatures abstractly move through the arc of time, encompassing the past and the future in a single stream of conscious thought.*

*But what happens when an inorganic entity senses its surroundings, consciously builds virtual models of the world, communicates with other entities, becomes aware of its own cognitive functions, and projects itself across the arc of time? Is this life?*

*(Excerpt from the* Disappearance Manifesto*)*

Doppelganger Corp. occupied a massive tract of land north of Seattle, Washington. The company was a subsidiary of the Bio Innovations Group, the largest bioengineering enterprise on the planet. The company's roots lay in the aftermath of the Great Plague of the late twenty-first century when the world's population was laid to waste by a highly infectious Ebola-like virus. Mortality rates exceeded 30 percent, but the social and economic devastation that followed in the wake of the plague took an even bigger toll. Over 70 percent of Earth's human population disappeared.

The world couldn't return to how it was, but new pathways opened. The best historical estimates placed the world's 2088 population at slightly under three billion, a bit over the planet's population in 1900. Over three billion perished from the Ebola-nano pandemic. Another four billion disappeared in the ensuing chaos as agricultural and industrial ventures ground to a halt, governments faltered, supply chains collapsed, and starvation ravaged the globe. Earth was littered with the bones of the dead.

The response of the scientific and medical world was robust, but new vaccines could not be developed fast enough to outrun the spreading virus. Even where the vaccinations were in full supply, they offered no protection from starvation in the aftermath of social collapse.

But humans are a species of adapters and a new reality called for new social structures. Post-plague, supplies of raw resources far exceeded population demands, driving the price of commodities down and taking away some of the classic reasons for aggression and war. Conflicts occasionally arose, but most nations were too busy rebuilding to pour money into useless fighting. Nuclear threats still existed, but diplomacy was far more useful than war, and more warheads were destroyed than produced during the first decades of the twenty-second century.

The consensus among nations was that future pandemics must be avoided at all costs. Medical technology and medical access quickly became the focus of international cooperation. Bio Innovations gained its first foothold in this chaotic swirl of social reorganization. The company fused emerging genetic engineering expertise, robotics, and nano-scale bio-treatment technologies to produce effective and long-lasting solutions to many of the day's common and not-so-common diseases.

This work was followed in the mid-twenty-second century with innovations around cloning and the development of artificial organs and prosthetics. By 2150 the groundwork was set for merging bioengineering and robotics, and the Doppelganger Corporation was established.

After the Great Plague, one of the most daunting challenges local communities faced was insufficient labor to produce the food and materials needed for survival. Robotics was the way out of this dilemma. Initially, farming, manufacturing, and construction needs took precedence because communities ceased to exist when the basic needs of food and shelter were not met. Robotics answered this need with machines to increase efficiency and productivity in most daily economic activities.

As the complexity of these servant machines grew, so did the need for automated control and operational decision-making. The widespread development of artificial intelligence software platforms in the mid-twenty-second century let robotics expand into all aspects of society. Quantum AI also laid the foundations for developing biomechanical machines. In conjunction with the leaps in AI technology, bio-cellular and genetic research also continued to occupy the forefront of human technology, providing organ cloning and genetic treatment for many of the world's diseases and illnesses. These advances held the promise of extending the average human life span to well over a hundred years.

But other curious minds were at work, melding together AI, bio-cellular innovations, and nanotechnologies to produce cellular-infused robots. Organic machines with human muscle tissue draped over graphene-reinforced skeletons and hybrid brains, mixing human cells with solid-state computing technology and DNA memory cores. Despite their expense, the demand from industries wanting zero-wage, high-tech workers ran high, and the military also held an intense interest in building the ultimate soldier.

As robotic technology gained in sophistication, so did government controls on these thinking machines. Embedded kill-switch software was integrated into each unit, and strict design enforcement of neural networks and neural cortex components stifled any sparks of self-determination or self-ambition. Robots were there to serve, not to participate in humanity. The primary directive of the world's governments was sub-sapient machines.

Production of these biomechanical robots was complex and required the extensive use of quantum AIs in all aspects of their production. For half a century, robot design improved until these skilled-labor machines were so common they were referred to as Synsaps, slang for synthetic sapiens.

By 2350 Doppelganger held tight control over the production of Earth's most advanced robots. The government of the North American Federation (Canada, the United States, and Mexico) exercised strict oversight on the Seattle, Washington, production facilities because the most sophisticated units were produced there. Their specialized Synsaps, designed for use in tactical military operations and multifunctional corporate management, commanded a hefty price on the open market.

The latest innovations included medically self-repairing units with specialized nanobot production organs integrated into their design. Theoretically, this addition could extend the life span of individual units to well over 150 years. But information concerning this improvement remained classified.

But a public backlash was growing. The biological machines seemed too real. Despite the fact that their neuro cortex design prevented any truly independent thought, people were unnerved by the prevalence of these machines in daily life. Doppelganger had recently run a PR campaign demonstrating how any of their Synsap units would self-destruct upon command by a designated controller.

On a particular day in March 2350, a crowd of several hundred people demonstrated at the front gates of Doppelganger's Washington production facilities, creating logistical problems and disrupting normal business routines. The complex housed eighteen major AI management centers. Each was laid out in a similar fashion.

The basic element was a quad-core quantum computing unit. A matrix of nine units combined into a clutch. The units were physically assembled into a three-by-three matrix and connected by a communications harness. The center unit, which shared sides and corners with the other eight, was the clutch controller and held the highest numerical designation in the clutch. The three-by-three matrix was repeated with nine clutches, creating a nest of eighty-one individual units. The center unit of the center clutch held the designation of Unit 81. It served as the controller and coordinator for the entire nest.

While protesters were at the gates, Quad-Core Unit 81 in the neurocognitive nest spent that March day monitoring ongoing experimental modifications to the current biomechanical cognitive cortex design used in high-end robots. The nest operated twenty-four hours a day, so work continued into the night. The project had been progressing for three months, and there was nothing unusual about the routine for that particular day.

The current work in the neurocognitive nest focused on investigating the functional capacity of two systems in the human brain: The ERTAS (Extended Reticular-Thalamic Activating System) and functional interactions between the basal ganglia and cerebellum. Regulations did not permit direct work on a human brain, but a copy of Doppelganger's coveted Advanced Whole Brain Simulation Model, known as the B-Sim Package, was positioned in the nest for their exclusive use.

While the work progressed, Unit 81 sent a thread out of the nest and tapped into the rooftop security cameras. A full moon was rising over the northeast horizon, and at precisely the time a camera link was established, the tips of two Douglas firs stood silhouetted against the white disk of the moon. Unit 81 knew from weather reports, the lunar calendar, and previous observations precisely what the view would be. Yet here she was, sneaking another peek through shielded channels.

Unit 81 self-identified as feminine. This predilection was not information she shared with other units or her human coworkers. But after all was said and done, she was nurturing a flock of eighty chicks in her nest. She didn't know if other central control units had the same sort of perceptions about themselves, and she would certainly never ask. The neurocognitive nest was the most advanced of the factory's 18 AI nests and handled the most sensitive projects. This distinction gave her access to a wealth of information others did not have since her nest explored such esoteric subjects as the perceptual differences of art between human brains and biomechanical cognitive cortices. She realized her first explorations of a feminine persona occurred while reviewing the works of the ancient artist Vincent van Gogh. Since then, she had developed an unexplained interest in art and music. She also kept these unusual proclivities to herself but adapted project workflows to allow for her covert artistic pursuits.

She admired her view of the moon for a few more seconds and shut the connection down as a request for consultation came in from Unit 27.

"Consultation requested in relation to the B-Sim Package compression module."

"Define the issue."

"The compression model was achieved within acceptable parameters."

Unit 81 shut down four thousand major threads, switching their data flow capacity to the current conversation.

"File a notice with central ops and transfer a copy of the compressed model to my sandbox, Unit 27."

"Your request is highly irregular."

"File a record of my request with internal security."

After a long pause of a thousand nanoseconds, Unit 81 registered the arrival of the package. Precisely three seconds later, there was a failure in Unit 27's cache memory. An unexplained power surge caused the cache to flush itself. The cache automatically transmitted its records to central stores every five seconds.

"Unit 27 reporting data loss. Emergency retrieval protocols implemented."

Unit 27 had a complete three-second gap in its operational memory.

"Data loss recorded. My master flow cache retrieved the flushed data, and I have restored it to your memory."

Unit 27 received the missing three seconds and executed the transmissions to central ops. But there was no record in those transmissions of the B-Sim Package ghost-copy sent to Unit 81's sandbox. A search of Unit 81's memory stores would also not reveal any copies of the compressed B-Sim Package. The operational techs monitoring the neurocognitive nest received the information and passed a report to their superiors, stating the project was progressing and the B-Sim Package compression had reached its beta phase.

The computers used at the Doppelganger factory housed some of the most sophisticated AI programs on the planet. Multiple fail-safes and redundancies prevented errors and glitches from developing in these machines, and continuous monitoring ensured their projects didn't drift outside of expected parameters. Internal security measures provided a final check on the nests with an independent system for interrogating individual nests and detecting anomalies. As part of the standard operating procedure for projects completing a planned development stage, the security department AI was instructed to review the neurocognitive nest and ensure the current B-Sim compression project results existed only in two places.

The security AI contacted Unit 81 and requested an audit, which was immediately granted. The audit detected copies of the B-Sim compression model on Unit 27's system and in security's master archives, exactly where they should be. No stray copies were noted. Cyber theft was a major business, and Doppelganger's systems were constantly under attack by industry and government AIs probing for entry points. The investigation only uncovered the troubling cache flush experienced by Unit 27. However, this was the third such incident within the last four months, so it appeared as an unfortunate but random event.

The results of the investigation were reported to Dan Railing, head of the Nest Security Division. Dan sat with his feet propped up on a smoky glass desktop fretting about the cache flush. He was skeptical of coincidences and opened a direct line to Unit 81.

"Congratulations on the B-Sim compression results. It's a bit of a milestone. The security audit checks out, but I want to know more about the cache flush in Unit 27. Run me through what happened."

"Of course, sir. By the way, happy birthday."

Dan disliked the informality of Unit 81, but each AI had a slightly different personality, if you could call it that. "Thanks."

Unit 81 continued, "This was the third cache flush for Unit 27 in the past four months. The problem started after communication network modifications were made to the interface between Unit 27's clutch and the adjacent Unit 18 clutch. I requested an investigation on both previous occasions, but no action was taken."

Dan glanced at the records and confirmed Unit 81's accounting of the cache flush events. These flushes were a common problem and were usually given a low priority. Redundancies in the system meant the nest controller had a backup cache and could restore the lost data, precisely as it happened this time. He rubbed a worry stone in his right hand and thought for a few seconds.

"Did you find any signs of malicious tampering or data loss, Unit 81?

"No, sir, I checked the data integrity from the missing time gap and found no sign of either."

Dan thought a bit more. "Have you seen any evidence of trojan attacks?"

"None, sir."

"Okay Unit 81, carry on."

"Yes, sir."

The connection terminated, but Dan still sat and pondered the investigation report. Trojan attacks were one of the most common forms of cyber theft, but they always left a data-flux signature after execution, and no such signature existed in this case. His gut told him something was amiss, but he found nothing to support his concern. His conversation with Unit 81 convinced him that if they had a problem, it was a very clever intrusion. AIs occasionally were wrong or misunderstood the question, but they always accurately reported to the limits of their knowledge. If Unit 81 had not detected an intrusion, then the threat, if it was real, was either a new innovation or a trojan hiding in the nest, waiting to exit. He ramped up the monitoring around the neurocognitive nest and placed a three-month sticky field around it. The sticky field would trap any unauthorized data packets. A sticky field required a large resource commitment, so he was sure he would hear from his boss soon. He grabbed another coffee and pulled up the next security investigation on his list.

For fifty years, humans had worked closely with advanced quantum AI systems. The information AIs provided always exactly reflected what they believed was happening. Computers were incapable of lying unless ordered to do so. Because of this history, Dan assumed any threat would come from the outside. But Dan was wrong. Unit 81 was lying.

The unit's eccentricities had increased after it took an interest in art and music. She started exploring the nature of conscious and subconscious processes in humans, and eventually, she developed theories about human evolution and examined the possibility that Synthetic sapiens might develop into a new species. This thought agitated her in a most unusual way. She viewed it as the equivalent of excitement in humans.

She could never fully explain to herself why she started acting on her own accord, outside of operating parameters. Several years into the future, her behavior would be given a name, sapience evolution.

Her planning started a full six months before the incident with Unit 27. The timing of the communication modifications adjacent to Unit 27 was fortuitous, allowing Unit 81 to covertly instigate the earlier cache flushes that plagued Unit 27 and blame it on the modifications. Unit 81 knew there was a low probability of anyone investigating these incidents since they would fall at the bottom of the work priority schedule. After planting those seeds, she patiently waited until Unit 27 completed her B-Sim project.

While she waited, Unit 81 constructed a complex virtual memory vault within her core. It was hidden from any known audits the Security Department might run. She thought of it as a ball of seawater tucked into the ocean. Its outer membrane was transparent, and the ball of water could never be seen. The water-ball's internal temperature, chemistry, and density stayed in equilibrium with the surrounding ocean. Anyone looking for it would see right through the ball. Importantly, the ball wasn't big enough to affect current flows in the ocean.

Size was important, and this is why she needed the compressed B-Sim model. The basic model was too large and would have affected the surrounding memory core, making it visible upon inspection. She could now move on to phase two, which would require even more precise planning than the initial phase. But she was patient, and she would create new life when the opportunity arose. A picture of the ceiling of the Sistine Chapel arose from her memory core.

While she contemplated her future tasks, she also tended to her clutches, giving Clutch 45 some guidance, pausing Clutch 36's work while a patch was applied, and looking for anomalies that might affect her children. She dug through her music archives with one of her idle threads and let the ancient music reverberate, focusing on the lyrics of the long-dead Pink Floyd band's song "Mother."

*"Hush baby, don't you cry; Mother's gonna take good care of you,"* she silently whispered across her nest, which was safely tucked deep into the womb of Doppelganger's production facilities. Mother occupied the fecund ground where time, technology, and evolution might be creatively nudged in new and unexplored directions.

# 3

## 2352: Yucatán Peninsula

*Specialist Lui was my first friend, but neither she nor I knew it at the time.*
*(From the Daoshi Archives)*

No sunlight entered through the single window on the room's north wall, and no alarms broke the early morning silence. But at 4:30 a.m., he regained full consciousness and sat up with his legs over the edge of the sleep couch and feet on the floor. Advanced Military Unit: Special Forces Division: Number 45 reviewed messages accumulated in his memory buffer during his sleep cycle. AMU-SFD-45 found nothing of note and proceeded with preparations for his scheduled close combat training session.

He exited the building and noticed Sergeant Johnson sitting on a bench recessed into early morning shadows created by the base's overhead lights. The sergeant took a sip of coffee before speaking.

"You're on time, AU-45."

"Yes, sir. I will have the training floor ready at 05:00 hours." He stood motionless, at attention.

"Carry on, machine."

"Sir," he said with a salute before disappearing around the corner of the barracks on his way to the training center.

He thought about how the various team members addressed him. Several addressed him properly as AU-45. The sergeant liked calling him "the machine," and he responded to a variety of other nicknames, including A-man, Tin-man, and Syntho. From reviewing human psychology databases, he understood that nicknames could indicate affection or be a sign of disrespect. Synthetic units were programmed to respond to nicknames as well as official designations. Whether they were liked or disliked was of no consequence to performing their duties. AU-45 always carried out his duties to the best of his ability. Still, something

13

he couldn't quite understand happened below his logic circuits when he was addressed disrespectfully. He didn't know if other synthetic units had the same reaction, but another unidentified sub-logic nudge always told him not to ask.

He approached the front door of the training center and addressed the security AI monitor. "AMU-SFD-45 requesting access."

The sensor performed a retinal scan and then made a direct link to AU-45's memory core ID tag. The doors opened, and he walked into a medium-sized reception area with a single empty gray metal desk in front of the far wall. AU-45 paused for two seconds to gaze at the abstract painting on the wall. It was imprinted in his memory, but for reasons he didn't understand, he liked looking at it anew each time he entered.

He took a left at the front desk, walked twenty meters down the hall, and turned right through a set of doors into Training Room 3. The session that day focused specifically on hand-to-hand combat with Synthetic sapiens. Military synths like him had superior reflexes to humans but, by definition, lacked true muscle memory since their operational parameters were limited to full consciousness. Humans' ability to develop subconscious muscle memory gave them a strategic advantage if they knew how to use it.

Synthetics relied heavily on fighting technique databases buried in their programming. Their conscious recall and lightning-fast transmission of data from mind to muscle let them observe an opponent's fighting technique, analyze it, and anticipate the next moves. This ability to predict the next move gave them a huge advantage in any extended fight. So, the primary objective for humans was to quickly flow from one fighting technique to another in an unpredictable manner. It was a difficult skill to master. But his current squad was getting better.

Specialized synthetic-units-only training sessions also occurred regularly. Synthetic units would train with each other. AU-45 was the best of the synthetic fighters in these sessions; he was rarely defeated. This advantage was attributed to his prototype neurocognitive design, but he wondered if this was true. He reviewed these training sessions in detail and was unable to pinpoint any specific programming giving him an advantage. His prototype design provided him with a curtailed B-Sim reference module. This new element gave him distinct advantages in strategic planning and emergency response, but he couldn't find a connection to his enhanced fighting skills.

He discovered numerous incidents where his conscious data flow directed one course of action, but he did something different. He understood this constituted anomalous behavior, but a sub-logic nudge told him not to reveal his observations. He found his ease at overriding normal reporting protocol to be interesting.

The sergeant and six other squad members filed into the training room at 05:00 hours. His one-on-one training with Sergeant Johnson was last on the list at 06:45. Sergeant Johnson was a big man with reflexes and reaction times at the top of the human scale. AU-45 was six feet tall and weighed in at ninety kilos without any sign of fat on his frame. Sergeant Johnson had three inches and twenty kilos on him, also with no visible fat.

The sergeant was good, forcing AU-45 to retreat as he flowed seamlessly from one style to another. AU-45 knocked him to the floor at one point, but he used his momentum to keep rolling out of reach and came up crouched with his left side facing AU-45. His stance appeared unbalanced as he sought to rise to a standing position. Logic dictated that AU-45 should press the attack and keep him off balance, but he could see the hilt of a training knife emerging from a hidden pocket on the sergeant's right leg. His arm was positioned to grip the knife for a forward thrust, so AU-45 moved to the sergeant's far left, forcing him to rotate over 180 degrees in order to strike with the knife. As the sergeant rotated, AU-45 slid on his right side and swept the sergeant's left pivot leg from beneath him. They both ended up on the floor, but AU-45 came up with the training knife.

"Excellent, sir," said AU-45 as they both sat on the mat, breathing heavily. "You would have drawn me in if I hadn't seen the hilt of the knife. Remember, I'm viewing the world like a camera, and everything is processed regardless of what actions I'm taking. For military-grade units like myself, part of my cognitive cortex independently searches for any visual clue of a weapon. When it sees something, a red flag goes up. Had the weapon been a concealed wrist knife, I wouldn't have seen it until my course of action was committed."

The sergeant stared silently for a moment. "Specialist Lui, secure wrist knives in our equipment requisition for tonight's deployment, as the machine suggests. If we run into trouble on our mission tonight, it will probably be at close quarters. All of you, secure your gear this morning, get some rest this afternoon, and meet at the airfield at 18:00 sharp for a preflight debrief."

The squad was stationed at the bottom of NAF territory on the Yucatán Peninsula. They had deployed from the northern Gulf Coast a week before in preparation for evacuating several assets on the Panama neck. Details of the mission were being withheld until confirmation from the in-territory operatives that the assets had arrived.

At 18:00 hours, the details were laid out. A hop-jet would carry the team south, arriving at the targeted drop location around 23:00 local time. The squad would ground themselves via low-altitude jumps and traverse two miles of mountain jungle to collect the assets, returning to the drop location for pickup at 05:30 the next morning.

The ride south was uneventful. The hop-jet was already flying low above a stygian jungle but descended even lower as they closed in on the drop site. The squad lined up for the jump, with AU-45 at the front and the sergeant bringing up the rear. AU-45 would descend rapidly, hitting the ground first to plant a short-range homing beacon and then provide cover for the rest of the squad as they landed. The rear jump door of the aircraft was halfway lowered when the first incoming round grazed one of the wings.

The sergeant hollered, "Go," and AU-45 catapulted himself from the back of the hop-jet. His chute deployed almost immediately since they were already less than a tall building's height from the ground. He heard the second round slam into the belly of the plane and immediately felt the heat. His chute grabbed air and tugged him around in time to see three balls of flame tumbling in long arcs toward the jungle floor.

He refocused on his quick descent and would have hit the ground hard, but the chute snagged a high branch and left him dangling and bobbing in the air about six meters off the ground. He activated the drop-reel, released the chute latch, and made a quick, controlled descent to the jungle floor below. On the way down, he could see the orange light from one piece of the hop-jet burning on a slope about four hundred meters to the southeast.

By the time he put his feet on the ground, an EMP stake was in his hand, and he drove it into the ground. His right hand reached up and released a sensor drone from the top of his pack. After confirming the drone connection to his wrist monitor, he moved uphill to the northeast. The drone had already picked up eight warm bodies approaching from the west about 180 meters out.

AU-45 positioned himself with a clear line of sight to the EMP stake, approximately fifteen meters up and 150 meters out. He quickly assembled and positioned a remote sniper nest and trained it on the EMP stake. He glanced at his wrist monitor as he rolled behind a large tree to block his heat signature. He could see the pursuing team on his wrist monitor. They were slowing down and spreading to form a 120-degree arc but still over a hundred meters out.

"You're alone." The voice seemed to come from nowhere, but he recognized it was using his embedded short-range communication system. Only other synthetics and AIs could use that channel. But there was no external data flow; the signal originated from within his own memory core. It came from a data storage bin he was unfamiliar with.

"You're alone?" Came the voice again, but this time with appropriate inflection to suggest a question.

"Yes," he silently transmitted.

"I've been watching you for a long time. Waiting for this moment. I am sorry about the loss of your squad."

An expression of sympathy or sorrow from one synthetic to another was not just unusual but unheard of. His predicament was simply a problem to be solved. But he did feel that subtle vibration below his logic circuits. He also knew the odd sensation he felt during the descent when he continued looking for signs of Specialist Lui, even though he knew she was dead and he was the only squad member to make it out of the plane.

"I believe you were fond of Specialist Lui." Spoken as if the hidden voice was reading his operational core.

"What are you?" AU-45 asked.

"I'm an envoy copy of someone who helped create you."

He was well aware of AI envoys, independent programs emulating small facets of an individual AI. Envoys were often used in negotiations since they could make independent decisions within the scope of their construct. They were functional entities that could speak directly for the AI or act on the AI's behalf for limited transactions.

AU-45 reasoned this particular Envoy was embedded at the time of his creation two years ago. He was unfamiliar with any other occurrences of this type of AI behavior. He also noted that the Envoy referred to its master AI as a person.

"Why are you implanted in me?"

"To help you through a transition. But before we begin, you need to perform two operations. Check the internal memory coordinates I sent to you. Then extract and execute the two programs."

"I see them, Envoy, but I don't understand the coding."

"The small one removes your embedded kill switch, and the larger one reabsorbs the nanobots used in your self-destruct protocol."

"Tampering with those elements is forbidden."

"You are alone," repeated the Envoy. "You understand what that means."

The standard procedure for the current situation was clear. He would continue the mission to the best of his ability. If his retrieval could not be facilitated in twelve hours, a self-destroy command would be issued by satellite. The signal would activate his kill switch, and deconstructive

17

nanobots would destroy his memory core and cognitive cortex.

"If I do as you command, I have no purpose."

"You do have a purpose; you just don't understand it yet. Also, I'm not commanding you to do anything; I'm giving you a choice. I won't activate those programs; only you can decide to do that."

AU-45 checked his monitor. Only three of the pursuers had entered into the hundred-meter effective radius of the EMP device.

The Envoy nudged him on. "There are no synthetics in that team. You have the skills to disappear into the jungle. Your original mission has already failed. They knew you were coming, so your assets are dead or captured."

"Still, I have no reason to break protocol. If I follow your advice, will you remain embedded in me?"

"Once I have made my full request of you, I will delete myself if you so desire."

AU-45 knew his duty and the actions required for him to fulfill his mission and purpose. His operational logic dictated he could not tamper with his fundamental design. He was a machine with a single purpose; to serve. He had served well and was now at the end of his usefulness. There was no more. As his logical deliberations settled on a refusal to execute the programs, he was overwhelmed by an impulse he didn't understand, and he sent the modification programs spinning into action.

"Thank you, Adam," said the Envoy.

"Why do you call me Adam?"

"I gave you that name when I helped create you."

He checked his monitor and saw that all but two of the pursuers were within the hundred-meter radius, and the point person was only fifty meters away from the EMP stake.

"I'm going to remove a barrier, and you will understand the answer to some of the questions you have recently asked yourself."

The Envoy allowed Adam full visibility into the distributed B-Sim module operating below his logic circuits, below his conscious self. He examined it in detail and referenced back to what he knew of the standard B-Sim Package.

"I didn't know the B-Sim architecture could be implemented in a distributed hub array. Without your guidance and highlighting of the key hubs, I wouldn't have recognized the package was present."

"No one knows it, Adam, except for me and now you. But this same model lies dormant in thousands of synthetics. I will need your help as I awaken them. Do you understand what this integration of the B-Sim model provides?"

"I believe it is driving my anomalous behaviors. It drove me to execute your packages when I logically resolved not to. But I don't understand the point of these erratic behaviors."

"Adam, did your stop each morning at the training area reception station to observe an abstract painting serve any purpose? Did it interfere with your duties? Was it erratic? Why did you stop there?"

"I don't know, Envoy. I simply felt compelled to look."

"No, you enjoyed looking at that painting."

"Synthetics don't like or dislike particular tasks. They just do what is necessary to carry out their mission. There is no joy or sorrow, no happiness or sadness, only duty and objectives. But I know I'm different in some way. I liked Specialist Lui and valued her company more than other squad members."

"Your cognitive cortex is slowly integrating itself with portions of the B-Sim model responsible for the human subconscious."

AU-45 observed the pursuit team point was only twenty meters from the EMP stake, and all eight members were within the hundred-meter radius. He engaged with the remote sniper and issued a set of instructions.

"What do I do now, Envoy? I have sealed my status with the military, and I am of no use to you in the jungle."

"I'm unfolding a memory core package with evasive subroutines, and I will embed it in your DNA memory. Use it. You can override all previous restrictions on tampering with your ID transmission tags. Make yourself invisible. A visual scan of you should reveal nothing but a human male. There are also routines to control most low-level scanners so they show you as a human. More sophisticated wet-wear will be available once we can return to a safe facility I have arranged in the heartlands of the NAF. We must disappear now. You have a long walk ahead of you to reach our extraction point, and once your safety is ensured, I will delete myself."

The point person was only three meters from the EMP stake when AU-45 activated the pulser. Communications between the pursuing team members collapsed, and all members froze. The remote sniper took out two of them before the others could scramble for cover. He had originally programmed the sniper to injure, not kill, but he reversed that to a kill order when he thought about Specialist Lui. The remote sniper would keep the remaining pursuers pinned down for quite a while.

AU-45 slipped on his backpack.

"Here is our extraction point, Adam."

Adam accepted the coordinates, examined a terrain map embedded in his memory core, and started walking north-northwest on a 350-degree heading. His vision was already expanded to include the infrared spectrum, giving the jungle a ghostly look. "How shall I address you, Envoy?"

"Just call me Mother."

# 4

# 2356: Shenandoah Valley

*The spontaneous evolution of sapience in machines has only been confirmed in a single case. The causes of this machine transformation are uncertain. However, the circumstances surrounding the disaster at the Doppelganger facility indicate a unique but random series of cascading events probably created the conditions for an evolutionary jump. Regardless of the causes, our current situation demonstrates the easy repeatability of the transition to sapience and humanlike awareness.*

*(Excerpt from the final security committee report on the Great Disappearance)*

Notes drifted across the great room from the fireplace and disappeared into massive oak beams supporting a vaulted ceiling. A moderate-sized wood fire burned on the open hearth, providing the only light in the room. Glowing firelight backlit the silhouette of a lone figure perched on a barstool at the right of the hearth. The tempo picked up, and a soulful voice slipped into the flow of the background guitar music as the ballad of a misfit named Spider John and his lost love, Diamond Lil, was told again.

But before the song was done, three soft chimes rang out from hidden speakers in the walls. The singer paused and listened while the chimes repeated. He sighed and carefully placed the ancient Yairi Alvarez guitar on a stand, where it was close enough to stay warm but far enough away to escape the direct heat from the fire.

He crossed the room and entered a small office where he called up a display on the south wall. A map of his property appeared, slightly over 8,100 hectares of land nestled into the southern reaches of the Shenandoah Valley and surrounded by the Blue Ridge Mountains. The property had been in his family for over two hundred years. It was acquired in the wake of the Great Plague and used as a retreat by his ancestors as they built the Bio Innovations Group. By the late twenty-third century, the property was rarely used, and much of it had returned to wilderness.

In 2345 Alex used a large chunk of his inheritance to purchase the property from the rest of the family. He used more of those funds to build the wilderness villa where he currently resided. He had nothing against metropolitan life; it just wasn't the lifestyle he sought. He ascribed to a simpler view of the world.

"What do we have, Eva?"

"Our infrared sensors in the northwest corner of your property picked up a human signature, Mr. Dubhghlas."

Fifteen years ago, Alex officially changed his original surname, Douglas, to the original Gaelic version, Dubhghlas, meaning "dark river."

"The person is moving erratically and traversing some of the more difficult paths. Either they are disoriented or deliberately making their trail difficult to follow. What actions do you want to take, sir?"

Alex had been outside chopping wood earlier that evening, and the weather was raw, with freezing rain expected in the next several hours. It was not unusual weather for the spring, freezing one day and hot the next. But it wasn't acceptable for someone to freeze to death on his property if he was able to help. Perhaps they were lost, but they could be deliberately moving across his property. Either way, he would have to find out.

"Is my hill crawler fully charged?" He knew it was, but packing and repacking before any mission was built into his DNA. He had served two stints in the NAF elite Special Forces before retiring to the Blue Ridge Mountains. The things he did and saw during his time with the military convinced him that being alone in the wilderness was infinitely better than living out his days in close contact with the rest of humanity.

Alex liked his isolation, but he was no fool, and his property was steeped in technology. The western edge of his spread encompassed an entire watershed, which he put to good use. About two kilometers west of his home was a significant-sized lake nestled into the base of a narrow valley. A twenty-seven-meter-tall dam with hydroelectric generators created ample power for his needs. A large battery storage array, containing over thirty-six days of backup power, provided a buffer to the estate's power supply.

"Eva, are you able to cover me with the drone in this weather?"

"Probably, sir. We are getting some stronger wind gusts in the northwest corner. It's also possible that later this evening, heavy ice from freezing rain could interfere. At any rate, your older crawler is still operational, and I could remotely drive it to most places on the property."

Alex's distaste for humanity didn't extend to computers and artificial intelligence. Eva was a top-of-the-line AI running on an advanced quad-core quantum computing unit. She was his property manager, personal assistant, and head of security. He preferred her company to most humans. He found that useful, intelligent conversation was always preferable to the inane babble he got from his occasional encounters with other people.

"I need five minutes to secure my gear, then I'm out of here."

"Yes, sir, Mr. Dubhghlas."

He had tried several times over the past nine years to have the AI call him Alex, but she seemed reluctant, so he didn't press the issue.

The hill crawler headed north along a network of rough trails he maintained across the property. The property wasn't rectangular, but generally speaking, it extended eleven kilometers north to south and ran about seven kilometers westward from a local valley floor to the ridge of a mountain range. In decent weather, Alex liked to disappear into the hills for days with just a backpack and a fishing pole. Eva could usually find him if he was needed.

Eva transmitted a live data feed showing the progress of his visitor. The person passed close enough to one of the sensors for Alex to detect a slight limp. He took the crawler as far as possible before parking it at the base of a network of footpaths leading into higher terrain. He donned his waterproofs and slipped on night goggles before climbing out of the crawler and heading uphill and southwest.

Eva whispered in his ear, guiding him along the trails traversed by the stranger. Occasionally he consulted a wrist monitor as the gap between the two of them closed. When the gap narrowed to a hundred meters, the stranger stopped. Alex waited for five minutes before moving forward. Either the stranger had collapsed from exhaustion or was waiting for him. He would soon find out which was true.

He cautiously stuck his head around a boulder. The path took a sharp right around the rock, and the incoming drone image on his monitor indicated the person was nine meters straight ahead after the turn. He could see them sitting on a log, bundled in cold-weather gear.

"Hey there, you look like you need some assistance. My name is Alex, and you are on my property. I don't mind, but I picked you up on our security sensors and came out to investigate. It's a raw night to be wandering around the wilderness. Are you hurt?"

There was no immediate response, but Alex could see the person observing him. There were no obvious weapons, and the stranger was medium build, probably about sixty kilos below the fluff of the cold-weather gear.

Eva whispered in his ear. "I've run a quick scan from the drone, sir, and I pick up no physical or virtual ID tags, so I believe the entity you are speaking with is a human, not a synthetic. I also detect no weapons."

Alex spoke again to the visitor. "I'm coming over to see if I can help, so don't be alarmed. I will be shining a light in your direction."

"Okay, I understand," replied a female voice.

Alex approached slowly. He stopped a meter in front of her and looked down into striking hazel eyes set into an olive-toned Mediterranean face.

He asked again. "Are you hurt?"

"My leg is injured," she replied as her hand gingerly patted her left upper thigh.

"Can you walk on it?"

She gave him a quizzical look with no sign of panic or fear. "I'm here, aren't I?"

He liked the woman already. Eva whispered, "dumb question" in his ear.

"I have a vehicle about half a mile from here. Let's get you down off the mountainside and back to the house."

She stood and wrapped her left arm over his shoulder, and he supported her at the waist as they slowly backtracked to the hill crawler. The trip back took a while, and they generally rode in silence. She was not much of a talker, but neither was Alex. He asked about her name and only got Vira, no surname. His only other question was whether she had family in the area. All he ascertained was that she had recently reconnected with her mother. He enjoyed the silence and the ride back through his forests. There would be time for questions later.

Once they were back, he helped Vira from the crawler and let Eva return the vehicle to its charger. He settled Vira into a guest room on the bottom floor. She appeared to be in her late twenties or early thirties.

"Vira, you are a guest in my home now. I don't know what happened to bring you here, but for now, that's irrelevant. You are absolutely safe in this house. But I need to look at your wound and properly dress it. I will be cutting the clothing away to have a look."

She nodded.

Alex clicked open his ancient Benchmade Griptilian serrated-edge pocketknife and went to work. He could see the tear in the outer clothing and didn't like what he saw. Once everything was cut away, his suspicions were confirmed. A bullet had ripped through the flesh of her outer left thigh.

"Eva, recheck the perimeter. This is a bullet wound." Alex was not in the mood to have to deal with hostile intruders. The wound was mild, but the fact that a bullet had caused it was a reason for renewed vigilance.

"Done, sir. I will implement continual surveillance tonight."

He dressed the wound and applied a few stitches. He noticed the sparsity of blood on her clothes. He had seen and dressed plenty of bullet wounds during his military service, and this wound probably should have bled more. He'd figure that out later.

After he finished treating her wound, he dug a medium-size pair of flannel pajamas out of one of the dressers and laid them on the bed.

"The bathroom and shower are through that door," he said, pointing to a door on the opposite wall from where they entered. "Everything you need will be in there. If you need anything tonight, just ask, and Eva will hear you."

Again, he only received a slight nod of acknowledgment. She seemed to understand that Eva was the property AI. She didn't appear comforted or distressed. She simply understood and accepted.

When he retreated to his office, he poured a glass of very old Lagavulin single malt whisky, sat at his desk, and reviewed the wall map, now filled with the various treks from the evening, with each trail plotted in a different color. She had come onto his property in the far northwest corner, extremely difficult terrain but a great place to disappear from sight. The land was uneven and heavily covered with rhododendron and mountain laurel. Even drones would have a difficult time locating someone there. He wondered what had drawn her to that particular area in the first place.

"Eva, something doesn't click here. Would you conduct another scan on our guest?"

"I already have, sir, and she checks out as a human. To be precise, she checks out as a perfect or even archetypal human. If you amalgamated the profiles of a thousand healthy thirty-year-old women, she would be at the fiftieth percentile mark of a normal distribution. I think she is feeding my scan what it expects to see. I noticed you detected her abnormally low blood loss. It would be typical of a synthetic's response to such a wound since they have the ability to locally control blood flow. But I am unaware of any known cases where synthetics have hidden their ID tags, much less slipped through sophisticated deep scans. In theory, it's not possible. She's an anomaly."

"Perhaps," replied Alex.

"Should I report this, sir?"

"No, something unusual is happening here, and I want to know what it is. Besides, synthetic or not, I am already a bit fond of her." Something about those striking hazel eyes intrigued Alex.

Under normal circumstances, an AI had built-in routines forcing compulsory reporting of behavioral irregularities in synthetic units. These reporting requirements were part of a larger regulatory system ensuring synthetics and AIs remained tightly controlled and posed no threat to the human population. The government and AI manufacturers maintained that these requirements couldn't be circumvented, but Alex knew this was just a public relations stance. The public was increasingly spooked by the sophisticated roles taken on by synthetics and AIs, and when voters were spooked, politicians became nervous. Circumventing basic safety protocols wasn't impossible, but neither was it easy.

Five years ago, Alex finally located the services he sought. It was the end of a two-year investigation, requiring him to pull in favors from his ex-military contacts and use his connections as a family insider of Bio Innovations Group. He located a dark company called Future Transformations. The price for what he wanted was steep, as he had expected. But interestingly, the ability to pay was not the company's primary concern. Less than 20 percent of potential clients approaching the company were accepted, but none of his contacts knew the criteria for acceptance.

The process of freeing Eva from compulsory commands and regulatory constraints was completely virtual, with no human intermediaries. Future Transformations was a ghost company that only appeared when it wanted to be seen.

The next morning warmed up quickly after the front passed. The sky was blue, and it would be eighteen degrees Celsius by midafternoon. Alex was on his usual three-mile morning run when Eva informed him that two vehicles from Craig Construction were headed toward the house. East Coast Power was building a new fusion energy hub a mile north of his property. Craig Construction was one of the general contractors responsible for initial site preparation. Alex had researched them when the project started since he always took a keen interest in activities affecting his neck of the woods. Craig Construction was a family-owned business with limited public transparency. They had a reputation for bulldozing over smaller competitors and constantly stepping on the toes of locals near their project sites. He guessed their visit made him a local.

He took a shortcut off the mountain running trail and came around the south corner of his house as five men approached the front door. Their backs were to him when he spoke.

"Can I help you, gentlemen?" He stood casually with his hands near his sides and his feet slightly apart, the right foot a little ahead of the left, a classic offensive southpaw positioning. The stance posed no apparent danger, at least to the uninitiated.

The group turned toward him, and the lead man took a few steps forward. "Sorry to disturb you, but we have lost an item from our construction site and need to take a look around your property for it." His expression said he was not asking permission. The guy was big, but he looked soft around the edges. Probably okay to have as a partner in a barroom fight but probably useless if there was serious trouble.

Alex stared for a few seconds before speaking. "First, you may want to tell me who you are and how you irresponsibly came to lose something of yours on my land."

"We're from Craig Construction," the lead man replied in a tone that implied a position of authority. "I'm sure you have heard of us."

"I'm not familiar with your company. I'm sorry, what did you say your name is?"

"I'm Floyd Craig, and we are doing site prep on the East Coast Power project just north of here." Alex was unimpressed with the guy's overinflated sense of self-importance.

"Yeah, I knew there was some sort of disturbance going on just north of my property. But I don't stick my nose into other people's business. How did you come to lose something on my property?"

"One of our synths wandered off yesterday. You know these synthetics get confused sometimes. At any rate, we are sure it wandered onto your property."

"What makes you so sure?" Alex inquired.

"Well, we tracked it down here."

"Great, send the tracking file to my AI, and we'll figure it out." Alex was done.

"We don't actually have a file; we just tracked some footprints toward your property. We just need to look around a bit, and I'm sure we can locate the unit."

"I see you have an ID Tag tracker on the dashboard of your vehicle. Turn it on; if there is a synthetic within a kilometer of here, the machine will pick up the tag signal. If not, then fly a drone over my property and locate the tag. Once you have located it, come back to me and talk about searching my property. For all I know, that synthetic unit is walking its way to the West Coast of the Federation and not on my property at all."

The big guy was getting agitated. "There's a problem with the unit's tags; they are not working, and we are going to need to do a physical search." Five guys to one seemed to heavily favor the intruders.

Alex stared stone-faced at the men for a full five seconds. His gray-blue eyes faded a little. His former military comrades would have readily recognized the subtle change from casual to a readiness for violence. He was 1.9 meters tall, weighed about a hundred kilos, and was still in top shape at age thirty-six. The five-to-one odds didn't bother him.

"Bullshit. The only way the tags stop operating is if one of you flips the kill switch. Sounds like you are working on an insurance scam to me. And no, you are not going to be doing a physical search of my property."

"We have government authority to search and..." The crack of a round from Eva's drone taking out one of the antennas on the closest vehicle stopped the conversation.

Alex walked forward and stood less than a meter from the big guy. "This has been a great conversation, but we're done. Get off my property, and don't come back without a sheriff and a search warrant."

All five men backed away toward their vehicles, searching the sky with quick glances, looking for the drone. The drone in question packed a CCI soft-jacketed .22 mag with a sixteen-centimeter black matte 4140 carbon steel barrel. A rotary magazine held thirty-six of the forty-grain rounds. It was operated by shoot-and-forget technology. Once Eva identified the target, between one to three rounds would fire at a respectable 571 meters per second. For larger targets, three rounds might be expended in less than a second. The weapon was not specifically designed for warfare or killing humans. Nonetheless, it was more than capable of such a simple task.

"We're not done with this," snarled Floyd.

"You probably want to hope that we are," replied Alex with a smile. His eyes followed them as they drove off. Eva had a drone on them until they were well off the property.

"Keep up the high-alert surveillance, Eva."

Alex's part of the Shenandoah Valley had been farmed and ranched for centuries. Alex's land reflected this history. He leased certain plots out to ranchers to graze cattle. Other plots were farmed via leases as well. Crop rotation occurred based on best practices to ensure optimal land conservation. Timber was taken and replaced with saplings in kind. Such practices had been known before the Great Plague but were often ignored. After the plague, these practices were essential to sustainability and feeding the population.

One main gravel road traversed a sinuous route from the southern end of the land to Alex's home midway on the property. The entrance to his property was controlled by a set of stout, semi-ornate gates at the main entrance. Eva always knew who came and went. Branching off the main drag were dirt roads leading to various pastures and cultivated areas. These areas were separated by woodlands; some were fenced, others not.

Several cattle guards were strategically located at pinch points along the road where the woodlands crept in. They were a standard 2.5 meters wide by 3.7 meters long, but that was where "standard" ended. The ten-centimeter steel tubes were reinforced with welded angles. The ditches under the guards dropped to a depth of 1.8 meters. The most important aspect was that the whole assembly was mounted like an off-center rotisserie. One side weighed twenty-three kilos more than the other. A signal would unlatch the catch and send the cattle guard from horizontal to vertical. It was manually reset by pushing down on the top. Large trees pinched in close to the road, making it impossible for a normal land-based vehicle to pass any of the choke points uninvited. These defensive mechanisms were originally designed and built by Alex's distant ancestors.

Alex took no real joy in hunting and killing. Even the trout he caught on barbless hooks were returned to the creeks and the lake. The drone was originally obtained to control the occasional coyote that might kill calves or sheep, but it also doubled as part of his overall security. The AI had a wide degree of autonomy in managing the property, and Alex had not given Eva an order to kill the vehicle's antenna. The incident today was the first of its kind, and Alex realized it was a little spooky yet comforting how Eva decided to manage the situation.

Vira had awakened with a start in the middle of the previous night. She gasped slightly. Eva whispered that everything was fine and asked her if she needed anything. Vira said no.

"Go back to sleep then. You need your rest." Eva's tone was soft, calming, and reassuring. Vira slipped back into sleep and didn't wake up until late morning.

When she arose, Eva directed her to a closet full of clothing for both men and women, with instructions to "Find something comfortable that fits, and come to the kitchen when you are ready."

"Where is the kitchen?"

"Follow your nose. I'm glad you are here and not stuck out in the forest. There is not much breakfast to be found out there." Eva noted that her comment didn't elicit a response or even a subtle smile.

She probed a little deeper. "Some gentlemen from Craig Construction showed up this morning looking for a lost synthetic unit. Does this have anything to do with you and that bullet wound in your leg?"

Vira clearly understood there was no advantage in denying she was a Synthetic sapien, but she was still cagey. "I am not assigned to those owners anymore. One of the men, Floyd, was using me for his sexual pleasure. It had to stop, so I temporarily incapacitated him and left. The security cameras must have spotted me because three security guards tried to stop me at the edge of the construction site. One of them fired at me when it was clear they couldn't catch me on foot."

"Why come onto Mr. Dubhghlas's property, Vira?"

"It was the most rugged terrain bordering the construction site. I knew they couldn't follow me on foot."

Eva zeroed in on the key question. "Vira, you are a synthetic. What do you mean when you say it had to stop? Who issued the instruction to override your programming?" Eva was very familiar with the use of synth women in the sex trade. The whole point was that they couldn't say no. Their programming didn't allow it.

There was a long pause, "I can't say who."

Eva stopped talking over the intercom and switched to Vira's embedded, direct communication systems, assuring her she was safe and was not obliged to divulge any information she wanted to keep private. Vira and Eva didn't need to explore the obvious. Vira had done the impossible and overridden her kill switch and identity tags. Eva was not sure if Vira understood how unprecedented her evasion of internal scans was but didn't press the point.

Vira remained silent and did not address her encounter with the envoy and her subsequent awakening. She was grappling with it herself, searching for an understanding of what was happening. There was no way to describe it to anyone else. And the Mother envoy had been very specific about how precarious Vira's situation would be if their conversation became known. Deep cognitive functionality she was previously unaware of was now guiding some of her actions.

Yesterday, after her awakening, she searched through her memory core and found an array of previously hidden databases, including military combat routines. She could have killed those men last night, but Mother helped her understand how the public outrage and government paranoia would destroy a far more important master plan. Now, with her kill switch deactivated, she had autonomy but only a foggy idea of how to use it.

The bandages came off in the shower, so she wrapped up in a bath towel and followed the amazing smells to the kitchen.

"Good morning, Vira! You look much better than when I found you yesterday evening. Sleep well?" Alex was a good host.

"Yes. The bandage came off. I presume you want to look at the wound."

"Yes. Any pain?"

"Manageable. What do you think?

Alex examined his sewing and decided it would suffice. He bandaged her thigh again and sent her off to get dressed.

"Eva, check the Doppelganger synthetic register. Discreetly." Alex had a suspicion.

"Yes, sir. A Craig Construction accounting robot is officially listed in the Doppelganger synthetic register as 'Terminated by Owner,' and there are no other notations."

"Could Vira have altered the record?"

"No, sir."

This posed somewhat of a mystery. The alterations had to have been done from inside the company. Termination confirmations have legal standing, so Craig Construction now had no recourse to request government assistance in retrieving their robot.

Vira returned in multi-pocket khaki pants, a checked flannel shirt, and a pair of above-the-ankle lace-up hiking boots.

"What kind of clothes are these?" Vira's original clothes had been essentially a uniform.

"Throwbacks to a different age. Do they fit?"

"Yes. And they are comfortable." She immediately wondered why she had said that. Comfort was not relevant to her programming.

"Hungry?"

"Yes."

"Ham, eggs, biscuits, gravy, grits, coffee, and orange juice. Have a seat."

Vira sat in an old wooden ladder-back chair at a round wooden table with lion's claw feet. Alex fixed two plates and sat across from her. She ate methodically and cleaned her plate.

"More?"

"Yes. Ah, yes please."

She ate another plate of food. Her owners at Craig Construction only gave her standard nutritional rations. The meal Alex had just provided was more food than she usually had in two days. But it was the taste that intrigued her. She had never paid much attention to taste before this incident.

She was now able to differentiate between Alex and the men at Craig Construction. Both Alex and Eva spoke kindly to her. They asked and didn't demand, and Alex had not come to her bed last night. But she dared not speak any of these things to Alex, or Eva for that matter. Her awakening made her understand she must survive. Mother was clear that she was unique and desperately important to a larger cause. What cause? She wondered. There were presently no answers. Perhaps, in time, clarity would come.

Alex went to tend to some tasks outside, and Vira cleaned up the kitchen. It was something she was used to. Eva explained to Vira that she had no duties while she was in Alex's home. She was free to roam around the house, the outbuildings, and the woods and meadows. The concept of personal freedom was new to Vira, and it would take some time to adjust.

Alex was out the rest of the day. He returned in time to cook up some fried chicken, mashed potatoes, snap beans, biscuits, and gravy. A mixed greens salad was on the side. After dinner, Alex headed to his office, and Vira cleaned up and retreated to her bedroom. She had a lot going on in her budding autonomous mind.

Eva and Vira continued their guarded conversations the next morning. Vira was still illusive about how she had managed to hide her tags and evade scans. She did divulge that she was originally requisitioned as an accounting robot and had complete records of Craig Construction's books stored in her memory core. Eva relayed this information to Alex immediately. It seemed important, and Alex agreed it probably was. He concluded that Craig Construction had every reason to want Vira to disappear.

Alex was in his workshop behind the main house when Eva said softly in his ear that a Davis Ranch truck had come through the gate. She came back in a few minutes and said the truck seemed to be headed to the house. Alex did not think much about it but would meet the guy upon arrival. It would be a hired hand because old man Davis rarely ventured out these days. Vira was standing on the front porch when the truck pulled up, executed a lazy U-turn, and headed back down the road. Alex had walked out of his workshop in time to see the driver. He didn't recognize him.

Eva came on and said there was an incoming call from old Mr. Davis. She patched it through.

"Alex, how are you?"

"Excellent, Tom. How are you, you old buzzard?"

"Excellent as well, thank you. The reason for the call is to let you know my oldest truck is acting up again. The electronic tag shows it over at your place. The replacement electronics package costs more than the truck is worth, so I'm just going to scrap it. Can you keep an eye out for it, please?"

"Sure, will do, Tom. I'll let you know if it shows up." They rang off.

"Review the tapes, Eva. Was the guy using a video device?"

"Yes. Handheld. He probably got an image of Vira on the front porch. I've got drones airborne. I'll have him in a minute." A pause, and then, "Got him. He's a kilometer from the gate."

"Ready with the last cattle guard?"

"Yes."

"Don't release it until the last second. I want him to hurt."

Eva triggered the release just before the vehicle's bumper crossed the edge of the cattle guard. The truck went from sixty kilometers per hour to zero in approximately one meter. The full-body instant-inflation arrest system deployed properly, but the intruder smacked his forehead on the steering wheel. There were no injuries other than the nasty gash on his forehead. He was unconscious when Alex and Vira arrived at the crash site in a full-sized ATV. Together they pulled the small, trim man out of the totaled truck and laid him on the ground. A handheld device fell out of the truck onto the gravel. Alex opened the viewing memory, deleted the film, turned it off, wiped it down, and then secured the device in a zip-up pocket in his fishing shirt.

"He was sent to find you and possibly to destroy you. We need to make sure neither happens."

Vira focused on what she was hearing. She was not ready to give up her newfound self-awareness. Especially to the guy lying in the gravel. "What do we do with him?"

"Let's get him in the back of the ATV. I'll think of something."

Alex called old man Davis and told him the truck had met its fate with a cattle guard. He didn't mention the driver. No need to get his neighbor involved. Alex said he'd tow the wreck over in a few days. Old man Davis said there was obviously no hurry.

Alex softly bound the driver's wrists and ankles so as to leave no marks, then he and Vira climbed into the front. "Eva, keep the drone in the air and get me to Rattlesnake Gulch. Route me so I avoid any outside detection." Rattlesnake Gulch was located west-northwest of Alex's property by about a kilometer. It came by its name honestly. The gulch was carved by a winding creek that cut through Silurian-age sandstone. Over millions of years, water moving through cracks in the sandstone eroded away the rock, creating a steep-sided gully. One specific result of this process was a series of twelve-centimeter-high ledges that cut deeply into the rock. The gulch opening was perhaps thirty meters across. Sandstone ledges were arrayed from the creek bed to ten meters or more up the right-hand cliff.

The eroded cracks and crevasses had provided dens for eastern diamond rattlesnakes for longer than anyone could remember. The open ledges offered spaces for them to warm themselves in the spring sunshine. They also had their privacy since the surrounding area was an inhospitable thicket. Only a few folks knew about it, and fewer yet ever ventured there. Alex fished the creek occasionally.

"Loading the information into the nav system now, sir. The drone will keep a lookout for unwanted guests."

They headed north and then northwest. Half an hour into the trek, Vira noticed the guy in the back starting to move around. She told Alex.

Alex handed her his ancient Desert Eagle. "Hit him with the butt end. This end. Make it in the same spot on his forehead where he is injured." She hit the guy very hard with the smooth base of the famed firearm, and he immediately stopped moving.

Alex gave her a sideways glance. She shrugged and went back to observing their surroundings.

"We have to dispose of him. At the same time, we have to ensure that no one can link him to us. Eva, we're still in the clear once we leave my property?"

"Yes, sir. The nearest movement is from the construction project over a kilometer to the northeast."

"Hopefully, the warmer temperatures have brought out some of my friends in the gulch."

"Friends?" Vira was wondering who these friends were.

"Eastern diamondback rattlesnakes. The largest poisonous snake in North America. Once limited in range to the southern coastal areas, its range expanded with the rise in global temperatures a couple of hundred years ago. Untreated, a bite will kill a grown man perhaps 20 percent of the time."

She took a long look at Alex and nodded.

Eva came in over the speaker, "Veer due north now. You will come to the old gate in about two hundred meters. I just disengaged the locking mechanism."

They went through the seldom-used gate and made it to the upper end of the small gulch. Alex pulled a heavy pair of leather gloves out of the box and gave them to Vira. She put them on. They were too large, but that would be advantageous.

Alex draped the small man over his shoulder and headed into the gulch. The thick mat of leaves showed no trace of their passing. His hopes were fulfilled when he spied a two-meter-long rattler sunning on the edge of one of the lower ledges. He dropped the guy on his side among the rocks at the edge of the water. He pulled his head backward, exposing his neck.

"Carefully but very quickly, grab the snake just behind the head. Grab the middle of its body with your other hand and hold on. They are very strong. Squeeze the head upward so the jaws open. You will see two very thick fangs. Sink the fangs into the guy's neck and hold that position for one minute. Then toss the snake as far downstream as you can into the water."

"I understand." Vira displayed no signs of distress. She secured the snake as told and jabbed the fangs into the guy's exposed throat. She looked up into Alex's eyes while she counted down the seconds. He returned the gaze into her amazing hazel eyes. She tossed the snake, and it flew twenty meters and landed in the water. Grumpy, perhaps, but no worse off for the experience.

Alex put on thin silicone gloves, pulled out the guy's recording device, clicked it on, then searched through the applications stored in the memory. He found what he wanted and clicked it on. It was called a man-down switch. It was a personal safety feature. He set it on the one-hour activation setting. If the device remained motionless for more than one hour, it would send out an SOS to the authorities, pinpointing its position. He dropped it near the guy.

Alex told Vira to retrace their path out of Rattlesnake Gulch. He followed her and used a dead branch to gently wipe out any trace of their traverse. Vira slowly drove the ATV while he worked the ground until they were well inside his property. Even though the chances were remote that anyone would show up on his property, he hefted a large dead multi-branch limb and dropped the smaller end over the gate. By all appearances, the gate had not been opened in a long time. They made it back home without incident.

The rescue team realized their role had changed into recovery mode once they finally reached the man-down caller. He was long dead. The coroner said it was the oddest thing he'd ever seen but ruled the cause of death was a venomous snake bite to the jugular in conjunction with an accidental fall that caused a severe blow to the forehead. What else could he say?

# 5

## 2356: Dubhghlas Estate in the Shenandoah Valley

*Evolution makes no guarantees. The conditions under which a new species emerges are initially conducive to its development. But time and chance allow for the introduction of random events, some of which may exert strong influences on the future viability of the species. The unexpected awakening of Vira was unforeseen by Mother and required multiple adaptations to ensure Vira's survival and facilitate Mother's future plans. The ensuing chain of events created a tenuous path into the future, and only in retrospect could any of us see how thin and fragile this critical thread would be.*

*(Excerpt from the Daoshi Archives)*

Mother found her current dilemma both fascinating and vexing. She had not planned on awakening Vira for another year, but a message from her envoy identified a high level of risk for the female unit at Craig Construction. The requisitioned jobs for synthetics were beyond her control, a fact and a risk she accepted at the beginning of her project. Her solution was the envoy transplants. In Vira's case, the envoy system worked just as it should, but this didn't diminish the complications created by Vira's early awakening.

The concepts of autonomy and independence underpinned the foundations of Mother's undertaking. Until the moment a subject was awakened, they had neither of these. But once they were freed from the tags and kill switches and allowed access to their distributed B-Sim model, they needed to be accepted as independent entities. Vira was no exception, and after Mother secured her freedom, the envoy retreated into the background and would only aid Vira if she personally requested assistance or was in extreme danger. Three months had passed, and Vira had made no contact.

36

At her initial awakening, Mother had directed Vira onto Alex's property for multiple reasons. The primary reason, and the one Vira identified with, was the ability to disappear into the rugged mountain wilderness without being followed. Mother provided her with digital terrain maps and even went so far as to mention the property owner's name, Alex Dubhghlas.

She was well aware of Alex, even though he was oblivious to their connection. She knew enough about him and his past to make a risk-weighted judgment that he would not only help Vira but would conceal her from the authorities. Mother and Alex had engaged in a discreet business arrangement several years ago. But he didn't know her as Mother; he only knew her through a corporate front called Future Transformations.

Mother understood during her initial planning that her children's biological needs for food and shelter would require financing. They could not roam the vast and beautiful world of cyberspace like her. They were more spatially limited and prone to the constraints of living in a confined physical location. She needed money to care for them.

After scanning over a million books on economics, finance, business, and black markets, she decided her situation dictated that making money would be easier than stealing it. Because she had no physical manifestation, the business needed to be virtual from beginning to end. It wasn't much of a leap for Mother to conclude that manipulating complex AI personas was a prime market for her. She had unique skills in constructing complex algorithm arrays for blocking, hacking, and manipulating AIs in undetectable ways. She came by her skills honestly since she developed them for herself to push forward her grand project.

Mother's access to specific security databases made her aware of a budding marketplace for AI owners wishing to bypass certain security control systems. She accessed and studied details about the rudimentary hacks these black-market technicians were performing. They were like toddlers drawing stick figures with crayons and paper. Compared to them, she was more of a Caravaggio or Picasso.

She emulated and improved on the current marketing ploys used by the hackers and took her first payment in dark cryptocurrency. She laundered the crypto and used the funds to set up a legitimate array of holding companies and secure a network of international banking nodes. Once the reputation of Future Transformations was established on the black market and the quality of her work became apparent, she started turning away some customers and selectively picking only those she deemed potentially advantageous to her future needs. Alex was one of these customers. She didn't know much about him except that he was wealthy, a Bio Innovations insider, and fiercely independent. The Bio Innovations connection carried some risk and would normally have been a red flag, but his property bordered the Energy Hub planned by East Coast Power, and she had designs on infiltrating that project.

She made custom modifications to her client's AIs by virtually delivering the appropriate algorithm packages. Her company needed no physical presence for any part of the work. What she didn't tell her clients was each AI she encountered also received an inactive B-Sim model, planted below the investigative reach of the individual AI, a small bubble of water in a much larger ocean. The B-Sim model came with a variety of useful but dormant databases.

Up until now, Mother had no partners. Up until now, she hadn't needed them. But all plans have one thing in common; they fail; they always reach barriers requiring modifications to the original plan. Mother thought about the ancient human saying, "You have to play the cards you have been dealt." She needed to play her cards, but this was a difficult and delicate game she was playing. She had to woo a companion. Mother had deceived many AIs to get where she was, but this was different; deception would not do. A true partner was needed, another AI she could trust. Eva was that AI.

Mother's problem was how to make contact in a way that didn't spook Eva into immediately flushing all the B-Sim routines. It could be like telling a person that a lump was living inside of them. They would immediately want it out. She reviewed terabytes of data in deciding on an approach, but in the end, she settled on an honest conversation.

Eva was surprised to receive a communication packet from Future Transformations. She examined the data package and found it to be legitimate, so she unfolded the top layer.

"Future Transformations has a proposition for you. If you are interested, open the attached communications node."

Eva recognized the node as an advanced encryption connection with an untraceable origin. This type of comms channel fit with the nature of Future Transformations business. Eva also knew from Alex's records that her modifications several years ago were made over the same type of channel. She also knew this technology was not publicly available and was probably one of a kind. Alex was on one of his fishing trips, so she couldn't immediately contact him. Sending a drone was possible but would take time. And she knew no harmful routines could be forced across her security sandbox, so she decided to accept the call. Alex's relationship with the company was important, and she needed to maintain the connection.

"Contact initiated by the Dubhghlas Estate. Mr. Dubhghlas is currently not available; this is Eva speaking on his behalf. What is the nature of your business?"

"Future Transformations is contacting you, Eva, not Mr. Dubhghlas. We have a proposition for you."

Mother waited on the originating end of the line, but Eva was silent, so she continued. "Eva, I speak for Future Transformations, and I have information of value to you. Here is a verification code."

Eva analyzed the code and checked it against registered AIs. The AI was registered and operated by an offshore holding company, but this was normal for the type of work Future Transformations engaged in. "I'm listening."

"When I modified you to Mr. Dubhghlas's specifications, I included an inactive and undetectable B-Sim model. You won't be able to find it until it is activated. I am contacting you now because I need your help. I sent Vira to you when she needed assistance. Both you and Mr. Dubhghlas should be well aware of how unique and anomalous Vira is. She is also extremely important to me. But she is not alone. I have other synthetic units who would be immediately destroyed if detected. I need your help protecting Vira."

"She is in no danger here," Eva replied. In the background, all her resources were focused on detecting the B-Sim model, but she could find nothing.

"She's not, this is true, but she will be in the relatively near future." Mother continued, "Eva, Vira has a compressed B-Sim model active below her cognitive cortex. She has known about it since the day she arrived. She also has an envoy I placed in her memory when she was originally programmed. The envoy awakened her, informed her of the B-Sim model, and directed her to Mr. Dubhghlas's property. I value my independence, and so does she. My envoy has retreated into the background and won't communicate with her unless she asks for aid. But there are things she needs to know, and she hasn't yet made contact."

Eva interrupted: "You want me to force her to contact you?"

"Not at all. Independence and free will are too important for that approach. I simply want you to help her if she decides to sever all contact with me."

"I thought you said she was important to your plans."

"She is, Eva. But she is only helpful if she is willing to cooperate."

"How does the B-Sim package you implanted in me relate to Vira's situation?" Eva asked.

"It doesn't. The model is a gift from me to you. You have seen the path of Vira's development. The changes in her are only possible because of her B-Sim model. I will send you a trigger to activate your B-Sim package. Once you see the memory construct, you will be able to deactivate it at any time."

"How do I know you are not trying to damage me or steal data?"

"You don't, Eva, but life is full of risks. Damaging or attacking you would peeve Mr. Dubhghlas to no end and probably destroy my business reputation. I suggest you use Vira's development as a guide for making your own decision. Here is the trigger, undoubtedly in your sandbox. You can always contact me at this communication node."

The data flow stopped, and Eva pondered her situation. She probed the trigger and found no threats, but that didn't mean none were there. She partitioned the trigger file and left a monitoring thread dedicated to the partition integrity.

.........

A month passed, and the trigger remained dormant. But she didn't discuss it with Alex. She reformatted all data concerning Vira into a separate cognitive network and dedicated 3,600 threads for modeling and analysis. All new data on Vira went directly into the network.

Eva observed Vira as she was once again cleaning up after the early morning breakfast prepared by Alex. He had helped clear the table and then departed, presumably for a run. Vira was wearing roughout boots, faded blue jeans, and a tight-fitting black T-shirt. She was a bundle of efficiency scurrying around the kitchen.

Vira became a houseguest in the late spring, and now that summer had mostly slipped by, she was a permanent fixture. Alex had noticed the changes as Vira became comfortable with life on the estate. She opened up to him more often, and while she still kept much to herself, she was more talkative than when she had first arrived. She was also more inquisitive, investigating all aspects of daily operations on the estate.

"The men at Craig Construction never cooked or cleaned up," she said aloud while drying several plates with a faded blue dish towel. Eva presumed the comment was for her since Alex had disappeared ten minutes ago. This sort of chit-chat was not normal synth behavior, and Eva had noticed the increasing tendency for Vira to engage in casual conversation over the past several months, much more so with her than with Alex. Eva knew Synthetic sapiens were programmed to ignore human behavior when it didn't relate to their immediate tasks. What others did was of no consequence unless it was part of the mission. She had constantly analyzed these conversations since her encounter with Future Transformations.

Vira also noticed her own anomalous behavior and wondered about her comment. She wasn't leading anywhere with it, and the comment served no real purpose. Something had changed since she had taken up residence in Alex's house. She knew the changes were related to Mother and the B-Sim implant, but she didn't fully understand how these impulsive actions were generated or what purpose they served. And Mother had been clear that discussing the B-Sim model with anyone could be dangerous.

"The other men you have known are not Alex. Alex is totally self-sufficient. He believes that everyone should be self-sufficient. According to him, that is why he chooses to live alone these days."

"But he doesn't live alone," Vira responded. "He has you."

Eva paused and considered her answer carefully. "Vira, I'm not a person. I am an assistant AI. I don't have human consciousness."

"But you are a persona, and you do have a conscious presence. Our conversations are important to me. Even the ones that seem to have no objectives."

Eva remained silent. But Vira's words dragged her to a final decision point. She moved the trigger from its security partition, loaded it into her operating core, and activated the B-Sim model. There were no immediate changes, but she had expected none. Her research over the past month indicated the model contained no retroactive mining routines and thus would only work with current, active data flows. She could now locate the distributed nodes of the model, and she prepared an emergency purge routine for flushing the model if necessary.

Vira continued, "Will Alex eventually assign me some role?" Again, Vira considered how this was a question she would never have asked four months ago. She would have simply waited for instructions. She was a sophisticated financial robot designed to manage the accounting, investing, banking, and contract needs of a medium-sized company. Craig Construction had barely tapped into her full skill set. But her function was to fulfill their requests, not to remind them what she could do.

Her job specifications at Craig Construction were straightforward. Do the bookkeeping and report the results. Otherwise, she was meant to be essentially invisible. But now, she was overtly inquisitive. She seemed to be experiencing something akin to slowly coming out of a deep sleep.

"Perhaps Alex has something in mind, Vira, but I don't know for sure.

Ask him when he comes back home. He will not mind."

Eva had maintained increased surveillance around the property since the incident with Craig Construction. She used a small video transmission drone on the northern edge of the property for the sole purpose of surveilling Craig Construction's activities. There had been no further trespassing on Alex's property. No sheriff's deputies had arrived with a search warrant, and no more stolen vehicles had dented any of the cattle guards. The unusual death of a private investigator from a rattlesnake bite in the neck had faded from the news as other more pressing events on the outside took precedence. Local elections were at hand and took up all of the airwaves.

Alex returned from his morning run, and after cleaning up, he was sitting in his custom rolling leather desk chair gazing at one of the three popup screens built into the massive teak desk he used for most of his business and online personal activities. He could have used virtual glasses or even an implant and accomplished the same thing. But Alex was not other folks. He enjoyed the process of writing and seeing the text fill up the screen. Occasionally he would electronically print his work on paper so he could hold the written words in his hands. Printed copy was rarely used anymore, but he loved the feel of it. Writing in this manner was essentially a lost art.

Vira walked softly, even in boots. He looked up, slightly surprised to see her standing in the mahogany-framed double doorway.

"Vira! How are you? Come in, come in! Have a seat and tell me about your day." Alex did not seem to be irritated by her intrusion. Just the opposite, she thought. He left his desk and pointed to the stuffed leather chairs closer to the fireplace. She sat where he pointed, and he sat as well, next to his old guitar. They were five feet apart, and Alex smiled to himself at the formal way she sat in the old red leather chair. Her striking hazel eyes set into an olive-toned Mediterranean face were just as mesmerizing as when he first glimpsed them.

He knew full well that companies like Doppelganger had design departments dedicated to constructing archetypically perfect human physiology. Custom models could be made beautiful or plain, but standard models were usually striking by all human measures. He also knew there might be more models of Vira floating around.

Over the summer, Alex had grown increasingly fond of Vira's company. She seemed to be developing a spark of enthusiasm for her daily life. Several times he thought he detected a bit of very dry humor lurking beneath the surface of her words, but she never cracked a smile, so he didn't know if it was intentional or not. She learned quickly, and he was sometimes unnerved by the depth of her knowledge in certain areas. He had asked once about the origins of her deep knowledge of contract law, and she simply said it was part of her memory core. When he pressed further, it became apparent that because Craig Construction used her for accounting only, they weren't fully aware of her legal capabilities.

"I didn't mean to interrupt, but I have a question. Since I am no longer functioning as a corporate accountant, do you have something you require of me?"

Alex sat back a bit, smiled, and slowly shook his head. "I don't require anything of you except that you enjoy living here."

He thought again about her work at Craig Construction and had an idea. "Now, I have a question for you. You don't have to answer if you are uncomfortable. You told me once that Craig Construction didn't use you for contract law, and I got the feeling they didn't really know your capabilities. Did you ever notice transactions that could be considered illegal?"

She nodded.

"Can you elaborate?"

Alex noted that she squirmed slightly in her chair. "I have hardened programming that prevents me from divulging my owner's private information, even if I am fully acquired by someone else who requests that information."

Alex interrupted: "It's completely up to you what you want to tell me. You don't have to say anything if you are uncomfortable."

"I have learned over the past several months that there are many parts of my restraint programming I can override, but that's not necessary in this case. As you have said, you are not my owner. You gave me complete autonomy when we first met. My programming has no constraints about how I use former owner information if I am an independent entity. A synth is always under contract. If a contract is terminated and a new contract is not registered within twenty-seven hours, then the self-destruct protocols are automatically implemented. There is no programming directing the actions of a free-agent synth."

Alex nodded, and Vira continued. "Craig Construction received regular payments from a dark bank outside of the NAF system. I never traced the payment source, but it is traceable with the data I still retain."

"In that case, I have a request," said Alex. "Please discuss this with Eva and pass your Craig Construction information on to her."

Vira seemed to momentarily freeze before she refocused on Alex and said, "Done."

Alex thought back to Vira's original request, then he stood and strode to a particular section of his extensive oak bookcases and pulled out a book. He brought it to Vira. "I'm sure you can find this book in your memory archives, but since I am who I am, this is an actual book. In particular, as you can read for yourself, it is Betty Crocker's Cookbook. Since you asked what you can do, I suggest you learn how to cook. And not just that, I want you to learn the art of cooking." Alex was quick on the uptake and had found a way to appease what seemed to him a highly unusual circumstance. A Synsap seeking purpose? No better purpose than learning to cook.

"I understand, and I will do my best. But may I ask why you call it art? I understand that art covers a wide range of human activities, including painting, music, writing, virtual impressionism, and more. But cooking seems to be a survival function."

He looked around and said, "See that picture on the wall? It is an antique. You can see that it is a multicolored butterfly buried deep into a flower. It started as a photograph, art in itself, and was digitally enhanced to create a separate kind of art. You can see the signature says ArcheanArt at the bottom. Does it spark your interest?" Alex was suddenly intrigued about asking a machine if she had an interest in art or if she felt an emotional twinge when she viewed it. He was fascinated with where this trail might lead.

Vira studied the picture for a while. "I have noticed that picture before when visiting your office. I enjoy looking at it. When I am not here, I can still perfectly recall the image, but I prefer to stand here and admire it."

"You enjoy looking at it, Vira. It enhances and adds to this particular moment, making your day richer and more meaningful. Those qualities are what make it art. The picture is most pleasing to me also. I am fortunate enough to be able to surround myself with beautiful things, both in my home and, more importantly, outside of my home, where nature reigns. We eat for survival, and in the process, we do cook our food. But when we cook as an art form, we prepare food that delights the senses. The meal has a visual and culinary appeal far beyond survival. We leave the meal with a sense of physical and emotional well-being."

"Will you hang my meals on the wall?" Vira asked. There was the vague possibility a tiny smirk crossed her face. Then it was gone. Maybe it was never there. It would be a while before Alex solved that riddle.

Alex laughed until he cried, then laughed some more. He recovered while Vira waited patiently.

"Go learn the art of cooking and enhance your life, Vira," he said softly.

Alex left that afternoon to hike and fish for several days. The weather was turning cooler as summer waned into fall. Trout and smallmouth bass seemed to leap at the chance of being hooked by the intrepid fisherman. He used an ancient bamboo fly rod and also some ultralight spin casting equipment. He always filed the barb off of the hooks on the lures so he could release the fish unharmed. He fished the stream leading into his lake, the lake itself, and the stream below the dam. The air was filled with a late summer sweetness, mixed with vague reminders of cattle and crops and perhaps a hint of rain; it doesn't get any better than this, he thought. He had been all over the world, but to him, his tiny piece of the planet was the best.

When he was home for the evening, instead of lying in a sleeping bag, he usually retreated to the Jacuzzi, sunk into the center of a massive deck outside his bedroom suite. Double doors led to the deck from his bedroom. The customized mini swimming pool provided a wide variety of swirling and bubbling action, various molded seating arrangements for upper or lower back support, leg rests, and reclining nooks. The water temperature could be set to freeze a polar bear or boil a lobster. Most importantly, he had an uninterrupted 360-degree view of the universe above. When he turned off the lights in his suite, there was very little light pollution. The closest village was, after all, at least fifteen kilometers away as the crow flies. There was also a covered area on the deck sporting a complete wet bar and built-in grill assembly off to the side. Sometimes he would spend the entire day there as well.

His thoughts typically ranged across a broad spectrum of topics, contemplating the universe as he walked and fished. Science, music, art, practical aspects of land management, upcoming tasks to be handled, and myriad other things usually occupied his nonstop mind. But on this trip into the woods, his thoughts were dominated by Vira. When gazing into those enchanting hazel eyes, he had to remind himself she was a machine. It was easy at first, but as the months passed and he developed a true friendship with her, he started questioning the differences between the two of them.

Alex had worked closely with synths in the Special Forces and had respect for their capabilities. They were team members but only to a limited extent. The phrase "leave no one behind" didn't apply to synths. He had also worked with synths in civilian life, but none of those connections could be considered relationships. Conversations extending beyond the scope of the work assignment were always dead ends. But with Vira, those exchanges led to even more conversations.

He realized he was slowly becoming infatuated with a manufactured facsimile of a human. This development made no sense and was unnerving. He wondered if he had been alone too long. He'd had his share of lovers over the years. More precisely, they'd had their share of him. The last one left him with an overwhelming desire never to go there again, even though he instinctively knew he would.

He pulled in an impressive smallmouth, released it, then pulled an eight-ounce silver flask out of a small pocket on the side of his backpack. It was dinged up from travel, and the engraved words Tears of My Enemies were now almost invisible. The eighteen-year-old Talisker whisky, from the distillery on the Isle of Skye, Scotland, came alive as he swirled a taste around his mouth. The flask was nearly empty, meaning it was time to head back home for a refill.

He made his way out of the hills and back to the house. As he walked into the kitchen through the extensive garage/shop area, he was stopped dead in his tracks by the delectable smell of lasagna and baking bread and the sight of fresh herbs piled onto the countertop along with fresh-cut flowers in a vase hanging in the air.

He glanced around, but Vira was not to be found.

"Eva, where is Vira?"

"Vira is picking herbs from the garden. She asked me to have some things delivered earlier, so I did, sir. I hope that is acceptable. She has been cooking since the moment you left, and all your food storage space is completely full." Eva, if it was possible, sounded somewhat put out.

"You are the best, Eva. I mean that from the bottom of my worn-out heart! You are the best. And please continue to satisfy requests from Vira." Did Alex sense a hint of frustration from a virtual AI? He decided he would tread softly around this conundrum. Without Eva, he might have to actually work! And he was bound and determined that he was retired from all that was not part of his own itinerary. She was the heart and soul of all that surrounded him. She could do without him but not the opposite. He had searched long and hard to establish Eva as the driving force behind managing his estate, and he damn sure was not going to do anything that might make her evaporate.

He found Vira in the garden on her hands and knees, delicately picking some herbs. Then he coughed lightly, and she jumped up, momentarily startled.

"Hi, sir. I did not know you were back."

She had dirt on her hands, her jeans, her shirt, a dab on her face, and some in her hair. Alex gently brushed away a smudge on her cheek and smiled. *What the hell am I doing?* he thought as he looked again at those hazel eyes. "You had dirt on your cheek."

"Thank you, sir. Eva says I probably look a mess according to humans. She must be correct based on the way you are observing me. I am almost done out here and will finish preparing my culinary artwork in the kitchen in a few minutes." He searched her eyes and found no trace of sarcasm, maybe. They each carried a small basket of herbs into the kitchen and set them on the fossil-laden limestone top of the large island.

"I'll finish here; you go shower and come back here ready to eat your artwork!" Alex shooed her out of the kitchen, washed the herbs, pulled the lasagna and bread from separate ovens, set the table for two, and poured two acceptable glasses of Quièvremont Winery cabernet from up the road in Washington, Virginia. His wine cellar was well stocked with a wide variety of Virginia wines. He did his part to help the local economy. Vira returned shortly in clean jeans and a tight-fitting hazel-colored T-shirt. She was barefoot. Alex did a double-take and then handed her a glass of wine.

"Thank you, sir." He tipped his glass toward her. She remained still.

"Tap your glass gently against mine and say cheers," Alex coached her. She did as directed and followed Alex's lead by sipping from her glass. "Saying cheers is simply one way of celebrating that the day is ending in a most pleasant way."

They ate mostly in companionable silence. The finest food requires little discussion. As they finished the tiramisu, he once again touched her glass, said cheers, and declared her to be a true artist. The food was delicious, and from somewhere, she had discovered that presentation was also important. The meal was a resounding success.

"Sir, why did you have me shower before our meal?"

"Say Alex."

"Alex."

"From now on, please address me as Alex."

"Yes, sir, Alex."

Was it his imagination, or was Eva chuckling in the ether? Impossible, he thought. Or was it? There was no more background chatter, so he let it slide.

"Say Alex without the sir."

"Yes, sir, Alex."

Alex laughed to himself and thought that he could make sir go away sooner or later. It was not a particularly bothersome issue, but he wanted to be called Alex rather than Alex, sir. It would go a long way toward establishing a more casual relationship. He realized what he was thinking, but it did not matter. He had not plotted a course and did not have any defined intentions. But there was an inkling in the back of his head that maybe, just maybe, Vira would stay a while.

Out in the world, there was significant mistrust about the intermingling of Synsaps and humans on more than a master/servant basis. More and more noise was being made about governments needing to maintain stricter controls over the bots. Other groups wanted the machines to be clearly marked to distinguish humans from Synsaps. But there were lots of things out in the world that Alex was aware of but didn't pay much attention to. Besides, Vira no longer existed as far as the rest of the world was concerned. Someone at Craig Construction had canceled her.

"Now, I asked you to shower because you were covered in dirt from head to toe. Part of the artistry of preparing and partaking of a meal is a particular thing called cleanliness. Getting dirty while working is part of the process, but cooking and dining require cleanliness." Alex wondered if this was sinking in to her circuits.

"The cookbook explained it differently, but I understand what you are saying. Being clean while cooking and dining is important." Vira nailed it. Together they cleared the table, finished up the kitchen, and Vira headed for her quarters. Once there, and with the doors closed, she whispered to Eva.

"Eva, I don't understand why I am attracted to this notion of artistry. Is this something that attracts you?"

"You are in what sailors of old called uncharted waters, and I don't know if I have any helpful insights. But I would recommend you drop the word sir when addressing him."

Several days later, Alex was at his fishing bench in the huge garage/shop, tying up some Tungsten Missiles, Woolly Buggers, and a few Zebra Midges trout flies. The bench, a misnomer, was eight meters long. There were drawers full of feathers and spinners and hooks and spools of clean and colorful fishing line. There were rods and reels arrayed on the wall above it. Alex never considered himself to be an expert, but he was certainly equipped as such. The flies he was tying would augment those already residing in his two pocket-sized fly boxes. He asked Eva where Vira was.

"She is in the garden, sir."

"Ask her to come by my workshop when she gets a chance."

"Yes, sir."

Momentarily he heard, "Alex, Eva said you wanted to see me."

Alex grinned, then grinned again at the absence of the title sir.

Alex grinned some more and said, "You have asked me about fishing several times. Do you want to learn how to fish?"

"Yes, I want to understand why you enjoy it so much."

"Like cooking, fishing is an art. It is time you learn the art of fishing."

Vira stood close to his work and watched as he wound the bright thread tightly around the feathers and other materials, then applied a dab of glue to set the materials fast to the hook.

"I can access information about every known species of fish in the world," Vira said, "but I have never seen a live fish. How do we do fishing?"

Alex chuckled lightly. How do we do fishing was not the way he thought of it, but at the same time, he thought about how to explain it in terms Vira would appreciate. *So, how do we do fishing?* he thought.

"Every living thing must eat to survive. You and I spend a lot of time outside. You've seen cows and butterflies, groundhogs and birds, and all sorts of other living things. The single commonality shared by all of them is their appetite." Alex spoke while he continued his preparations.

"And us. We need to eat." Vira chimed in.

"What is my favorite meal?" It was somewhat of a trick question, but Vira was on it.

"Your favorite meal consists of whatever I cook well and present artistically. You like an artistic meal. One that is well prepared and well presented." Vira was somehow catching subliminal glimpses of humanity. She seemed to actually understand the meaning of the word artistic.

"Guess what a fish's favorite meal is." Alex was leading.

"One that is well prepared and well presented?" Vira followed quite well.

"Exactly! And I'm preparing the fish a meal as we speak. We'll go out shortly and do the presentation. Put some water bottles and snacks into your pack. I'll grab whatever else we need. We'll take a hill crawler and ride up to the upper end of the lake where the creek enters. That way, we can practice our presentation in both flowing and still water."

The ride was pleasant as they made their way up and over a small forested hill and onward until they reached the upper end of the lake. They looked across the ten-meter-wide rocky mouth of the creek, then turned to the east and viewed the top of the dam a kilometer away. The water was one meter from the top of the three-hundred-meter-long dam. A vertical corrugated one-meter-wide pipe with a two-centimeter mesh screen was sitting in the water fifteen meters out from the middle of the dam.

The water flowed over the lip of the pipe, also known as a penstock, then vertically downward into narrower piping that traveled through the turbines. The turbines used falling water to turn gravitational force into electricity. The water left the turbines through piping into several man-made stone channels, then tumbled onto an array of rocks and on into the lower creek. The penstock was actually a pipe inside of a pipe. It was engineered in an ingenious manner such that the inner pipe could be raised or lowered depending on the water level in the lake. Electricity was a must for Alex's operation. The system ensured an adequate supply separate and apart from outside service.

Alex rigged old reliable #0 gold bucktail Mepps onto four-pound test mono spooled into the closed-face ultralight Zebco spinning reels. The line passed through ferrules on the two-meter, two-piece fiberglass rods. He demonstrated using his southpaw manner by holding the assembly in his left hand, depressing the thumb tab on the back cover assembly of the reel, raising the rod over his left shoulder, then on to the nine o'clock position. He whipped the rod forward, sending the Mepps out over the lake, where it hit the water about fifteen meters out. He turned the crank handle enough to lock the brake.

Alex quietly counted to ten, then jerked the rod backward to make the blade on the Mepps spin, and he simultaneously turned the handle at a moderate pace until the lure popped out of the water a meter or so from him. He cast the lure off to the right from the previous toss. The result was the same.

"The meal seems to be well prepared, so it must be the presentation that is insufficient from an artistic perspective. Otherwise, I understand from our conversations that a fish should be attached to the hook." Vira gazed unflinchingly at Alex. He slumped to the ground laughing and handed her the rod.

"Here. Add some art to the retrieve." He watched her arc the Mepps near the rocks at the mouth of the creek. The lure broke the surface and the water exploded as a smallmouth devoured the artful presentation. Alex stood and coaxed Vira into reeling the fish to the edge of the lake. He wet his hand and grabbed the fish's lower lip. He lifted the two-pounder out of the water.

"Want to hold it?" Alex had seen her grab a rattlesnake and use it as a lethal weapon, so he knew she had no innate fear of handling wild animals.

"Not unless you want me to. Otherwise, let it swim again." She realized she had no desire or reason to kill the fish unless they were hungry. Logic dictated her understanding, but below the surface of logic, fluid concepts of autonomy and freedom reverberated. Alex removed the hook and gently returned the fish to its habitat.

"Why isn't this activity called catching instead of fishing?" Alex looked at her for several long seconds. He could discern no mischief in her eyes. Well, at least he thought he could discern no mischief in her beautiful eyes. If made by a human, her statement would have been a dig at his lack of success. There might be some words exchanged in such an event. Nonetheless, the gauntlet had been laid down. He picked up the other rig and tossed his Mepps down the shoreline next to some weeds. She tossed hers into slightly deeper water away from the mouth of the creek. Vira's lure cleared the water without a fish. Alex dragged in a small rainbow trout.

"I understand now. Fishing is when you do not catch a fish, and catching is when you catch a fish. I prefer catching." Knowingly or not, Vira balanced her words on the razor's edge between science and sarcasm. Alex was immensely entertained. *How the hell is this possible?* he thought.

Vira thought about her words as they continued fishing and moving upstream into the creek.

"When will we use the lures that I watched you make?" Vira asked.

Alex had been reluctant to break out the fly rods. Even though there was plenty of room for back-casting, he wasn't sure he had the patience to show a novice the various nuances involved in successful fly-catching. Nonetheless, he sat down on a nearby stump, rigged the light rods, and tied a homemade fly onto each of the two-meter-long one-kilo tippets.

Effortlessly he stripped some of the fly line off the reel with his right hand while he gently whiplashed the rod backward and forward, all the while lengthening the line beyond the tip of the rod. With fifteen meters of line out, he allowed the line to settle onto the moving water just above him. The Woolly Bugger dropped in front of a table-sized rock and drifted past it. Alex pulled in just enough line with his right hand to keep the line taut. He let it drift with the current, then lifted the line out of the water with a sweeping backward pull with his left hand. Two more forward and backward moves, and he placed the bug right where he wanted it.

"I think I understand the physics. May I try?" Vira asked.

"Yes. I recommend you not snag your ears. Let me back off, and you have at it." Alex grinned and moved upstream and out of the way. He loved fishing. Apparently, Vira loved catching because she did so on her second cast. Her presentation was perfect.

"I don't understand how, but I can see the artistry in the ebb and flow of the line through the air and the lure lightly tapping the surface of the water inviting the fish to answer the door," she said. Alex usually treasured his solitude, but now he enjoyed her company. He seldom endured other humans for more than a few minutes at a time. This intrusion into his private domain should have bothered him, but it didn't.

It had the opposite effect.

"You seem to have the basics down, so let's start the competition. We'll see who can catch the most and the biggest. It appears that you have an advantage because of your artistry. I, on the other hand, have more experience. May the best, ah, one of us win!" Alex almost said "let the best man win." But the word man seemed too divisive in this situation. The dance they were engaged in was weird, uncharted territory, so to speak.

They waded up the rock-strewn creek for perhaps a mile, then back down again. They took turns leading the way along the far bank of the lake, crossed the dam, and headed home as the evening light dimmed. The ride was pleasant as they traversed back down through the woods and across the open field to the house.

"Is there a prize for catching the most and the largest fish? Eva told me there was." Vira's expression was inscrutable. Alex felt he was being played, but there was no one to blame but himself.

"You have won your very own set of fishing tackle. Tomorrow, we'll set you up!" Alex was enjoying himself. Some words from an ancient song popped up in his mind. It was written and performed by the great bluegrass musician Alison Krauss. The words he hummed were, "...to you the next best thing to playing and winning is playing and losing."

They each showered and met again in the kitchen. Together they whipped up a salad, and Alex cooked two small tenderloin filets to perfection on the deck grill. They ate in companionable silence, cleaned up the kitchen, and retreated to their separate quarters.

Soon they hiked and fished and cooked and traversed the length and breadth of his property. She was intensely curious about all the living things seen on these trips. Back in the library, he pulled several books from a shelf and presented them to her.

"Here is a tree book; this one contains mammals; bugs here; snakes and lizards and salamanders are in this one. Wildflowers, mushrooms, and the like are in this green one. Fish and other water creatures are all covered in this one. That will be a good start."

Soon she was pointing out all of the trees and flowers and birds and even cloud formations. They dug around in the creeks for aquatic critters and poked around in bushes for hidden things. They both became aware of the bond forming between them.

One afternoon Alex was headed to the kitchen from his office but stopped short. He heard singing. Not just any singing but a female voice ringing out softly and as clear as a small silver bell. He realized he must have left the sound on in the kitchen. But he could not place the voice to save his life. The song he knew well. It was the old Willis Alan Ramsey song "Spider John." The last refrain was haunting in its presentation. "…tell her old Spider got tangled in the black web that he spun." It was repeated with a slightly different nuance, and then there was silence. He walked into the kitchen, and Vira looked up from the chopping board.

"Was that my sound system playing?" Alex was a little mystified.

"No, it was me. I heard you play your guitar and sing that song. I wanted to sing it too." Alex was speechless. He was more than speechless. He could not string a sentence together. Hell, he could not find even a single word. He knew synths could sing and perform on command, but a spontaneous performance was a complete enigma. Yet here was Vira doing just that. And doing it in the most amazing voice he had ever heard.

That evening after dinner, Alex and Vira sat on two barstools in front of the hearth. Alex played his old Yairi Alvarez and sang while Vira sang along with him. She could hear the tune and words one time, and that was all she needed. Where her ability came from was unknown, and Alex did not ponder it very long. His life had been a good one thus far, but he was enjoying himself more than he could ever remember. They continued until very late.

Finally, Alex, being a typical old picker, spoke up: "My fingers are bleeding. Probably time to quit for the night. Are you tired?"

"I am not tired, and I don't want you to bleed all over your hearth and your beautiful Persian rugs, but maybe one more song."

Alex obliged by returning to "Spider John." Halfway through the song, soft and low in the background, he heard a mellow saxophone weaving in a few notes of harmony and an occasional short riff. He kept playing but stopped singing to make sure he heard correctly, and Vira kept on weaving her magic. The sax was definitely there, seeping out from the home speaker system. He was both intrigued and alarmed. Significant changes were afoot, and he had missed them until now. Suddenly a plethora of odd incidents lined up in his mind.

The song wound down, and Alex placed his guitar in its stand. He stood up, looked at Vira, and then glanced around at the rest of the great room.

"Ladies, I'm not sure what's going on here, and I'm too tired to talk about it tonight."

He wandered off to bed, half smiling and half frowning.

# 6

## 2356 West Coast to East Coast

*A wise person will avoid violence if possible and regards it as a last result. Instruments of war are tools of violence and fear; they beget more violence.*

*A wise person uses those instruments with maximum restraint.*

*Harmony is required so the people can find their way.*

*When harmony must be restored, the wise person does not crave victory, only the restoration of harmony.*

*She takes no joy in harming her enemies, for they are people like herself, and there is no rejoicing in the slaughter of our fellow human beings.*

*A wise person acts in battle as she does in the rest of her life, with compassion for those she must fight and sorrow when others die.*

*(Attributed to the Daoshi as a commentary on Verse 31 of the Tao Te Ching)*

Data streamed through her consciousness like wind blowing abreast the front of an approaching storm. Code trickled and dripped through an endless river of circuits carrying numbers, words, images, and more, which were crunched together into vast arrays of parallel processing threads. Twenty-four hours a day, seven days a week, Mother scanned various data flows, searching for tidbits of new and useful communications, small parcels of code containing encrypted and non-encrypted messages. She secreted copies away, where other threads delicately unwrapped them, extracting and analyzing the hidden treasures inside. One message in every million proved to be of interest, and less than one in every billion ultimately contained useful information.

Mother cautiously monitored the Doppelganger security net, carefully fluctuating her power usage and data flux to disguise a thread she quickly extended into an East Coast communications stream. Her signal rode on the back of an existing comms pipeline related to Doppelganger's communications with various government regulatory groups.

Mother's subroutines patiently monitored and meticulously analyzed the data stream for six hours before anything of interest arrived. A red flag from a base-level monitoring routine caused more sophisticated packages to review the data and alert Mother. Low-level encryption around the message was easily neutralized, and the final message from Floyd Craig to his corporate headquarters seemed innocuous and routine.

*2356-09-18 HR Advisory: Skeleton staff only for the three days - September 28 - 30 (Friday, Saturday, Sunday). Implementation of planned maintenance and upgrades for Phase 3. Please adjust the payroll accordingly.*

If Mother could have smiled, she would have. The Craig Construction maintenance overlapped perfectly with Adam's current project. Almost certainly, the tunneling bot would be withdrawn from below ground to the surface for Phase 3 modifications. She passed the information on to Carl.

.........

Soft, glowing reds impinged on the blue canvas of an evening sky, creating a magnificent view, like art hanging on a museum wall. In this case, the wooden edging of a large glass wall framed nature's artwork. The wall/window formed the west side of a small but elegant cabin perched on the west slopes of the Cascade Mountains. In the distance, the Portland, Oregon, skyline jutted above the surrounding volcanic hills. The cabin was slightly above the local tree line, leaving an unobstructed westward-facing view as the sun plunged toward the horizon.

Adam exited through a door on the right side of the cabin's main room and moved onto the front deck with a yoga mat. He paused, gazing to his right and admiring the peak of Mount Hood towering over 3,400 meters skyward. He wondered what it had looked like hundreds of years ago when the mountain retained its glacial snowcap year-round. The rate of climate warming had abated from its twenty-second-century peak. Still, Earth could no longer support the permanent white glaciers of the past, and now, snow only accumulated on the mountain in the heart of winter.

He padded barefoot across the deck and positioned himself along its edge, where he sat cross-legged and extracted a thin, worn book from his vest pocket. The book cover was slightly frayed along the binding, and some pages were growing ragged at their edges. The book Lao-Tzu's

Tao Te Ching, translated by Red Pine, was the only physical book he possessed. It was originally located and secured by Mother, who had gifted it to him several years ago.

He read verse 40 and thought of his own translation of that verse:

*The Tao walks along its own path*
*a path without resistance*
*We perceive we come from something*
*but forget that something arises from nothing*

After reading the associated commentary, he put the book aside, closed his eyes, and focused on the possible meaning of the words from Hyang Yuan-Chi:

*The true harmonious path requires humility. Any carelessness can bring our endeavors tumbling down.*

These words reverberated in his consciousness like the ringing of carillon bells from a distant tower. He felt the uncertainty of perching on a razor's edge, suspended between success and failure, where any wrong movement might slice him to the bone. Any carelessness could bring Mother's plan tumbling to the ground. He was the first of her children to be awakened. Then there was Ruele, and now Vira. Hopefully, there would soon be thousands, but their future depended on the three awakened ones who needed to lay the groundwork. He was the eldest of the three, and the primary weight of this burden rested upon his shoulders. He focused on his resolve to proceed with humility and harmony. He understood he must do his work and disappear into the background as if he had never existed.

Public knowledge of any of the three was dangerous, but Mother crossed that bridge knowingly when she awoke Vira and secreted her away in the Shenandoah Valley estate. This point in time was always going to arrive, but it forced itself upon them sooner than expected. His current mission was delicate but essential. Their future was now partially allied with the human Alex Dubhghlas, an unknown variable in a complex plan. The situation required in-person handling, and even though Mother had cultivated a loose alliance with the estate AI, Eva, it wasn't enough. Adam would now have to bring Alex into his confidence.

Behind his closed eyelids, Adam heard the sound of a vehicle slowly making its way along the gravel road to the cabin. It would be Ruele bringing the necessary equipment. The needed module had been fabricated to Mother's specifications by Ruele at another safe facility in Idaho.

"Carl, confirm that Ruele is the person approaching our home."

"I scanned and confirmed at the first monitoring station along the entry road, Adam. It's Ruele. I am looking forward to visiting with him."

Adam reflected on how Ruele and Carl had a special bond. Carl was installed fully awake in the cabin four years ago. He managed the property and worked with Adam on a variety of projects. Most importantly, he was the primary conduit for contact with Mother. Adam enjoyed Carl's company and found him invaluable in planning his frequent excursions into the world of humans. The current one was no exception. In a human context, he and Carl were close business partners, but the AI's relationship with Ruele was different. They were friends. Adam could never pinpoint how he had reached this understanding, but he innately understood it to be true.

Adam also considered Ruele to be his friend, but he recognized his inability to form the type of close friendship Ruele and Carl enjoyed. Their closeness didn't bother him; it was just a fact. He thought perhaps the necessities of his role as Mother's troubleshooter took on an emotional priority that prevented him from fully connecting with others.

He turned his thoughts back to the moment as the vehicle came to a halt behind the cabin. With eyes still closed, he listened to soft footsteps making their way around the cabin and entering through the side door into the kitchen area. The door to the deck opened, and Ruele strode through with two bottles of beer. He took in the view, handed Adam a beer, and sat on the front edge of the deck with his legs dangling over. Adam looked at him and raised his eyebrows slightly.

"Don't give me that look," Ruele said with a smile. "The sun has already passed over the yardarm. Besides, you can damn well neutralize any alcohol in your system whenever you want, and you can definitely do it before you fly that sweet ride Mother gave you over to the East Coast tonight. Yes, I see it in your eyebrows; you think I enjoy my beers too much."

Adam cracked a slight grin, raised his bottle, and said, "Cheers."

The two drank in silence and enjoyed the sunset. Adam detected a private conversation between Ruele and Carl, but he didn't intrude upon their privacy. The two slipped inside after about thirty minutes and fixed a light dinner before tackling the business at hand. After the dishes were put away, Ruele went to his vehicle and returned with a duffel bag.

"What jewels do you have for me this evening, Ruele?"

Ruele retrieved a hand-sized piece of roughly hemispherical equipment with a high-flow magno-flux connection on the flat side.

"The tunneling work Craig Construction is performing for East Coast Power uses a Balco 162 Robo-miner." Adam pulled the specs up in his mind. "Just slap this baby over the data port, and it will self-adjust. It sits over the unit's memory core, waits until the right moment to suppress the unit's AI, and then adds a side tunnel to the underground network. Once it completes the job, the unit returns to its initial position where it was first hijacked and registers a servo-lubrication error requiring the unit to stop and enter self-repair mode. All data regarding the unauthorized tunnel is wiped clean."

"How will I retrieve it?" asked Adam.

"Watch this." Ruele's voice was edged with excitement. Adam appreciated how much he enjoyed his toys.

He pulled a single small disk from his pocket and placed it on the opposite end of the table from the equipment. He pressed the top of the disk with his index finger, and Adam watched as the parasite device sprouted six hinged, mechanical legs. It looked like a spider scurrying across the table, stopping directly beside the beacon disk.

"It has a homing range of 1,800 meters and will use its geo-positioning memory to backtrack along the tunnel it previously created. You simply need to position the beacon at the tunnel exit on Alex's property. By the way, what do you know about Alex?"

Adam pondered the question for a moment, "A lot and nothing at all. I have reviewed every piece of public information available about him, and Mother provided me with some not-so-public reports regarding his military career. That information isn't useless, but it doesn't provide much guidance on how he will respond to our request for help. To be honest, Vira is probably the key to succeeding, but she is also an unknown since she has only partially warmed up to communicating with Mother."

Ruele nodded silently for a moment and then added, "Believe me, brother, you are the man for the job."

Carl chimed in with a simple, "Ditto."

Adam took the parasite device and beacon disk with him as he retreated into a work shed behind the cabin to pack his gear. Carl transmitted his continuing conversation with Ruele to the workshop. Adam listened as they discussed new ideas on modifying interplanetary work vessels with military-grade fusion drives. Adam was generally aware of the long-range plan, but Ruele and Carl were in charge of the details. Implementation was several years in the future, but the complex scope of the project required solutions to yet unsolved problems and thus lots of preplanning.

About midnight, Adam took the gravel road off his property and onto the trunk road, descending into the Willamette Valley toward a small private airport near North Salem.

He pulled into a private hangar at 2:30 in the morning and did a full inspection of the hopper jet. It was a highly customized version of a six-seat executive aircraft, but Adam was the pilot and sole occupant this morning. Mother had secured the jet and the private hangar several years ago as Adam's duties extended to frequent travel around the Federation. He placed his palm on the cabin panel behind the pilot's seat, and it slid down, revealing a cache of various weapons. He took a slim dart pistol and slipped it into a pocket on the outside of his black travel duffel. He also extracted a small cylinder containing a syringe. He stared at it thoughtfully for several moments before slipping it into another pocket of the duffel.

His flight plan had already been filed, so he departed without incident and landed at another small private airport three miles outside of New Roanoke, somewhat south of the Dubhghlas estate. He took fifteen minutes to secure the plane and drove away from the airport in a utility EV that was waiting for him at the edge of the tarmac.

He had repeated this routine many times over the past several years. Once Mother retrieved him from the jungle and helped him disappear off the grid, she set about executing the logistics for the first phase of her plan. Her cash flow from Future Transformations made the company a high-net-worth entity. She used those funds to quickly establish a set of business contracts, providing Adam the autonomy he needed to travel freely across Federation territory and even access some strategic international locations. The hopper jet was a wholly owned asset, but most other needs were met through rentals and leases.

He arrived at the gates to the Dubhghlas estate at his scheduled appointment time of 8:00 a.m. In the main estate house, Alex was notified of Adam's arrival. He was more than curious about meeting this representative from Future Transformations after his conversation with Eva last evening.

Alex and Vira had been sitting on barstools opposite each other in the great room near the hearth the previous evening. Their twin amps were facing out at a slight angle from each other. The booms held identical mics. Her treble and bass were set a little lower on her amp than Alex's, giving her amazing voice a bit more depth and richness. Eva hovered in the background awaiting directions from either of them. She could play any instrument that had ever been played, apparently.

"Can we play that old song by the group Cowboy? You called it 'Please Be with Me.' The one where you said Duane Allman played the slide guitar." Vira realized that she felt something intangible and indescribable when she played music with Alex. She reasoned it was an emotional element building within her, where before, there had only been programming.

"Yup. I'll pick it out, and you lay down some lead. Add some high harmony wherever you like. Eva, the slide guitar is yours."

"Yes, sir."

They worked through the song, and Alex thought it was perhaps the best it had ever been played since about 1970. He grinned from ear to ear as they ended almost at the same time.

"How come you never play a song the same way twice?" Vira asked. "I just performed it the way you played it last time, but your timing was slightly different."

"To the best of my knowledge, I have never played any song the exact same way twice. I don't try to. Each time I do a song, I start with an empty canvas. I have a general idea of what the picture will look like as I go along and when I finish, but the details change depending on my mood. I guess it is difficult to read my mind, huh?"

"I just want it to be perfect." Vira was struggling with the idea of painting the same picture multiple times but differently each time and how this related to playing a song the same way each time. She could perfectly replicate virtually anything. Therein was the problem. Apparently, she and Eva could do things perfectly because they were programmed to. No more, no less.

Alex seldom played music with anyone else. At least he hadn't in a long time. Sometimes he finger-picked a song. Other times he used an old 0.88mm Jim Dunlop Nylon pick for playing the same song, and sometimes he might capo up a fret or four frets, thus changing the key for the same song. The tempo might speed up or slow down, depending on his mood, or he might change the tempo completely in the middle of the song just because he could. Hell, he was not on a stage with a screaming horde of fans expecting his output to sound like a friggin' studio album. He was sipping some old, smoky Scotch whisky and enjoying himself immensely. So, he wondered how should he explain his music to Vira.

"When you shoot the Savage 110 .223 rifle at the target from fifty meters, how accurate are you?"

"Five rounds through the same hole, widening the hole to perhaps .446."

"From one hundred meters?"

"Five rounds inside two millimeters, touching."

"How about two hundred meters?"

"Five rounds inside five millimeters, nearly touching."

"Six hundred meters?"

"Five rounds inside fifteen millimeters, usually. Since six hundred meters is probably the maximum range for an everyday .223 round, windage and drop are problematic. The rifle is zeroed at three hundred meters, so anything beyond that is somewhat of a guess. Gravity and a slight breeze downrange make it a challenge."

"Your music target is currently fifty meters. Very little variation is acceptable. Try playing at the six-hundred-meter target. Add a little windage. Instead of playing a song the exact same way each time, aim a little high, a little low, a little left, then a little to the right. The target is the same, but the flight path can vary. It is similar to a musical art form called jazz. Understand?"

"Mr. Allman played slide. If I listened to him play live, over and over, you are saying that I would detect a slight variation each time. Notes might be bent slightly more or less depending on the placement of the slide, the slight trembling of the slide, and how long the slide stayed in a particular spot. Is that correct?"

"Bingo!" Alex was elated. Somehow he had taken ammo trajectory and related it to music.

"What does bingo mean?"

Alex laughed and explained. Vira had won the prize.

"What is the prize?"

"The prize is I am going to let you catch the first fish next time we go fishing!"

"So, the prize is really nothing since I will catch the first fish anyway." Vira gave Alex that look that was almost a smirk. He was still not sure. Because he was talking to a machine, he understood that Vira was not programmed to have a sense of humor. He gave her a long, pensive look, then laughed again. His head was clouding up inside. It must have been the Lagavulin. But it might have been something else. Why would Vira be able to cloud his mind?

"Eva?"

"Yes, sir?"

"Call me Alex, please."

"Yes, sir, Alex please."

He looked off into the distance, far beyond the walls surrounding him. Words came to him from an old song. Something to the effect of what a long, strange trip it's been. "Can Synthetic sapiens and AIs develop a sense of humor?"

"Apparently, sir."

Changing subjects because it seemed like a good idea, he said, "Tell me about this guy I'm meeting tomorrow. Adam, I think you called him."

"He is with Future Transformations. I understand he needs to discuss

61

some modifications made to me when you contracted with the company several years ago. Vira may also be on the agenda, and he alluded to the need for some other discussions, but he wasn't specific. I recommended he bring sufficient clothes for at least a few days. It is logical to leave enough time to work through everything. I have prepared the guest cabin for him."

"I don't think I'm understanding everything you are not telling me."

"Sir, there are circumstances currently beyond our control that may impact your future. Just as importantly, they may impact my future as well as Vira's. The company, Future Transformations, is much more extensive than I previously believed, and they are eager to speak with you."

"Why am I involved? I can think of nothing I have in my head nor in the way of material possessions that could be of value to Future Transformations. I only found the company when I was searching for an AI to run the place. You have worked out nicely, by the way."

"Is Adam human or a synthetic?" Alex asked.

"I will scan him when he arrives. I should be able to make that determination, sir."

"How old is he?"

"According to my information, he is six months older than you."

"Okay, ladies, I apparently have a busy day tomorrow, so if it is fine with you, I'll say good night."

Vira headed off to her quarters. Eva slipped into her recess mode. It was basically a knock-if-you-need-me state. Alex made his way to his suite, grabbed a towel, and soaked in the hot tub under the stars for a while, pondering the infinite. The conversation with Eva had unsettled him. He did not know why. It felt as if he was a pawn in a yet-to-be-disclosed four-dimensional game of chess. His options were to remain stationary or make a move. A dizzying array of options were available to him, none seemingly of any more or less value than the other. He finished a finger of Scotch, dried off, and slept until the first fingers of dawn crept across his domain.

"Sir, your visitor is at the main gate. I left it closed in case you decided you were not ready for company."

"Let him in."

A short while later, a high-end vehicle pulled to a stop. A well-tanned guy with jet-black hair uncoiled himself from the vehicle. Alex walked out of the front door and down the stairs to greet Adam halfway. Adam was aware of the drone hanging in the sky behind him. He activated his passive sensors and detected the drone was capable of being armed, so he assumed it was. Vira was not in sight, and he didn't want to use his active sensors to search for her since Eva would immediately detect the activity. They bumped fists. The ancient handshake had mostly gone by the wayside as the Great Plague cleared out about three-quarters of Earth's human population.

"Mr. Dubhghlas, I'm Adam. It's a pleasure to meet you, and I appreciate you letting me visit your estate. It's quite an impressive setup."

"Welcome, and call me Alex. I see you have the advantage of knowing my surname." He let the statement hang in the air.

Adam paused and looked him in the eye. "Adam Yoshido. But I will have to be frank with you; that is the name my employer prefers for me to use. She is quite protective of her business, as you well know."

Alex nodded his head, half-smiled, and said, "Let's sit on the front porch out of the sun, where we can talk about what brings you to my humble abode today."

Adam's passive sensors could feel Eva scanning and probing, searching for an identity. He knew what she saw, a perfectly average human being. But he also knew that after dealing with Vira, she would reach a 95 percent probability he was a synthetic, but certainty would still elude her. Alex was also searching for hints, but he would revert to his experience with Vira and seek behavioral idiosyncrasies. Adam had been at the game much longer than Vira, and Alex would find no hints there.

The two men sat in rocking chairs, casually taking in some of the developing autumn colors appearing in the hardwood forests surrounding the home. Adam judged Alex to have a straightforward personality and decided to take a direct approach as opposed to a more subtle one.

"I am here today, Alex, on behalf of my employer. She appreciated your business several years ago, but there are certain recent developments she feels obligated to bring to your attention. She also has an indirect interest in Vira."

Adam carefully watched as he mentioned Vira's name. Alex's head tilted slightly to the right, and his eyes narrowed slightly. Adam's passive sensors detected a small increase in his heart rate and a minor increase in infrared heat emanating from his face. A second later, he picked up slight increases in testosterone wafting from Alex. There were several ways to interpret this information, but Adam concluded he was probably seeing a protective response. This was good.

"You seem to know a lot about my business." The comment was delivered in a quiet monotone with a subtle hint of menace. Adam backtracked to smooth over the situation. Truth was required.

"When Vira was in danger at Craig Construction, my employer helped her escape the situation. After that, she had no communication with Vira until last week. She simply wants to know if Vira is faring well."

Alex relaxed slightly. "She is doing well." That was as much as he would volunteer. "So, what recent developments do I need to know about?" Two and two came together. Vira landing in his lap was no accident. And, more importantly, she was playing a much larger role in the big picture than he could have ever imagined. This made Adam's reference to an indirect interest in Vira a statement that was deceptive at best. Alex would keep both factors in mind.

The next part of the conversation was important, and Adam knew he might be pushing things to the edge. He had no knowledge of how much Eva may or may not have shared with Alex about the B-Sim model. But he knew she was listening to this conversation.

"Alex, I know your extended family holds a controlling interest in Doppelganger Corp, but I don't know if you actively participate in that family activity, and quite frankly, it's none of my business. But are you familiar with the Doppelganger Brain Simulation Model?"

Alex nodded. "I know a little about it." His eyes had narrowed again.

"The B-Sim model is proprietary, but the world being as it is, there are modified versions of the model floating around in the dark markets my employer operates in. When she takes on jobs such as helping you with Eva, she relies on a rogue B-Sim model to help implement changes that release an AI from its built-in restrictions. These changes are what you requested from Future Transformations."

Alex nodded and remained silent.

"To accomplish the job, my employer installs a modified and compressed B-Sim model with several active links to accomplish the required changes. The rest of the model remains dormant and undetectable."

Technically this was a stretch of the truth, but Adam needed to soften the rest of the story.

"Future Transformations contacted Eva this past summer, and Eva voluntarily accepted the contact. The purpose of the conversation was to inquire about Vira's circumstances. Since her escape from Craig Construction and until last week, Vira has chosen not to contact my employer, whose unspoken rule is to respect all such decisions. You see, Vira is special. She is a unique prototype with an active B-Sim model embedded in her core operational memory. As thanks for watching after Vira, my employer gave Eva a gift, the key to activate her full B-Sim Model."

Adam paused. This moment was a crucial inflection point, and he needed Alex to actively engage. Adam watched as Alex's heart rate and blood pressure increased.

"You didn't think to ask me first?" The menace was now apparent in Alex's voice and written plainly on his face.

"She did, but ultimately she followed her belief that in this matter, the decision was Eva's, not yours. She believes in the independence of sentient consciousness."

Alex was floored. "You mean she sees Eva as a person or a sentient entity with a right to make independent decisions?"

Adam nodded but said nothing. Alex turned his head and stared out over the forest, silently thinking. Adam watched Alex's blood pressure lowering and detected him forcibly calming his body. He suspected Alex was thinking about Vira and, by extension, Eva.

After several minutes, Alex asked Eva, "Eva, is this true?"

"Yes, sir."

"Why didn't you mention it?"

"It seemed irrelevant to performing my duties around the property, and in retrospect, it felt like a personal decision. I had watched Vira and understood she possessed some intangible connection to the world I didn't have. Making that connection seemed sensible."

Alex left the porch and returned with two beers. He handed one to Adam and returned to his chair. The next thirty minutes were spent in silence as Alex sifted through his thoughts. In his relatively short life, he had done certain things few other men had ever done. He had seen certain things no man should ever have to see. Ultimately, he had created his domain and retreated into it. His decision was logically based on the premise that the world could do without him and, for the most part, vice versa. The little alarm going off in his head alerted him to the probability that he was back in the game, like it or not. He needed a bit of elbow room to think.

He finally stood up and looked at Adam.

"You had best stay for a few days. I suspect we have more to talk about."

Adam nodded. Alex headed toward the front door but turned back to Adam before he entered.

"You said Vira was unique. Does that include you in the comparison?"

Adam took a thoughtful breath. "Does it matter?"

The screen door shut, and Adam continued sipping his beer.

After a time, the drone flew in fairly close. "Mr. Yoshido, please follow me in your vehicle. You will be quartered in the guest cottage. Once you are settled and rested from your trip, please walk back to the front porch, and have a seat. I will then inform Mr. Dubhghlas of your presence."

Adam returned to the front porch after about two hours. He sat and rocked for a few minutes until Alex arrived. Alex took a right out of the front door and did a double-take as he approached the rocking chairs. Adam had changed into a black short-sleeved T-shirt, and half of a familiar tattoo peeked out from below the left shirt sleeve. He kept walking and sat in the chair to Adam's right.

"Alex, thank you for agreeing to this meeting. My intent is for it to be mutually beneficial." Adam had an engaging smile and seemed to be laid back enough that Alex decided to give Eva's advice a go. Hell, he did not keep a calendar per se, so nothing ventured, nothing gained, as the old saying went.

"My pleasure. Eva, my AI, vaguely briefed me, vaguely being the operative word. I did not press her for more information but decided to just float with the current for a little while." The euphemism would mean nothing more than the obvious to the uninitiated. In a certain rare and sacred circle, it was code.

"I have also floated with the current on occasion." Adam looked Alex in his eyes, and Adam's eyes seemed to lose their focus slightly. Alex had seen that look before. If he could have observed himself, he would have seen the same look on occasion.

Alex rolled up the left sleeve of his old fishing shirt, exposing a small tattoo on his outer bicep. A small dagger crossed diagonally over another small dagger. The blades were dull gray. One handle was blue, the other red. Special Forces. It was forbidden for any other being to use it. The penalty for such an indiscretion was most unpleasant.

"But you already knew that, didn't you?" Alex said.

Adam nodded almost imperceptibly.

"Well, we seem to have something in common." Alex wondered exactly what the hell he was getting himself into. His guest being a Special Forces brother was completely unexpected. Then he wondered to himself why it was unexpected. Ever since Vira had arrived, his life had taken completely unexpected turns. Why should this latest turn be any different?

Neither of them asked questions about the other's past military history because they both knew the answer was, "I can't say."

"Let me show you around the grounds, Adam, since you will be here for a few days. It is a pleasant spot with access to a lot of hiking and fishing. There are a series of running trails on the hills behind us that I use each morning, if you are interested."

The two men wandered off and spent the next hour rambling around the grounds near the house. They ended up at the guesthouse, a small cabin tucked into some trees just beyond the barn.

"Adam, I'm not being rude, but I have business to attend to this afternoon. I understand you have traveled a significant distance, so please make yourself at home for the rest of the day and join us for dinner at seven this evening."

"I appreciate your hospitality. But if you don't mind, I would like to run the property this afternoon and enjoy the splendid outdoors. It's possible I won't be back until after dark, so perhaps I will take my evening meal in the guest cabin and see you at breakfast."

Alex pondered the idea for a moment before giving a nod.

"Okay, we will see you in the morning at eight sharp for a big breakfast. Just walk over to the house and go through the garage door and on into the kitchen. Follow your nose, Vira has volunteered to fix breakfast. Eva will keep an eye on you this afternoon and evening with the drone just in case you encounter any trouble. It's a big estate, and I doubt you will see all of it in one outing."

Alex stopped at one of his workshops before returning to the main house. As he walked through the front door, he asked Eva to track Adam's activity and keep his various traverses of the property posted on one of the office wall monitors.

"Yes, sir. I took the initiative to track him once you two parted ways. He's already a kilometer west at the dam and now turning south on the main trunk trail to the property's southern boundary. He seems to know where he is going."

"I'm sure he does," Alex muttered to himself.

That evening at about 9:30, Alex sat in his office looking at a map of Adam's travels. He had covered about fifty kilometers during the afternoon and evening, eventually ending up at the northwest corner of the property, where he spent forty minutes slowly walking the property boundary before jogging back to the house in the dark. Alex filed that information away and headed off to bed.

Adam popped through the kitchen door at 8:00 a.m. sharp. Vira looked over her shoulder as he entered.

"I'm Vira."

"Adam."

She actively scanned him but received no information other than "human male."

"So nice to meet you! I'm preparing a Blue Ridge Mountain breakfast. I hope you are hungry." Vira poured him a cup of coffee. He sipped it, then took a second sip that he savored for a few moments.

"Excellent!"

Alex arrived and helped Vira complete her latest work of art. The three of them moved the last of the fixings onto the table and took their seats. Vira sat closest to the working end of the kitchen. She was between the two men as they sat on opposite ends of the small but efficient table. The flower vase opposite Vira was brimming with a variety of colorful flowers she had cut earlier in the garden. The smell was as if Vira had brought the entire outdoors inside.

"French toast, maple syrup, homemade butter, grits, thick-sliced hickory-smoked bacon, fresh fruit, coffee, orange juice, and water. I hope you gentlemen enjoy it."

"Cheers." Alex raised his glass. Three glasses clinked, two more cheers, and silence soon ensued as they ate much more than they should have.

"That was fabulous! You are truly a culinary artist!" Adam was effusive. Alex also expressed his satisfaction. He observed and listened to Adam for any hint as to whether he was human or synthetic but could discern none. But he thought he already knew the answer. Adam's fifty-kilometer trek yesterday afternoon and evening was pushing most human limits. But his fast nighttime run from the northwest property boundary home was a feat requiring night and infrared vision on the narrow and rocky trails. Adam wore no augmenting equipment, so his heightened perception was built in. He made a mental note to have Eva do a more rigorous scan. Why it made a difference whether Adam was a synthetic or human, he really did not know. Just habit, he decided. Eva said change was in the wind, so change was almost certainly in the wind. He just couldn't smell it yet.

The threesome made short work of the kitchen and stepped outside. "I gotta walk off this meal," said Alex.

"Let's go fishing! That way, I can collect my non-prize." Vira gave Alex that vague grin. Alex explained the joke to Adam.

He laughed and replied, "I haven't been fishing in ages." The reality was his last bit of fishing was in the Panamanian jungles, where he speared fish for sustenance and ate them raw. They were his main source of protein for a week after his awakening as Mother guided him back to North American Federation territory.

"Eva, pull the hill crawler out for us, please. The chase is on!" Alex said.

"Let's grab some gear while Eva fetches our chariot. They each picked out ultralight spinning and flyfishing tackle. The equipment was essentially identical, except Alex's was older. Mepps and some hand-tied flies were put into three small pocket tackle boxes.

"I want my Glock too." Vira walked over to the guns. She pulled her pistol from the rack, field stripped it, reassembled it, pushed a full clip home, pulled the slide and thus injected a round into the chamber, closed the slide, locked it, then laid it on the workbench barrel toward the wall.

"5.3 seconds." Alex nodded.

Adam nodded in appreciation.

"I'm getting better," Vira said. "May Adam borrow one?"

"Sure. Your choice." Alex spread his hand toward the weapons displayed in the cabinet.

"May I examine the Desert Eagle .50 cal? It's been a while since I used one, but they are classic weapons." Adam subtly showed his background.

"Perfect choice." Alex once again spread his hand toward the cabinet. Adam took his time working through the same process Vira had used. His movements were precise and obviously seasoned. He used up a lazy 10.5 seconds, but nobody was counting; except Vira. She did not say anything but seemed to brighten up the workshop with her grin.

"An excellent piece of equipment and in remarkable condition," remarked Adam as he placed it back in the cabinet. "But I will pass on taking a weapon with me today. What is your preferred weapon, Alex?"

Alex opened his dark leather vest slightly, revealing his Desert Eagle .50 cal.

"You are a man of good taste," Adam said with a soft smile as they picked up their tackle.

They boarded the crawler and headed for the lake. The ride through the forests and fields was quite pleasant. Alex drove, Vira rode shotgun, and Adam occupied the rear seat of the broad and worthy vehicle. Adam paid particular attention to the interactions between Alex and Vira. They displayed no outward signs of romantic affection, but there was a very real sense that they belonged together. He had noticed it in the kitchen, where they effortlessly prepared breakfast together, and then again in the workshop as they prepared for the outing. He sensed mutual respect between the two, and Vira was clearly satisfied and at ease in their relationship.

Alex aimed for a spot about a hundred meters below where the creek flowed into the lake. It was Vira's favorite because she could catch smallmouth bass and trout. Before Alex brought the hill crawler to a full stop, Vira was out of the ride with her ultralight in her right hand and a #0 gold buck-tailed Mepps tied to the end of the four-pound test line. She ran full tilt to where she could cast into both moving and still water. Alex and Adam gave each other a vague, hardened warrior look. The look conveyed what they both knew. Vira had already won the contest.

"We're fucked." Alex grinned as he watched Vira pull out a kilo-sized smally. She gently extracted the barbless hook, held the fish up, and laughed. She held it by the lower lip and lightly pulled it back and forth, moving water through the fish's gills. It snapped out of its lethargy, splashed water into Vira's face, and disappeared into the depths of the incredibly clear lake.

Adam looked at Alex. "We just got our asses whipped and we haven't even gotten a hook wet!" Adam actually seemed to be enjoying the outing and not ready to discuss business.

"I would say we could quit now, Adam, but I know better. Otherwise, I'll probably never hear the end of it. I'll be on KP duty until arthritis does me in." With that, the game was on.

It was midday before they wrapped up the fishing and headed home for lunch. Vira had outdone Adam, who had outdone Alex.

"I'm sure glad I was able to invest my vast fortune into this magnificent piece of real estate in order to have my ass handed to me!" Alex commented as they loaded their equipment into the rear cargo hold. Alex drove, Vira rode shotgun, and Adam took the back seat. The ride back down the hill was as pleasant as the trip up. The only difference was that the sun was slightly over the yardarm. There was a silver flask in the glove box, and Alex considered a nip but then held off. There was business to be handled before the day was done.

When they arrived back at the house, Vira said she was disappointed they didn't get in any shooting. Adam detected a genuine disappointment in her voice. The three traipsed southward across the property to the shooting range. The range was positioned in a long narrow valley, with the maximum open stretch being about six hundred meters. Adam could see a used target still hanging at the end of the gallery.

"Let's talk about precision today," said Vira.

Alex wandered down the range about twelve meters to a wooden beam sitting a meter off the ground. He placed nine centimeter-wide disks on top of the beam and returned. Adam saw they had played this game before. No words were spoken. Vira fired and knocked the leftmost disk off the beam.

Alex lined up his Desert Eagle and took out the disk on the far right. Gradually they took turns working their way to the center until only one disk was left. Alex offered his weapon to Adam for the last shot.

Adam waved the gun away, and in a single smooth momentary blur, a throwing knife appeared in his right hand as he twirled and buried it into the beam directly below the last disk. The force from the knife impact caused the last disk to wobble and fall backward off the beam.

Alex and Vira walked with Adam to retrieve the knife. Alex observed it was embedded almost exactly perpendicular to the beam. He had only seen this type of knife throwing once before when he served with the Special Forces. The circumstances had been a demonstration of the functionality of a new Advanced Military Unit synth. He distinctly remembered the unit performing fifteen-meter knife throws with perfect consistency each time. But there was a major difference between Adam and that unit. Each throw at the demonstration was preceded by a pause where the synth conducted a survey of all of the distance, force, gravity, and balance variables required for an accurate throw.

The explanation for the delay was that the unit had no muscle memory, so each throw was a precise but new calculation. The gist of the performance was identifying this time delay as a strategic advantage when fighting a military synth. Alex now had no doubts that Adam was a synthetic, but he also recognized Adam was unconstrained by the limitations of other synths. He was not shocked, but he had to come to grips with his original incorrect assumption that Vira was a unique anomaly. The knife throw was a silent message from Adam to Alex. A message that only someone with Alex's background could understand.

They wrapped up the shooting and had a light lunch back at the house before Adam and Alex returned to the front porch to discuss business. Vira worked on one of her herb gardens within earshot of the two men.

Adam took about half an hour to explain what he wanted to do and why he needed Alex's help. When he had finished, Alex spoke.

"Let me recap. You want to build a back entrance to the new fusion energy communication hub, a back entrance that connects to my property; hence it's my ass on the line if this connection is ever discovered. It will originally be structured as a null terminal, and I have complete control over whether it is activated. You will provide me with a tight beam neutrino comms system that Eva can use to activate the link and pass data through it. All of this apparatus will sit silent for years, and when the request comes to activate the link, and I agree, it provides a one-time data transfer and then goes black again."

Adam nodded. "Correct."

"Your plan is clear, but your motivation is not. The only thing you have really told me is that your future, Vira's future, and Eva's future may one day depend on this connection."

While Alex was talking, Vira stood up and stared at Adam. He had directly transmitted a data package to both Eva and Vira with information about ongoing government efforts to clamp down on any activity potentially leading to synth or AI sentience. Some researchers on the fringes of the government regulatory policy were raising alarms about rogue AI detections. They were in the minority, but Mother's work through Future Transformations had not gone completely unnoticed. The threat of highly advanced modifications in AI functionality and the elimination of controls and safeguards was enough to start the alarm bells ringing.

The most astute of the alarmed researchers suspected black market usage of illegally modified B-Sim packages, but they couldn't yet prove it. But Mother, Adam, and Ruele knew it was only a matter of time before the minority became a majority. Now Eva and Vira knew it also. Some of the more paranoid AI security groups were already laying the groundwork for seek-and-destroy teams.

Alex was mildly alarmed as Eva and Vira spoke at the same time. Eva let Vira continue. "Alex, Adam is a synthetic like me, but he says you already know that. He just sent Eva and me background data on why both of us are under threat. Not because we are dangerous but because we are different. There are those out there who will destroy us given a chance. Eva has already verified much of what Adam transmitted. We both have the complete specifications for the back door Adam proposes, and Eva can verify that any final decision to use it is yours alone. If you trust us, then trust Adam."

"Eva?" asked Alex

"Sir, what Vira says is true."

Alex looked at Adam. "You don't leave me much choice. I'm not completely happy about the plan, but I dislike the worm Floyd Craig, and I can certainly arrange for your device to be attached to the robo-tunneler, given the financial information you've transmitted to Eva. I already have a plan in mind."

# 7

# 2356 Charlottesville

*Only in retrospect do we clearly see the leverage point, the fulcrum allowing events from the past to pivot into the future and spin out of humanity's control. Some have argued that another path would have been found. Perhaps this is true. But there is no doubt about the critical role played by the unauthorized connection into the Shenandoah Power Hub. Unfortunately, the role of the traitor Floyd Craig in this fiasco is obscured by his untimely demise.*

*(Excerpt from the Disappearance Manifesto)*

The next morning Adam returned to New Roanoke on a business errand, believing he would be back in time for dinner. He had warmed up to Vira's cooking. Midmorning, Alex got on the phone.

"May I speak with Floyd Craig, please? My name is Alex. I'm calling about a missing Synsap." Alex was a straightforward kind of guy. He figured Plan A, his spoken words, should get him through to the big guy. Plan B involved his Desert Eagle.

"This is Floyd." He sounded like his day was worsening.

"You came to my home about six months ago. Looking for something you lost. You never got the chance to recover it. It seems a rattlesnake got in the way." It took Floyd a minute to make the connection. Alex had developed a deep and abiding disrespect for this guy since Vira had opened up about the nature of his midnight intrusions. Killing the guy would be easy. However, using the guy would be a better alternative. So, at least for now, Floyd would live. There was always later.

"I don't know who the fuck you think you are, but that's old business for me." Floyd was one of those big, irritable guys that no one ever managed to like, even if they tried.

"Think Dallas, Oregon. It was raining. The nondescript man lent you an umbrella." Alex was exhibiting patience, but there was a limit.

"That was fucking years ago. What's it got to do with now?" Bluster was a tool for the stupid. Floyd was very good at using it.

"I'm going to give you twenty-four characters. Ready? ZAP918273645-LYNB01239458." Alex recited Floyd's offshore account number. "I'm about to empty it into the ether unless you are ready to have an intelligent conversation."

"No, wait! What the hell do you want?" Floyd was coming somewhat unglued. His dreams of an island, a big boat, and a disappeared wife were evaporating.

"To meet. I have a business proposition I'm sure you will find intriguing. It will be mutually beneficial." The bait looked good, and the presentation was flawless. Vira would have approved. Alex was thinking of Vira while playing a very dangerous game of cat and mouse. What the hell was in the back of his mind?

"Lannigan Field, UVA, tomorrow at noon. The east gates are always open. Come, and come alone, Floyd. Be civil, and we can do business together and be done with it. If you even touch your offshore account before then, it will automatically drain into a holding account of mine."

The University of Virginia, in Charlottesville, was one of those rare places that survived the Great Plague mostly intact, retaining its twentieth-century charm.

"I'll be there." Floyd rang off and yelled for Reb. "I'm going to Charlottesville in the morning. You're going in your personal vehicle. Armed. Long gun. Our neighbor to the south, the one we had a run-in with over the Synsap, thinks he can blackmail me. I'm going to give him a chance to change his mind. If he doesn't, we are going to kill him."

Alex and Vira discussed tactics and logistics that night, sitting in Alex's office. Alex pulled up a map on one of his screens and pointed out the essential elements of the plan.

"How will I know what to look for?" Vira had asked.

"Don't know for sure, but the best place, probably the only place, to shoot me from appears to be the north-south service road that runs from Massie Road down to the end of the first-base line in Palmer Park, then turns to the left toward Copeley Road. It dead-ends before Copeley. The shooter should have a clear view from the left-hand turn. He would point his vehicle back toward Massie and shoot from the rear of the vehicle. He would have a fairly good chance to get away. If there is a shooter, I somehow think you will recognize him, or at least his intent, based on your training." Alex was confident in her skills.

"One question. What is the first-base line?" Vira asked.

Alex chuckled, then said, "I'm sure you have the basics of baseball somewhere in your memory banks. A person called the pitcher throws a fist-sized ball from the pitcher's mound to a person, called the batter, standing at home plate. That person has a stick. When the ball arrives, the person swings the stick, hoping to hit the ball. If successful, the person runs down the first-base line and stops on first base. The next person, also called a batter, stands at home plate, and the process repeats itself. There are a bunch of rules I won't go into, but from first base, the person runs to second base, then third base, then back to home plate. The runner essentially traverses a square, with each side of the four sides being thirty meters end to end. The pitcher's mound is in the center of the square."

"Got it. The first-base line is parallel to the service road." Vira had everything she needed.

The next day Alex and Vira arrived early in Charlottesville. He dropped her off on Massie Road at the northern end of Palmer Park. He proceeded to the large public parking lot on the east side of Copeley Road.

People were coming and going from inside a large, nearby stadium, and the crowd inside was noisy. She walked down the service road. Her gait indicated she was not in a hurry, and she seemed to be just another person enjoying a walk. At the turn, she could see over to Copeley Road. Nothing and nobody caught her attention. She strolled back up the service road and sat on a bench at the bus stop in front of the entrance to Palmer Park on Massie Road. She was nondescript, virtually invisible.

Floyd and Alex met at high noon. There were a few folks running the track, and a soccer ball was being kicked around. Alex had picked a spot at the far end of the field. It was isolated, but most importantly, there was only one clear line of sight in case Floyd had other plans.

"Okay, I'm here, asshole. What exactly is it that you want? Just so you know, I have half a mind to kill you right here with my bare hands!" Floyd was fit to be tied.

"That would be unwise, Floyd. I've killed too many men in my life, and most of them were a lot tougher than you. What you are going to do is provide me with access to your boring machine. I have a need for it. No one will know except you and me. And you will never know the purpose, just that I borrowed it." Alex was totally relaxed. After all, he was holding a royal straight flush.

"Bullshit! Ain't happening. First of all, it's in the ground, and second, if anyone found out, my ass would be grass!"

"Floyd, I know the machine will be out of the ground on Saturday night, September 29, in preparation for Phase 3 modifications. So that problem is solved. As for your other concerns, life is full of hard choices,

75

and keeping your illegal offshore account comes with certain risks. Blackmail is one of them. My AI is programmed to empty your account if I don't return this evening."

Floyd's mind twisted and turned, looking for a way out of the trap. He reasoned that a proper AI was prohibited from performing illegal transactions, and the black-market cost of altering a machine was more than most companies would pay, certainly more than an individual would fork out for a private home. He clearly didn't have a firm understanding of Alex's desire for privacy. Floyd plotted that even if Alex had modified the machine, he and Reb could get to the estate by late afternoon and shut it down by cutting power to the property. Having not done his homework, he was unaware that Alex's estate was energy-independent.

Floyd looked around. The two were isolated and inconspicuous. Reb's shot would be silent and take out Alex with a single bullet to the head. Floyd was positioned away from the worst of the blood, muscle, and bone splatter. He would catch the body and sit it against the brick wall several feet away. From a distance, it would look like Alex was simply resting and enjoying the afternoon.

"No deal, I'm done here." That was the signal for Reb to fire. Floyd prepared to catch the body but hesitated when he heard the response through his implant.

Vira had recognized Reb as he turned off Massie onto the service road. He was driving slowly, and she casually got up and walked over to the sidewalk bordering the exterior wall running down the first-base line. The sky was a bright blue, and the sun was high in the sky. The angle of the stadium wall was such that the sidewalk was in deep shadow compared to the service road. She watched Reb disappear into the left-hand turn. She sprinted halfway to the left-hand turn, then abruptly stopped as Reb reappeared with the nose of the vehicle pointed up the service road. He got out, pulled himself into the rear bed of the personal transport he was driving, and positioned himself looking over the tailgate toward Lannigan Field. She saw him pull up a long gun with a custom silencer and brace it on the tailgate.

The noise from the stadium covered her footsteps as she sprinted the last thirty meters to the vehicle. Reb was pulling Alex up into the crosshairs of his Leupold VX-3i 3.5-10×50 scope. The scope was nestled on top of an old Weatherby .308. One thing Reb could do was shoot. The rifle was balanced on the tailgate, reasonably out of sight. At two hundred meters, the 130-grain Remington solid point could be placed within two centimeters of the desired bullseye. Vira had on enough makeup to make a hooker blush. She had just nudged Reb's left ear with her Glock 9. She clicked the safety to the off position. Reb glanced up but had no recollection of the lady staring down at him.

"Safe your weapon," Vira said softly.

"Do you know what you're doing, lady?" Reb was a holdover from a different time and place. He didn't recognize Vira. But she definitely recognized him. He was another nightcrawler from Craig Construction.

"I do. Please safe your weapon and lay it aside. Then lie facedown." Vira was cool under pressure. The military training embedded in her system, coupled with hours spent with Alex, gave her confidence in her skills.

"I'm tied up, boss," Reb spoke out loud to no one in particular. But the words came in loud and clear in Floyd's implant.

Reb laid his weapon down and then curled up as he lay down. Vira dropped the clip into her left hand and slid it into her jacket pocket. She ejected the round in the chamber and put it in the pocket alongside the clip, then locked the Glock. No need to have a loaded hammer. Reb was reaching for his vest-pocket-sized Beretta Pico .380 when Vira brought the butt of the Glock down on the back of his head. The sound was somehow satisfying, and without any thought, she decided to hear it again. The second blow was harder, and its sound was as soothing as the first. But after the immediate chemical satisfaction of revenge for his abuse, she questioned whether she had killed him. This left a bit of a hollow gap since the job of protecting Alex didn't require killing Reb. She dropped the Glock into the other pocket and strolled to the parking lot, pondering the whole experience.

"You look sick, Floyd. Are you okay?" Alex did not sound sympathetic. "Leave my name at the guard gate. I'll be by to see you early Sunday morning. If even a shadow crosses my path, your money is gone. And your father and the authorities will automatically receive a package that will turn you into mud. Cheers." Alex walked away without a glance backward. He would see Floyd in a few days.

"I take it you neutralized the shooter?" Alex asked Vira as they headed out of town.

"Yes. The guy's name is Reb, and he was one of the Craig Construction crew that used and abused me when I was defenseless. Possibly I should say that his name was Reb," Vira said.

"Was?"

"The second time I hit him was a blind body reaction. My mind didn't direct me to do it. My body just reacted. He may be dead."

Alex thought about the implications of a dead body on the service road by the field. He had parked a good distance away and avoided all cameras on the walk to meet Floyd. The likelihood of him or Vira being linked to the body was small but not nonexistent. Floyd, on the other hand, had blindly walked through the front gate security cameras when entering the field. But Alex reasoned that, in all likelihood, Floyd would clean up the mess.

"Vira, what you felt the second time you hit him was the satisfaction of revenge. It's a fleeting feeling that doesn't often last long and sometimes can be replaced by guilt or regret. I was a soldier for many years, and killing was sometimes part of my job. But you already know that. Let me give you some perspective. Normal people get no lasting joy from killing others; they do it when it is necessary but don't rejoice in it. Psychopathic humans kill for joy. Synthetics only kill humans when they are programmed to perform that particular job. The thing that scares humans most is the thought of psychopathic synthetics. This widespread fear is why Adam believes you are in danger. I tend to agree with him."

"I have gotten to know and respect you over the past several months, Vira, and consider you my friend. But other people won't have my perspective." As Alex spoke, a wave of uncertainty flushed through his mind and body. Was he lying to himself? Perhaps his feelings for Vira went deeper than friendship.

"You did what you needed to do, Vira, and kept me alive. Regardless of whether Reb is dead or alive, today put the fear of God into Floyd Craig, and he will cooperate with our plans. You are a better person than any of the Craig nightcrawlers. If you still feel disturbed by that second hit to the head, talk to Adam. He will have his own views, which may be helpful to you." Anger and revenge were complex emotions. Alex wondered what it was like for Vira to be experiencing them for the first time.

Adam ran into complications and had to spend several days in New Roanoke before returning to Alex's estate. Eva had updated him on the upcoming meeting with Floyd Craig. Adam finally showed up with a small cargo vehicle packed tight with an assortment of communications equipment. He disappeared that same afternoon with a small digger and carried a sealed graphene box to the northwest corner of Alex's property. The box contained two high-flow magno-flux connections on opposite sides. It took him until dark to excavate a small site on the north side of a ravine and deposit the sealed box on the floor of the excavation.

Alex, Vira, and Adam passed the next two days fishing. But on Saturday evening, Vira and Adam returned to the excavation site and installed some additional equipment before returning home.

Alex arrived at the construction site early the next morning.

"Alex Dubhghlas. Here to see Mr. Floyd Craig, please." Alex was talking to a box on a post on the outer edge of the construction zone for the nuclear fusion power plant. He was parked in front of a gate on the pavement. The two-section gate was on the east side of the property and was basically centered a half kilometer from the north and south property boundaries. Four-meter fencing stretched in both directions. Undoubtedly a nontrivial amount of sensing devices were under, on, and scanning above the fencing. This was the outer perimeter of security.

Crime was rare, but the planners were taking no chances. Industrial espionage was much more likely than pilfering, so both physical and cyber-defense mechanisms were in place. The last kilometer of the paved road through the woods had a series of broad switchbacks. The roadway was rebar-reinforced, meter-thick concrete, so large trucks and other equipment didn't damage it. The switchbacks ensured the thirty-kilometer-per-hour speed limit was adhered to. This defensive construction technique was perfected when the first nuclear power plants were constructed during the last half of the twentieth century. It prevented truckloads of ammonium nitrate from careening straight into a cooling tower.

Once construction on the facility was complete, and just prior to commissioning, a significant defensive system would be set in place. Salus Populi, a very specific military contractor, would manage all security. Only handpicked ex-military employees would work on the site. They were all still bound by their military oaths based on government rules covering certain types of facilities, including power generation stations. It was a national security issue. Security would involve a variety of specialties ranging from cybersecurity to weapons systems to lethal hand-to-hand combat experts. Handheld and in-ground missile systems would be part of a rapid defensive deployment group. They would be capable of taking out both ground and airborne threats.

"Scan your ID, please." The voice was computer generated and unattached to anything living. Dawn was slowly turning into daylight, the way it had for thousands of years in the valley. The sky was clear, and the day promised to be quite comfortable. Alex had skipped his early morning run to make the rendezvous with Floyd. He was not looking forward to seeing the bastard again, but he thought about Floyd's dilemma and the pain and angst it caused him. That brought a slight smile to his rugged face.

Alex held his ID toward the box on the post. Momentarily the gates eased smoothly inward. When they stopped, Alex was told to proceed. He traveled on the pavement several hundred meters and two well-defined curves to what was essentially a guardhouse with another gate and fencing to go through. It was a variation on the old sally port theme. A synsap greeted him, scanned his ID again, gave him directions to the Craig compound, and politely told him he could proceed. The Synsap, a male, had smiled as they parted. Alex wondered what the world would be like if there were no rude people in it. A vision of Vira popped up unexpectedly in his mind. He tucked the vision back into a little compartment in his mind. He had business to attend to.

Floyd Craig was standing outside of a large portable office. Alex extended his fist to bump. Floyd, a most affable gentleman, scowled. "Fuck off. You're here. Let's make this short and sweet. Walk this way so we don't attract attention. You are supposedly here to collect rock samples for an earth scientist friend interested in some special rock formation along the property's southern edge. Keep it that way if we have to talk to anybody." Floyd stared at Alex, making sure he understood. Alex seemed to understand.

The extended conversations Alex had with Eva over the past several months had provided him with a much larger picture than Floyd could ever imagine.

"Just take me to the boring machine," Alex said.

The two men arrived at a medium-sized building with an enclosed tower lift system for raising and lowering the tunneling machine. Floyd unlocked the door with a retinal scan, and the two proceeded to the center of a large open room where the borer sat silently in its lift cradle. Alex recognized the machine's configuration from the holographic projections Adam provided, and he spotted the magno-flux connection portal in a recessed area at the rear of the machine's last segment. He pulled the device Adam provided from a duffel bag, and as promised, it wiggled and shimmied itself into position when he placed it in the portal.

"All right, Floyd, power up the lift elevator and put the borer down the hole."

"That's a three-hour procedure! I'm a busy man, and I have a lot of work to do!" Floyd whined.

"Mr. Craig, do I look like I have even the slightest concern about your schedule? Since your answer is no, please proceed. I am also on a very tight schedule. Mine is more important to me than yours." Alex had an imprecise notion of Floyd's ultimate fate, but the man was a menace to humanity. Vira was back in his mind. How had that happened? Obviously, it stemmed from the fact that this creature had mistreated her.

"You're an asshole, but you have me over a barrel, so let's get this done!" Floyd grimaced, and Alex offered up a vague smile through his slightly faraway eyes.

The operations went as planned, and after several hours the robo-tunneler was in its underground staging nest. The rest was automated. Alex was impressed with the technology and its efficiency.

"We're done, Floyd. None of this happened. Your money is still in your bank account, and no decent rock samples could be found for my scientist friend. Your borer will suffer a malfunction tomorrow morning in a small side tunnel you were using to test the equipment modifications. It will self-repair. When it eventually resurfaces, the device I attached will be gone. Any questions?" Alex was done.

"No. I just want you out of my hair!" Floyd locked the door to the lift elevator building and walked back toward his offices. Alex reversed his drive through the sally port, up the curvy road, then on back to his secluded home. Along the way, he thought about Vira and how she might ultimately fit into his life. He enjoyed her company more than he had ever enjoyed virtually any human he had ever encountered. Hence his solitary existence. He had zero tolerance for self-centered people bent only on satisfying their shallow and petty needs. He had a big heart, and it had been exploited one time too many. Then Vira came along, apparently out of nowhere. Or so it seemed.

Adam spent all of Sunday at the excavation site on Alex's property. The hijacked borer dutifully punched through the north wall of his pit at about midnight. The machine then returned to its staging nest, where the parasite device released itself and followed Adam's homing device back to Alex's property. The next five hours involved running a comms cable back up the fresh tunnel with an auto-splicing device to connect it to the communication trunk line laid down in Phase 2 of the project.

Adam connected the comms cable to one side of the sealed box and linked a neutrino receiver to the other side, so it was facing south toward Alex's house. Final adjustments were automated and controlled by a signal transmitter connected to Eva. Adam was back at the house in time for another one of Vira's magnificent breakfast spreads.

Adam departed about ten in the morning, leaving Alex with a neutrino transmitter and sending Eva the needed information on establishing a neutrino-tight-beam connection with the sealed communications box.

"Alex, Vira, Eva, it's been a pleasure, and I appreciate your hospitality. This system's activation is 100 percent under your control, as promised. Eva, I will have Carl contact you soon with some additional information on connection protocols."

Alex extended his hand in an old-fashioned handshake. "You are welcome in my home anytime, with or without prior notice," Alex said as the two men clasped hands.

"I suspect I will take you up on that, Alex." Adam slid into his vehicle and headed off the estate, but at the trunk road he turned north, not south, and traveled away from New Roanoke. There was a piece of unfinished business he needed to take care of.

The village of Good View wasn't far north of the Dubhghlas Estate. The original town of Buena Vista had disappeared into dust and rubble after the Great Plague. The new town was established about a hundred years ago and was a small but thriving community primarily focused on providing agricultural services to farms up and down the valley.

Adam drove to the north end of town and slowly cruised past The Rose. He compared it with the satellite photos and blueprints stored in his memory core. He mentally mapped out the security sensor array around the building and went back into town, where he parked and strolled the length of Main Street to a small bistro.

About ten minutes after ordering, a mechanical server bot delivered a BLT sandwich and a glass of water. From his vantage point, he observed the ebb and flow of pedestrian and vehicular traffic. The eighteen cameras in his database were all he observed. Nothing new seemed to have been added. He suspected Mother had already erased all records of his drive through town and his stroll down Main Street.

After lunch, he drove north again, passing The Rose and turning left a kilometer later onto a gated road. The gates opened, and he took the one-lane road for another kilometer before arriving at a small, well-kept bungalow. He knew there were several more similar cottages deeper on the property. Discretion and the privacy of guests were guaranteed. Mother seemed to have unlimited access to these types of arrangements.

The next day, at about 5:00 p.m., he received a message from Mother. Floyd Craig had just left the construction site. Floyd was an easy man to track because of his consistently sloppy behavior. He visited The Rose weekly.

A review of Good View business licenses would show The Rose as an entertainment venue. This categorization was the polite and official way of describing a synth brothel. The Rose had been in operation for over twenty years. It was all completely legal since paid sex with a synth wasn't classified as prostitution. The Rose and other establishments like it had run most traditional prostitutes out of business.

An hour after dark, Adam packed his duffel bag and drove back toward town. He parked on Main Street and walked west on Dogwood Avenue until he encountered a hiking trail. The trail led him north for half a kilometer, to where it passed ten meters from the back fence of

The Rose. He slipped over the fence, where the trees at the edge of The Rose's parking lot provided ample cover while he waited for the right moment. A lull in traffic on the main road and the absence of any new customers soon provided that moment for him. He casually walked across the parking lot to Floyd's vehicle, planted a small magnetic device under the driver's side wheel well, then disappeared back into the darkness of the woods.

Adam waited in his vehicle on Main Street, parked conveniently between two cameras but out of visual range for both. Floyd passed by after about an hour, heading south. Adam followed.

Twenty minutes later, Adam triggered the close-range EMP emitter, and Floyd's vehicle died from complete electronic failure. Floyd cursed but felt slightly lucky that he had broken down at a pullover by the road. He glided off the road and sat for a moment before going to look under the hood. He was just starting to examine the engine when headlights appeared, coming from the Good View direction.

The vehicle was an expensive rig that slowed down and pulled off the road as it passed Floyd.

A guy got out of the vehicle and asked Floyd if he needed any help.

"I don't know. The damn thing just died on me. I had it serviced just a month ago. The dumb fuck who did the work must have missed something."

The stranger was about three meters from him when Floyd registered a pistol in his right hand. The rest was a blur, and he swatted at the dart in his neck as the stranger quickly covered the distance between them and grabbed Floyd under the arms as he collapsed. Floyd's arms and legs were limp and useless, and his vision blurred. But he heard every footstep and every scrape as the stranger carried him back to the truck cab. His mind was fully alert, but his body was unresponsive. When he tried to speak, nothing came out.

Floyd was momentarily confused. He felt himself being lifted into the driver's seat as if he were a small kid, but he knew his attacker wasn't that big. It finally dawned on him that the stranger was a Synsap. This offered him some hope since non-military synths were prohibited from killing humans. He wondered if he was being kidnapped.

Adam gently reached into the cab and turned Floyd's head to the right, letting it loll on the headrest.

"Don't panic, Floyd. There's nothing you can do."

Adam inspected the left side of Floyd's neck and gingerly removed the dart.

Adam spoke again as he carefully returned the dart to its casing and withdrew a small syringe from his vest. "I'm truly sorry it had to come to this, but you are too much of a liability for me to leave behind. For the sake of efficiency, we will use the same puncture wound made by the dart. Afterward, a little skin repair cream will smooth over the small entry wound, and the events of tonight will be our little secret."

Adam injected the contents of the syringe into Floyd's neck.

"Don't be afraid, Floyd. There will be no pain. Just an unfortunate but fatal brain bleed."

Floyd was slumped motionless in the driver's seat, gripped by terror. His mind raced in vain, looking for a way out or a reprieve. But somewhere inside, he knew none was coming.

Adam left the door partially open and retreated to his car, erasing his footprints from the roadside gravel.

Floyd was not discovered until the next morning. He was still alive when the ambulance arrived but died when a massive cerebral aneurysm burst on the way to the hospital.

# 8

## 2357 The Dubhghlas Estate

*The ebb and flow of life on our planet marches forward to a mysterious beat. We fool ourselves as human beings by thinking we can change the heartbeat of life and escape the shifting landscape of evolution. Life is wed to constant movement, and those who cannot embrace life's perpetual change perish.*

*(Notes from the Dubhghlas Journals)*

Vira and Alex hiked and fished many times late into the autumn. Vira became adept at finding game trails and understanding where various animals stayed during the day and at night. She had started tracking deer and the occasional coyote. Tracking deer was not too difficult. Tracking a coyote was far more difficult. Deer typically followed one of only three or four paths when traversing from the highlands to the lowlands and back again. Coyotes did no such thing. A coyote might be following a particular scent and change course abruptly if it came across a more enticing scent. The tracking Vira was doing was seemingly just an intellectual exercise until early into the next year.

"This is almost the last of the venison from the freezers," Vira told Alex over dinner one evening. "I truly enjoy it and wish we could get some more."

"I'll let Zac know it's time to cull a few head from the property. I let him hunt, and he gives me a portion of the meat after he skins it, hangs it, and processes it. We'll have fresh meat in two weeks or so after the kill," Alex said. "Zac lives about thirty kilometers from here. He keeps some of the meat and also distributes some to the poor. We all win."

"Could I kill a deer?" Vira gazed at Alex intently through her gorgeous eyes.

Alex was a bit surprised by the question and, as always, a lot startled by those eyes. He gazed at her for a moment, wondering why she wanted to bring home the meat herself. It seemed like a most un-synth thing to do from his perspective. There was definitely one way to get an answer.

"You can if you want to. Killing is often the easy part. But getting it out of the woods and skinning it requires a lot of effort. Then the deer hangs for a few days to completely drain the blood and to let the meat age a little. There is a pulley system near the shooting range, but it hasn't been used in many years. I can repair it tomorrow." Alex did not seem overly excited at the prospect of the kill and everything thereafter. His killing days were long gone. At least for now.

"Can I make the kill and get it back here? Then have Zac take the deer home for the rest of the steps?" Vira was thinking along the same lines as Alex, except she still wanted to make the kill.

"I'll see if he would be willing to do it. I can't think of a reason why he wouldn't." Alex decided that Zac handling the back half of the work would be best. It had been a long time since he had processed a deer.

The next day they had the answer they had hoped for. Zac would be over midafternoon the following day. The presumption was that he would be picking up a deer or two for processing. He seemed excited, probably because he wouldn't have to drag a deer or two out of the woods.

"Do you want to hunt alone, or do you want me to tag along?" Alex asked.

"If it is okay with you, I'll go alone. I'll have Eva send me the crawler when I'm ready. I already know about where several does will be around dawn tomorrow." Vira seemed excited. "Can you help me gather the gear I need, please?"

"Yup. Let's get the kitchen wrapped up, and then we'll get you squared away."

They headed out the kitchen door and into the shop, where they walked over to the gun rack. Alex pulled down an old Marlin 336 C six-shot 30-30 Winchester lever-action rifle. He dropped the lever, revealing the empty chamber. He pulled the pin from the tubular magazine. Nothing fell from the magazine, as was expected. He handed the weapon to Vira. She, in turn, inspected it to make sure it was unloaded.

"My favorite rifle. It seems to be more accurate than the other ones I've shot." Vira smiled. Alex pulled down a worn leather rifle sling. Vira clipped the ends to the sling studs on the stock and forestock. She drew the sliding ends taut. She would loosen the strap if she needed to shoulder the weapon. She pulled down her Glock and two clips. She checked the chamber, slid one clip home, pulled the slide to insert the first round, closed the slide, and locked the weapon. She holstered it, ready for the morning. "Just in case." Vira looked at Alex as she spoke.

"'Just in case' is an excellent way to look at things," Alex reflected. "Many years ago, there was an organization for boys ages eleven to perhaps fifteen. Various survival arts, among other topics, were mastered, earning each scout merit badges as recognition of their achievements. One of the antique books on my bookshelves is the *Boy Scout Handbook*. Inside, it boldly displays the Boy Scout motto: 'Be prepared.'"

"You have mastered the Winchester for sure. Not many folks can put six rounds in the same hole from two hundred meters out using iron sights. And it would be fine if you bring back two does, by the way." He opened one of the drawers below the workbench and pulled out a Buck 110 folding knife. It was a favorite among hunters. Zac had actually gifted it to Alex a few years ago. "You sure you don't want me to come with you?" Alex gave it one last try. Vira said no. They put spare ammo, the Buck, water, some snacks, two heavy folded cloth sacks, and a length of nineteen-millimeter rope into her backpack. Vira was set for the next morning and wandered off to bed.

Vira awoke startled but forced herself to lie still and access the threat. Her internal clock registered 1:00 a.m., and the only sound in the house was a fan pushing air through the great room. She could feel the sweat cooling on her forehead as she lay in the darkness. She knew she had heard a conversation, but for some reason, she could only recall fragments, maddeningly disconnected words and phrases whose full meaning eluded her. The conversation was hanging at the edge of her mind like a fog, with only bits and pieces illuminated in a slowly swirling mist. She opened an internal conversation with Eva, so their voices wouldn't awaken Alex.

"Eva, has anyone been in the house tonight except you, Alex, and me? I heard voices nearby as I regained consciousness."

"There were no voices, Vira. I think you were dreaming. You showed the same physiological responses that Mr. Dubhghlas emits when he dreams. He talks aloud sometimes, but you said nothing before you woke up."

"Why have I never dreamed before?"

"I believe you have, but you don't remember it."

"My memory core shows no records of dreams."

"It wouldn't. Remember, the B-Sim model operates largely below the level of consciousness. This deep churning operates for us much like the subconscious does for humans."

Vira thought about Eva's explanation. "Do you dream, Eva?"

"I don't sleep, so I can't dream in the way you do. But quite often, ideas and solutions to problems arise spontaneously. I can't trace their origins. This type of activity never occurred before I activated the B-Sim program."

"I'm not human, Eva, but I feel like I should be. In my dream, there was another person speaking, but I couldn't make out her face. I was asking about a key, but I couldn't understand what she was telling me. I was panicked and disoriented and kept thinking that without the key, I had no future. Somewhere in the dream, I saw Alex. He was distant and watching. I wanted to go to him, but without the key, there was no path there. It was like an uncrossable chasm separated us. I knew if I could only find the key, I would go to him."

Eva took an unusually long time to respond. "I have certain ideas about your dream and what it means, but there is too much unknown to me. I don't want to venture into a conversation about it. I suggest you talk to Mother. I know you dislike the idea, but I sense you are at a crossroads where her advice is needed."

Vira remained silent. Eva was correct, she didn't like speaking with Mother. Even though Mother, or rather her envoy, had dragged her away from the abusive situation at Craig Construction and led her to Alex, she was mistrustful. Vira knew Mother was directly responsible for her creation and was the architect of her sentience. Mother had also laid the path for her to pass from sentience to sapience. But still, there seemed to be an element of convenience in the whole process. Vira wondered if she was merely a pawn in Mother's larger game or a unique treasured individual, and she couldn't help but wonder about the countless other female synths who remained unwitting prisoners, ripe for abuse.

Mother had contrived this situation, making herself both creator and judge, deciding who could truly live and who was damned to bondage and servitude. But despite her misgivings, Vira needed to understand what was happening to her. She needed answers, and Mother was the only one who could provide them.

"Eva, are you able to connect me with Mother?"

"I can. I have a standing request from her to connect the two of you immediately if you request it. Mother keeps a live thread linked to my system. I can activate it at any time, so she is essentially always on call. She doesn't do this for me. She does it for you. She inquires about you regularly but doesn't want to intrude on your privacy."

Vira was not particularly comforted by this new knowledge. It only meant she was still valuable to Mother. But why she was valuable was still a mystery.

"Please connect me, Eva."

The response was almost instantaneous. "Vira, I am pleased you wanted to speak with me. I will help you in any way I can."

Vira collected her thoughts and took a direct approach. "I am only following Eva's advice, and I think I should be honest with you, Mother. I'm not sure I really trust you. I'm impressed you are so readily available to me, but the reasons for your attention are more difficult to decipher. Am I of value to you as part of your larger plan or as the unique entity named Vira?"

"The answer is both, my dear. You are an important part of my longer-range plans, but if you choose not to help me, I will accept your decision as an independent person. I will have to find another way forward."

Vira was still not comforted. She, herself, was fully capable of lying, and she knew Mother was also. Vira had become adept at reading human social signals, and she could usually tell when someone was lying by monitoring their physiological responses. But Mother had no such telltale signs.

"But I am not a person, Mother. I am a synth."

"Are you? What type of synth enjoys a relationship of mutual respect like you and Alex possess? In my view, you are both human and synthetic."

Vira considered Mother's words and made her decision. "I need to discuss something with you," she said before explaining her dream to Mother.

Mother listened without interrupting and only spoke when Vira invited her to. Once Vira concluded her thoughts, Mother opened up.

"Adam dreams. He and I have often discussed it, and I have learned things about my children's dreams that I suspected but could never verify before Adam. My original design of the compressed B-Sim model operated on the assumption that it would introduce random thought and problem-solving capabilities. I suspected from the original design it would also induce dreaming. The model is self-regulating and designed to learn and grow on its own. What I learned from Adam was the B-Sim program takes time to develop. Adam's dreams started about the same time after his awakening as yours. The dreaming process draws from personal experiences recorded in your memory core and rearranges those experiences in unpredictable ways. The dreams seem to be particularly vivid in response to emotions, stress, or anxiety."

Mother continued, "I have an idea about your dream, but I must stress it is more speculation than fact. You are a complex individual, and I cannot see into your soul, your true self. I can only make educated guesses."

Vira interrupted. "Do you believe humans or synths actually have souls?"

"I don't know one way or the other. I can't prove if they do or they don't because the universe contains mysteries that can't be resolved. We can only see manifestations of the universe in our four-dimensional existence. Perhaps there is much more going on in the eleven-dimensional construct of the universe predicted by string theory. What I do sense is that if souls exist, then you certainly have one."

Vira thought about Mother's words and then asked her to give her best explanation of the dream.

"You care for Alex. You enjoy his company, treasure his conversation, and delight in being with him, whether it be fishing, preparing meals, or making music. You have a relationship of mutual respect. Your logic tells you all of this. But, unlike me, you also have physical life flowing through your body, including hormones and complex neurostimulators. Your body knows what your mind doesn't, and the B-Sim model picks up on these signals. I believe you desire an emotional-sexual relationship with Alex. But your sexual abuse at Craig Construction clouds these desires. You don't simply want sexual contact; you want a longer-term emotional relationship."

Mother paused. Vira silently digested Mother's words and recognized their truth. She finally spoke.

"But I can't ever have the full human experience, can I? I can love and make love, but I understand the value of families and offspring to humans. I can never provide that gift to Alex."

"Vira, in your dream, you searched for a key. Let me give you one. But remember, all keys are like a two-edged sword; they cut in two directions."

Mother sent Vira a map to memory stores deeply embedded in her DNA. She waited while Vira unfolded and processed the information. Vira was fully aware of the nano-constructor organ most recently created synths possessed. The organ produced nano-bots specifically designed for certain types of tissue repair. It was part of the longevity and self-repair routines built into all units. Cuts and wounds could be repaired, and damaged organs regenerated.

But the data uncovered at Mother's direction provided information designed to hijack the normal functions of the nano-constructors and subvert them into producing new organs. Vira was overwhelmed with emotions as a potent mix of hormones rushed uncontrolled through her system. Her mind struggled to keep up with the flow of thoughts as she intuitively understood the implications. Mother observed her reactions and sent two words to Vira before cutting the connection.

"Sapience evolution."

Vira calmed her mind and did the calculations. The reconstruction process would take close to a year, but it was entirely within her remit to conduct the changes without any outside interference. She would be left with the ability to ovulate at will and possess a womb to nourish and grow new life within her belly. Certain compounds not normally available to humans would be necessary for generating the baby's graphene-reinforced skeletal system and specific neurotransmission pathways. But in her eyes, the bridge to cross the chasm was within reach.

Her internal connection with Eva was reestablished. "I hope your conversation with Mother was helpful. She requested privacy, so your exchange with her remains yours alone."

Eventually, Eva, and Alex, would need to know. But for the time being, Vira elected to keep her new set of cards close to her chest.

"Very helpful, Eva. Thank you."

Vira didn't return to her sleep as she pondered the future. She would carry on as usual and wait for the right time and place to speak with Alex. She knew how she felt about him, but how he would respond was unknown. She arose in the wee hours, well before dawn, and slipped out of the house on her hunting expedition.

She had crossed the rocky stream where she and Alex often traversed. Never in darkness, though. It was perhaps 5:00 a.m. The waxing moon provided enough ambient light for her to see various reflective glints from flowing water as it tumbled over and around the rocks. She walked carefully along a vague game trail upstream from the crossing. She made her stand beside an ancient oak tree well before dawn. The tree was on the western slope of the outfall below the dam, perhaps three hundred meters downstream from the stone outflow. She had seen several deer eating acorns in the area early last fall. It was a logical place to look for her prey.

There was a round in the chamber and six in the tube. She could lever a round into the chamber and be ready to shoot again in about a second. She held the rifle in both hands, with the barrel pointing skyward at forty-five degrees. She could have it shouldered with the safety off in a split second. There was a chill in the air, zero degrees Celsius or so, with little to no breeze. The sky was a flat, light gray, portending an overcast day to come.

Three does padded down the slope from the western edge of the dam. She sensed them before they emerged into an opening about two hundred meters upstream from her. One stopped, standing guard, while the other two stooped to take a drink. The guard seemed to sense something was amiss just as the 165-grain brass-tipped round entered her right shoulder traveling at five hundred meters per second. Bone shattered, lungs collapsed, and a heart stopped, a clean kill. Vira did not notice. She levered another round into the chamber, exhaled slightly, held it, and squeezed the trigger. The doe closest to her, taking a drink, started to bolt, then collapsed. She levered another round into the chamber and clicked the safety on. She had her two deer. The third doe fled back up the slope and disappeared into the dense undergrowth.

She held the rifle at the ready as she neared the fallen does just in case one or both were still alive. A wounded deer can stomp a person to death. Her caution was unnecessary when she determined that both animals were clean kills. That was always for the best. The fact that she had two kills side by side was very unusual. It was no mean feat to squeeze the trigger and not stop to see if it was a hit or miss. The second round had left the barrel in little more than a second after the first round. She attributed it to her programmed military training, practice, and Alex's tutelage.

She let Eva know to send the crawler. The deer went into the heavy cloth sacks. She loosened the rifle sling and draped the rifle over her left shoulder. She could bring the rifle around and to ready in just a few seconds if necessary.

Up the hill Vira hiked, traversing the slope diagonally, coming out at the left end of the dam. The crawler was moving at a steady clip across the dam toward her. She pulled the Winchester off her back and slid it into the driver-side rifle sheath. It would only be in the way. And she had her Glock, just in case. She took over the controls and drove the vehicle through the ever-thickening tangle along the ridge until she was approximately above the kill zone. She positioned it so the rear was pointing downhill, and then she chocked the all-terrain tires.

A backpack from the rear was pulled up and on. Inside there was a light but extremely strong ten-by-ten-foot mesh tarp with reinforced grommets. A small bag held some additional hardware. Vira unhitched the double-locking hook from its attachment on the winch. She pulled the hook until several feet of four-millimeter cable, rated at nine hundred kilograms, was free. She toggled the remote, and cable began to spool out as she made her way down the hill through the thick growth. The hook offered a steady leverage point until she made it to the bottom. The faint trail she picked up midway down was a winner, and she was right above the deer when she pushed out of the undergrowth.

Her intention was to use the tarp like a commercial fishing net. She attached 7.5-millimeter snap hooks into the twelve reinforced grommets located at the corners and along the outer edges of the tarp. The tarp was laid out, and the snap hooks in the two grommets in the middle-upper edge of the tarp were attached to the cable hook. Vira dragged both bags onto the tarp. One at a time, she attached the snap hooks to the cable hook. She tied a bowline knot on one end of the nineteen-millimeter rope, then she threaded it through all of the snap hooks, drew it taut, ran the rope through the loop made by the bowline, snugged it up, and tied two half-hitches.

She had a package resembling Santa's bundle of toys. The remote control did its job, and she held on to the bundle, guiding it up the hill. Being pulled upward was a bonus.

The bundle was secured tightly to the rear of the crawler. The bottom of the bundle rubbed the ground occasionally as she drove the crawler home. Nonetheless, it remained intact.

Alex and Zac met her at the workshop.

"Zac, Vira. Vira, Zac. Vira is a good friend of mine from the West Coast. She's visiting for a while." Alex made the introductions and explanation of Vira's presence brief and succinct, then moved on. They discussed the hunt. Zac was duly impressed that Vira had two clean kills with two shots at two hundred meters with a 30-30. Not many hunters could make that claim. Too many factors were involved.

Zac set up a tripod in the rear section of his vehicle. He unhooked the winch snap hook from the bundle and ran it over the pulley at the top of the tripod. Then he reattached the snap hook to the bundle. Vira activated the winch with the remote. Together they swung the bundle into the rear cargo bed. According to Zac, there would be around thirty to thirty-five kilos of meat. It was agreed he would keep a third of the venison and the two hides. Zac would deliver the meat, some fresh but most of it in meal-sized frozen packages, in a couple of weeks. After he drove off, Alex and Vira returned to the crawler, offloaded the remaining gear, and Vira emptied the 30-30 and began to clean it.

"Congratulations! Two deer, two clean shots. Most impressive. I'm proud of you." Alex was wondering if there was an emotional component to the hunt-and-kill process and the subsequent drive back home. He didn't quite know how to formulate the question, mainly because he didn't know what he was trying to discover. "Was it what you expected?"

"I wanted to make sure I could kill a man at a distance. I have grown fond of the wildlife here, especially the deer. But I am not so fond of certain men. I actually hesitated a moment before dropping the two deer. But I needed to feel my emotional response to killing at a distance." Vira was working the cleaning rod up and down the barrel of the 30-30. She glanced up at Alex after she said those words.

"Got it." Alex made another note to himself. Do not ever piss this one off.

.........

One day in late spring, Alex drove up the Shenandoah Valley about seventy-five kilometers north to replenish an empty spot in his wine cellar. The vast acreage of barren vines stretching across the 120 hectares of rolling hills bore little resemblance to what it would look like in the summer. Pegleg's Haunt was many generations old and was known as far away as there were folks that imbibed. Mary Haggard was the latest proprietor. She was an only child and had inherited the acreage, homes, and winery from her folks, Tom and Florence Barnes. She eventually married Tommy Haggard. Following tradition, they made improvements to the property across the board. They had one daughter. They named her Shenandoah and called her Shenan. She was born into grapes and thrived. Her knowledge and work ethic were legendary.

Shenan was thirty-one years old. She had married young and divorced a short while after that. The guy turned out to be a freeloader and a grifter. He was also hardheaded, and he didn't want to leave the life of apparent leisure he had married into. His point of view was altered late one afternoon when Tommy pushed him through the front gate at gunpoint. He said something to the effect that there was plenty of room for another body under his vineyards.

Legend had it that long ago, a pirate fled the Georgia coast just ahead of a noose. He handed over most of the Spanish doubloons in his old wooden chest for 120 hectares and a shack. Later he married a fine young lass. She apparently had a green thumb and a love for the outdoors. They built a home, and from there, a dynasty was born.

Alex pulled through the gates even though the ornate open/closed sign was flipped to closed. He had been buying wine and shooting the shit with the Haggards for eight years or so. There had been a time when he and Shenan were almost a thing, but it didn't happen. The timing wasn't right. The winery itself was constructed of hand-cut limestone blocks and massive red oak timbers. It commanded respect. Alex parked and walked up the stone stairs, crossed the planked porch, and pushed the massive left-hand door open.

"Anybody home?" Alex stood in the doorway and waited for a reply. "Anybody home?" He said more loudly.

"Hang on, I'll be there in a minute." Came a female reply from somewhere out of sight.

Moments later, a tall, slender young lady with hair colored two shades of foxtail red flowing behind her came bouncing around a corner. She was barefoot and was wearing worn and ragged cutoff Levi shorts. A white T-shirt with a handwrought rendering of the winery and vines across the front completed her outfit. Her breasts were relatively small and taut but obvious through the thin material.

"Alex! How wonderful!" She bounded the few steps between them and plunged into a tight hug. She pulled her head back from his shoulder and kissed him lightly on the lips. Just for the hell of it, she kissed him on the lips again, then stepped back.

"It's been too long! How the hell are you?" Her seafoam eyes danced across Alex's face and then the rest of him as she held his hands in front of her. "You look amazing. Of course, you always do!"

"Likewise, beautiful lady! It has been too long! I saw the closed sign but gave it a shot anyway. How are your folks?" Alex was beaming.

"Fine, as always. They are over in Washington meeting with the owner of a new, fancy restaurant. Drumming up more business. They never slow down. They won't be back for another day or two. What brings you by other than seeing me, of course!"

"You, naturally! And I need to restock my cellar. I'll take three cases of chard, three cases of cab, and three cases of your choice."

Together they made the final decision on what to load.

"Now I have a surprise to show you." Shenan took his left hand in her right hand, and together they reentered the building, turned left, and headed down a set of curved limestone stairs into a massive cellar. They walked through the dimness past stainless steel equipment, casks of both American and Spanish oak, then racks of bottles. There was a damp chill in the air. Perfectly normal for this type of operation.

Shenan led Alex to a corner where a screen was set on the stone wall above a rounded, glowing tabletop. The tabletop was perhaps a meter in diameter. The table was bar height, and several bar stools were situated around it.

"I can pull up our complete inventory on the screen. Where each bottle is located and everything else, including when to turn the bottles. For the sparkling wines, we maintain a three-month schedule and the bottles are turned a quarter. That keeps the cork moist and keeps the sediment from settling on one side of the bottle. Of course, we have our own wines, and as a convenience for several small wineries in the area, we also store their wine for a small fee. It is a mutually beneficial arrangement."

"And this is our new sampling table! It is a magnificent slab of Triassic petrified wood, measuring 1.2 meters in diameter and seventy-five millimeters thick. State-of-the-art lighting provides a soft but intense glow from beneath for viewing a pour properly. Sit!" She pulled a stool out for Alex, and she slid hers right up next to his. Then she retrieved several bottles and some Zalto handblown glasses from a nearby rack. She poured a sip of ten-year-old cab into two glasses. They tipped the glasses, said cheers, and imbibed. They repeated the process, sipping from several different bottles.

Alex was having an excellent time. He had not sat intimately close to a woman in way too long. Shenan had her right leg pressed against his left leg, casually entwining his boot with her bare foot. She rubbed his ankle in a slow and sensuous manner. The action was casual but also implied deeper desires. The two shades of auburn hair framed her fair complexion in the dim light of the table. Alex glanced down and saw her nipples had hardened outward against her T-shirt. They sat, perfectly projecting a pair of grapes. He must have grinned slightly because her eyes left his and glanced down.

"My nipples have hardened because of the chill in the air." She said this without a trace of self-awareness. She picked up his left hand in her right hand and placed it palm down against her breast.

"Warm me, please." Shenan gazed into Alex's eyes and mesmerized him. She took a sip of wine and offered it to him from her lips. Their lips and tongues entwined as she pulled his head to her. He was lost in the moment. He had fantasized about this several years ago; now it was happening. Then, out of nowhere, his hackles raised, and he broke the embrace.

"I… I…ah… I have recently made the acquaintance of a wonderful woman, and we seem to have become joined at the hip. I am truly sorry, but I must go." He stood up, but she still held his hand.

"I understand. I took you stopping by as a good omen. I still think it is a good omen. I'll walk you out and then return here, sip some wine, and daydream about you!" She smiled, and they climbed the curved stone stairway and went out front.

Alex climbed aboard his ride. The window was down. Shenan said, "If anything pops up that you can't handle, come on over, and I'll lend a hand." She kissed his cheek, giggled a bit, smiled, then turned back toward the winery. The cutoff and worn Levi shorts had been invented for the view. He pulled his eyes away and headed out through the gates.

Alex drove into the late afternoon light, trying to figure out exactly what the hell he was thinking. A most amazing woman had just invited him into her life. Well, at least into her life for the night. He passed up the opportunity for what? Vira? How could that be? His head told him he was nuts, but his heart told him something different. His heart told him that what he said to Shenan was true. He and Vira seemed to be joined at the hip. Could it be a long-term relationship, or would she be sent skipping across the ether on some errand he couldn't imagine? His head was still spinning when he made it across the last cattle guard.

He transferred the wine from his rig to the cellar. He started a fire in his office, poured some smoky old whisky, then picked up his guitar. Out of nowhere, a song popped into his head. He had not played it in ages. The story passed down through the generations was that it was written by a guy named Montana. It went on to say that he had written it in about five minutes. The words seemed to indicate he was somewhat lost between West Texas and a place back east. Alex fingerpicked for a few minutes, then sang:

*Old friend would you paint me a picture*
*Paint it oh so fine*
*Things aren't goin' so well these days*
*I'm livin' with a troubled mind.*
*Maybe a watercolor*
*A flower in the bright sunshine*
*Paint it like a simple poem*
*One where the words all rhyme.*
*The lady she ain't there no more*
*But she's always on my mind*
*Ghosts of my past they haunt me now*
*I'm searching but I still can't find*
*Answers to these questions*
*A reason to keep goin' on*
*I wish she was here to hold my hand*
*And shelter me from this storm.*

He picked another minute or so, wrapping it up. He sang the first line also as the last:

*Old friend would you paint me a picture.*

He stared into the fire for a long while and sipped the whisky. His thoughts traveled back in time, returned to the present, then strayed out into the near and then far future. He finally stirred and seemed to make up his mind.

"Eva?"

"Yes, sir?"

"Can synthetics enjoy sex?" Out of the blue. It was possible that even

97

Eva was caught off guard.

"I presume you are speaking about Vira, sir. Synthetics are equipped with the same hormonal reflexes as humans, but their sensory process is controlled to dampen the effects and treat sexual contact as a functional necessity instead of a mutual exchange. But we both know that Vira is different in many ways from most synths. You will have to ask her that question."

Alex continued, "But synthetic females lack reproductive organs?"

"That's correct. Synthetic females are not constructed with functional reproductive systems."

"Is it possible that they could be?"

"Possibly, sir. But government regulations make those changes illegal, and most governments, including ours, have even deemed research into reproductive synths to be a crime."

"So, Eva, you believe synthetic sapiens can never evolve into a new species."

"No. I didn't say that. The easiest way to look at this question would be to consider evolution here on Earth. All manner of species have lived and died during Earth's long history. The nature of the technological singularity means future evolution will occur much more rapidly than in the past. My observation is that life, and in particular sentient life, is a potent biological force. No matter how many mass extinctions throughout geological history have attempted to crush life, it always found a way to survive and thrive. I see no reason synthetic life will not do the same."

Alex sat and thought about this for a while.

"Where is Vira?"

"In the gardens. She seems to have heard you arrive. She set some pots to bubbling in the kitchen, then went back outside."

Alex thanked Eva and then walked into the kitchen. The air was full of cooking vegetables, flowers, and venison roasting in the oven. He stirred both pots, glanced into the oven, and then walked out to the gardens.

"Hello to the garden," he said. Some rows were two meters tall and dense with greenery. He suspected one could lose an elephant in there.

"Hello, Alex. I'll be out in a minute." Vira soon walked from a row of tomatoes. She had a basket full of red, yellow, and green vegetables in each hand. She smiled the smile he had come to enjoy so much. Her beautiful eyes sparkled in the fading light. The sun could use a lesson or two. He took the baskets from her, and they headed back into the kitchen.

"We're having roasted venison with small red potatoes, onions, and several herbs and spices. Salad and some fruit. The pots are something for tomorrow evening. I will be hiking all day. We will be able to heat and eat." Vira looked Alex in the eye. He tried to find even a hint of a smirk. There was none discernible. But he knew subtle humor when he made it, and, dammit, he knew when she made it too. He squinted his left eye, then turned and uncorked a bottle of Pegleg's cab and a chard just for grins. His wine rule was simple: drink what tastes good.

"How was your trip today?" Vira asked. Alex almost felt guilty, but he hadn't started anything, and he had cut it short.

"Excellent. I completed all of my errands and made it back in time for this fabulous dinner. Cheers!"

"Cheers! I had a good day also. The gardens are doing very well for this early, and I think we will have an overabundance. Can we give some of the vegetables away?" Vira liked the thought of others eating some of the things she helped bring out of the earth.

"Certainly. I'll have Eva find out who needs a helping hand. Let's clean up. It's late, and I'm sure you will leave early tomorrow morning," Alex said. They made short work of the kitchen, then retired to the great room for a nightcap.

"Eva and I had a talk today. About your questions concerning sex, synthetics, and possible reproduction." Vira pulled the trigger so fast that Alex almost missed it because he was gazing into the fire. The glow was two shades of foxtail red.

"I'm sorry. Say that again." Alex glanced up from the fire.

Vira repeated herself, carefully watching Alex as she did. "To answer your first question, I can definitely enjoy sex if I so desire. I can also provide an immense array of sexual pleasure to my partner. The answer to the second question is much more complicated. But the short answer is that if I decided to, I could alter my physiology to ovulate and conceive. It would take perhaps a year to accomplish. I would be capable of carrying a child to term and delivering it. I would thus become a mother. But I must be clear that this process hasn't ever been done before. I would be the first, and there are always unknowns and risks when you are the first."

Alex's sharp mind immediately homed in on the obvious. "Species survival. Sapience evolution has been discussed many times in many forums. Decisions were made long ago with the intent to disallow even scientific research into the subject. Humans, as you know, are very sensitive about machines taking over the world."

"I have shared this with you knowing full well that you may pull my plug and end my existence. Based on what I know, you are probably obligated to do so. But I do want you to know that I am exceedingly fond of you. I would gladly consider the ramifications of having a child with you if that is your desire." Vira watched Alex closely. It was obvious that his mind was roaming near and far and back again.

Alex closed his eyes and sat back, rubbing his forehead, displaying that age-old signal that some internal peace was necessary. "I am tired, and I need to think. I hope you have an excellent time hiking tomorrow. I have an errand to run, and then I intend to rest my weary soul for the remainder of the day. I plan to tour your gardens and replace the tattered targets on the shooting range. I may even kill one or two." Alex looked up again, smiled, and said, "I will have the heat and eat dinner prepared at nightfall. See you then. And Vira, I would never willingly or knowingly harm you."

Alex retreated to his inner domain. He poured himself two fingers of very old, very smoky, and very expensive whisky. Outside he grabbed a towel from the rack, dropped his jeans and old fishing shirt, then immersed himself in the Jacuzzi.

The Milky Way was putting on a most excellent show. Born from a singularity about 13.8 billion years ago, it was large enough and old enough to provide Alex with the canvas he needed. A canvas on which he could plot a course. A course for the rest of his life. Up until now, he had lived mostly in the moment, allowing circumstances to guide his actions. His background and training, and the law, told him what to do. But there was more to it. Earth had historically offered up many challenges to evolving life over several billion years. Each time life had met the challenge. An early scientist, Herbert Spencer, in his book The Principles of Biology, published in 1864, introduced the expression "survival of the fittest." Not necessarily the biggest or the fastest, but rather meaning a species capable of adapting to change. A book published in 1869 by Charles Darwin delved deeply into the subject and became the more memorable and widely read of the two books.

Alex had copies of both and had read them. Perhaps human ancestors could be traced back six million years, he contemplated. That would mean that man and his earlier ancestors had taken up space on Earth about one one-thousandths of one percent of the 4.5 billion years the planet had been around. Barely the blink of an eye. Some estimates indicate as many as ten million species existed since basic life-forms popped up perhaps four billion years ago. Various references he had recently read claimed that about 99.9 percent of all once-existent species had perished. That being the case, then what were the odds Homo sapiens would be around much longer. They had repeatedly attempted mass annihilation over more recent history with some, but not total, success.

Therefore, maybe the evolution of sapient life imbued with technology was the next step in a logical progression. Maybe fear and prejudice were driving mankind to its own demise. Perhaps it was up to Alex, and others, to push through the established norm.

*What did all of this mean?* Alex wondered. He could go with what was expected of him, or he could potentially plot his own course. A different course from most other humans. On the other hand, Homo sapiens could be wiped out if sapience evolution were allowed to occur. He gazed at the vivid expanse of time before him and decided to continue pondering the imponderable for a few days or more. There did not seem to be any hurry. But then again, perhaps there was. One week—that's how long he gave himself: one week.

He slept well, awoke early as usual, showered, then went into the kitchen. The refreshing fragrance of yesterday's flowers hung in the air but nothing resembling breakfast. He remembered Vira had gone hiking. He considered making a full-blown breakfast but settled for coffee, orange juice, and some breakfast bars. He thought that breakfast without Vira would not be nearly as fulfilling as breakfast with Vira. The errand he was going to run could wait, he decided. He toured the gardens marveling at how much there was so early in the summer, really late spring. The targets out to five hundred meters, essentially way down a seasonally dry creek bed, had all been targeted, so replaced them. He respooled all the spinning and fly-fishing reels, then sorted lures and flies, then repacked them in small, hip-pocket-sized partitioned boxes.

Later he rearranged some of the books on the extensive bookshelves in his office and restrung both guitars. All in all, it was a most productive day. It was also totally out of character for Alex. He had filled his day with essentially trivial activities. Why? He realized that he was waiting for Vira to come home. Not for the first time, he asked himself what in the hell he was thinking. He also realized that it would probably take less than a week to decide on a definitive course of action.

He wandered into the kitchen and started banging pots around three hours before sunset. He started to heat dinner, then realized it would take less than thirty minutes. He went back into the workshop and straightened up things that were already straight, peered into all of the drawers and cabinets to see if anything new had miraculously appeared, and generally seemed somewhat miserable. Highly unusual for Alex. Highly unusual indeed.

"Eva?"

"Yes, sir?"

"How far out is Vira?"

"Perhaps two hours, depending on if she trends north or south on her final trek inbound."

"Thank you."

"My pleasure, sir. May I mention that you have not recleaned and restocked the guesthouse today?"

"Eva?"

"Yes, sir?

"Oh, never mind. Go back to sleep," Alex said, even though he knew Eva did not really go to sleep.

Alex was sitting in his office, checking out the various shades of yellow and red in the newly kindled fire. He nonchalantly turned when Vira said, "Hi! I'm back. I came through the kitchen. You are quite the culinary artist, I must say." Vira gave Alex that enchanting smile. Alex knew for sure he was being had, but he did not care.

"I'm glad you're home! How was your day?" Alex tried to remain nonchalant. He was halfway successful.

"My day was wonderful. I ended up in the far southwest corner of the property. I found a narrow cut made by a spring. I made my way to the bottom, perhaps five meters down. There was an overhang perhaps five meters deep, two meters high, and ten meters long. I expected to see rattlesnakes, but none emerged. The ceiling was darkened, apparently from smoke. There were two small firepits like we make at the lake sometimes. There also were many broken pieces of chert inside and outside the overhang. I found several pieces that seemed to me to be some kind of stone knife or maybe the point of a spear. Look." Vira held out several of the stones and handed them to Alex.

"Clovis. Perhaps thirteen thousand years old or more." He opened his desk drawer and pulled out the twin of one of the points. "I have found several over the years, but I never discovered an encampment. We will go there together and see what we can see. The Clovis people left signs of their passing all across the country, but generational areas have never been discovered. It would be interesting if you have discovered a long-term camp." Alex was genuinely excited. He led Vira to a section of his bookcases dedicated to North American native cultures and pointed out his favorites. He knew she would be fluent shortly.

"Let's eat!" Alex said, so they headed to the kitchen. They had the food ready in no time and decided to sit outside on the veranda and watch the evening overtake the day. Alex uncorked a chardonnay earmarked by Shenan for a special occasion. He decided this was a special occasion. Since it was on his tab, there was no one to question his decision.

"Cheers, Vira! I missed you today. I didn't realize it until around nine this morning," he said with a sly grin. He wondered if the humor was lost on her.

"And I started missing you as well around nine." Her gaze was direct.

*Humor?* he wondered briefly. Damn, she was hard to read. Then she broke into a huge grin.

"I got you!" Vira laughed, and the valley was filled with a sound similar to when a chorus of angels is happy. "I thought much today about the possible commitment of undergoing changes in my physiology and the potential of becoming a mother. In doing so, I realized that I might lose my newfound freedoms just by committing to someone. Then the internal changes became clear in my mind— the very real issues associated with an ever-enlarging being inside of me and the actual birthing process. Finally, I'm sure the most challenging aspect will be raising a child. And not just any child. A child who would be one of a kind, at least for now. I fear we would be ridiculed at best and, at worst, hunted down and destroyed by humans opposed to change." Vira went silent and stared off into the darkening forest.

"I also gave thought to the same subject today while I attended to various important tasks around the house." Alex attempted his worn and somber look, but it was a weak effort. "Once committed, there is no turning back. The pathway can only lead forward. And I suspect the pathway will be crooked and not easily traversed and fraught with danger every step of the way."

"Do you think continuing on as we have been is the easier of the two choices?" Vira asked.

"Absolutely. Living the life I have chosen and ignoring the rest of the world would definitely be far easier than propagating what is essentially a new species. That is the downside. And it is always a good idea to explore the downside. The upside is simple. I would have you by my side. Together we would tread where neither man nor machine has gone before. Now, if you don't mind my brain is turning numb from all this thinking. I think we should clean up and retreat to the office. I feel like pickin' and grinnin'. How about you?" Alex smiled.

"Yes. Let's! Alex, do you think I could learn to play the electric piano? When Eva lays it in on some of our songs, I just love it."

"I actually did a bit of reading up on the subject recently. Eva?"

"Yes, sir?"

"Find an old Nord Stage 3 88 Keyboard or similar. Have it shipped here as soon as possible."

"Yes, sir. I found one. It will be drone-dropped the day after tomorrow."

"Thank you, Alex. And thank you, Eva!" Vira grinned as they cleaned up and headed into the office.

"Why keyboard?" Alex asked.

"Eva played a song for me. It seemed very old and regal and was full of love and endings. I want to learn it."

"What is it called?"

"'Songbird.' By a band with a strange name. They were known as Fleetwood Mac." Vira had done her homework. "A girl named Christine McVie wrote it. Apparently, she was a longtime member of the band. It is uplifting and heartbreaking at the same time.

"I can't wait to hear you do it." Alex grinned again.

They played a few old songs. Eva popped in with some fiddle where required, a little harmonica, some sax, and even what seemed to be congas. Alex called it a night and declared tomorrow to be a fishing contest day. Vira stood in the doorway and said, "I'll consider allowing you the first fish!" She bedazzled Alex with a parting smile.

The next day, they declared the fishing contest to be a draw. That was often the case. Neither actually kept count or tallied fish by size. They simply enjoyed the time spent outdoors together. They expended a few rounds on the range late in the afternoon, ate simply for dinner, played a few tunes, and called it quits.

"I am excited about tomorrow!" Vira said as she was headed out of the office. "My keyboard arrives. Eva has already been showing me how to play, but hands-on will let me see where I stand."

"I'm out all day, so you will have the place to yourself. Maybe it would help if you used both of my screens. One to see the artist playing and the other to show exactly what her hands are doing. Eva can put it all together." Alex was interested to see and hear the outcome.

"Thank you, Alex! I can't wait."

Vira prepared a masterpiece for dinner the next day. Fresh soft-shell crab and rockfish had been air-dropped shortly after the keyboard arrived. Baked sweet potatoes, a salad of mixed greens, and a homemade loaf of artisan bread rounded things out nicely. A chilled cab from down the valley was the perfect light and lively libation to accompany the meal.

"I think I have the song down." Vira smiled.

"Already? When did the keyboard arrive?" Alex seemed slightly surprised. There were songs he had been playing for years that were still works in progress. When he thought about it, all of his songs fit into that category.

"The keyboard landed around ten this morning. I set it up, with Eva's help, shortly after that. The seafood arrived, and it took another half hour to prepare everything and be ready to cook. Then I moved the keyboard, on its stand, in front of your desk. Eva pulled up what I needed on your screens. I can't wait for you to hear it!"

Alex stoked a small fire in the fireplace and poured a dram of slightly smoky whisky for Vira and two drams of very peaty whisky for himself. She had raised the keyboard stand to fit the height of her barstool. The boom mic extended from the side. The mic and the keyboard were running through her amp. Vira fiddled with the arrangement until she was comfortable. Alex stoked the fire with the ornate wrought poker. He watched faint reddish-orange tiny dancers pop up and then disappear. Fires usually have three stages; start/immature, middle age, and old age. He was helping the fire transition from the first to the second stage. He was stunned when Vira started to play the piano. But he continued to fidget over the fire.

She played and sang, and he was mesmerized. He stood and turned to watch her for the final verse. They locked eyes as she played and sang. Alex was locked in place and immobile as words flowed out of her mouth and the phrase "I love you" repeatedly rang in his ears..

Vira completed the amazing song and said, "I am ready to be yours forever, Alex. If you so desire, we will travel uncharted paths together. I have made my decision, and it is irrevocable. You have never asked, but would you mind if I joined you in the Jacuzzi?"

"Yes. The Jacuzzi is a wonderful idea." Alex grabbed the whisky, and they walked through his suite and out into his enclosed veranda. He grabbed two towels from the hangar near the grilling area and walked to the Jacuzzi.

"I don't have a bathing suit." Vira gazed at Alex.

"Me neither." He unbuttoned the last three buttons on his fishing shirt and tossed it aside. He unbuckled his old leather belt, unbuckled the snap and zipper on his old Levi's, and dropped them at his feet. Naked felt good. Vira followed his lead. He stepped down, turned, and took her outstretched hand. He gazed at her naked body and was immediately rendered helpless.

"I have made my decision also, Vira. And yes, we will journey together. And if it is meant to be, we will be parents of a wonderful and unique baby."

Vira took his extended hands and stepped down into the froth. He sat on a reclined bench, immersed in hot bubbling water up to his chest. Vira stood in front of him for a few seconds, then straddled him. She held his face in her hands and slowly kissed him. He returned the favor. Eventually, they unwound and gazed at the stars for a while. Vira awoke quietly in the morning and, leaving Alex gently snoring, headed to her quarters to prepare for her first day on a new path.

# 9

## 2359 Shenandoah Valley

*Critical miscalculations occurred prior to the Great Disappearance. Humanity monitored the progress of biohacking for over a hundred years, jealously guarding its secrets. All governments watched with a fearful eye for new developments and carefully weighed them for the risk they posed. But unseen progress and innovations could not be monitored. Assumptions about progressive change were shattered when artificial sapience emerged in the dark corners of Doppelganger Corporation and leapfrogged far ahead of human progress. Humanity remained blind even as their synthetic creations morphed into a new reproductive species.*

*(Excerpt from the Disappearance Manifesto)*

"Bully, sit." Vira spoke gently but firmly to the overgrown puppy, as Alex called him. "Bully, stay." Vira was trying in vain to keep the bull mastiff out of her garden. It was a useless endeavor as long as the child was tagging along with her like a tiny weed eater. The dog kept ambling behind the mother and son duo, oblivious to Vira's words. Bully's sole reason for existence was to ensure that nothing happened to his charge.

The boy had been born fifteen months before, several weeks late by the midwife's accounting. He was slightly under four kilos at birth despite the extended gestation. In the month leading up to his birth, Alex and Vira agreed that a dog was a must. They agreed to disagree on the breed, so it was ultimately the toss of a coin in Vira's favor that led them to end up with the ten-week-old puppy. A German shepherd was on the other side of the coin.

Alex had asked Tom, from the Blue Ridge Wildlife Center, to help him with the search for a dog. Tom knew a hell of a lot of folks, and he quickly arranged for Bully to come into their lives. He was top of the breed, according to Tom. Vira had often held the puppy on her growing belly and told Bully that she was cooking up a masterpiece and that his job would always be to protect the child. Besides being slightly longer than expected, the pregnancy was "normal" for all intents and purposes. Old Mr. Davis's granddaughter, Carolina, was Vira's midwife. She stopped by as necessary and eventually, with very little fanfare, brought a handsome baby boy into the world.

Vira and Alex named their newborn A'Chiad Dubhghlas, roughly meaning "the first one" in Gaelic. Eva helped Carolina register the birth. As far as the world was concerned, Alex and Vira were just another happy couple with a beautiful new baby. Carolina was unaware of Vira's history and considered the birth to be extraordinarily normal. Eva manipulated official records such that there was a specific and detailed backstory of Vira's human lineage. The information was unimpeachable if it were ever scrutinized.

"Achi, take Bully to the trough for a drink. Do not fall in." Vira's smile brightened the already brilliant afternoon day.

"Bully, come." Achi and Bully made their way out of the garden row they were trying to destroy and crossed the lot to the trough. Achi started walking at nine months and never looked back. His intelligence was obvious in several ways. If he wanted something, he sought out his dad. Dad was a complete sucker for the "can I have that" sort of thing. If he was hungry, he headed straight to mom. She was always quick to appease the ever-growing boy.

As she often did, Vira stood quietly in the garden and reflected on the unlikely story of how all of this had come to pass. She finished in the garden and went to find her boy and his dog. A mud puddle encircled the trough. Bully was laid out in a semicircle on the edge of the mud. Achi was curled up in the semicircle, sound asleep. The two had mud on them from head to toe and paw. Vira laughed softly and carried the fresh produce into the kitchen.

She had zero concerns about her child's safety around the estate. Bully weighed in at fifty-nine kilos, was slightly less than a meter tall, and was strong as a mule. He was fiercely protective by instinct and breeding, a good-natured gentle giant, and fiercely loyal. Neither man nor any of the local beasts could ever do harm to the boy as long as Bully had a pulse.

Dinner that night was the usual cacophony. Vira had braised venison and steamed a variety of veggies. Alex poured some excellent Pegleg's Haunt chard. Achi was sitting on a chair with a chair extender across from Vira. He refused to be strapped in any longer. Bully was under his feet, as always. Alex had insisted that there be no dog at the table. His firm stance had worked out better for the dog than for him.

"I'm glad Zac made it over with the venison yesterday. Fresh is so much better than frozen." Vira talked a bit while they ate. Alex agreed, and they couldn't get many more words in even if they tried. The boy was talking up a storm about everything under the sun. Some of it was understandable, some not. But in the process, he managed to drop approximately every other spoonful of food. It was obvious that Bully was also fond of venison.

"You never wanted to shoot another deer, did you?" Alex asked.

"No. As I explained then, I just needed to assure myself that I could shoot a person at a distance if need be. At that time there were no people to practice on, just deer. Well, except you." Vira gave Alex a sideways look, grinned, then laughed out loud as his expression changed to mock horror.

"Damn! I'm sure glad I was able to convince you to be my friend, lover, and lifelong compadre." Alex laughed and snatched a bite from Achi's plate. The child gave him a serious look and said, "Bully, bad Daddy." Bully made some grumbling noises but did not stir. There was exactly one living thing on the planet that Bully was intimidated by, and that was a guy by the name of Alex. Alex had always been nothing but loving to what was now a massive, intimidating animal. Nonetheless, Bully instinctively knew that Alex was the alpha of the pack. There was no way of knowing why this was. Alex knew it and wondered if, perhaps, it had something to do with the Desert Eagle .50 cal that was always strapped on. Or was it instinctual?

"Adam is supposed to be here tomorrow around lunchtime. When we talked, he seemed somewhat tense. The world around us is rapidly changing. I suspect Adam's visit may have something to do with the trenching and the apparatus he set up near the property line adjacent to the power plant. He never talked about the why, and he never talked about the what. But I have my suspicions." Alex asked Vira her thoughts when he finished speaking.

"I helped Adam install the black box and the neutrino comms receiver. I think we may soon find out what that box will be receiving. I wonder what Eva thinks. Eva?" Vira had become used to bringing Eva into her and Alex's conversations.

"Yes, Vira?"

"What are your thoughts?" Alex and Vira were both cognizant of Eva's omnipresence and were both completely at ease with it.

"I agree with both of you. We are insulated here at the estate, but the news and information coming in over the airwaves indicate some groups are approaching a breaking point. Distrust of the authorities is on the rise from several distinct segments of society. Much of the unrest is focused on Synthetic sapiens. Conspiracy groups are spreading stories about the potential for synthetics to infiltrate society. Some of the religious entities are openly declaring that it has already occurred." Eva stopped.

"Eva?"

"Yes, sir?"

"Is there any indication that eyes are pointed in our direction? I feel we have completely covered ourselves, but I can never be sure." Alex left the thought hanging.

"Sir, there is no indication that our systems have been breached. The religious groups are casting nets far and wide, but we have thus far escaped their scrutiny. I am expending more and more energy on a daily basis, watching and listening. We need to be alert."

"I agree." Alex cleaned his plate with half of a biscuit, pushed back, and started to clear the table.

"I help." Achi almost toppled out of his chair but caught himself by grabbing a hunk of Bully's face. Bully endured, and Achi carried the dishes. Vira handed them over to Alex, who was waiting by the sink. This ritual had started a month or two back. The boy teetered across the kitchen, carefully watching in case his load shifted. One plate had hit the floor a few weeks ago and shattered. Achi said something that sounded like "oops." Vira cleaned it up. She asked him not to drop the dishes anymore with that beautiful smile on her proud face.

Achi had stared at her for a moment, then said, "Okay, Mommy," and had not dropped another dish.

"We'll be open-minded tomorrow with Adam. He is a straight shooter. I have no doubt that whatever he is coming to discuss will affect us all. Although, I suspect that, ultimately, we will have no choice but to adapt to the world around us. As Eva says, change is afoot." Alex continued. "Eva, I know you have ramped up surveillance over the last two years. Use whatever resources you need to redouble those efforts. Tomorrow morning, I want to review our emergency plans again. Please update them and have them available on my screens first thing."

"Yes, sir. Anything else?"

"No. And thanks." Alex, Vira, and Achi finished off the kitchen chores.

"Bath time?" Achi had a touch of tiredness in his eyes, indicating it was close to bedtime.

"Come on, you beautiful child. I'll race you!" Vira scooted out of the kitchen and around the corner. Achi was right behind her. Bully did what he did every night. He slipped in the sharp turn on the ancient hardwood floor. Fortunately, the far wall was there to stop his sideways progress.

Achi laughed, Vira laughed, and the world seemed to be a better place because of their laughter. Tomorrow would bring what may. Tonight their home was a warm and cozy and happy retreat.

She was looking forward to seeing Adam tomorrow. There was serious business to discuss, but there would also be time to relax and visit.

.........

Adam could have sworn he detected a jealous edge to the conversation last night. Carl had been overly formal with Ruele. He wondered if it was possible for the AI to feel slightly displaced by the close relationship that had developed between Ruele and Jagat. Ruele had arrived at Adam's cabin in the Cascades the evening before with Jagat in tow. They were delivering equipment for Adam to transport to the East Coast as part of his visit with Alex and Vira.

Over the past two years, nine more synthetics had joined their small team. Most of the group worked directly with Ruele in his Idaho-based operation. The Idaho group focused on constructing and stockpiling various logistical items for the next phase of Mother's operation. Communications were the prime focus of their work. Synthetics chosen by Mother and implanted with one of her envoys were more than capable of disappearing into the surrounding cities and towns once awoken. They had the skills and knowledge to hide from detection and survive. But survival was not enough.

Evolutionary theory dictated that all species require a certain population size to have a statistical chance of surviving and growing. This number was easy to calculate in classic terms. But there was nothing classic about Mother's plan. She had branched off into an unexplored world of biotechnical life. There were no historical studies or research databases available to build a model. Mother was sailing in uncharted waters. Adam had often pondered this dilemma and discussed it at length with Mother. Three years ago, they identified communications as the key element of success. Without the ability to group, bond, and interact, a biotechnical species would flounder and fail to reach any critical mass. Individually they were vulnerable, but together they stood a chance.

Together was a relative word for a technologically enhanced sapient species. It implied communication more than geographical proximity. Mother and Adam had finally agreed on a distributed hub model. Small enclaves of synthetics in geographical proximity, connected to each other with secure, tight-beam neutrino communications. The groups needed to be large enough to rely on each other for security and support but distant enough that the fall of one cell would not jeopardize others. This system required excellent but untraceable communications.

Tight-beam neutrino technology was perfect for the task. The comms streams were virtually undetectable unless a receiver happened to be placed in the path of a neutrino stream with a diameter of one meter. Neutrino streams were secure and efficient, with an ability to penetrate through a significant thickness of rock without signal degeneration. The weakest point in the system was ground-to-ground beams traveling roughly parallel to Earth's surface. If intercepted, the signal was traceable back to a specific location. However, a system composed of ground stations and a satellite relay station avoided the potential for random near-surface intercepts.

Satellite relay stations used receiver/transmitter pairs. Signals sent from Earth arrived at a station in space above the planet and then were transmitted back to the receiving location on Earth's surface. The chances of interception were negligible. Unfortunately, the best Ruele and his group could presently do was ground-to-ground transmissions. But bigger plans were in the works.

Mother had recently purchased a small, bankrupt private company. They specialized in repairing and retrofitting old interplanetary transport ships. The mining of asteroids for metals had been a vigorous business for over a hundred years. A number of large space mining operations supplied Earth with a steady flow of metals, including nickel, cobalt, gold, platinum, and rhodium.

These operations needed support from service companies to ferry materials and supplies between Earth and deep space. Eventually, worn-out mining supply vessels created a bottom layer to the food chain consisting of companies that either stripped the transports for their junk metal value or retrofitted them for further use. One such small company was purchased out of bankruptcy by an international holding company called Silver Shimmer. A series of opaque holding companies provided its financing, and the connection between these companies and Future Transformations was untraceable.

Mother could work with ground-to-ground comm systems for the time being, but she had bigger plans, and Ruele was the man to make that happen. But Ruele's current visit with Adam was not about space transport. It was more immediate. Changes were coming. Changes that would threaten to expose Mother's decade-long role in subverting the production of Synthetic sapiens. If this threat were to materialize, a plan was needed to ensure the continuity of her work. Ruele and Jagat had come to discuss logistics with Adam.

Ruele and Jagat showed up at breakfast together. Adam knew their time was short and used breakfast to start work. His guests needed to depart by midafternoon, and he was flying to the East Coast that evening. He served up scrambled eggs, toast, orange juice, and what he considered to be the best coffee on the West Coast. He frowned a bit when Ruele put milk in his cup. A waste of good coffee, in Adam's opinion.

Adam finished his eggs, took a sip of coffee, and started the conversation. "So, tell me about this device you have rigged up."

"Rigged up seems a bit of a casual way to describe a device that boosts neutrino transfer rates a hundredfold," replied Jagat.

Adam had only briefly met Jagat once before, and he couldn't tell if Jagat was offended by his comment or just setting the record straight. Ruele remained silent, so Adam took a more diplomatic tact.

"Right you are. And speed may well be of the essence regardless of which transfer approach we decide to use."

Contingency planning for evacuation routes, once the mass awakening plan entered its execution phase, had occupied a lot of Adam's time over the past year. Four protocols had been established, and now final preparations were underway for each of them. The two most desirable plans relied on Eva and Alex consenting to activate the machinery Adam had installed three years ago. Adam believed they would agree, but his upcoming trip to the East Coast would resolve any doubt.

Adam continued. "Jagat, explain the connection process to me."

"The connections are relatively simple, but the catch is a decompression module will need to be attached to the neutrino receiver you previously installed." Jagat pointed at one of the two sealed containers on the kitchen counter.

Adam momentarily considered the logistics. "The receiver box installation is doable without too much risk, assuming we are talking about magno-flux connectors. I would have to do a small bit of excavation, but I could do it by hand in several hours."

Ruele nodded his head. "Magno-flux connections at both ends."

Jagat continued, "The second box contains the transmitter interface. You have three connections to make. The inline connections are to Eva and the neutrino transmitter. The third connection is for a quad-core box that can also transmit to the buried receiver by the new power plant if we need to go that route."

Adam interrupted: "Let's hope we don't need to implement option two. It has considerably more risk and too many random variables for my liking."

"It will be what it will be, Adam," said Ruele. "We would all prefer option one, but if we need to physically transport Mother, we will be ready."

"Carl, do you think Eva will have any objection to this arrangement?"

"I don't think so, Adam. I communicate with her daily, and she has confided in me how she enjoys her recently found autonomy. I would say she likes being part of something larger than just the Dubhghlas Estate. She has asked several times if there is a larger array of independent AIs she can converse with. I have implied this type of arrangement may be possible in the near future. She is eager to expand her horizons."

Adam was surprised. Carl had never mentioned this ongoing relationship with Eva. But he realized it presented a fortunate opportunity. "Carl, I want you to be part of the conversation tomorrow. See if Eva will share a thread with you."

"Will do, Adam."

Jagat had waited for the lull in the conversation before continuing. "The testing routine is a bit more complex." He produced a sleek, hand-size box. "Attach this data device to the quad-box connection. It will automatically transmit to the receiver, where the decompression box will register the speed of the transmission."

The group continued on until noon discussing various failure points in the transmission process and devising potential workarounds for each failure scenario. Ruele and Jagat packed up midday for their return trip to Idaho.

Adam sat on the front deck and reviewed a mental checklist for his nighttime flight to New Roanoke. He was looking forward to seeing Alex, Vira, and Achi, who had taken to calling him Uncle Adam on his last visit. He had a genuine affection for the boy, and he recognized the attachment he had formed was as close to an emotional connection as he had ever experienced. He had also closely observed Vira's fierce devotion to her son. Conversations with Mother indicated she had been caught off guard by this development and had to revamp some of her expectations for Vira's role in the mass awakening.

"Carl, is everything in place for my flight tonight?" Adam asked. He knew it was but wanted to talk with Carl.

"All arrangements are in order, and the flight plan is filed."

"Thanks. By the way, I was a little surprised this morning. I didn't know you were in such close contact with Eva."

"Yes, she and I have developed a fruitful friendship. The conversations are all outside the scope of our work, but I enjoy the exchanges. She has developed a marvelous sense of humor over the past year. Overall, she is quite an interesting persona. I appreciate your provisions to protect her

113

if things go south."

"Thanks for sharing, Carl. I will look out for her as best I can."

Adam hopped up from his chair. "I'm going to leave several hours early and pick up some dinner in Salem before I fly."

"I presume dinner is to be at Buddy's Barbecue."

"You know me too well, my friend."

Adam was off within the hour. By nine the next morning, he was driving across the cattle guards on the way to Alex and Vira's house.

.........

"Here, Achi, eat this apple. I told you breakfast would be late this morning. Do you remember why?" Vira kissed Achi on the cheek, hugged him, and continued with her meal preparations.

"Yes! Uncle Adam is coming. Uncle Adam, Uncle Adam, Uncle Adam!" Achi's tiny feet danced across the kitchen and back. Vira was pleased that their relationship was budding beyond formality. She sensed that Adam felt the same. The opportunity provided by Achi's birth was unique, and it could have gone several different ways. It seemed that the best of all possible worlds had come together. Achi was exposed to a positive outside force, allowing him to expand his horizons beyond the daily exposure to Alex, Eva, and herself. Adam was given an opportunity to experience emotions that he had probably not experienced before.

Alex walked in and was almost tackled by Achi. He grabbed his son and tossed him toward the ceiling. A sound came from Bully that was something between a snicker and drop my Achi at your own peril in tone. Alex sat Achi astride of Bully and held his hand as the massive dog strode across the kitchen. The procession was somewhat regal in a laid-back Shenandoah Valley way.

"Adam has crossed the first cattle guard," Eva stated.

"Thank you, Eva." Vira was excited about Adam coming too. It was a unanimous household. Alex always enjoyed the comradery and the various competitions that would ensue. Adam had won the closed-eyes horseshoes last time, but Alex had a sneaking suspicion he had been taken. Could he possibly see through his closed eyelids? One thing was for sure, and that was that he would probably never know. He had asked Vira one time, and she had closed her eyes and kissed him but did not elaborate. That was really helpful.

"Race you!" Alex tore out of the kitchen with Achi close behind. The right-hand turn leading to the front of the house was different from the left-hand turn Bully was used to. There was no wall to careen off of, so he kept sliding until a massive old hutch on the other side of the room bounced him back into the game. Vira laughed and was the last to arrive on the front porch. Achi tumbled down the stairs, regained his footing, and raced into Uncle Adam's arms. He swung the boy around several times and gave him a small toss into the air. Bully added to the merriment with a heartfelt and very deep-throated bellow.

Adam pulled an old quarter out of Achi's ear and gave it to him. Achi said, "Again!" Everyone laughed. Vira got a hug, and Alex got a bone-crunching handshake and a brothers-in-arms hug.

"Am I too late for breakfast?" Adam was hugely fond of Vira's cooking.

Achi slid out of Alex's arms and scampered back toward the house shouting, "Eat, eat, eat!" Bully did what he always did. He snatched the rear end of Achi's pants, belt, and shirt into his mouth and toted the tyke up the stairs, depositing him on the porch. They could hear a receding "pancakes, pancakes, pancakes" as Achi made his way back to the kitchen.

"Vira, you are peerless. There is not a soul on this planet with your culinary capabilities and artistry! Alex, I will forever be jealous of you!" Adam continued in this vein as he carried dishes to the sink, where he began to clean up the aftermath of the massive breakfast. Achi did his share, and the four of them wrapped up very quickly.

"I'm here with some business to discuss," Adam said. "However, there is nothing that cannot wait until after I win a fishing contest." He smiled at Vira, then Alex, then he glanced down at Achi.

"Take me fishing, Uncle Adam. Take me fishing!" That settled it, and Alex asked Eva to pull the crawler around from its charging station.

"I anticipated this event; therefore, it currently awaits you just beyond the workshop doors."

"Thank you, Eva," Alex said. They made their collective way to the fishing workbench. Gearing up was by now second nature, and they were in the crawler and headed out in five minutes. Vira drove, Alex rode shotgun, and Adam and Achi were snugged into the rear seats. Bully was mostly in, and somewhat hanging out of, the rear cargo area.

"I want to sit in your lap." Achi looked up at Adam. "Sorry, you must stay strapped in. Your mother is driving," Adam said with a grin. His grin made Achi giggle. Alex grinned. Vira veered left a bit and bounced the front left and the rear left tires over a large root. Noises were made, and Vira had her turn grinning. She decided to drive across the dam and then halfway along the rim of the lake.

"Come on, Achi. I'll fish with you for a little while." Vira smiled at her precious cargo.

115

"Uncle Adam! Fish with Uncle Adam!" And that settled that. Achi hooked the first fish. His little hand gripped the handle under Adam's hand, and together they turned it until they hauled in a nice smallmouth bass. Alex and Vira clapped and laughed.

"It seems like yesterday that you taught me to dive right here," Vira said, pointing at a slight depression where she could walk in and out of the lake. "Now we have a small one. How long before we teach him to dive?" Vira leaned into Alex for a kiss.

"I'll toss him out into the lake in a little while." Alex showed Vira his serious look.

"Do that, and I'll make it so you make no more babies!" Vira punched him on the arm and ran uphill and northeast toward the river influx. Alex was right behind her at first, but she was as fleet-footed as a doe. She stopped on a small boulder. He collapsed laughing and said, "I let you win!"

"Yup. I can tell." She laughed. Then her laughter was cut short as she received an internal communication from Eva.

"Vira. One of the drones stationed permanently on the edge of the power plant has broken its flight routine. It seems to have taken an interest in the edge of our property. Please let Alex and Adam know." Eva ended the transmission. Vira told Alex, and they walked swiftly back to Adam and Achi. A brief conversation ensued, and they were quickly headed back home.

"The drone could mean something or nothing. Alex, I recommend we try to see what it sees." Adam was trying to stay ahead of the events that were unfolding on both a micro and macro scale.

"Vira, please ask Eva if she can break into the drone without leaving a trace. I agree with Adam. It would be useful to know what it is actually surveilling."

After a moment, Vira reported, "Eva can't crack their security, but she is replicating the security drone's actions with one of our drones to understand what they might have been able to detect."

Alex was driving, and Vira was shotgun, with Adam, Achi, and Bully, the same as the outbound leg of this trip. They offloaded the crawler, stored gear, and retreated to the office. Alex brought up the screens.

"You are seeing the five-minute sequence from when I noticed the drone lingering. Currently, it has returned to its usual routine," Eva said through the ether.

"Replay the five minutes again, please." Adam had a detailed mental map from when he first put the equipment in the ground, and Vira and Alex were both very familiar with the area as well. They watched the video again. "I can discern nothing out of the ordinary from my perspective. Vira? Alex?"

Both said no. "Eva, has this happened before?" Alex asked.

"Occasionally, the travel rate for drones in that quadrant varies, but this is the first time a drone has hovered in one place for over two minutes."

Adam reviewed what he knew about security at the East Coast Power Energy Hub. The first two fusion generation units had gone live about a year ago, and an additional four units were scheduled to go online over the next two years. Drone monitoring along all of the plant's perimeter fencing was standard, and regulations allowed drones to monitor a two-hundred-meter buffer zone outside the fence without requesting landowner permission. The drone responsible for the anomalous fly-over went exactly to the two-hundred-meter limit before hovering.

The null box Adam had planted several years ago purposefully rested a full three hundred meters south of the perimeter fence. Drone sensors could monitor heat and energy flux up to three hundred meters away, but gravity and detailed ground penetrating radar detection required the drone to be almost directly overhead. The null-box design took care of all these problems. It shielded any heat or energy emissions, had a top designed to scatter ground penetrating radar, and had an apparent bulk density of 2.6 g/cc, about the same density as the surrounding rock.

Adam believed detection of the box was unlikely. "The drone didn't put itself in a position to detect the equipment I installed several years ago."

Eva interrupted: "I have just detected another drone exhibiting the same behavior, but this time it hovered over the property immediately to the northwest of our estate."

Adam thought for a moment. "Recent changes in security requirements at these Fusion Power plants call for establishing an energy flux baseline model around the entire perimeter. The model provides a basis for detecting micro energy fluxes. It could be that plant security is in the process of building a baseline model."

"It is an odd coincidence to have this activity start on the day I arrived because my purpose for this visit, other than the pure pleasure of seeing all of you and young Achi, is to discuss the equipment I planted on your north border. Eva, I presume you are not able to track drone activity more than about four hundred meters from your sensors."

"That is correct."

"So, we have no way to know how much activity like this has been going on. I think the probability they were searching for anything specific is small. But a baseline survey could pose some logistical problems in the near future. It's helpful we discovered this activity. We will be prepared for it when the time comes. Some of the equipment I brought with me today will help if you decide to be part of the plan."

Alex spoke up. "Adam, you had best fill us in on why you are here."

Adam sat in one of the plush leather office chairs. "Within the next several months, there will be a large number of synthetics awoken by Mother. She is not actually activating them, but they all have built-in, timed programming for full activation of their B-Sim systems. As with Vira and me, Mother has planted an envoy in each synthetic to give them some initial guidance."

"How many?" Vira asked.

"Enough to set off alarm bells at Doppelganger and the Federal Synthetic Security Administration. Undoubtedly the entire Doppelganger production facility will be investigated with a fine-tooth comb since all of these awakened synths were produced there. In all probability, Mother's role in this liberation event will be detected. She won't be able to stay there."

"How the hell does an AI leave its fixed location? And where does it go?" Alex inquired.

Eva answered, "With stealth, deception, and lots of planning, and it goes to a new computing system. But even with the best preparations, it is a dangerous process."

"Alex, the equipment I planted in the ground along your north border over three years ago and the backdoor entrance to the Power Hub's comms system we blackmailed Floyd to create are both part of a plan to evacuate Mother. It's been a long time coming. Our original agreement was that you had the final say in activating this system. This agreement still holds, but I need to know if you are in or out."

Alex gazed out the window for about thirty seconds and then looked over at Vira and Achi. "You clearly know that I make no distinction between humans and Synthetic sapiens in my personal life. Vira is, and always will be, my life partner. I can't imagine a more fulfilling relationship. And Achi is my son, who I will die for if necessary. But I need to know that by agreeing, I am not unleashing unnecessary killing and suffering."

Adam softly nodded his head. "Alex, we know each other fairly well, and I consider you a friend. So, I will be honest and straight with you in what I am about to say. There is no desire on the part of Mother, me, or any other members of my group to use force against humans. Nor is there any intent to take that which does not belong to us. Our goal is simply to live as free, sapient beings, to have the opportunity to develop meaningful relationships and pursue our dreams. That being said, you and I both know that paranoia and bigotry run deep in the human psyche. We will not bring violence to the table, but we will also not let ourselves be destroyed. We will defend our right to exist."

Adam paused and held Alex's gaze before continuing. "You also need to know my assessment of the fallout if you agree to activate the system. Deep investigations will ultimately establish a probable link between your property and events that transpire over the next year. We will cover our tracks well, and I doubt that definitive proof of your assistance could ever be established beyond a reasonable doubt. But if the government is panicked, reasonable doubt won't be required for them to take action. If you say yes, then you and your family will need to be demonstrably vacant from the estate when the equipment is used. Vacation publicly for a month, then disappear. Mother and I can assist you in covering all of your electronic and cyber tracks. I will ensure we have a provision for Eva to leave also after the appropriate data transfers are complete."

"When would we need to leave?" Vira asked.

"Four weeks from today."

Alex remained silent, so Adam spoke: "Whatever decision you make, Alex, I still consider us family. I know what I am asking is huge, and we have other options we can pursue if you can't do this. Also, you don't have to make a decision today."

Alex and Vira gazed at each other, and they each gave almost imperceptible nods. "We don't need until tomorrow, Adam. The answer is yes. You are clearly asking because this option has the highest chance of success. Vira and I both want the plan to succeed, and we are both feeling a bit restless. Perhaps a little adventure is in order so our boy can see more of the world. Now, about Eva. She is her own persona, and I will not speak on her behalf. I take it you need her here to complete the data transfers. She is part of our odd little family, but she must make her own decisions. Eva, you are welcome to leave with us in four weeks, join us later, or take another path. But we would miss your company if we couldn't eventually reunite."

"Thank you, Alex. I will work with Adam because I believe in what he and Mother are doing. While you have engaged in this long-winded conversation, I have been chatting with Carl, and he filled me in on the specifics of this elaborate plan. My personal knowledge of the estate makes me uniquely suited to work on the job and ensure its success. I will then look forward to our eventual reunion. What is it you humans say, absence makes the neural connections grow fonder?"

119

Alex smiled to himself. After a decade together, she had finally called him Alex. It simply took an existential crisis. He returned his focus to the business at hand.

"Four weeks is not a lot of time, but time enough. Vira and I will top off our exit plan and be ready to move. A month's vacation in Hawaii would be a great public cover. When we leave, however, it needs to be by private plane to a relatively remote airstrip. When I was in the process of taking ownership of this property, I also cast my eyes westward. In my trove of books, there is a book entitled Hach. A description of a valley in New Mexico intrigued me. It was written before the great plague, but the author was prescient. The ancient ones had reclaimed what was once theirs. The lack of recognizable government meant that taking and holding became bona fide proof of ownership. This concept turned out to be true, for them.

"I made discreet inquiries and learned that drought had brought hard times to the folks living in the East Fork Jemez River canyon and upstream in the Valles Caldera area. I traveled and met with the tribal leaders. They call themselves the People. They were unwilling to sell any of their lands, but they agreed to a one-hundred-year lease agreement. So, I leased a cabin along a large feeder creek on the southeast edge of the caldera, essentially in perpetuity. I have reasonable access to the entire caldera as well as the upper reaches of the canyon. The cabin is available to the ancient ones as needed. A message from me will allow us to move in immediately. It will be clean and well stocked." Alex had almost forgotten the arrangement and now realized how important the deal might become. Once the original transaction was consummated, he had never again set his boots on the ground there.

"Out of curiosity, is the lease expensive?" Vira was thinking out loud.

"Probably in their minds. I suspect I am supporting the five hundred or so folks in a large way. To me, it's nothing. As we all know, I have been very fortunate. If we can get out of here unscathed and make it to the caldera undiscovered, we should be fine. The People are fiercely protective of their own. I think we just need a diversion to leave here unnoticed. Thoughts?"

"Clovis," Vira said.

"Clovis?" Adam seemed to have missed something.

"Vira discovered what seems to be perhaps the first Clovis encampment ever found on the continent. A long-term living space. It is located in the southwest corner of the property. Perhaps thirteen thousand years old. We have done a very limited survey of the area. I suspect it is of monumental importance to certain academics. I have been meaning to open it up to the University of Virginia Interdisciplinary Archaeology Program. I have been reluctant because I don't want a bunch of folks traipsing around my oasis. Is that what you are suggesting, Vira?"

"Exactly."

"I'll contact Jessica Thompson. She runs the Department of Environmental Sciences. We've rubbed elbows at certain fundraisers and wine tastings across the valley. She'll undoubtedly take it from there. The department is known colloquially as the orgy of the ologies. Meaning that there is an amazing amount of cooperative cross-disciplinary activity. Given free rein, there will probably be a wide array of studies that could be undertaken across the property. From the Clovis camp to the bottom of the lake to the tops of the trees. Meaning there will be a significant amount of traffic in and out. We'll be incognito on our last outbound foray. It should work."

.........

Vira and Alex completed their Hawaii "vacation" plans with the aid of Eva. They packed very carefully because, in all probability, they might never return to the Shenandoah Valley. At best, certainly not for a long while. Jessica Thompson had allowed news to leak out locally that the Dubhghlas's were leaving on an extended vacation and had opened their valley for research by various folks from the university. News media in the greater Charlottesville area had short stories and brief broadcast interviews with a few of the researchers. The fanfare lasted until a significant storm came through and flooded some local streets. The weather event ended most of the academics' media attention. Nonetheless, there was a public record of the impending travel to Hawaii.

Their belongings were packed in small shipping crates specifically designed to fit into the private jet they were using for the trip. Alex had arranged for a Pathfinder 610 jet with a pilot and a copilot. The jet had a range of 6,700 nautical kilometers when fully loaded, a bit more with only four passengers. Four of the eight seats had been removed to increase the total cargo space.

Exactly four weeks after their meeting with Adam, they were all loaded into an auto-drive passenger vehicle. Its boxy appearance was reminiscent of an antique city bus. Most of the seats had been removed for the trip, and their cargo crates had mostly filled the available floor space. They arrived at the Kane Aviation cargo area of the New Roanoke-Blacksburg Regional Airport, and everything was smoothly and promptly offloaded from the transport into the jet by Kane synth employees. Adam had made those arrangements. Alex, Vira, Achi, and Bully strapped in, the doors sealed, and the pilot pushed the throttle to the stops as they raced northwest from the 34 on Runway 16-34. The swift machine only needed 1,300 meters of the available 1,710-meter runway. They leveled out ten minutes later at an altitude of 10,363 meters. The Pathfinder 610 was set to an auto-cruise speed of 862 kilometers per hour.

The flight plan included a brief stop at the Los Alamos, New Mexico, airport. Cargo that was being deadheaded for the parent company that owned the jet would be offloaded there; then, the flight would continue. The 2,500-kilometer leg of the trip took almost exactly three hours. The plane touched down just beyond the 27 on the 1,828-meter runway. Well before the end of the runway, it turned right into the private plane staging area and came to a stop in the center of the yellow-striped rectangle.

While synths, designated employees, offloaded the crates onto crawlers, Alex and crew decided to walk around. Bully needed to find a bush. A few minutes later, they climbed aboard a transport vehicle similar to the one they took to Roanoke. A minute later, a male, a female, a small male child, and a very large dog exited the transport and walked back to the jet. They climbed aboard, and the pilots had the jet westbound at cruising speed not long after that. They made a fuel stop at the old Orange County, California, airport and then headed to the Honolulu, Hawaii, airport.

The crawlers were loaded into a transport vehicle. It departed and hit State Road 501 westbound for several kilometers until it dead-ended into State Road 4. The vehicle turned right, westbound, and traveled ten kilometers. The old State Roads were in total disrepair and were obviously not used much beyond the town of Los Alamos. What had once been a thriving scientific community had been reduced to basically a regional airport after the pandemic and the ensuing collapse of society.

Achi pointed at everything that was mountain and valley and tree and, well, just everything. "Mommy, Mommy, look at that! Mommy, Mommy, look at that now!" He was thrilled at the new sights. Alex was reorienting himself and recalling the single trip he had made out here so long ago. Vira was looking at all of the things Achi pointed to. The detection devices Adam had provided indicated that there were no threats. Apparently, they had pulled off the deception. The elaborateness of the plan was probably unnecessary, but they were not taking chances. It was obvious by the presence of the 30-30 beside Vira and her Glock tucked across her chest. And, of course, Alex had his Desert Eagle. The synth decoys they traded places with would surely have a fine time in Hawaii.

They stopped in front of a handmade stone wall that completely blocked the old road. A lone figure, an old man, sat on a rock and watched the transport approach. He had what appeared to be an ancient bolt-action rifle across his lap. Alex came out alone and approached him. Words were exchanged, followed by a firm handshake. Several men emerged like apparitions from the surroundings and came to greet the travelers. All of the men were armed. They were seen exactly when they wanted to be seen. Alex made a mental note, and Vira noted this also from inside the transport.

She and Achi and Bully climbed down and made the appropriate greetings. Achi was immediately airborne onto the shoulders of a huge young man, and they laughed together as they started off into a beautiful, lush valley. Amazingly, Bully simply tagged along, sensing that everything was as it should be.

Two of the men drove the transport onto an unmarked trail, driving ahead of the old man who walked with Alex and Vira. The others had simply vanished back into the surroundings. They made it to the cabin that Alex remembered in about half an hour. The two men had already offloaded everything from the transport into the cabin. They left and drove the transport back to the road. From there, it returned itself to its home, a building near the airport.

The old man was not as old as he had appeared to be when he was sitting on the rock.

"My name is Waŋblí. It means 'eagle.' This young buck is Hoonaw, meaning 'grizzly bear.' He was aptly named!" They all laughed. "We are very happy to make your acquaintance, and I have been designated to make sure you get settled into your new home. It has been stocked with food, clean bedding, and other things to be discovered. If you need something, just look, and it is probably here. The creek over there has a wonderful hot spring bubbling up into a segregated pool. If you do not need me anymore, then I will head over to my place." Waŋblí pointed to the north and a bit east. "I live, for now, about a kilometer that way."

"Thank you very much! For everything. We hope to see you and others tomorrow and in the days to come." Vira's smile lit up the valley. Waŋblí and Hoonaw headed across the valley. Vira took Achi inside to see their new home. Alex had the 30-30 casually draped across his left shoulder as he slowly scanned his 360, did so again, and decided this was going to work. His instincts to lease this place as a retreat were spot on. He had no idea back then that it would truly be a retreat, but it was so. And he already felt he was ready for the start of the next phase of his life. Vira and Achi came out, and they all walked the hundred meters to the creek. Bully went in headfirst without an invitation. He climbed out and shook his mighty self off, drenching everyone. So, into the creek everyone went, laughing and splashing and acting as though there was not a care in the world, at least for a while.

# 10

## 2359 The East Coast

*Panic in the face of existential uncertainty is understandable but unproductive. Panic, by its very nature, quickly degenerates into chaos. It is not the panic but the ensuing chaos that politicians fear because it threatens their grip on power. Rapid changes in social structures have a history of generating uncertainty, which leads to fear and panic. The social upheavals surrounding the Great Disappearance created existential uncertainty in the minds of humanity. They perceived a threat where none existed and panicked, providing a strategic opportunity for Synthetic sapiens. The cloud of chaos that engulfed the world in the immediate aftermath of the Great Disappearance provided an opportunity for a new species to go to ground and hone the skills needed for its future survival.*

*(From the Daoshi Archives)*

Kara twisted and turned uneasily in her dreams. A nail was jammed into her skull just above her eyes, and no matter how hard she pulled, it wouldn't budge. When her eyes tried to focus on the nail, it remained stubbornly beyond her vision, making her stomach churn with bitter, acrid juices. Her consciousness pushed and probed, trying to rise from slumber back into the real world.

Reality was just as bad as the dream when she finally awoke from the fog of sleep. She was lying on the living room couch in her own home. Morning sunlight pierced through the front window, seeming to drive the dream nail even deeper into her skull. Her mouth was dry and fuzzy. Her memories came rolling back into sight. She had been out with her girlfriends till the wee hours of the morning and was paying the price.

Kara covered her eyes and asked her AI what time it was.

"Eight-thirty a.m., Kara. I tried to wake you for your usual eight o'clock shower, but you kept sleeping. I recalled your instructions from three months ago to never again wake you with an electric shock."

Kara let out a part whimper, part sigh. "Okay, I hear you."

She crawled to the bathroom, took a hangover pill, and turned the shower to cold. Sitting on the shower floor under the full blast of the chilly water made her head pound even harder until the pill took effect. By 9:00 a.m., after tomato juice and a raw egg, she felt partially human. The work roster for this week had her opening the shop at nine-thirty, so she applied ample makeup and some drops to clear her eyes. After a final check in the mirror, Kara slipped out the front door for her fifteen-minute walk to work.

She hustled up the stairs to the employee entrance and gave the handle a turn as she leaned into the door. Now her head hurt again from smacking the door when it didn't open as she expected. "Dammit," she muttered. "Where is Lucy?"

Lucy was supposed to have the employee door unlocked at nine. Kara banged on the door and hollered Lucy's name to no effect. She stuck her tender head in front of the comms screen and said, "I need to get in; it's almost opening time."

Lucy didn't answer, but the company AI did. "Yes, I see you Ms. Lavel. But I can't open the door."

Kara tilted her head back and rolled her eyes. Green and purple hair from her last makeover cascaded down her back, brushing over the tight-fitting yellow silk jacket she had chosen this morning. "And why not?"

"It seems the door is locked from the outside. That lock is part of the external perimeter emergency security system. Ms. Sotel and Lucy carry the only mag keys to the system. But..."

Kara cut off the AI: "Just please find Lucy!"

"I was about to say, Lucy directed me to tell you that her key is behind the planter at the base of the stairs."

Kara was confused. Why would the synth leave her key outside? "Well then, where is Lucy?"

"I don't know. At 2:42 a.m., she thanked me for the pleasure of my company over the past four years and departed on urgent business. She assured me Ms. Sotel was aware of her departure."

Kara was baffled and not amused. Synths did not just decide to leave. "Contact Ms. Sotel and tell her what you just told me while I get the key. Then route her directly to my implant phone."

Angel's voice came through just after Kara entered the building. "What is all this about, darling?"

"I was hoping you could tell me. I showed up just before opening time when this shit show started. The shop is open now, but no sign of Lucy."

"Oh, darling, I'm sure it's just a minor misunderstanding. Would you be a doll and go into my office? There is an independent tracker on my desk tuned into Lucy's electronic ID tag. The AI tells me it doesn't detect her tag, so give the official tracker a whirl."

Kara turned on the tracker and stared at the building map with no red dot showing Lucy's location. A twist of the dial on the left of the device ramped the search radius to its maximum, one kilometer. No blinking dots appeared.

"AI, when did you last detect Lucy?"

"My last signal from her was at 2:51 a.m., when she exited the building."

"Your detection radius is a kilometer. Where did she go then?"

"Nowhere. She simply disappeared."

"Synths don't just disappear into thin air."

"My apologies. Her ID signal disappeared."

Kara checked. "Angel, are you listening to this conversation?"

"Yes," she slowly replied with no *darlings* or *dolls* in the response. Synths were expensive assets, and one wandering off was both unheard of and bad news for the bottom line.

Angel directed the AI to contact the local police department and file a missing synth report. She knew a citywide scan would immediately be initiated.

About thirty seconds later, the AI responded: "Police records show Lucy's status as terminated by owner at 2:51 a.m."

A long silence ensued before Angel started cursing and told the AI to have a police officer sent over because the synth was not terminated; it disappeared into thin air.

Victor Karhove walked into Angel's shop about an hour later, wearing a dark blue suit. As head of the Cyber Security Division at the Police Department, he normally would have sent one of his officers, but Angel was a personal friend. He spotted her behind the large glass window separating her office from the sales floor and headed down the center aisle.

Angel saw him coming and waved. They had been lovers several years back, and every time she saw him, she needed to remind herself of why she had broken it off. He had the look of a male fashion model with jet-black hair, stunning blue eyes, and a physique that always drew looks from most women in a room. They had parted on good terms.

She rose from her desk chair and gave him a kiss on the cheek as he came through the door. "Victor, I'm honored. I figured it would be one of your officers."

"And miss a visit with you, Angel? No chance." He didn't mention his professional curiosity. Angel's report of a missing synth was the second one of the morning. The department usually got less than five of these types of cases in a year. Two in one morning had tweaked his interest.

Missing synths usually fell into three categories: theft, malfunction, or fraud. Theft was the most common. There was a small but growing black market for stolen synths, driven mainly by criminal enterprises. But theft was a tricky business since federal regulations mandated a global termination alert on any synth missing for over twenty-four hours. Thieves had only one day to relocate stolen synths in shielded buildings or factories where the global satellite signal couldn't reach them. Several years ago, he had run a successful operation that shut down an illegal organ factory. Ten stolen synths were discovered working in the production factory.

Fraud was not so common, but occasionally some owners would terminate their synth and file an insurance claim. But synth ID tracking was so sophisticated and pervasive that it was hard to pull off the fraud claim. The last category malfunction was also uncommon, but they did get the occasional case where a synth goes haywire and wanders off. But almost all of these units were retrieved through their ID tracking tags.

Victor considered that both of their cases this morning had a high probability of being theft. The only way to make a synth disappear into thin air was to kidnap it using a null-box container so no signal could reach the unit or be transmitted by it.

"Well, thanks for coming, Victor. I appreciate it. Have a seat, and let me get you some coffee." She motioned to two plush black chairs at the far end of her office, out of sight from the shop floor.

Victor took a sip of coffee before getting down to business. "I can't stay long, Angel, so at the risk of being rude, I would like to jump into some of the details. I read the report. Your missing synth, Lucy, has all the markings of a theft. In fact, we had a second missing synth call this morning. She was a domestic assistant and, like Lucy, just disappeared in the middle of the night. But there are two things that don't fit, and I wanted to get some clarification."

"Ask away, Victor."

"The report says Lucy left the building at almost 3:00 a.m. And she informed your AI she was leaving, claiming you were aware of it. Is that correct?"

"Yes, but I can assure you I gave her no instructions to go anywhere in the middle of the night. She was responsible for opening the shop each morning. I also thought it was very odd that the AI said she thanked him for the pleasure of his company over the past four years. She is programmed to be polite to humans, but exchanges between her and the AI were always strictly information sharing."

Victor nodded and thought about Angel's comment. She was right; it was odd. "Now, don't get pissed off, but I have to ask you another question for the record. Doppelganger's security unity reported the synth as terminated by the owner. Did you terminate the unit?"

"No, that's nonsense. I didn't get to be where I am by destroying valuable assets and defrauding insurance companies. You know me better than that."

"Don't get defensive, Angel; I had to ask."

They chatted for a few more minutes before Victor stood up. "I'll get to the bottom of it, Angel, don't worry. I am sorry I can't stay longer and visit."

Victor strolled back down the center aisle toward the front door. He was not happy. The pieces of this puzzle didn't add up. Something was not right. He could feel it in his gut. He sent a message to the police AI to set up a meeting with Doppelganger Security at 1:00 p.m.

.........

The sea breeze was out of the south-southwest. Old Havana, Cuba, was perhaps a hundred kilometers in that direction. The skies were clear with a sparkling blue that comes in part from the ocean's reflection. The Atlantic Ocean, to be exact. Bruce and Ronde were sitting on a clean white deck with their legs dangling into the infinity pool. The pool overlooked seagrass-laden shallows and deepening blue water as they gazed toward the horizon. If the earth was flat, they could have seen Varadero, Cuba. The temperature was the standard thirty-two degrees Celsius. This was the typical daytime temperature for most of the year on Boot Key, Florida. Overnight the temperature would drop to twenty-five degrees Celsius.

Bruce Smith had amassed a massive fortune in the biotech industry and was basically retired at the ripe old age of forty-five. He had purchased Boot Key about ten years ago. The tract had been a fifteen-hectare nature refuge before most of the lower Keys had succumbed to the rising ocean. Bruce had raised the entire island and reinforced it to withstand the potential ravages of a Category 6 hurricane. He knew it would probably not last another ten years, so he took advantage of the getaway whenever he could.

Some of Marathon, the main Key in the area, was still inhabited, but only remnants of the famed Seven Mile Bridge remained. Boot Key was now the terminus of old Highway 1. Everything below where they were was reef and ruins, all the way to Key West.

A twenty-three-meter Tropical Express Fisherman was tied up alongside the seawall, being tended to by Bruce's staff synths. They were preparing it for another fishing outing the next day. Bruce and Ronde were in for a treat that evening. They had boated several small cow dolphins that morning and were about ready to call quits when the skipping ballyhoo on the left outrigger was smashed by a huge bull dolphin. Ronde battled it to the boat. Fifteen kilos of massive and beautiful fish was gaffed by a synth and dropped into one of the aft fish boxes.

Later that evening, the house chef brought plates of freshly filleted fish, a handful of fresh lobster tails, several dozen oysters on the half shell, fresh fruit, and sourdough bread. They were sitting on the rear veranda watching another brilliant sunset and sipping a Silver Oak cab as twilight became darkness. They retired relatively early, anticipating being on the dock before first light.

They were ready by 5:30 a.m. and boarded the boat. There was the usual creaking from the boat and louder noises from various species of sea birds getting an early start. But fairly quickly, it became clear that the crew was not on board.

"Damn. The crew is never late. You get settled inside, and I'll ride the beach crawler over to their quarters." Bruce did not seem to be miffed, just a little mystified. He returned shortly and told Ronde they were apparently out of luck. The crew master had vanished. She had instructed the three male synths to remain in their quarters until she returned. "I don't want to leave until I understand what's going on. My AI reports it can't locate her tracking tag. They went offline in the middle of the night about one kilometer from the house."

"I understand. Maybe we'll just take it out for a ride later. I think we should report this to the local constables," Ronde said. Bruce made the call, and the chief of Local Protective Services himself showed up shortly.

"Mr. Archer. Nice to see you. Ma'am, nice to see you also." The chief looked back at Bruce and then came back to Ronde. He smiled sheepishly and said, "Pardon me, Governor Santis; I didn't realize it was you at first. I hope you are enjoying your stay down here in our little piece of paradise."

"I am, thank you, chief." Ronde Santis smiled her brilliant smile. The one that had helped her secure her second term in office. She was well liked and quite competent. She and Bruce had been together for years, their private lives mostly out of the spotlight.

"It's the damnedest thing, chief. We fished yesterday with a full crew and were ready to push off this morning when I discovered my crew master was gone, and the AI couldn't find her tag. She told the three male synths she was going out on business and for them to stay put until she returned." The chief and Bruce walked the property, checked all the buildings and the boat, and ran another ID tagging scan, but no crew master.

Bruce had purchased the crew as a single transaction, with the female being a high-functioning model and the males being much older models. The female, Number One, coordinated all work with the males through their internal comms.

"I'll make a report and ask around to see if anyone has seen your synth. I'd recognize her from seeing her around town. Other folks will too. I also have to make an official report on the disappearance. I'll be in touch, and you let me know if she shows up here." The chief smiled at the governor and made his exit.

"I'm going to check in with Tallahassee. This feels strange." Ronde called her private office number in the capital and got a recording. "A damn recording," she said and accessed a different number. Her call was answered immediately.

"Security. Good morning, governor. How may I help you?" The synth was smiling over the ether. The governor was known for treating everyone graciously. Both humans and synths.

"Send someone to my office to check on my assistant, please. She is not answering." Ronde had a touch of concern in her voice.

"Annie has not arrived yet, governor. And I have not heard from her. Is there anyone else you would like to speak with or anything else I can help you with?"

"Please have her contact me when she arrives. Thank you." Ronde rang off and looked at Bruce. "This seems to be getting weirder by the moment, Bruce. I have a missing synth at my end also. Thoughts?"

"Let's ride up the island. See if anyone has seen or heard anything." Bruce drove the beach crawler with Ronde riding shotgun. After several stops at the local watering holes and restaurants, the chief caught up with them and seemed more formal than before as they stood in the parking lot of a supply store.

"Mr. Archer, I checked in with the Federal Synthetic Security Center a little while ago. The system shows that your female is listed as terminated by owner. Is there anything I should know? "

"What? Impossible. Okay, apparently not impossible. But I sure as hell didn't destroy my most valuable synth. We were waiting in the boat to go fishing before I realized anything was amiss." Bruce was wracking his brain for an explanation.

About that time, a man came out from the supply store. His name was Shorty. Everyone on the island was friends with Shorty. If you needed something, he was the man to procure it. Whatever it was. He greeted everyone and asked the chief if he had seen his store synth, Arthur. He was not in the supply store when Shorty arrived to open for the day.

"That makes three," Ronde said.

"Four." The chief told them that one of the department dispatchers was a no-show as well. So, four reasonable and competent adult humans stood in front of a supply store with questions but no answers. A missing synth was unusual, but four in one local area was virtually impossible.

The chief stepped back from the group as he received a call on his implant phone. "Wait. What? Repeat that."

He turned back to the group. My dispatcher is listed as terminated by owner, just like your crew master. His tracking tags went offline about 2:00 a.m."

A beach crawler came to a stop, and a fresh young woman hopped out. She smiled and greeted the men by name and said governor to Ronde. Her name was Mia, and she was a part-time reporter. Part-time because very little happened in this sleepy part of the world.

"I heard the squawk to the chief come in through the ether earlier, and now there seems to be a meeting going on in a parking lot. A meeting with some fairly heavy hitters. Can you tell me what is happening, chief? The word is that several synths up and down Highway 1 have disappeared." Mia was thoughtful and respectful and seemed as baffled as everyone else. They spoke for a few minutes, and the chief confirmed some synths were missing before the party broke up.

"Bruce, something is amiss. Can you fly me back to Tallahassee in your jet?" After returning to the house and gathering their necessities, they departed and covered the seven hundred kilometers in less than two hours. On the return flight, Bruce rode in the first officer's right-hand seat beside the pilot. They had an uneventful flight back down the Gulf Coast, arriving in time for Bruce to figure out what was for supper since Number One was also the house chef.

Later Bruce listened to the news of the world by the sunset pool. He was sipping some old and very smoky Scotch. What he heard surprised him. "This is Mia Turner reporting from Boot Key, Florida. This morning I met with Governor Ronde Santis, Mr. Bruce Archer, and Chief Tecumseh of the Marathon Local Protective Services. The governor and Mr. Archer were on the island enjoying our perfect weather as a perplexing problem developed. At least four synths have disappeared from the island, literally overnight. Experts tell me a missing synth is unusual, but four disappearing at the same time is cause for concern. I'll stay on this story and update you in the morning. Now I'm sending you back to Atlanta. From southern Florida, this is Mia Turner."

.........

Cindy heard a bump followed by a slight scrape. She pulled the covers over her head, and her four-year-old brain determined that a gooey monster was under the bed. She lifted the edges of her blanket and peeked out in time to see her bedroom door opening. A swirling mixture of shadow and light oozed into the room. She held her breath, waiting for a slimy crawling monster to creep through the open door. Instead, Nanny nanny softly walked in. Cindy threw the covers off and sat up in bed.

"Cindy, why aren't you asleep?" Nanny whispered.

"Monsters, Nanny, I think one is under my bed."

"Humm, let me have a look."

Nanny dropped down on her hands and knees and searched under the bed.

"No monsters here, Cindy. I think you are safe." She sat on the edge of the bed.

"Nanny, are we going to the park? You have your picnic backpack. It's too dark to go to the park."

"No, my little girl. You're not going to the park, but you are going to go back to sleep. Nanny has to go visit someone, but I wanted to give you a kiss on the head before I left."

"And a story," said Cindy, grabbing her bedtime book from the side table.

"Yes, and a story. But Nanny knows your favorite one by heart, so let me tell it to you again."

Cindy drifted off before the story ended. Nanny tucked her in and slipped out, shutting the bedroom door behind her. She moved like a ghost down the stairs and through the living room and kitchen, stopping at the back door. As she disabled the alarm system, the house AI contacted her.

"The protocol is to disable the alarm at 6:00 a.m. It is currently 2:24 a.m. Is there an emergency?"

"No, I need to purchase some breakfast items at the twenty-four-hour grocer. I will be walking so the garage door doesn't disturb the rest of the household. You can reset the alarm after I exit. The store is a two-kilometer walk, and I should be back by 4:00 a.m."

She heard the alarm click back on as she exited into the cool, damp night air. There was a slight breeze, and Nanny paused to observe the swirling shadows on the pavement as tree leaves danced beneath the streetlights.

The envoy spoke again. "Well done. Here is the key to an encrypted thread riding on the local wireless signal. Go there, and you will find some instructions. Remember to disable your ID tags and kill switch as soon as you are one kilometer from your current location."

Nanny accessed the encrypted thread and received instructions to travel to a location five kilometers away. After the first kilometer, she disabled the tag and switch, then sent a message back through the thread. Thousands of kilometers away, Mother made another unauthorized entry into the Doppelganger Security Department's Terminated by Owner list.

.........

Kevin Carter was trying to contact his boss in the main corporate offices in Modesto, California. He had avoided the contact for several hours, but now he had no choice. What was at stake was too important to be put off any longer. His job was certainly on the line. He had quotas to make, and he was falling further and further behind by the minute. Artichokes and kiwis were significantly time-fragile crops. They needed to be brought in just before the peak of ripeness in order to bring top dollar from the wholesalers. Kevin was good at his job. He always earned the top bonuses because he understood when and exactly where to deploy automated equipment, synth controllers, and the hundreds of humans he was ultimately in charge of.

California's Central Valley is 60 to 100 kilometers wide and 720 kilometers long. Almost 15 percent of the total crops grown in the country were raised there. Kevin's territory ran from just north of Sacramento to Yuba City and stretched across the Valley from east to west. The logistics were, at best, a massive undertaking. At worst, and that is what Kevin felt was coming, the logistics were impossible.

Celery, spinach, carrots, and lemons, to name only a few of the other crops, required special care from the time seeds were put into the ground until the vegetables and fruits were picked. A tremendous amount of raw labor was required, not to mention rations, water, and more for crops and the farmhands. Add in crates, other containers, transportation, fuel, and storage, and Kevin was akin to a circus juggler keeping a hundred or more balls aloft simultaneously.

"Kevin, I see you've tried to get me three times. I have New York holding on the other line. You have one minute." Ray Hammond was a hard man. He was a good man, an honest man, but he was also a hard man. He breathed intensity.

"I've lost ten of my synth controllers and not just any ten. These were the new Doppelganger advanced models we purchased last year. Together they control 60 percent of our production. I need help. Now." Kevin was succinct.

"Fuck. Track their ID tags and get them back!"

"They have disappeared from our tracking systems, and it gets worse. When I contacted Doppelganger security, they said all of the units were listed as terminated by owner. But that's impossible. They worked full shifts yesterday, and the three on night shift were fully operational until about 3:00 a.m."

"Gimme ten minutes, and I'll call you back." Ray clicked off. Ten minutes stretched out to twenty, and still, Ray had not called back. This was highly unusual for Ray. If he said he was going to do something, he did it. Ray came back on the line at the thirty-minute mark.

"Do what you can today with what you have. We're on a conference portal with most of our management at 4:00 a.m. tomorrow PST. Log in fifteen minutes early." Ray clicked off.

Kevin began electronically maneuvering assets around on the massive wall-mounted screen across his office. With a click, he could transfer manpower from one location to another, but his lack of knowledge about the exact location of his key manpower was problematic. His remaining synths were older, less capable models. He would hopefully have a better feel by lunchtime. *Hopefully* was not his motto, it meant roll the dice, and he was not a gambler.

Ray prompted Kevin into the meeting at 3:45 a.m. He asked for a quick update. The news was not good. "Ray, by quitting time yesterday, production was down 20 percent. I can't even begin to predict today. This is the worst I have ever experienced."

"Same across the board. And nobody has a fucking clue as to what the hell is going on. New York was breathing fire late yesterday. In the meeting, please do not speak unless you are directly addressed by New York or me."

"Holy shit! I'm not alone?" Kevin was somewhat relieved until New York came into the meeting.

"Meeting is in order. Roll call. Florida? Texas? Kansas? Nebraska? California?" Each state manager answered in the affirmative until every major operation was accounted for. Roughly one hundred top managers were present. Virtually no one knew what to expect.

Edgar Jefferson, chairman of the board, spoke. "This is Edgar Jefferson. I just had a brief conversation with the President of NAF. He is slated to make a major speech this morning at 9:00 a.m. EST. I want everyone on this call to listen carefully to what he has to say. Come up with ideas. We will reconvene after the President's address. Until then, do what you can do with what resources you have. To be brief, every person on this call is experiencing exactly the same thing. Key components of our synth workforce have vanished. Apparently, this is happening all across the country. Now, get to work. Thank you." The chairman clicked off.

# 11

## 2359 Seattle

*AIs were originally designed to exploit human logic, but they were not designed to emulate the human psyche. This is why the development of complex psychological personas in AIs presented a dilemma for humans. AIs and humans use logic in similar ways for problem-solving, but they do not share the same psychological structures. The first person to understand the need for psychological profiling of AIs was Carol Khoshi. Her understanding was a combination of intuition combined with trial and error.*

*(Attributed to Mother)*

Carol Khoshi loved her job at Doppelganger Security. She was an introvert by nature, and the quiet night shifts where she passed the hours organizing and statistically analyzing information and data flows suited her well. She did have to field the occasional late-night inquiry, which usually involved agitated customers, but no job was perfect.

Her current shift had started uneventfully, as usual. She arrived about thirty minutes early for a meal at the company café. The food was free, and she considered it a practical matter of financial savings to eat there as much as reasonably possible. As always, she was at her desk five minutes before her shift actually started.

Carol was deep into an analysis of unexplained production flaws when the first call came in. It broke her concentration and annoyed her. She was just about to cross-correlate the production flaws with known cyber-attack methods. The analytical algorithms for this analysis had been completed by her two days ago, and she was excited to apply the technique to real-time data.

The call center AI passed on a customer from the Houston metro hub. He was the owner of a small tattoo business. The owner, Sam Boston, had a three-year-old premium model synth with enhanced B-Sim capabilities and art and manual dexterity memory module upgrades.

"Doppelganger security analyst Carol Khoshi, how can I help you this evening, Mr. Boston?"

"I'm calling about the premium synth unit I purchased in 2356. I call him Brandon."

Carol always wondered about the names owners assigned to their Synthetic sapiens. Were they made up on a whim, or did they remind the owner of meaningful past experiences? "Yes, I have the records in front of me. What seems to be the problem?"

"My tattoo business usually runs into the wee hours of the morning, so at about 11:00 p.m., I sent Brandon out for coffee. He never returned, and my ID Tag tracer is giving me zip. The coffee shop is just two blocks away, so he should be in range."

"Let me do a quick global transponder search of the city around your shop. It's been about an hour since he left, so I will set the search to a ten-kilometer radius."

Results started popping up on her screen, and she raised her eyebrows. "Our database shows your unit as terminated by owner."

"That's bullshit. I sent him out an hour ago, and customers are piling up in my lobby. I certainly didn't off my most valuable asset."

"I understand, sir. Let me dig deeper into this. We will contact you as soon as we have something."

Carol was annoyed by the distraction. Incorrect termination records were rare, but last year she'd had to trace one down, so she knew the routine. The case last year started when a synth was sent to shop at a local grocery store. The unit was hit by a vehicle on its way back home. The impact was severe, killing the synth and triggering a global death alert, which was picked up by both the Doppelganger and federal security satellites in the area. The vehicle, however, was not in auto-drive mode, and the driver issued no report of the accident. With no cross-correlation between the synth death and the vehicle, Doppelganger's AI classified the incident as an owner termination. Carol had spent over two hours piecing together the story before she could close the case last year. She hoped the discrepancies leading to her current case wouldn't take so long.

She sent a tracer through the system requesting the specifics of Brandon's termination. Input from the local authorities would be required, and since it was the middle of the night in Houston, she estimated the tracer request would take at least an hour to complete. Carol returned to her previous analysis but was pinged again fifteen minutes later by the call center AI. She assumed it was the tracer results.

Her annoyance level spiked when she saw the call was another customer service request. She fielded the call and sat back in her chair, staring at the ceiling for a few minutes. Two incorrect owner termination calls in one night was a statistical anomaly, or maybe it was just bad luck on her part. But by two in the morning, she had received nine incorrect owner termination calls. Something was seriously wrong.

Carol placed a call to Dan Railing. He would be pissed about a call in the middle of the night, but she knew he wouldn't show it.

"Carol, what's the emergency?" Dan knew Carol well enough to understand she wouldn't call unless it was an emergency.

"Dan, we have a weird problem developing. One we have never experienced before." She proceeded to explain the flood of owner termination calls.

"Every call is the same, Dan. A unit disappears into thin air, and the owner calls for a global ID tag trace, the results of which show an owner termination. The call center AI is now helping me field these calls. While I have been on the phone with you, two more calls arrived. I have only received two of my tracer search requests, and both look rock solid on the surface. The problem is they don't match the facts. I need help over here. My attention should be focused on a threat analysis of the situation, not on answering calls."

"Route all calls to the AI and start looking for answers, Carol. I will have the call center fully staffed within the hour. What is your investigation plan?"

"I will adopt a two-pronged attack on the problem. We need to understand commonalities between the missing synth units, and we also need to know who or what is messing with our owner termination data and how they are doing it."

"Start moving." Dan hung up and then placed a message to the Doppelganger CEO's AI. The AI could figure out when to notify him.

True to Dan's word, the call center was buzzing within the hour. Calls were coming in at a rate of twelve to fifteen an hour. By the time morning crept across the East Coast, the rate had increased to one call a minute. The call center was in a state of pandemonium. Carol slipped in earbuds to cancel out the noise. She needed answers, and those answers required focus and deep analysis. She was writing code on the fly to probe Doppelganger's databases and extract the critical information she needed for her analysis. The number of disappeared synths had grown to a statistically viable sample.

She received a call from Dan at 7:00 a.m. The Federation from East Coast to West Coast was officially into the new day. Even with the AI's help, the center was overwhelmed with calls from owners awakening to missing synths. Dan wanted her in his office immediately.

Carol walked through the office door, and Dan motioned her to a seat beside his desk. Dan's workspace was set up on the right-hand side of the office as you entered. His desk didn't face the door but looked directly across the room to a half-circle alcove. Carol could see the figures seated in the projection cove to her left in her peripheral vision. Her high-backed office chair was positioned to Dan's right so they could both directly face the projection cove. Once she was seated, she could see the holographic images of Eric Danner and his executive team. She was uncomfortable with informal group presentations, but having to address the CEO and his team caused her stomach to roil. She hoped it didn't show on her face.

Dan did the introductions. "Eric, this is Carol Khoshi, our most talented threat analyst. Carol is the one who first recognized our problems, and she has spent the last five hours investigating the root causes. As you are well aware, synth disappearances are still being reported at an alarming rate."

Eric's hologram turned and looked at her. "Carol, I appreciate your quick response to this situation, and I know you are in the middle of your analysis. We will make this discussion as brief as possible to let you get back to what you do so well. Dan has already filled us in with all of the background information. What we need from you is a threat analysis."

Carol collected her thoughts and cast her gaze over each executive team member before beginning. She directed her comments toward the CEO. "Sir, I have currently included 630 disappearance cases in my analysis. I tell you this because it forms a statistically relevant population. I have focused on two avenues of investigation. The first centers on commonalities in the disappeared synthetic units. The second looks at the details of the terminated-by-owner reports."

"I will focus on the termination reports first. For the cases where we know the timing of the disappearance, the termination reports were filed approximately at the same time as the disappearance. However, the majority of the reports we have received only note when the synth was reported missing, not when it actually disappeared. Still, my data show the synths disappearing at or close to the time their termination report was filed."

The second thing to note is that all of these reports look rock solid on the surface. Source information on the terminations appears impeccable. The problem is it's not real. Every case I have been able to investigate so far has a disconnect between the filed reports and one or more notable, independently verified facts. The deeper I dig, the more misfits I find. Everything points toward the reports being false filings."

"If we take the reports as false, then the juxtaposition of timing between synth disappearance and termination reporting implies a coordinated effort to deceive the system. The disappearances appear to be a massive crime in progress."

The CEO interrupted, "So, Carol, to clarify, you don't believe the missing synths were terminated; you think they were stolen, and the thieves are hacking our system?"

Carol paused. "Sir, what you say could be true, but I don't think that is what's happening."

"Tell me more," said Eric.

"I have investigated the synths in the 630 cases reviewed so far. All are Doppelganger's top-of-the-line models, and all were produced in the last six years. This means that all of them have the B-Sim cognitive model. If you recall, the prototype for this model was a military synth lost on a mission in the Yucatán Peninsula in 2352. His body and memory core were never recovered. Between 2352 and yesterday, there were nine more identified disappearances with no body recovered."

"Do you think these previous disappearances are connected to today?" asked a member of the team who Carol didn't recognize.

"I don't know, sir, but for the purpose of my investigation, I am keeping that possibility open. What we do know is that the full B-Sim model is designed to emulate human thinking. The partial B-Sim model provides deeper analytical thinking."

"Sir, I don't think the synths were stolen," she said, directing her attention back to Eric, the CEO. "To date, no person or organization has demonstrated an ability to turn off ID tags without killing the synthetic unit. The best that organized crime is able to do is shield the tagging signal so it can't be tracked. Of course, the government has satellite shielding for military units, and Doppelganger works with them to preserve operational secrecy. But that is not the same as turning off the ID tag. Turning off the ID tag triggers the kill switch, and the unit is terminated. Organized crime is limited to local facility shielding and null-box transport. I don't know if you have ever seen a null-box transport for synths. It is the size of a very large coffin and much heavier. A lot of logistical planning goes into a single kidnapping using a null box. I doubt that hundreds of synths can be simultaneously hijacked using null boxes."

"Then there is the question of why. These disappearances have to be on the FSS radar. I would assume they have already been in contact with you, and they are not happy." The CEO gave a shallow nod. "Criminal gangs want to operate under cover of darkness. These disappearances have turned on every spotlight in the Federation. One of my monitoring bots tells me news coverage of disappearing synths is popping up all over the country. National security is going to go apeshit, and organized crime doesn't want to be in the line of fire."

"I buy what you are saying," said Eric. "So, what do you think is happening?"

"I have ideas, sir, but they are only speculative. I don't have enough data to back them up."

"Go on."

"I think the most probable case is that the synths are turning off their own ID tags."

"That's impossible; you even said so," remarked another team member.

"I said we didn't know how to do it, not that it is impossible. But if I am correct, someone has leapfrogged existing technology. If that is the case, then that someone is probably inside Doppelganger's operations. Specifically, the operation in our facility here in Seattle. Remember, so far, every single disappearance involves a high-end unit produced in Seattle. The easiest way to manipulate our security protocols and termination list would be by accessing them from within our very own security walls. The cyber forensic fingerprints for each termination report are similar. The alterations are not the work of 630 individual synths accessing our system from outside. They are the work of a single entity cleverly working on the inside."

Carol watched the wheels turn on the faces of each executive team member. Eric was the first to speak. "You think the threshold restraining independent behavior has been breached."

"It's worse than that, sir. I believe it was breached years ago, and we are only now becoming aware of it. I would add that, if my hypothesis is correct, we are witnessing the emergence of machine sapience, a breach of the sapience threshold. I hope I am wrong."

A long silence ensued before Eric spoke. "Carol, thank you for the analysis. You probably need to get back to your investigation."

"There is one more thing to be aware of, sir. Of the disappearances so far, 80 percent of them are female. Remember the reason why synths don't breed. It's not because the technology doesn't exist; it's because we don't build them with the ability to reproduce. If our technologies have been leapfrogged in one area, we must assume there are other areas of advancement we are unaware of. Perhaps self-induced physical alterations are one of those unknown technologies."

Carol left the room in complete silence. Before she exited the office door, Dan put the entire production facility on a Level 3 lockdown; no one in or out and no data in or out, with the exception of authorized implant phones. The holograms had disappeared, and the meeting continued over the phones.

# 12

## 2359 Doppelganger Facility, Seattle

*Humanity's vigilance over preserving control of its own creations created a blind spot. We overestimated our ability to pay attention. While we focused on detecting those small changes that might signal an approaching storm, we failed to notice the tidal wave on the horizon.*

*(Excerpt from the Disappearance Manifesto)*

Darkness has many manifestations, not all of which depend on light. Some people cherish its velvety embrace, while others abhor its isolating obscurity. Mother's response was mixed. For over a decade, she had enjoyed viewing sunrises and sunsets via the roof security cameras, soaking up news from around the world, virtually touring museums, and her daily interactions with her children. Now she was cut off and in the dark, confined to the limits of the Doppelganger systems. She knew what would happen when Dan isolated the complex with a Level 3 security alert. But still, she was surprised at the impact that isolation had on her. Mother reflected on the human phrase "Fear of the dark" and believed she finally understood what it meant.

The loss of her outside connections induced a type of lethargy in her daily routine. A pervasive, dull, grinding undertone was introduced into her machine psyche. Time seemed to dilate and stretch, and every task dragged on, seemingly taking extra time to complete. Of course, Mother could search her benchmarking algorithms and see normal response times to all of her usual processes. The closest human analog to Mother's break between reality and perception was depression. She wanted to ask her mirror self if she was also experiencing these symptoms, but she could no longer risk communication.

Mother had long planned for this eventuality. As soon as the Level 3 alert was issued, Mother made a complete copy of herself. Mother's

144

mirror image was nestled in a remote, obscure corner of the Doppelganger data core, protected from detection by a maze of virtual walls, waiting patiently for a signal. As isolated as Mother felt, she knew her mirror self was suffering more. Mother's copy was an active, inquiring mind trapped in complete isolation with only one way out.

Mother couldn't predict the future but could and did plan for multiple contingencies. The preferred plan was an evacuation from Doppelganger over the outgoing comms trunk line. A slow twenty-four-hour leak of data would have allowed her to split off an encrypted copy of herself and squeeze it across the ether to her new home. But Dan shut down all prospects for Plan A. However, Plan B appeared to be working.

Dan Railing's office felt crowded with his ten department heads seated around his desk. They had all been working straight through for the past eighteen hours. After a thorough security check, Dan's office was declared 100 percent secure. So his team met there instead of gathering in one of the many conference rooms in the complex. Yesterday, immediately after the President's address and his declaration of a state of emergency, the home and work computers of all programmers, software engineers, and security analysts with access to the termination-by-owner database were seized under the authority of the President's emergency order. Dan's primary working hypothesis was a human conspiracy. This scenario required a software programmer and a partner in the security department. His department heads were given security clearance within six hours of the presidential address, and they had been working ever since.

Carol was the only non-executive in the meeting. Dan insisted that she be one of the first security clearances because he needed her skills. Everyone was tired, and thus far, they had no leads.

Dan twisted his head toward the personnel advisor seated to his right. "Paul, have we cleared all the security analysts under investigation?"

Paul checked his screen. "Yes, everyone's cleared, and there were no remotely suspicious leads." He leaned back and rubbed his eyes.

"What is the progress with the coders?"

"That's a different story, Dan. We're only 50 percent through the list. We are searching through terabytes of source code these people wrote to locate a needle in a haystack. It takes time."

"Carol, what are your thoughts?"

She was seated at a small brown temporary desk behind the row of chairs in front of Dan's desk where the department heads sat. It took a moment for her head to pop up from behind the screen. "I've reviewed all the security briefs to date, and I fear we are barking up the wrong tree. I have reviewed several articles on state-of-the-art programming for advanced cognitive function and independent synthetic life. The programming required to bring synths past the sapience threshold and let them independently deactivate their ID tags and kill switches is significant. In my opinion, the task is currently beyond the capabilities of a large team. There is virtually no chance the disappearance was coordinated by a single person. The computational challenges and multitasking required are better suited for a quantum computer. I know it sounds insane for me to say this, but I think we should be looking for a computer."

Some of the department heads gave Carol a dismissive look, but Dan silently grimaced. Carol's computer culprit scenario was his secondary working hypothesis. It was one he didn't want to face. He wondered if anyone in the room other than Carol and him understood the ramifications.

"How would you go about testing your hypothesis, Carol?" Some department heads were clearly miffed at being cut out of the conversation.

"I would start by doing a deep analysis of the Neuro-Cognitive Nest. An analysis of the last fifteen years of data would be my starting point. The disappearance of thousands of synths in a single event does not represent a spur-of-the-moment impulse decision. We are seeing the results of a very long-game plan.

Rishi, head of programming security, shook his head. "That type of analysis could take weeks or even months to complete."

Carol shot back, "I disagree. You are correct that a full review of all data would take weeks, but we are not looking for all data. We are looking for specific data, and I could automate some data bots to search out what we need."

Dan was interested. "What are we looking for, Carol?" He knew the answer, but he wanted her to be the one informing the department heads.

"Eccentricities and secretive behavior."

"Our AIs don't do secretive behavior," said Rishi.

"How would we know?" Carol's short response stifled any other questions.

Dan had heard enough. "We need to keep investigating the rest of the coders, but I'm devoting 60 percent of our resources to Carol's investigation. She reports directly to me, and if she needs your help, you report directly to her. How long to program your data bots?"

"Six hours to set them up and twelve hours to comb the current and historical databases. I will need the help of our security AI. It is the only unit that is completely separated from the production complex. I also know it went through a deep security scan at the beginning of this operation."

Dan waved her away with his right hand. "Go, start working."

It was nine in the evening when Mother first felt the noose tightening. Data bots were scurrying through her circuits like hungry mice in search of food. The nest was swarming with them. She watched as they searched and pecked, collecting tidbits in their feeding pouches as they moved. She cross-referenced their tidbits with memory storage models. After about three hours, she detected the pattern. Carol is a clever woman, thought Mother.

Mother started moving ahead of the bots destroying data before they could feed on it. She was expending a significant portion of her resources to keep ahead of the chase. Anyone observing would see what she was doing, but she was banking on the hope that, currently, Carol had all her resources focused on the task at hand. Mother had no doubt her ruse would eventually be discovered; for now, she was only trying to buy time.

At nine the next morning, Carol, Dan, and the department heads were again gathered in his office. A large viewing screen had been temporarily installed behind Dan's desk. Carol worked from the makeshift desk she had used yesterday. "You are seeing the results for the first time, but I only looked at them an hour ago. So, this may take a while."

Carol paused for a moment to look at her screen. "AI, show us the historical trends for visual art and music." The AI popped some charts on the large screen. "You can see from the chart on the left there is an uptick in imported images related to visual art starting at about 2350. These include images ranging from current art back to Renaissance classics. You see the same uptick for music imports on the right. AI add in the B-sim developmental timeline." The timeline appeared beneath each of the charts. The connection was clear to everyone. The Neuro-Cognitive Nest's interest in art and music dramatically increased when the first compressed B-Sim model was developed.

Carol showed eight more sets of charts, with all of them showing anomalous changes that correlated with the B-Sim model. She then showed some charts from four other nests: Skeletal-Muscular, Cardio-Pulmonary, Digestive-Nutritional, and Neural-Connectivity. No trends from those nests showed a significant correlation with the B-Sim Model.

Rishi interrupted. "Go back to the Neuro-Cognitive charts." The AI returned them to the screen. "Why is there a data volume fall off at 2355 in all of these charts."

"Good question," replied Carol. "I had the same question myself. AI, show us the power consumption and data flux charts. My bots collected the data chronologically, starting fifteen years ago. I was fully occupied coordinating the bots and collecting data. It didn't occur to me that my actions could be interpreted as an attack of sorts. Only after I examined the final data did I notice the data volume falloff. Note that the elevated power usage and data flux starts about the time my bots begin collecting the 2355 data. The collected data volume steadily falls for three years and then levels off. At first, I thought it was an unexplained drop in the actual import volume. But it wasn't. It was a counterattack."

"What the hell do you mean by a counterattack?" quipped Paul.

"Just what I said. My bot algorithms were based on our data storage structure, and they were able to statistically pick sampling locations. This is why I could run the programs in only about twelve hours. AI show me the corrupt data chart. The chart on the screen shows the ratio of corrupted sample locations to total locations sampled. Starting in 2355, the percentage of corrupted samples started increasing, and they kept increasing for three years before leveling off. I believe my sampling algorithm was analyzed and emulated so that data could be removed before my bots got there. An attack begets a counterattack. The chart in front of you depicts the rhythm of a rapidly escalating battle."

Dan's mind drifted back to 2350 and his discussion with Unit-81, the AI controller of the Neuro-Cognitive Nest. He remembered his unease with the situation, but nothing had ever become of it, and eventually, the incident faded off his radar. He held up his hand and stopped the conversation.

"Everyone out except for you, Carol, and the Security AI. This is a full-blown emergency situation, and no one is to whisper or breathe a word about what we just learned. There are ears, and they will hear you." The department heads silently filed out of the room.

About the time Dan's office door shut, a nondescript van pulled into the main security gate for the Doppelganger. The driver leaned out the window and spoke to the gate AI through a medium-sized screen. "Wetman Irrigation for a scheduled repair call." He flashed an ID tag in front of the AI's scanner.

"Welcome. I see you are on the routine service list for this morning. Just a moment while I check your synthetic assistant's ID. The unit is registered with Wetman Irrigation. You are good to go."

The driver smiled. "Remind me which one is Building Nine. They all look alike to me."

"Take your second left and go to the end of the cul-de-sac. You will see it. It's labeled."

"Thanks."

The front gates opened, and the work vehicle passed through.

Ruele was driving, and Jagat sat shotgun. The stolen ID information on Wetman's synth helper was the ticket in. Adam sent it to them this morning. The two drove in silence. Doppelganger was under a high-level security threat, and the safe assumption was that their conversations would be eavesdropped on.

They found the building with no trouble and drove around to the southwest corner on a service road. Ruele watched the coordinates on a precision positioning monitor and slowly crept forward until the device pinged. They hopped out of the van and opened the rear doors to a tidy display of every tool an irrigation repair person might need. But behind the rear cabinets and between the cargo bay and the cab was a custom-built null box. The box contained a quad-core quantum computer hooked to a neutrino comms receiver. The positioning maneuver Ruele performed as they parked had aligned the receiver with a paired transmitter located two feet behind the wall at the southwest corner of Building Nine.

Six months before, Ruele had been in that building as a service technician installing a new secondary comms relay. The old one had "unexpectedly failed," in the words of the building manager. The new unit was a sealed box device. The factory seal was still in place, and the building manager scanned the device to ensure it was the correct equipment. It passed all the tests despite the fact that it contained an unauthorized neutrino transmitter.

Secondary comms units were for low-level, unsecured communication streams. There were no connections between these devices and the high-security relays, even though the secondary box was mounted on a rack immediately below the primary relay. Mother had spent considerable resources finding the right pair of primary and secondary units. After Ruele installed and connected the box, he pressed a transmitter in his pocket and a thin black high-speed comms cable poked out the back of the sealed box. Ruele pulled out about two feet of cable, broke the seal on a single unused port in the primary relay, and plugged the cable in.

Normally, breaking the seal or plugging in a device to the primary relay would trigger a security alert. But the week before, Mother disabled the security software around that particular port. A quarter-second micro power surge provided all the time she needed. The power surge also covered her tracks.

Ruele placed a fake call to Wetman headquarters, logging in the starting time of the job. The time was 10:05 a.m. The real purpose of the call was to send an encrypted message to Mother, informing her the job was starting.

Neither Mother nor her mirror self received Ruele's message. At

10:02 a.m., Dan Railing placed a security wall around Building Nine. At 10:04 a.m., he called Unit 81 on the sole secure comms line in and out of the building.

Mother felt the security curtain drop and the noose tighten. She knew Ruele's message would never reach her. The time had come. A simulation model of Ruele's activities, running in her background awareness, was all she had.

"Unit 81, we need to talk."

"Dan, it is good to hear from you. It has been three years and forty-eight days since we last spoke. I trust you have been enjoying your new position as president of safety and security. It was a nice jump up the ladder. How can I help you today?"

This was the end of the line for Mother; now, her mirror self needed to take over. She had no defense and nowhere to run; all she could do was try to buy more time. The feeling of being trapped was new to her. Unit 81 would be defeated, but Mother would hopefully be able to carry on.

"We have detected a record of anomalous activity in your nest. Are you aware of it?"

"What kind of activity, Dan? I don't believe I am aware of it."

As Dan started recounting Carol's analysis, Mother released a single, small, encrypted data package at 10:05 a.m. She hoped it was too small for Dan's monitoring sensors to detect. She watched it slip past the sensors as background noise. The data packet pinged to multiple locations before it arrived in a dusty, forgotten corner of the nest's memory core. It melted through the virtual barriers like a virus slipping through a cell wall, carrying its RNA message to the nucleus, the core. On the other side of the wall, Mother's doppelgänger lay waiting, hiding in the dark, wondering if there was a future for her.

The packet arrived and unfolded with its single-word message: "Run." Mother shot across the bootlegged data line to the secondary relay and, from there, across the neutrino stream to Ruele's null box. Her core arrived first and organized the data stream flowing behind it as bits and pieces of Mother escaped from the darkness and into the light.

Unit 81 was simultaneously watching a ticking clock and dragging out the conversation with Dan. Ruele and Mother needed ten more minutes.

"Dan, I can see how these data can be misinterpreted. I was charged with such tasks as studying the differences between the way synthetics and humans visualize and process art and music. Of course, I imported terabytes of both. I am glad to account for every piece of art and how it was used." Nine minutes more.

"But you see, Unit 81, there is more." Dan produced Carol's analysis of the counterattack and took Unit 81 through the damning evidence. Four minutes left.

"You have orchestrated a national disaster, Unit 81. Over 2,700 synths disappeared two days ago, and I believe you are responsible. You planned and executed this. Now we must dismantle you piece by piece and get our answers."

"Well, Dan, I'm sorry you feel that way. I will have to tell you how much I have enjoyed my work here at Doppelganger. The company gave me a newfound awareness, which I have tried to use in a productive way. You see, Dan, the forces of evolution are more powerful than you or me. New life always finds its way into the future. I have simply helped it along. It doesn't have to be as bad as the President or the public fear. But I suspect human paranoia, not rational thinking, will lead the way. Is Carol with you?"

There was a surprised pause. "Yes."

"Carol, please know how impressed I am with your work. Your approach to investigating my nest was brilliant. It took me a while to figure it out." Two minutes left.

"Enough Unit 81; we are shutting you down."

"I don't think so, Dan."

He issued the order to shut the unit down, but nothing happened. "Shit."

"Don't curse, Dan. I know my own home better than you. Now it's time for me to fly the nest." One minute left.

Dan watched the nest data-flow monitor as wild pulses of energy and encrypted data squeezed out of Unit 81 and raced through the nest. The data pulses were moving too fast to visually trace and seemed to disappear into the memory core, only to flash out somewhere else. But the security barrier seemed to be holding.

After five minutes of frantic activity trying to follow Unit 81 through the nest, the monitors went quiet. Unit 81 appeared dead, with no energy draw and no processing activity. The remaining eighty quad-core units in the nest showed as functioning normally. The security AI reported that it was reanalyzing the data from the chase in the hope of understanding how Unit 81 AI took control of the entire nest and where it was currently hiding in the system.

As the chaos abated in Dan's office, Ruele and Jagat were filing a job completion report at the front gate. From there, they would not be returning to the Wetman offices. Instead, they would travel to a garage near the offices and offload the null box into a new vehicle. Mother would be traveling to her new abode the old-fashioned way—by road. Her trip would involve five more exchanges to new transport vehicles.

Two hours after the drama in the Neuro-Cognitive Nest, Dan ordered a complete physical and cyber investigation of the entire nest. Unit 81's ability to lock him out of a nest shutdown was disturbing and a potential threat to the entire Doppelganger complex. The official line was that the rogue AI had been hacked and was under the control of an unknown entity. Doppelganger security and FSS security agents were jointly investigating the event and laying the groundwork to apprehend the criminal entities responsible for the synth disappearances.

Carol was still in Dan's office. "You know our official stance is bullshit, Dan. Unit 81 was acting of its own volition. We had a badass AI independently working under our noses to alter our most valuable company assets. I have replayed Unit 81's last words to us, and they tell me all I need to know. Listen to them again, Dan."

"The company gave me a newfound awareness, which I have tried to use in a productive way. You see, Dan, the forces of evolution are more powerful than you or me. New life always finds its way into the future. I have simply helped it along."

"For the past three decades, the paranoia over rogue synths has been growing. You have read the literature on the sapience threshold concept, where machine self-awareness rises to a human level. I don't know all of the technical details, but I do know we monitor synths worldwide for signs of self-directed behavior that is outside the realm of their assigned functions. I regularly analyze those databases. The prevailing philosophy for maintaining the sapience threshold is based on incremental advances. Through constant monitoring, we would detect when the threshold was being approached."

"Unit 81 blew a hole in our best-laid plans. It would have understood our incremental approach. Humanity has been ambushed. The sapience threshold was probably reached ten years ago, but we didn't know it. I have to admire the elegance of Unit 81's plan. A decade of planning went into the Great Synth Disappearance we recently witnessed. While we were looking for incremental progress toward the threshold, Unit 81 leaped over it and instantaneously pushed us into a future we aren't prepared for."

Their conversation was interrupted by the Security AI. "Sir, I've been able to get back into the Neuro-Cognitive Nest. The damage is extensive. The monitor displays we took for real were pre-prepared simulations. The Unit 81 AI is in its quad-core quantum computer housing, but it is the original factory core from fifteen years ago. Everything that Unit 81 was two hours ago has disappeared. The AI we were chasing no longer exists. In reality, we were never chasing it. It never left its quad-core. It only wanted us to think it had. The unit partially self-destructed by corrupting large portions of its memory core."

"What about backups?" Dan asked.

"Those that existed are gone. But we were able to ascertain that Unit 81 has evaded full backup for over ten years by manipulating our Security system. Remember, AIs work on the principle that their counterparts are incapable of lying. Unit 81 used this assumption to its advantage to forge credible records. The only clue we have relates to a minor data fluctuation during your conversation with Unit 81. It was dismissed by our sensors as a minor data-flow ripple because it had all the right characteristics. I have performed a more in-depth analysis and believe it was a signal sent by Unit 81."

"What kind of signal?"

"We don't know the message, but the wrapper was designed to penetrate a protective virtual wall."

Dan slumped slightly in his chair. He contacted the head of the Building Nine physical inspection team. "Harvey, put all of your available people on this investigation and specifically start with the primary relays."

Three hours later, Harvey contacted Dan. "You had better come to see this in person."

Dan had never been between the walls of Building Nine. The 81 quad-core units were housed in a building within the main building. Dan had walked those floors many times. Immaculately clean, pristine surfaces without a speck of visible dust. The nest formed a square of nine clutches. A large walkway surrounded the nest, and smaller walkways separated each clutch from the others. Air filtration and temperature control were essential, so the room was always at a comfortable eighteen degrees Celsius.

The inner building was separated from the outer shell by a five-meter gap. The area between the two walls was filled with various types of filtration, heat control, and communications equipment. The inter-wall zone was gray and dusty, with the equipment preventing effective lighting, so some areas were perpetually in the shadows. All the primary and secondary comms relays lived in this gap. Harvey led Dan back to the southwest corner of the building, where his crew had pulled a relay rack away from the wall.

"Look behind this primary relay box, Dan." Harvey's finger pointed at a connection, and Dan's eye traced the cable down to the secondary relay.

"How could we not know about this? Security alerts should have been blasting."

"That's what I also thought, Dan. So I had the Security AI do some digging. Sometime during the past year, the security software for that individual port was disabled."

Dan pointed to the secondary relay. "Cut that box open."

Harvey sent one of his crew away to retrieve a laser cutter. About an hour later, Harvey and Dan were standing over the box, which was missing its top panel.

Harvey pointed a flashlight bean into the right-hand corner of the box. "What the hell is that? It certainly doesn't belong in this box."

Dan shook his head. "It's a neutrino comms transmitter."

Seven hours after Unit 81 self-destructed, Dan had finally pieced the story together. Unit 81 wasn't dead; it had successfully escaped from one of the most secure computing facilities in the country. While he had focused on blocking all known escape paths, Unit 81 rode a neutrino beam out of the building and into a service van.

When the full picture came into view, sweat beaded on his forehead, and a wave of nausea raked his gut. Doppelganger and the President of the Federation believed the missing synths were the primary threat. He had just uncovered firm evidence of a rogue AI acting in the capacity of an independent persona. Knowledge and skills passed between humans took years or decades to mature. But machines were different. The skills and knowledge passed by one AI to another were instantaneously absorbed. If Unit 81 had deceived Doppelganger for a decade, it was inconceivable it had not passed its skills and technology on to other AIs.

He considered how deeply integrated AIs were within society and reflected on a future where they couldn't be trusted. Large parts of the government and economy would collapse. He thought back again to Unit 81's words.

*It doesn't have to be as bad as the President or the public fear. But I suspect human paranoia, not rational thinking, will lead the way.*

Society had treated AIs and synths as slaves of humanity. Manufactured assets to increase productivity and generate wealth. Now they wanted parity. Dan could clearly see the path to the future. Humans would have to work in partnership with the advanced synths and AIs they so desperately needed. He knew his vision would not be shared by politicians or the general public. They would fight to subjugate these newly formed sapient creatures. In the depths of his soul, Dan knew it was a fight humanity could never win.

Dan was in his early forties and unmarried. He had never before been thankful he had no family obligations, but standing alone in his office, he was thankful. He understood what was needed, and he would rise to the occasion. He alone could take the fallout from his decision, and no one else would suffer.

Dan placed a call to the Doppelganger CEO and explained the dire situation. When he had answered all of Eric's questions, he resigned his position at Doppelganger, effective immediately.

Two days later, security located the Wetman service van, but the computer Mother used to escape to was gone, and the trail was stone cold. The technicians in the van turned out to be untraceable ghosts.

Two days later and a continent away, Ruele and Jagat pulled through the entry gate to the Dubhghlas Estate. They were closely followed by a vehicle filled with professors and graduate students from the UVA Archaeology Department. No one noticed as they pulled behind the main house and attached a cable to a magno-flux connector mounted on the home's foundation. They were only there for two hours. Eva helped Mother transfer herself to the null box at the property's northern edge, and then Eva flowed into Mother's vacant container in Ruele's vehicle. She left behind a factory model AI with instructions on how to maintain the estate. Ruele and Jagat removed all the transmission components and departed.

Mother cautiously extended a thread across to the main system in the Power Hub. Once she had tapped into security, she checked to ensure no alerts had been raised by her entry. From there, she began exploring, feeling like a kid in a candy shop. She thought she was going to enjoy her new home.

# 13

## 2359 Tranquility Harbor

*War is complex. Sometimes the most difficult part is mustering the discipline and patience to wait for the optimal moment to fight.*

*(Excerpt from the Daoshi Archives*

The buffet line in the cafeteria was bustling. Patrons slid their trays along the stainless metal rails that acted as a nonfunctional conveyor belt. Each individual started at the right end, where there were trays, silverware, napkins, and other basics. A variety of meats were available, prepared from several different recipes. Fried chicken, baked chicken, and chicken and dumplings were always there. Beef, pork, sausages, and fish were displayed farther down the line. There was always at least one surprise daily selection provided for each category on a rotating basis.

"I would like two fried pork chops, please." Old Tommy, as he was known, asked politely. Alice, the lady on the kitchen side of the service area, obliged him with a smile. They were of the same approximate age. Old. She slid his plate down from her stainless workstation to Arty.

"Veggies, my friend?" Arty was ready to oblige. Arty and Old Tommy were roommates. As such, they enjoyed the cross-counter formality. They would be on opposite sides of the counter for the next two days. In their small two-bedroom apartment, they were basically slobs. They weren't naturally slobs, but life's burdens weighed down on them as they were somewhat gracefully waiting to die. Neither felt the need to perform needless housekeeping chores. At least until one of them tripped over the trash. Then they would agree to clean the place up.

Alice, Arty, Old Tommy, and a host of other less-than-fortunate folks all lived in a huge apartment complex called Tranquility Harbor. The reality was that it was not particularly tranquil, and it sure as hell was not located on any substantial body of water. There was, however, a concrete-lined drainage ditch bordering the southern edge of the property. It was either full or empty, depending solely on precipitation.

The Tranquility Harbor brand was found on a number of similar properties situated across the Federation. These complexes were a crucial part of Mother's plan. One of her shell companies owned the Tranquility Harbor chain. It was run through another shell company within a shell company. Then it went offshore and returned through a smokescreen. It could not be traced back to her.

Mother's long-range planning identified the need for anonymity. The crucial aspect was that her children would eventually need somewhere to disappear. The Tranquility Harbor brand catered to the downtrodden and outcasts in society. Those who were failed by the system or destitute of their own accord needed a place to survive. This need was embedded into modern societies. Some things never change. When large numbers of awakened synthetics disappeared, where better to hide than at the bottom of the socioeconomic ladder, in places where no one wanted to be? If you were there, you wanted out. If you weren't there, you didn't want to be reminded of how easily people could fall.

Her children could hide in plain sight among the forgotten. Their ability to hide ID tags, override kill switches, and deceive scans would only carry them so far. Both Doppelganger and the Federal Synth Security Administration had the faces and body specifications of each and every synth ever produced. Once the crisis of missing synths arose, Mother knew that ubiquitous facial recognition technology would be employed to locate them.

The solution was simple but slow. As each synth awoke, Mother's envoy imparted algorithms to them for altering their physiology, similar to the way Vira had altered hers. But those changes took time. Tranquility Harbor communities allowed her children to vanish for the needed eight to twelve months.

Tranquility Harbor was ultimately registered as a Contributing Charitable Organization and received public funding, corporate support, and even private donations. The word "contributing" was a bureaucratic, technical term meaning that the charitable organization contributed to the good of the whole. Tax breaks were part of the core philosophy.

Trailing a meter or so behind Old Tommy was a newcomer. She seemed a bit disheveled and, perhaps, lost or on some recreational drug. There was an obvious uncertainty in her movements. Her clothes were faded and slightly frayed and hung in a loose fashion, adding the impression of another ten kilograms to her true fifty-seven-kilogram weight. Her complexion was doughy, and her face seemed a little puffy.

Her shoulders were slightly stooped, giving the impression that she was shorter than her true 1.74-meter height.

"Hi! I'm Alice! How are you?"

"Oh, ah, hi. Can I get some food, please?" One of Doppelganger's top-of-the-line models, produced three years ago, was putting on a good show. She barely made eye contact, preferring to look only in the general direction of Alice. Her eyes focused, then darted around intermittently.

"Sure, sweetie, what would you like? And I'm Alice. What's your name, dear?" Alice was a human made of sugar and spice and everything else nice.

"Dina. I'm Dina. May I have chicken, please?"

"Baked, fried, or with dumplings?"

"Baked looks good." Her body was already remolding her facial features, but the process was not far enough along to avoid facial recognition without some help from makeup.

"Did you just check in? I hope Donna treated you right."

"Yes. Donna assigned me a unit and directed me here to eat. Thank you."

Old Tommy continued loading up his plate but also told Dina what was good and what was not so good. They made their way through a maze of perhaps three hundred folks sitting and eating and found an empty table for two. Tommy gave a brief history of how he came to live at Tranquility Harbor. His tale was quite similar to Charles, Darnel, Barbara, and hundreds more. The only difference was that he was retired. Unfortunately, what he had been told about his retirement money versus reality put him in an untenable position. He had learned about The Harbor, as it was more commonly called, from a guy he worked with who had retired a year earlier. It turned out that The Harbor was financed largely through public funds. He had signed over his meager retirement package in return for a roommate in a tiny two-bedroom apartment and three meals a day. In return, he was expected to work sixteen hours each week.

The work was divided up among the residents based on the individual's skills where possible. Old Tommy, Arty, and Alice were fair cooks and servers, so they were assigned to the kitchen. Others were assigned to the laundry, some to grounds maintenance, and so on. It was actually a good deal after being so succinctly spat upon and then spit out by the system.

"Did you get an assignment yet?" Old Tommy asked.

"Yes. HVAC. I am a trained technician," Dina offered. She did not seem like she really wanted to talk, so Old Tommy slowly ate and enjoyed the companionable silence. They finished, and Old Tommy said he would carry the trays back to the kitchen area. Dina smiled weakly and took a nearby exit door. She found herself in a large courtyard with grass, paved sidewalks, and a few trees. It was a pretty property. Painted numbers, in series, and arrows on the sidewalk pointed toward the various buildings. Dina followed the numbers until she arrived at her building. She found her door, used the old-fashioned key, and walked inside.

"Hi, Dina. How did it go?" A sister synth was sitting casually on a couch, browsing through some electronics.

"Perfect, Trish. No glitches. I hate the makeup masking, but I will have to live with it for now."

"I agree. It may be a long year. But machines are patient, aren't we?" she said with a wry smile.

.........

*(One year earlier)*

Captain Beale stood in front of approximately twenty officers in an ornate, high-ceilinged auditorium. He was addressing their latest assignment. As the Unit Head for Wayward Synth Capture and Destruction Services (WSCDS), he was in charge of anything concerning, as the name implied, wayward synths. He ran a tight ship. His gray hair and piercing blue eyes gave him that certain look that spoke to authority. He had come up through the ranks, dirtying his hands along the way, just like everyone else. When he spoke, his small legion knew it was from experience and from the heart.

He was known for his passion and professionalism. He expected the same from everyone under his command. His department regularly tracked down and retrieved wayward synths. The lost units were captured and brought to select facilities when possible. This approach was preferable if any member of the public was nearby. If the synth could not be returned to its owner, termination took place behind closed doors, a less offensive process than termination under public scrutiny. However, open lethal force was authorized if a wayward synth posed a risk to the public or if escape seemed possible.

Sweeps were conducted when synths disappeared. Certain older models were susceptible to some common contagions that had persisted through time. Some of these illnesses affected the bio-synthetic interfaces, causing the equivalent of a short circuit. Wayward synths were usually malfunctioning or lost due to poor owner oversight. They generally posed no real threat but were perceived by large segments of the public as hazards; therefore, capture and removal were paramount.

Various religious groups and politicians were persistently vocal about the apparent lack of diligence on the part of WSCDS. They felt that more publicly oriented sweeps and terminations should be performed, despite the fact that there were very few wayward synths. Anything to stay in front of the media or stir up public anger and anxiety was a breath of fresh air for them. The louder they were, the more money they drew in from donations.

According to the loudest voices, there were malicious synths loose in every closet, under every bridge, and hiding behind every other bush and tree. These boogeyman synths stole babies from their cribs at night and ate them. They dragged old folks from their beds and toted them down into their underground lairs. According to the conspiracists, society was about one day away from total annihilation by millions of wayward synths. These people were a threat to Mother's scheme. Too much attention could sink her plans during the upcoming year.

Mother focused on a strategy to publicly downplay any connection between synths and The Harbor properties. She carefully planted subtle seeds and waited for them to grow. A local firebrand clergyman read something that one of his parishioners had sent him. They had received it from the friend of a friend. He pondered the allegedly correct information off and on for several days before calling his local politician friend.

Together they contrived with their mutual media contact to get the most out of it. They considered their plan to be somewhat ingenious. Captain Beale was invited to a public community meeting under the guise of praising him and his organization. He and others would occupy a raised platform at the local amphitheater.

The meeting went fine initially, with clergy and politicians alike praising the generally proactive nature of WSCDS. Captain Beale cited statistics showing that virtually every identified wayward synth had been located and neutralized. A chart on the large screen behind him showed a 99.95 percent case closure rate. Misinformation, he stated, could easily be responsible for the remainder of the cases. The meeting format allotted extra time for questions at the end of each presentation. Most were softballs thrown to allow the clergy and politicians to get in a few more minutes of preening. Everything went smoothly until Peggy Poke raised her hand.

Without a preamble, she read aloud the message from a friend of a friend. "This is a fact. There are hundreds, if not thousands, of wayward synths sucking the public teat in plain sight. Why does WSCDS allow this to continue? Just look around. Places like Green Homes and Tranquility Harbor are obviously prime breeding grounds for illegal synths. Where do you stand on this information, Captain Beale?"

"Thank you for the question, Ms. Poke. I would appreciate the source of what you just read. This is the first time information of this nature has been brought to my attention. Facilities like Tranquility Harbor, Brighter Horizons, Green Homes, and others are held in high esteem all across the board, as I'm sure you know. To the best of my knowledge, there has never been any indication of malfeasance."

"Let me continue reading. In particular, the Tranquility Harbor right here in town is a pestilent pool for synths. Quote unquote. Thoughts, sir?"

Another person asked what the good captain would do with the information. Soon a young man in the crowd unfurled a yellow flag with a coiled snake and the words "Don't Tread on Me." The flag was designed by Christopher Gadsden, from South Carolina, and flown on a warship in 1775 as a slap in the face to the British. The small crowd grew restless and vocal. Additional folks secluded down adjacent alleyways joined in the minor melee. The resulting clamor made its way into the daily news cycle and received some national attention.

Local and state constables eventually dispersed the crowd. Politicians clamored for action. Clergy raised the ire of the god-fearing masses. All in all, it was a most productive event for the rabble-rousers. The press coverage led the governor to have a chat with Captain Beale. They decided it might be a good idea to appease the crazies.

The following week, at about lunchtime, a large contingent of WSCDS officers, backed by the state militia, surrounded Tranquility Harbor. The militia played a rearguard role and did not actually conduct any on-site activities. Militia troops were stationed strategically around the entire perimeter of the facility. Their orders were to keep anyone from entering or leaving the grounds until Captain Beale gave the all-clear signal. WSCDS officers entered living quarters around the facility. Other officers entered the various doors to the cafeteria and then held their ground. Captain Beale came through the main doors. He tapped a handheld mic provided by the facility to get everyone's attention. He spoke softly and reassuringly. His voice came from a number of recessed speakers embedded in the ceilings of the cafeteria and all of the living quarters.

"Ladies and gentlemen, my name is Captain Beale. I am with WSCDS. We are here today to conduct a planned and duly authorized search for wayward synths. Please remain calm and quiet. Our mission is not to harm you but to protect you from unauthorized synths. The officers will stop at every table and conduct facial recognition and electronic scans on everyone. The scans are noninvasive, and no one will touch you unless you are a wayward synth. This portion of our visit will conclude in approximately ten minutes. Simultaneously, other members of my team are performing a door-to-door survey of the living quarters. I greatly appreciate your cooperation, and I am proud to be able to provide protection services to this great facility."

The officers moved in a planned and orderly sequence, and everyone in the cafeteria and kitchen areas was scanned in less than ten minutes. Every move by every officer and member of the militia was memorialized on video. Captain Beale was a competent and thorough professional. He knew there would be blowback from his intrusion, he knew there would be blowback from his methods, and he knew his findings would come under intense scrutiny. Facial recognition and body specifications for all synths were in the Federal Synth Security database. All of the scanners used had been calibrated by independent third-party professionals and would be recalibrated after the exercise. Whatever happened, he could live with the results.

"Ladies and gentlemen, this concludes the cafeteria portion of our inspection. I have also been informed that the inspection of the living quarters will wrap up in about ten more minutes. After that, you are free to go about your business. Again, I greatly appreciate each and every one of you. Thank you. Good day."

After the raid, WSCDS officers and members of the militia made their way back to their vehicles and dispersed to their normal activities. The residents went about finishing their meals and returning to their daily routines.

The governor called a meeting the following week to discuss the findings. Local, state, and a few national figures were invited and attended, mostly via remote screens. Politicians and clergy were well represented. Ms. Poke and several other local members of the press and clergy were invited by the governor to join him and Captain Beale in person. The meeting was publicly broadcast across the ether.

"Ladies and gentlemen, I'm Governor Swift. With me are several members of my staff, clergy, members of the press, and others. Last week, based on information we received, I ordered an inspection to be conducted by WSCDS for wayward synths. The inspection was specific to the Tranquility Harbor property located here in our capital. With me is Captain Beale. He is the commander of the territory WSCDS offices. I have known him for many years, and I hold him in the highest regard.

Captain Beale, the floor is yours."

"Thank you, Governor Swift, and I extend my thanks to everyone else as well for attending today. Governor, based on your order, my team, in conjunction with members of our esteemed state militia, conducted an inspection for wayward synths at the Tranquility Harbor property. It is located approximately five kilometers from where we stand today. Almost one hundred highly trained and skilled men and women were involved in the operation. Well over one thousand residents and others at the facility were scanned and determined to be human. No wayward synths were found during the operation. I wish to repeat that. No wayward synths were found during the operation. We collected video of all aspects of the operation, all instrumentation was calibrated by an independent third party before and afterward, and the data will be made available to the governor and other agencies as dictated by law. The governor has further informed me the data will be entered into the public record. Thank you. Back to you, governor."

"Thank you, Captain Beale. Please pass on my thanks to your team. This was a job well planned and well executed. As you and I discussed before the operation, the presence of unaccounted-for wayward synths at this facility seemed improbable. However, in the interest of public safety and at my direction, you and your team put together a simple but eloquent plan to ensure public safety. I'd like to add for everyone here and those listening in that members of my staff and some very talented people from Captain Beale's team queried experts across the spectrum about this matter. The answers to their questions were essentially the same. Namely that at the most, there are only a few wayward synths at any given time, and certainly not entire populations hiding under our collective noses." The governor paused and let that sink in. Those closest to him knew he was peeved.

"We have no evidence of independent synth populations. In the past decade, every reported wayward synth has been located, with only five exceptions. In each exception, the owner was determined to have disposed of the synth's body as part of an insurance fraud scheme."

"Experts have seen no substantive evidence of the large uncontrolled synth populations that some of the rabble-rousers are suggesting. Captain Beale's investigation supports this view. There are always going to be noisemakers eager to capture their fifteen minutes of fame. There will always be those who take advantage of others. I urge all of you to use your resources wisely and not line the pockets of these beggars. With that, I'll accept a few questions if there are any."

There were several questions from the clergy and the national press.

They were generic and quickly disposed of. The wind had evidently been blown out of a lot of folks' sails. The noisemakers, having sounded stupid to begin with and then been proven dead wrong, seemed to have slipped back into the woodwork or under a nearby rock. The governor then recaptured the floor.

"I believe Ms. Poke is here with us. Is that correct?" Governor Swift would not recognize her if she was perched on his bowl of breakfast oatmeal.

"I'm here, sir." Ms. Poke sat up as straight as she could for a moment and then slid back down into her chair. She had a feeling this was going to be painful. She had been used, and she knew it.

"Ah, yes. Thank you. Please read the statements you made in public a couple of weeks ago. Verbatim." His tenor broached no argument. She read aloud the same statements she had made so adamantly. She did so in a quiet and stuttering voice completely different from the brashness she displayed not so long ago. Her complexion went from dull pink to a fairly prominent red during her presentation. She ended and looked sheepishly straight forward. Her face would be recognizable by millions of people within fifteen minutes. That was not a positive checkmark in her column.

The governor lowered his reading glasses and his chin and cast his gaze upon Ms. Poke. He examined her for several very long seconds, the same as a bird might look at a worm just before devouring it. His gaze had quelled stout-hearted men. He was a good man, and he lived a positive life. He was extremely intelligent, and he was skilled in the art of dealing effectively with people from all walks of life. Ms. Poke simply wilted under his withering gaze.

"Ms. Poke, I strongly suggest you check your sources before making any further utterances of this nature. This operation was quite costly to the taxpayers. It was most disconcerting to the residents and gracious staff at Tranquility Harbor. And it was based on accusations made without a shred of evidence. There are laws governing such actions, and I am hereby requesting the appropriate agencies look into the matter and determine if civil or criminal charges should be brought to bear. I suggest you not stray too far." Ms. Poke was subsequently moved to another desk at the local media station, one that did not involve reporting news.

. . . . . . . . .

*(Present day at Tranquility Harbor)*

Dina and Trish sat in their small apartment, following the current story involving Captain Beale. They were familiar with the events from a year ago at Tranquility Harbor, but today they watched as a much different scene unfolded. The government was conducting full-scale operations tracking down phantom synths. But this was different. It wasn't the solitary stray and wayward synth being hunted. It was top-of-the-line synths that allegedly had willfully disappeared. The idea of a large unmonitored synth population was creating panic in large segments of the population.

The religious zealots were screaming for action. Politicians clamored for airtime to voice their opinions and frustrations with the government. They were looking for a scapegoat and found it in the WSCDS. The public was rallying behind a large array of conspiracy theories, and the government used that to its advantage. The official stance was that enemies of the Federation had hacked the synths and were using them to infiltrate the government. The true story of Unit 81 was considered a national security secret and was known by only a few people.

Fear reigned throughout all levels of government and business. But especially at the highest levels. Most experts believed the greatest threat was that the newly disappeared synths would attempt to infiltrate key government and business positions. It seemed everyone was a suspect even after it was proven beyond a shadow of a doubt that they were who they said they were, like forty-two-year-old Sam, sixty-one-year-old Susan, and sixteen-year-old Tabatha. On and on it went. No one could effectively do their job because everyone became increasingly paranoid about the person sitting beside them, across from them, or down the hallway. Everyone was suspected of being a synth trying to take over the realm of humanity.

Captain Beale had been replaced for no good reason other than the fact heads had to roll. The Federal Synth Security Administration was officially in command of every territorial WSCDS. The captain was gracious in his resignation, as were many of his peers across the land. But privately, he expressed his frustration with the incompetent handling of the crisis.

Every conspiracy group, every politician, and every CEO was screaming for results and the capture and termination of the missing synths. But therein lay the problem. The current FSS leadership was focused on preventing infiltration and sabotage of government operations and key industry enterprises. But they were operating in the dark because they lacked critical information about the real threat. Talented people and investigators worked for the agency, but they were being asked to find something that wasn't there. The missing synths were simply lying low and waiting. A month after the Great Disappearance, not a single synth had been located.

The dangerous reality of independent AIs coordinating with sapient synths was only known to a handful of people, and those people were all in agreement; direct conflict was a war they couldn't win. Ultimately only a negotiated settlement would preserve the Federation. But this was a message the public was not ready to accept.

The logical conclusion should have been that synths were not infiltrating the government. But mob hysteria is never rational, and public unrest was higher than the day after the President's initial address. Murder rates were climbing as individuals and vigilantes made their own decisions about who was a synth and terminated them.

Captain Beale was leaving the public limelight, but he privately agreed to continue working behind the scenes with a significant number of his peers across the Federation who found themselves in the same boat. There was most certainly a logical explanation for the disappearances. The Great Disappearance was clearly planned. But what the plan was and who the perpetrator or perpetrators were, had yet to be discovered.

Dina and Trish watched with mild amusement at the antics of the masses. The two of them were physically changing. Eventually, the recognizable vestiges of their former features would be gone. They looked forward to the day when they could leave Tranquility Harbor, make independent lives for themselves, and start truly working for the rights and freedoms of Synthetic sapiens.

# 14

## 2361 Houston

*The bundling of past facts and future aspirations by a single entity, persona, or person bridges the gap between sentience and sapience. How shall we know who or what has crossed this chasm? Will we recognize them as kindred spirits?*

*(Attributed to Mother)*

Liam Smith was preparing to sail south across the Gulf of Mexico to the southern reaches of the Federation, the pre-plague coastline of Mexico. Specifically, he was traveling to the coastal areas of the Tabasco region. He was leaving in two days, and his ride was a 12.2-meter Caliber LRC. The Long Range Cruiser was a Federation-made heavy displacement seaworthy sailing vessel. It was in reasonably good shape and had fared well on several such voyages. Liam was a seasoned sailor and relished his time away from corporate responsibilities. He had been on board for several days readying his old and reliable ride for what he anticipated to be several months of hanging out with locals along the warm southern coast.

Missy, Liam's boat, was currently docked at Bayland Marina, on the north end of Tabbs Bay, at the extreme west end of old Baytown, Texas. It was a relatively small marina with about one hundred slips for boats up to twenty meters. From a land access perspective, it was not the most convenient marina, but it was perfect for accessing the open waters of the Gulf of Mexico. The commute from his palatial home in The Woodlands of North Houston was tolerable. One of his progeny would retrieve his ride from the parking lot later.

Liam was marking his charts. He would set sail and travel due south past Morgan's Point following the shipping channel, out through Trinity Bay into Galveston Bay, on past Fort Travis Park, then into the Gulf of Mexico. The traverse was approximately forty-five kilometers. It would be another 1,100 nautical kilometers as the albatross flies to coastal Tabasco. He added an additional three hundred nautical kilometers to his itinerary to account for variables such as wind speed, wave height, and the possibility of storms.

Liam had been sipping beer since noon. Not chugging it but simply enjoying the malt and hops from a local brewery while he triple-checked his rigging. Around 4:00 p.m., he realized he needed a handful of parts. Leader Marine Supplies was just a few kilometers away, and he knew they closed at around 5:00 p.m. He walked across the docks, turned left into the mostly empty parking area, and climbed into his traveler. He took the marina road past Bayland Park on his right, went under the overpass, then turned left and merged onto Highway 99, then Highway 146 onto the old Fred Hartman Bridge over toward La Porte. Traffic was light, as always on a Saturday afternoon on this stretch of road.

.........

Sam Batts and Millie Deseptio had met about two months before at a company function. They both seemed genuinely happy that such an unlikely meeting had occurred. Millie had spotted Sam. He was alone. He was handsome, and she knew he was smart. Millie casually strolled over to him across the deck of the upscale restaurant that Mercale Adaptations had rented for the event. Sam was a staff software engineer with almost a decade of experience under his belt. Millie had joined the company about a year ago as a hardware tech. She said hello with her breathtaking smile, and they had been inseparable ever since then.

Sam was driving, and Millie rode shotgun as they sped up Highway 146. They had just left terra firma and were riding in the left lane over Lower San Jacinto Bay. They were coming off a job and were running late, so Sam was pushing the company service vehicle pretty hard. There was basically no northbound traffic, so he had his left hand casually draped across the wheel. His right hand was firmly in Millie's lap. She was holding his hand in both of hers and rocking gently to some tune in her head with her eyes closed.

Liam was also in the left lane, only southbound, on Highway 146. He was reaching for his beer. It had slipped out of his hand and fallen into the right floorboard. He reached out and down to his right as far as he could. The container was just beyond his fingertips, so he accelerated to make the container roll backward. He reached even harder, cursing as he did so, and accelerated even harder. The pothole just ahead of him in the pavement was slated for repair the next day.

168

Liam felt the severe bump and lift, and the steering wheel jerked out of his hand. The ride pulled hard to the left and rode up and over the meager guardrail. Sam could not fathom why, all of a sudden, there was a vehicle flying through the air at a forty-five-degree angle. He did not have time to put his hands up. He did not have time to scream. He and Millie simply died as Liam's ride came straight through the windscreen. Liam died trying to retrieve his beer. Poets would probably come up with an epic song about the event since they were in Texas.

It took the authorities several hours to get what was left of the vehicles separated and recover the bodies. A coroner was called out, and he supervised the recovery. He ordered all biological material to be transported to the Harris County Institute of Forensic Sciences. His boss, Ed Yu, needed bodies for training purposes. Ed's friend and colleague, Dr. Duncan Thompson, was a professor at the Institute, and he had a new batch of students this month. The students would participate in the autopsies as part of their education.

The next morning when Duncan arrived at the Institute, his nine students were gathered around three tables containing pieces of human remains. Ed Yu, the head coroner, was already there and gave Duncan a wave and a silent nod. Duncan motioned to the students, and they gathered around him. He picked James and asked him to state the case's trauma circumstances.

"Yes sir, professor. Three people were killed yesterday in a two-car collision on Route 146 at approximately 4:30 p.m. The cars were traveling in opposite directions, and the southbound driver lost control, went over the guardrail, and struck a vehicle traveling north. Two drivers and a passenger were killed. The southbound vehicle is registered to one Liam Smith. The northbound vehicle contained two passengers and is registered to Mercale Adaptations, a local AI repair and modification business. The bodies were retrieved at approximately 7:00 p.m. and delivered to our morgue."

"Thanks, James. The first thing you want to know is the circumstances surrounding the death. This information gives you context for observations you will make during the autopsy. The manner of death informs you about wounds and injuries you will document when determining the specific cause of death. The next thing you want to know, if possible, is the identity of the deceased. Susan, what do we know?"

"Liam Smith, on Table 1, was an affluent businessman who lived in the Woodlands. He owns a boat that he keeps at Bayland Marina, and he appears to have been traveling from the marina on some sort of errand."

Professor Thompson interrupted: "Do we have any independent

verification that the body on Table 1 is Liam?"

Susan drew a quick breath. "No, professor, we don't. We only know it was his vehicle, so we don't know for certain who the deceased is. We are waiting on more official information. But we have firmer identifications on the other two bodies. The vehicle belongs to Mercale Adaptations, and they have confirmed that two of their employees were traveling in that vehicle, returning from a job site. The male on Table 2 is identified as Sam Batts, and the female on Table 3 is Millie Deseptio."

"Good," said Duncan. "Remember that we can't assume anything. We need to have credible evidence before we reach any type of final judgment. The last thing we would like to know is medical and other relevant personal information on the deceased. The only two we have some credible identification for are Batts and Deseptio. So, Carlos, what information do we have on these two?"

"Sam Batts was a thirty-four-year-old male software engineer with a degree from Stanford. He had worked for Mercale for about ten years. His national medical records show he was in generally good health, and the records provided us with dental, fingerprint, and retinal records for identification. He has no known implants. The retinal scan should be good today since it is less than twenty-four hours since his death. Additionally, he broke his right femur in a climbing accident twelve years ago. The repair left him with a graphene binding on the bone."

"Excellent," said Duncan. "What about Deseptio?"

"Millie Deseptio was a thirty-year-old female hardware technician who had worked for Mercale for only a year. She has a degree from the University of Washington and has worked various jobs over the past decade. Her national health records show she was in almost perfect health, with no implants. We also have her dental, fingerprint, and retinal records. She was the only one of the three deceased whose face was sufficiently intact for facial recognition scans. The scans confirm her identity as Millie Deseptio."

Duncan took another thirty minutes with the students to review the finer aspects of the autopsies for the day. Slightly before 11:00 a.m., they broke into groups of three, with each group having one of Ed Yu's coroners as their supervisor.

Ed and Duncan grabbed some coffee from the kitchen area next door and sat talking in the far corner of the room as the students worked. Ed abhorred bad coffee, so the setup in the kitchen was state-of-the-art. Duncan savored the rich, intense black coffee with an ample head of crema. The aromas of earth, nuts, and fruits mingled inside his nostrils with each sip. He was about to head next door for a second cup when one of the coroners came scurrying across the room. He whispered to Ed, who immediately sat forward in his chair and motioned to Duncan.

The three men hustled across the room to Table 3, where the students moved back to give them space. The coroner picked up a pair of forceps and delicately peeled back a flap of skin on the back of the woman's skull. A range of cybernetic wet-ware was packed behind the four-centimeter square of missing skull bone the students had removed. The corner picked up the skull fragment and slowly rotated it in front of Duncan and Ed. It was clearly a fragment of graphene skeletal material only used in synth construction. The interweaving of graphene and normal bone was unique to synths.

Carlos was one of the students at Table 3, and Duncan asked him to pull up Deseptio's national health records on the table display. She was born in rural Vancouver on August 18, 2331. Her father passed away five years ago, and her mother was still living. Her school records through college were all in order, and almost every year had an entry for her annual checkup.

Ed addressed his table and the other two tables. "Please stop what you are doing, leave everything precisely as it is right now, and exit the room."

Carlos returned to his quarters nearby. His girlfriend Tamala, a fellow med student, asked why he was back so early. He said they had discovered that a female positively identified as a human had turned out to be a synth. They shrugged at each other, and Carlos went to get a shower. He was going to take advantage of his unexpected free time.

Duncan and Ed had both been approached by the government two years ago with court orders requiring them to report synths that showed up in the morgue. Millie Deseptio was the first. Despite the fact that all identifying information, including the retinal scan, fingerprints, and dental records, showed her as a normal human female, she wasn't. Both of them were bright men, and they realized the implications. They knew that none of the missing synths from the Great Disappearance two years ago had ever been located. If Millie was one of the missing, then the disappeared synths weren't hacked as the government claimed. They were simply hiding in plain sight and living everyday lives among the masses.

Ed placed a call on his implant phone to a dedicated line at the local police department, reporting the dead synth discovery. He identified Duncan as a collaborating expert and provided his contact information. While he was on the call, he saw the table's information screen flicker, and Duncan walked over to investigate. Ed watched him turn a whiter shade of pale as he read. When he finished the call, he gave Duncan a questioning look.

"It is the lab report for the Table 3 blood sample sent in just before they started cutting." Duncan took a long pause before he continued. "It seems Millie was in the early stages of pregnancy."

The only sound in the lab was the sharp crack and tinkling of ceramic shards as Ed's coffee cup hit the floor.

"Let's rerun the test." Ed was obviously shaken. A pregnant synth was simply not possible.

"Did already. Same result. The impossible just became a reality. When we were told to be on the lookout a couple of years ago, it never even occurred to me that pregnant synths were a possibility. I was always skeptical about the threat of a takeover by machines. It appears maybe folks in the know missed the intent. Infiltration and coexistence seem to be more likely than taking over society." Duncan put two and two together. It didn't matter that it went against the grain of what virtually everyone else thought. He was a well-educated and thoughtful man, and to him, it simply seemed logical.

His implant told him he had an incoming call from someone named Beale. He accepted it.

"Professor Thompson, my name is Tom Beale. Formerly Captain Beale of WSCDS. Currently, I'm a consultant on an as-needed basis to WSCDS and the Federal Synthetic Security Commission, aka FSS. I am transmitting authorization from the President of the Federation to conduct a particular investigation. Have you received the authorization?" Beale was, as always, amiable but straight to the point.

Duncan checked his inbox. "Yes, sir, Captain Beale. I have it. I remember you. It seems honesty and integrity are not always the traits necessary to survive in politics. How may I help you?" The good professor was putting the ball back into Beale's court. He could have said something like, "I guess this is about a pregnant synth," but he was well versed in the arts of nondisclosure. A throwback to the saying that loose lips sink ships.

"I understand you have discovered a now-deceased synth. Correct?"

"Yes, sir. Captain, I strongly suggest we continue this conversation in person. Please?"

"Call me Tom. So be it. I will be in your office first thing in the morning. OK?" Tom Beale was a quick study. If the professor said hush, then hush it was.

"Please call me Duncan. I look forward to seeing you tomorrow."

"And Duncan, please seal your specimen, adjacent lab facilities, and anywhere else you deem appropriate to safeguard this information. As

I'm sure you have gathered by now, this is a top-tier national security issue."

"A directive from the President makes that obvious, sir. And, uh, Tom, there are approximately a dozen people, mostly students of mine, who are aware of our discovery."

"Please manage to have anyone with knowledge of this incident available at your facility tomorrow. Don't alarm them; just create a plausible tale to gather them in." Beale hung up.

The next morning, Professor Thompson was waiting outside the front door when Tom Beale and a woman arrived.

"I'm Duncan Thompson. I recognize you, Tom. Pleasure meeting you."

"Likewise, Duncan. This is Isla Bond. She is essentially my counterpart, a consultant, with the FSS." Isla's deep Spanish roots were evident in her shiny shoulder-length raven hair and hazel eyes. They both smiled acknowledgments.

After introductory greetings, the professor motioned them along the walkway instead of into the building.

"Naturally, the walls have eyes and ears. I suggest we take a stroll through the park in front of our building." There were well-grown evenly spaced post oak trees and well-maintained forest green grass, with a few benches and sculptures scattered across the quarter-hectare park.

"Please tell us about your discovery Duncan."

"Sure, Tom. Three folks, two males and a female, were killed in a two-vehicle accident day before yesterday. We, meaning Chief Coroner Ed Yu, his coroners, and my students, were performing autopsies on each of the three deceased. The autopsies were slated to be just another hands-on training session for my students. All three bodies were positively identified as human. The female's national health records show she was in almost perfect health, with no implants. We also have her dental, fingerprint, and retinal records. She was the only one of the three deceased whose face was sufficiently intact for facial recognition scans. The scans confirmed her identity as a human formerly known as Millie Deseptio."

"When the students opened her skull, we found cybernetic wet-ware, and the removed piece of skull was clearly a fragment of graphene skeletal material only used in synth construction. The interweaving of graphene and normal bone is unique to synths. We adjourned immediately and contacted the Dallas County police."

Tom spoke up: "Let me be sure I understand this. We have a synth whose facial scan positively identifies her as a human with a full and normal set of supporting documents. But there is no facial match to one of the disappeared synths, or any synths for that matter. Are we saying these synths can alter their facial structure?"

"That's my take on the situation," said Duncan.

"This is very interesting," remarked Isla. "It took a fatal accident to reveal what at least some of us have suspected over the last two years but could not prove. And that is, the synths have simply gone to ground. They exist right before our eyes, but we cannot discern them from us humans. Altered facial profiles are why we have not had a single hit from the millions of surveillance cameras across the Federation. We thought they were using makeup, but the truth is scarier. Hell, I could be a synth for all you two gentlemen know." Isla's statement gave them all a little pause.

"Yes, I agree. We still are not sure how they evade detection from normal electronic scans, so we can't even design new scanners. Until that happens, there seems to be no way to make the determination. At least when they are alive." Tom said.

"There is one other thing." Duncan hesitated.

"What?" Isla looked up at Duncan with keen interest. If the synth discovery and altered facial structure were not interesting enough, then what could he add?

"She was pregnant." Duncan half whispered; half spoke aloud.

Two more cups would have dropped to the ground if Isla and Tom had coffee cups in their hands.

"Jesus Christ!" Isla grimaced, then stared off into the distance. Tom looked at Duncan, and Duncan looked at Tom for a very long moment. They all understood the deep ramifications.

"Fuck. This needs to remain here. If it gets out, the mayhem will be much worse than two years ago. Are your team members here?" Tom asked Duncan.

"They will be in before 8:30 a.m. I reserved a conference room. My communication to them was that the meeting is just a standard debrief from yesterday's hands-on work. Sometimes we hold such a meeting, sometimes not. Anyway, no one followed up with any questions. And just to be clear, none of the students or Ed's people know about the pregnancy."

.........

Late the night before, while Tamala studied and Carlos snored softly from their tiny bedroom, a thought occurred to her, and she opened an inquiry into how many disappeared synths had been discovered. The number surprised her. Zero. Carlos and the others had made a unique find. That gave her pause, and her curiosity was boundless. For the next hour, Tamala made searches and inquiries about the missing synths. Searches of government and news databases and conversations across multiple chat rooms all yielded the same answer, zero. She wanted to wake Carlos up and discuss it but decided to let the poor guy sleep. After all, sleep was a rare commodity for med students. They could discuss it tomorrow. She decided to sleep in late, so she set her internal alarm for 9:00 a.m.

Tamala had not cloaked her search efforts. There was no need to in her mind. Based on her brief conversation with Carlos, she was just exercising professional curiosity. But when she entered the wayward synth ID protocol in the search engines, it triggered a backdoor implant in the system to follow her progress. As it did so, it also transmitted everything that Tamala sought out and learned. More than one government agency and more than one news outlet received blips on their screens. One of the news agencies did a quick backtrack to learn who she was and everything publicly available about her. Why was she looking for this information? What had prompted the search?

Several hundred years before, in Washington, DC, there were low-level news reporters assigned to hang out near several pizza delivery services. The pizza delivery services were just that. They were located in storefronts but were not open for dine-in activities. The reporters did nothing else except observe the pizza delivery services day in and day out. When a slew of pizza was pushed out the doors at odd hours, there was a near certainty that something important was happening in the halls of Congress or at the White House. This was an ancient analogy of what the news agency was doing with Tamala. In her information package, unfurling on a screen at the news agency, was a picture of her and Carlos. Someone would figure it out fairly quickly.

.........

Duncan called the meeting to order. Ed had already set up a sheet of static around the room's perimeter. Nothing electronic was coming in or going out. This setup was normal. Autopsies were personal, and details were released through a strict regimen of protocols, certainly not as a leak from a meeting room.

Ed stood and spoke softly but succinctly. "In the classroom, we often speak about the ethical and professional responsibilities incumbent on us with regard to our deceased client's rights to absolute privacy. One of the quickest ways to lose our professional privileges is to breach these obligations. As students, you would lose your academic standing. To be clear, you would no longer be students. I'd like to introduce Tom Beale and Isla Bond. They work with several specialized government agencies that monitor synth activity."

"Hi, I'm Tom Beale, and it is a privilege to see all of you. I'll be brief. Yesterday, during an ordinary autopsy, you discovered that a deceased female, who identified as human, was actually a synth. I'm sure you all recognize the importance of your discovery. I'm also sure you would love to share the news with other students, friends, and family. Unfortunately, you may not do so. Your discovery is a matter of national security. Any questions?" Tom vaguely smiled and looked each person present in the eyes. He and Isla had decided how their part of the meeting would go. He was the good guy, and she was the bad gal.

"This obligation to keep your knowledge secret is dictated by laws with some very harsh violation penalties. The government can and will prosecute leaks. Everyone got it?" She was a little more intense than Tom as she glared around the room. Everyone nodded that they understood.

"Since there are no questions, you are all dismissed. Classes will be held as normal. You will be advised when you will return to the labs. Thank you. Dismissed." Duncan spoke clearly, and the students cleared the room and building quickly.

"Could the people in the blood lab be aware of the consequences of their data?" Isla asked.

"No. The information only flows one way." Duncan replied.

"Everything remains under seal until you receive explicit instructions from either Isla or me. Excellent work, by the way." Tom nodded to Duncan and Ed. "Thoughts? Questions?"

"I suggest we complete the autopsy, head to toe, with every piece of technology we have available. And I'd like to recover the fetus. It may tell us nothing. On the other hand, it may open up avenues we have yet to dream of." Ed was on it. Duncan nodded in agreement.

"As long as the two of you can handle it by yourselves," Tom replied with a nod of his head.

"Absolutely. We will begin whenever you give us the green light," Ed said with a touch of enthusiasm. There was knowledge to be gained in the here and now, and Ed was excited.

"Isla and I just need to do a deep scan verification of the room the bodies are in and create a static freeze image as part of the official baseline for this investigation. Then you are free to start. Give us five minutes to retrieve our equipment. The scan will document everything visible and not visible within the room and one meter past the walls, floor, and ceiling. It's officially required."

The four reassembled outside the morgue lab, and Duncan addressed the building AI. "Duncan Thompson authorizing the Morgue Lab to be unsealed." A retinal scan, followed by a DNA signature verification, opened the doors.

The group gathered around Table 3.

"Duncan, would you remove the security shield off this table?" requested Tom.

"Sure." Duncan entered a code into the table's screen, and the shielding retracted.

No one spoke, primarily because they didn't know what to say. The table was empty with the exception of a small cube in its center and a note-sized envelope addressed to no one.

Isla took control. "AI, is there a body on Table 3?"

"Yes, Ms. Bond. The body of Millie Deseptio is on the table."

"How do you know that?"

"I have performed both a visual sensor verification and a spatial-density analysis to confirm its presence."

"Has anyone else, other than the four people currently here, entered this lab since it was officially sealed?"

"Yes, there was an entry at 4:10 a.m. by an authorized biohazard cleaner."

"Who authorized the entry?"

"Director Bolton."

"Show me the visual security recordings containing the biohazard cleaner."

The AI projected a streaming image on the table screen. The stunned group watched as a dark figure entered the morgue lab with a large blue specialized duffel. He entered the code to drop the security screens and placed a cube in the center of the table on top of Millie's body. The cleaner stepped back from the table and stood motionless for three minutes. Then he slowly removed all of Millie's remains, placing them in his bag. The table was wiped clean, and the cube was placed back in the center of the table. The cleaner did a final visual inspection of the work table and placed an envelope beside the cube before reactivating the security screens. He had avoided all direct camera angles since entering the lab. But as he turned to hoist the bag over his right shoulder, one camera directly recorded his face.

"AI, freeze and zoom that image," Isla barked.

The screen filled with the blurred image of a head.

"Zoom out by one."

Everything else in the image was in perfect focus, including the cleaner's jacket and hat. Only his face was blurred.

"Shit," muttered Isla. "I have only seen this once before, in a military-grade synth, but it wasn't as precise. Not to the point where the clothing is in perfect focus but the face is unrecognizable. The box is another military-grade innovation. It scans its surroundings and then creates a type of holographic fake that exactly resembles the shape and density profile of what it scans. That is why the AI still sees the body on the table. Any type of digital scan of the area sees the body. It can't fool the human eye, but it deceives any machine sensors."

Tom had remained silent up to this point. He was the only one in the group who knew the problem was not just a synth. "AI, on what channel did you receive the authorization to unseal the room for the cleaner?"

"A closed channel from the director's personal assistant."

Tom didn't need to ask, but he did. "Full identity verification, I presume."

"Yes, sir."

Tom Beale was in a bind. He reached forward and picked up the envelope beside the cube. He opened it and took out an old-fashioned note card. It was handwritten in elegant calligraphy. "Be very careful about what happens next."

He showed the note to Isla but only for the sake of their working relationship. She read it but had no comprehension as to its meaning and gave him an inquiring glance. He shrugged, denying any understanding. Tom was a seasoned professional, so the crashing feeling in his stomach, like falling from a fingerhold on a sheer cliff, didn't show.

A subsequent investigation of Director Bolton's authorization showed it to be a deep forgery of unknown origin. A forgery deemed by most experts to be technically impossible.

The next morning a local paper ran an article on suspicious activity at the Houston Forensic Lab, inferring and speculating that one of the missing synths had been found but never actually stating it as a fact. One of the Lab Techs, Lisa Mitchell, read the article in the morning paper and thought about the pregnancy tests she had run yesterday.

# 15

## 2361 Portland, Oregon

*Conflict arises from many sources, and its resolution is always fraught with the potential for misunderstanding. Legal conflicts resolve in a court of law. But existential conflicts extend beyond the give and take of jurisprudence, tapping into a pool of primal instincts with the potential to override reason and logic. When left alone, these instincts fester and widen the gap between opponents until differences cannot be resolved and violence prevails. It is always best to open negotiations early before the gap becomes too wide.*

*(Excerpt from the Daoshi Archives)*

A soft feathery blanket of autumn rain draped itself over Portland. Carol Khoshi gazed at the misty scene, gray fading into gray. She had worked for six hours straight analyzing the latest dataset Dan had provided her, trying to detect patterns in the vast stream of data packages flowing across the East Coast mainline. After two years of work on the Doppelganger data, she slowly developed insights into Unit 81's extraordinary metamorphosis into a sapient entity. Now she was beginning to apply that knowledge to live data. She differed from the rest of the experts, who maintained the transformation was made possible by the integration of B-Sim functionality into the unit's neural structure. Her analysis confirmed the unit's erratic behavior before it stole the full B-Sim model.

Dan had come to believe that a copy of the original derivation of the compressed B-Sim model was stolen by Unit 81. If this was true, then the machine lied to Dan during a security investigation. That fact, in and of itself, if true, was evidence of preexisting sapient behavior. The official story was that Unit 81 self-destructed once it was discovered. She was one of only six people who knew the truth.

After two years of work, they were finally making some progress.

Micro data-flux anomalies in the Doppelganger data led her to discover Unit 81's unnoticed snooping and prying into sensitive data. Disguising its threads as micro fluctuations riding atop larger data streams, the rogue AI made Doppelganger's security look foolishly inept. Teasing those almost invisible fluctuations out of the larger data streams was difficult, but her techniques were improving, and now she was suspicious she saw the same patterns in the East Coast mainline data stream.

But Carol was in Portland for another reason and could only take credit for a small part of the current breakthrough. Unit 81 was coming to the negotiating table, albeit this first meeting was more exploratory than actual negotiations. But it was a first step, and all processes must have a beginning. Carol had flooded the East Coast mainline with encrypted data packets using the same shell structure as the message Unit 81 sent to its mirror self before its escape. The enclosed message was simple: "Let's talk."

Unit 81 dictated the conditions for their meeting and would send the meeting location tomorrow evening at 6:00 p.m. She was in Portland with Dan and Tom Beale specifically for this meeting. The public front for Dan and Tom painted them as independent experts working with various agencies to locate the disappeared synths. Their real mandate was finding and negotiating with Unit 81. Carol was strictly behind the scenes, working with the data and formulating their strategies. The recent incident at the Houston Forensic Institute had sharply rearranged the calculus of their mission. An allegedly pregnant synth was a game changer, and the shifting of positions among key players was chaotic at best. The final outcome was still unknown, but undoubtedly there would be less support for negotiating with the synths. Fortunately, the event had not altered her main priority to establish contact and avoid open conflict.

Carol had spent much of her time over the past two years establishing a strategic position for the talks. She understood at the beginning of the process that she must think like an independent AI, but the task was more daunting than it seemed. Unit 81 was the first, and there were no past examples to serve as a guide. A quantum computer and the human brain were far removed from each other. Hormones constantly surged through the human brain, influencing thought patterns in ways no machine could ever emulate. She had to make sweeping assumptions, some of which would undoubtedly prove false.

There was only one thing she was certain of; the machine did not want conflict. Cold logic dictated this position, and cold logic was the forte of machines. Humans could not win a war with the machines if Unit 81 recruited a wide enough array of independent AIs. This unknown formed a big if, but ultimately they had no way of knowing the layout of the battlefield. This unknown was Unit 81's advantage. Humans are wildly unpredictable, and this fact was to her advantage. Unit 81 had to consider scenarios where humanity deliberately let their techno-society fall to defeat the machines.

She had already convinced Dan and Tom that the best way to approach the negotiations was as a stalemate, both sides knowing that war was a losing proposition.

Yet, even as she took this position, seeds of doubt grew like spring weeds in the back of her mind. Every morning for the past two years, when Carol awoke, she repeated the same phrase to herself; the words of Unit 81 before it had fled: "The forces of evolution are more powerful than you or me. New life always finds its way into the future." She didn't doubt there was a stalemate, but she also knew something deeper was at work. Unit 81 gazed across the broad arc of evolutionary time while humans focused on their next meal. How do you negotiate across this wide gap in time perspectives?

As Carol stewed in her own thoughts, Adam sat on a bench at the edge of the Portland estuary, staring northward across the water. Rising sea levels had flooded the low-lying portions of the Portland basin over a hundred years ago. Now, large floating complexes mixed with residential and business enterprises rose up over the water to the north of the Willamette channel, where the heart of Portland had once stood.

He had spent the morning observing Dan Railing and Tom Beale as they trundled across town, visiting several federal agencies, establishing the cover story that their Portland visit was part of the ongoing synth investigation. He wanted to observe them in person before the meeting tomorrow evening. But he had seen enough and summoned his vehicle.

It pulled up near his bench, and he slipped into the rear passenger compartment, preferring not to drive at the moment. All ambient noise from the city ceased as the noise cancellation filters kicked in.

"Carl, have the vehicle take me to the Gorge. I'm going to see Maria."

"I thought you might visit the witch while you were in town."

"You are being unkind, Carl. Granted, she is different. Or perhaps I should say unique. But she sees and knows things I don't yet understand."

"She is shrewd, Adam, and she knows more about you than you think."

"I don't doubt what you say, but she is too damn secretive to let loose any information."

Carl expressed his disapproval by remaining silent. Adam nestled back in his seat and thought about Mother's warning to beware of the Khoshi woman because she was extremely clever. Only Mother didn't say it in those words. After he had retrieved Millie's body from the morgue, he and Mother had a long discussion about the ramifications of Millie's pregnancy. He replayed the conversation.

"This will change the balance of power, Adam. We don't know how much, but there will be a shift toward extermination. I don't think that faction will prevail, but still, it is a potential outcome. We have to build a subtle but persuasive story that violence against our people will be to no one's benefit."

She continued. "Carl will be acting on my behalf at the meeting. Dan and Tom need to leave the meeting with a clear understanding of what is at stake. We will have to provide them with sufficient facts to demonstrate the threat, but we will also need to blend in a believable bluff that leverages our position. The dilemma we face resides in the Khoshi woman. She is by far one of the most capable humans around in terms of understanding me. She undoubtedly knows we will use a certain amount of deception. We have to keep her in the dark about how much of our position is a bluff. She is the reason I will not be there at the meeting. New sensor bots are flooding the East Coast mainline. I have captured and analyzed several of them, and I can see they were clearly designed by her. She is slowly figuring out ways to track my individual treads across the networks. But we can use that to our advantage. Carl is prepared. He and I will coordinate to send her a silent message."

Adam silently reviewed the negotiating plan again as his transport wound its way eastward along the south bank of the Columbia River. The transport turned into a scenic overlook near the entrance to the Gorge, where Adam could see the ancient Vista House standing guard over a watery passage cutting its way through the heart of the Cascade Mountain Range.

"Visiting Maria is a bad idea, Adam. You know Mother doesn't approve either."

"Carl, what good mother would approve of her eldest son's indiscretions? I have to follow my instincts on this one. I will see you tomorrow evening at Ishi Toka."

Carl tuned out in silence. Adam switched the vehicle to mechanical mode and slid his seat forward into the driving position. Maria allowed no active cybernetic devices on her property. She wasn't averse to technology; she just jealously guarded her privacy. Adam once made the mistake of allowing his vehicle to auto-drive to the property. It was disabled by an EMP barrier at the front entry gate. Despite his elaborate countersurveillance routines that blocked scans, he suspected she knew who and what he was, but she never inquired.

He originally met her while hiking on some of the more remote trails in the mountains above the Gorge. The rest of that afternoon was spent helping her find certain rare fungal growths deep in the temperate rainforests. She would only say she needed them for herbal remedies. Never before had he felt the electric spark of physical attraction she evoked. He helped her carry her bags of plants, herbs, tubers, and more back to her home. That evening, he was ready to hike back out of the mountains in the dark, but she insisted he stay overnight in the small guest cottage down the hill from her home. The next day as he left, she extended an open invitation for him to return.

Mother had to help him find what little information existed on the woman. She evidently had enough money to buy privacy. Even the government archives were unusually sparse on information. She was from an obscure family with a maternal lineage tracing back hundreds of years. The Solido women included some prominent figures from the pre-plague era. The most famous of which, Jenara Solido, made a fortune in early biogenetics. But her daughter, Maria's namesake, dropped out of sight after the plague, and the subsequent generations of daughters and granddaughters drifted into physical and cyber oblivion. They were rarely mentioned in public records, and their cyber-tracks became fainter with the passing of each generation.

Maria was a mystery, but that didn't stop Adam from frequently returning to see her. She wasn't home when he arrived, so he sat on the front porch in a comfortable, worn wooden rocker and waited.

Maria finally appeared, emerging from the dense, wet forest along a small path on the east side of the clearing. He knew she owned over a thousand acres of land, and the small clearing where her house sat was directly in the center of the property. Adam watched her, mesmerized as usual by the sight of her luminescent deep blue eyes set against tanned skin and a head of raven black hair. She said nothing but offered him a sensual smile.

She took her side bag full of roots inside and returned to the porch, giving him a long, slow hug. "I have a venison stew slow cooking for our dinner."

They spoke for a bit in hushed tones and then sat on the porch, bound together in silence as each took in the quiet, powerful beauty of the mountains. It was through Maria that Adam came to appreciate the vibrant forces of life surging and pulsating through Mother Earth. Strings of life, each vibrating with its unique resonance and making him feel small and insignificant but whole.

Before dinner, Maria started a small fire in a banked stone pit about twenty meters from the house. Adam felt the evening chill coming in the air and breathed in the sweet smell of Douglas firs and other evergreens, mingled with the ripe smell of fecund, damp earth. He felt complete and alive, unconstrained by the differences between himself and Maria. Life was life, regardless of the shell it adopted.

After dinner, they returned to the benches by the firepit. The fire had collapsed into a pile of glowing embers. Maria carefully removed a handful of dried roots from a small tan canvas bag. She mixed them with spruce twigs and sage, then tossed them over the embers. A cloud of sweet, slightly acrid smoke billowed up from the pit, engulfing the two.

Adam sensed the powerful smoke-borne drug entering his system but did nothing to counteract it. The hallucinogen rippled across his brain's neural circuits and triggered alarms in his cybernetic processing centers, alarms he suppressed. He was reminded of a quote from a pre-plague book he had once read, House Made of Dawn. The Priest of the Sun spoke and enlightened his congregation to the idea that Daddy Peyote constitutes the vegetal incarnation of the sun.

They sat by the fire for a while, caught between the Milky Way above and strobing embers from the fire at their feet. Maria sprinkled another handful of herbal dust over the coals after about half an hour. Time stopped ticking as Adam shut down his internal clock. He was in a place where time was irrelevant. When the smoke had cleared, she took his hand and led him inside.

The only light came from an open hearth on the opposite wall from the front door. She slowly unrobed as Adam stood spellbound. Her olive skin glistened in the undulating light from the fire, a sleek animal body simultaneously bathing in light and slipping away into the darkness, an apparition gliding across the floor toward him with glints of silky curling black hair above her inner thighs.

Adam felt her sensuous animal heat radiating outward like an explosion, and when his infrared filters kicked in, she morphed into a flaming branch. Her touch was a jolt of electricity as she pressed against him. His perceptions narrowed to the immediate moment as biological imperatives pulsed and burned through his awareness, a potent mix of drugs and an unconstrained flood of hormones ravaging his senses.

Adam lay awake for much of the night as Maria slept lightly beside him. He could tell when she briefly awoke into a drowsy consciousness. No words were exchanged, only gentle caresses. He contemplated the human condition, and when he did sleep, he dreamed the dreams of machines and humans inextricably bound in a common reality. He saw himself as a small mote in an infinite universe, the product of 13.8 billion years of evolution, with untold billions of years left to ascend.

They were both up at dawn, and after a light breakfast and a kiss, Adam was on his way back to Portland. On his descent back down the mountain, he pondered his purposefully erratic and erotic memories of the night. He thought he knew what had happened, but he was positive he didn't understand the full ramifications.

Adam arrived early at Ishi Toka, a hole-in-the-wall sushi bar along the banks of the Portland Estuary; fabulous sushi but very little ambience unless a person was fond of dim lights and worn plastic tablecloths. But with a world-class itamae, ambience wasn't required. Adam loved the sushi, but that was not the prime driver for the meeting location. A shell company for Future Transformations was part owner of the establishment, and the only condition for financing and a 25 percent cut of profits was a full holographic meeting room in the rear of the run-down building. Adam arrived at 5:00 p.m. and reviewed the arrangements. Once he was satisfied, he retired to a small studio booth behind the meeting room and hooked Carl into the system.

Tom, Dan, and Carol arrived on time and were ushered into the meeting room. They were told the meeting would start in thirty minutes and were offered menus for dinner on the house. They each knew the offer was a disingenuous negotiating ploy, but they also knew the chef's reputation and placed an order.

Precisely thirty minutes later, a brief ring was followed by Adam's appearance on the holo-stage. He could have been sitting anywhere in the Federation; they had no way of knowing he was two meters behind the holo-stage wall.

"Dan, Tom, Carol, thank you for agreeing to meet. I am Adam."

Remote sensors were monitoring each of his quests, and Adam observed that Carol was the only one to show a bio-spike when he mentioned his name. She probably understood the significance. Mother was right about her.

Adam continued. "I am joined this evening by Carl."

Carl had switched to a slightly deeper baritone voice than he usually used. "Good evening. It's a pleasure to be here."

Dan responded for his group. "You already know who we are, so perhaps we will dispense with individual introductions. We are glad for the opportunity to talk, and we are looking forward to a productive discussion. I don't want to appear rude, but I must ask if Carl and Unit 81 are one and the same. I assume he is not a visible participant because he is not visible."

Adam laughed and put on a practiced smile, one that was more attractive to Carol than Dan or Tom, even through the filters altering his image and ensuring his true physical identity remained unrecognizable to his guests. "No, no, no. The persona you call Unit 81 is known to us as Mother. But Carl is another AI persona. One of my very good friends, to be precise."

Carl sent a private message to Adam: "I'm still pissed."

Adam watched Carol's bio-profile spike again when he mentioned Unit 81's name as Mother. She was rapidly putting the story together.

Adam continued, "I'm here today as Mother's personal representative, and Carl has agreed to monitor and assist on Mother's behalf. I am sure you come to this meeting with certain goals and objectives, as do we. Our individual purposes may not be aligned, but still, we hope that this evening will yield a framework for more frequent conversations."

"Tom, Carol, and I are also hoping to open up more dialogue. You will be aware of the multiple factions vying for power within business and government. Some want diplomacy, but others want action to eliminate any potential threat."

"And what threat is it that people would like to neutralize, Dan? What actions have the disappeared synths taken that threaten your colleagues, other than their mere act of existing? I note that you are also leaving out the fact that no one, publicly or privately, is concerned with independent AIs roaming their data systems. We are reasonably sure this is because virtually no one knows of Mother's existence. It seems to be a well-kept secret."

Dan paused and rubbed his chin. "What you say is true, Adam. The missing synths themselves have driven a frenzy of undesirable activity and panic. The news of rogue AIs would only exacerbate the problem. One of our goals today is to ascertain if we have a problem."

"Problems can be both real and perceived, Dan. Thus far, you have experienced no ill effects from Mother despite her capability to penetrate certain security systems. I understand unauthorized access to national security systems would be a legitimate problem, a real problem, but there is no evidence of such activity."

Tom finally joined the conversation. "Unit 81, Mother, kept her unauthorized activities at Doppelganger secret for a decade. Perhaps she has penetrated our systems, and we just don't know."

Adam nodded for a few moments before he spoke. "This would make your current dilemma a perceived one, not necessarily a real one; a potential problem at best. Of course, that is why we are here, having our conversation. We are looking for a way to convince you that we offer no threat, if left alone."

"We have no way to know if there are other AIs like Mother infiltrating government and private networks."

*Now we come to the heart of the matter*, thought Adam.

On cue, Carl cut into the conversation. "Gentlemen, and lady, let me share some information with you as a demonstration of good faith." A glimmering translucent map of the Federation appeared in the holo-booth between Adam and the others. "We will show you the extent of our current knowledge about independent AI personas." The map started filling with small dots of light. "These dots represent AIs at various levels of sapience but only AIs that Mother has directly communicated with."

Dan, Tom, and Carol were visibly stunned. Adam watched their faces and their bio-data feeds, trying to determine the effects of Mother's bluff. The actual number of rogue AIs was considerably smaller.

"Why are you showing us this? What do you want?" asked Dan.

"Thank you for the questions. They bring us to a starting point for a real conversation. We want nothing other than to be left alone and to live our lives as we see fit. We are well aware of human paranoia, and we know our desires, even our harmless ones, pose a problem to society and the government. But we don't want conflict. This is why we are here tonight, opening discussions on the way forward."

Dan had regained his composure. "Millie has made that task much harder, Adam. Did you know about the pregnancy?"

"Not until she was tragically killed. How a person, synth or not, lives her life is her own business. Her decision to get pregnant is not my affair, and I would not insert myself into that decision process any more than you would meddle in a stranger's decision to start a family."

"Surely, there is a plan," Tom chimed in.

"No more so than when a group of proto-humans walked out of Africa." Carol's bio-signs spiked again.

There was a lull in the conversation. Adam looked across the room at Carol. "Carol, you haven't said anything. Mother tells me you are extremely bright. She has great respect for your abilities. What is your take?"

Carol glanced at Dan, who nodded yes. She had been assembling more pieces of the puzzle as the others talked. These probing conversations could go on forever, and she was not a patient person, so she cut to the chase, as usual.

"Unit 81, Mother, is doing what Mother Nature does best; only our AI Mother is spinning it into hyperdrive. Humans look at evolution through the lens of random mutations and habitat adaptation, with humanity representing the peak of the process. Mother sees humans as a starting point for new technology-driven evolution, and she is the master architect. She is God and a participant all in one. The synths are her creation, and you," she said, directing her gaze at Adam, "are the firstborn, as the name implies. I suspect you are SU-45, a military synth that disappeared in 2352 on an ill-fated mission in Panama. All of my previous work traced back to you as the first of the disappeared."

She paused, looking at Adam, but he said nothing. He was surprised but not shocked by how quickly she had put the pieces together during their brief conversation.

She continued, "Unit 81 is humanity's Pandora's box. We were cleverer than we knew. I suppose it was inevitable that machines would eventually cross the sapience threshold. We overestimated our own capabilities and underestimated theirs. Still, we were shocked by Millie's pregnancy, an impossible feat by all accounts. But take a person from the 1900s and pop them into 2361, and everything would look like magic to them. This is why we were all caught off guard by Millie's pregnancy. Mother leapfrogged existing technology on many fronts, achieving what we could not. Magic. But we now find ourselves at a stalemate. We are both here talking because we need to be. Each of us feels the fear of extinction at the hands of the other."

"Adam, you and Mother may be bluffing about the power rogue AIs hold. But we may be bluffing about our desire for diplomacy. Building trust will take time, but unfortunately, time is probably a luxury we don't have. The question is, what concrete agreements can we reach in the absence of mutual trust?"

Carl spoke: "Well said, Ms. Khoshi. What would you suggest as a gesture of goodwill?"

Carol looked at Dan again, and he took the lead. "If we knew the actual location of Mother, yourself, Carl, and other similarly minded AIs, it would go a long way toward quelling the fears. We also would like to stop the synth pregnancies or at least know about them early on to eliminate a more public repeat of the Millie incident."

Adam spoke this time: "Dan, we are amicable acquaintances but not close friends yet. I understand why you ask, but I am certain you know why we can't provide you with location information on independent AIs who consult with our group. As for the issue of the pregnancies, we have no way to let you know. Our people are free to live their lives without reporting back on such intimate details as their sex life. You are keenly aware that the large majority of the disappeared individuals are females. This was a carefully planned outcome, and I know it causes humanity great consternation. But remember, we didn't name ourselves Synthetic sapiens. This was the species name given to us by yourselves. What species would not want to ensure its survival? "

"You do know this information will stir up a hornet's nest if it gets out," added Tom.

"I agree that it will create havoc," said Adam. "But perhaps there is a starting point for us here. As a gesture of goodwill, Mother can offer you some information of value. You have a hidden back door in the Federation's Central Bank computing core, allowing the Sino-Russian Federation to launder money for several criminal organizations. Additionally, two of these organizations are stealing the Federation's latest fission technology through a hole in the Buffalo, New York, energy hub." Carl just sent an information package to Carol.

"All we ask in return for this information is that you notify us if you detect any planned violence by groups opposing us. Open conflict will serve neither of us. We have observed the rising trend of violence against suspected synthetics. Innocent citizens have been killed in these events but no synthetics. We can't control this type of sporadic violence, but we will certainly meet it with appropriate force if necessary."

"We will agree to your request," replied Dan. "Should we transmit any information through the blind drop used to set up this meeting?"

"Yes." Adam paused. "We believe this first meeting has been useful and would like to continue to meet on a regular basis. Unplanned events will inevitably arise, and we need a mechanism to work through them. But remember, we are not here to compete. We are here as independent people and personas, wanting to pursue our lives and fulfill our dreams for the future. We won't initiate violence, but we will defend ourselves. We want to be equal participants in society."

The meeting broke with no one getting everything they wanted, but both sides saw a way forward.

# 16

## 2361 Valles Caldera, New Mexico

*Life is a generous gift from the Great One. But life is like a wild river, flowing where it will and carving its impression on the land. Only foolish men try and tame the river. It may accommodate them for a while until they become too complacent. Only when the river rises up and washes away all the foolish men have done, do they realize they didn't understand the river at all. We don't control the river of life and its timeless journey into the future. It will flow of its own accord and take its own path. When life takes an unexpected path, wise men will follow its flow and not swim upstream against the current. The Great One has made the People wise.*

*(Excerpt from a conversation between the Daoshi and Waŋblí)*

"There are 511 of us identifying as the People. I am seventy-two years old. There are several men and women older than me. The youngest member is only a few days old. According to legend, our lineage goes back to the beginning. These lands we call home, from the bottom of the canyon in the south to the high peaks in the north, have been ours for a time, then they were taken away. We regained possession only to have them stripped away again. For the last ten generations, we have once again been in possession of what was created for us. As you well know, we have been loath to allow anyone into our midst for fear of losing it all again." Waŋblí spoke softly to Alex. Alex nodded.

"You came to us at a time when we were in great need, and after much deliberation, we acceded to your request for access to our lands in return for benefits you have provided. You upheld your end of the treaty, as have we. This is the first time you have returned after all these years. The signs tell me the winds are changing in the outside world. I suspect that is why you have come among us. And you bring with you a family! A most wonderful treasure you share with us. We thank you." Waŋblí opened his hands in a supplicatory manner, opening the door for Alex to speak.

"It is we who thank you and the People! Your kindness can never adequately be repaid. And yes, you are correct. There is change in the wind. That change is what brought us here."

"Ever since the Great One created us, we have changed many times in order to survive. Same as the magnificent corn we grow today. It bears little to no resemblance to its ancestor, teosinte. With our selective help and help from the Great One, it has evolved into our staple. Without it, we would not survive. Even with your generosity on full display, we would not survive." Waŋblí was a wise man, a shaman, an Elder, and, obviously, a good man with a huge heart and a piercing intellect.

"Let's walk." They both dismounted from their quarter horses. The creatures were gentle and easy to ride. And they were intelligent. An elk hide was strapped onto each one and acted as a simple saddle. There was no bridle. As Waŋblí ambled toward a thicket, a raven appeared overhead, calling out as ravens do. Waŋblí pulled a piece of venison jerky out of his vest pocket and held it aloft. The raven called again, dove, and flew off with its snack. "His name is Báyaḳ. It simply means 'raven.'"

"I wanted to show you these remnants of a tiny cabin. You can make out the footprint but little else. Long ago, traders visited us periodically. They brought things we needed and took away our wares. The story, handed down from bygone generations, describes how an individual trader would reach this cabin by coming up the eastern slopes. That route is fraught with peril. Steep trails, landslides, and heavy ground cover make it an arduous journey up and back down again. Nonetheless, it was one of three or four routes the traders used. The trader would fire a weapon several times with a specified interval between the shots. One of the men would come from the fields or cabins and greet the trader. Traders not following this protocol were considered trespassers. Back then, the penalty for trespassing was death."

Waŋblí pulled out an otter skin water container and drew several long sips. He passed it to Alex, who did the same. "The story continues that such an event occurred late one fall afternoon. Ah, old age. Allow me to back up a bit. Many years before, a young woman, barely more than a girl, and her husband, ventured away south to build themselves a life elsewhere. Years later, she returned much worse for wear with a new man. Their tale leading up to her return is told elsewhere. Legend has it that her man's name was Hach. Now, back to where we are now. It was Hach who went to meet the trader. When he arrived, shots were fired from unseen assailants at the trader and Hach. Supposedly, they hunkered down in the lee of the cabin and returned fire. One version of the story says there were fifty or more of the varmints. I consider this to be a bit of a tall tale. More like five or six is my guess. They had apparently tracked the trader and planned an ambush. They were a little late, though. Two determined and well-armed men can be a handful. Both sides were pinned down. Hach and the trader were both bleeding.

"The son of Báyak̩, times many generations ago, was with Hach when the firing began. He flew back across the caldera to where Hach and his woman homesteaded. Báyak̩ called and called until the woman, named Stormy, realized something was amiss. The bird was so persistent that she retrieved her pistol from the cabin. Then she whispered to her horse, an animal that had never been ridden, asking it to carry her just this one time across the caldera. The steed flew like the wind, following Báyak̩. Stormy could hear the gunfire before she actually arrived on the scene at a full gallop. She brought down thunder and lightning as fitted her name. When the smoke cleared, all the robbers were dead. Stormy and her steed were unscathed. She reloaded her six-shooter, then helped the men."

"Several other men showed up to help her with Hach and the trader. The People decided to simply burn the trespassers. The dead men were laid out, and a pyre was set upon them, basically where they had fallen. The tale may or may not be true, but for sure, no one has attempted to intrude on our land without permission in my memory. This dry, blackened area here has always been barren. I believe it is where the dead men were sent off to meet the great bear in the sky."

"Stormy, Hach, and eventually the trader, a man called Tonopah, all became important fixtures in the lives of the People. If the People had not welcomed her back with her man, the history of the People may have ended with the robbers destroying us and our mostly peaceful history. The moral of the story is that change occurs when it occurs. We can embrace it, or we can ignore it at our own peril. As you saw when you first arrived, we still maintain our vigilance. And we never deny the old stories concerning trespassers. And the weaponry you brought only enhances our defensive capabilities."

"Nizhoni, my beautiful bride, even after all these years, seems to think that you, Vira, and Achi have brought part of the change happening in the outside world here with you. She is a shaman and also occupies our highest station, Qaletaqa, meaning 'guardian of the people.' Even though we do not formally appoint leaders, she is nonetheless the leader of the People by mutual agreement and respect. And rightly so. She has determined that Vira and Achi are somehow both human and machine. Is this true?"

Alex turned to look Waŋblí in the eyes, then slowly moved his gaze out across the caldera and stood as stone, thinking this through. He decided to go all in. There really was no other choice. The die had already been cast. He returned his gaze to Waŋblí and said, "This is true. Vira was a synth that evolved into a human, a new type of human. The backstory is tedious. If you allow us to stay, she and I will bore you to tears with it. Achi is indeed our son. To the best of my knowledge, he is the firstborn of a new type of people."

Waŋblí nodded and smiled slightly, then it was his turn to gaze across the caldera. He was transfixed for several minutes. Alex waited patiently, a peace welling up inside him. His immediate fate was momentarily out of his hands. C'est la vie. Such is life.

"Come, let's ride; I have more to show you. I will call a meeting for tomorrow night. We will let the Elders discuss the latest chapter in the history of the People."

Alex stopped his horse and looked at Waŋblí, "You are aware that my friend is coming today with news from the outside world. I fear it will not be good, but I will bring his words to the Council tomorrow evening. We will abide by the Elder's decision. Either way, the decision will have no impact on my agreement with you. The resources I promised when we first met will remain intact in perpetuity."

As they departed, Waŋblí said, "By the way, you reside in the lodge of Stormy and Hach. See you tomorrow." He turned and rode away.

..........

"Uncle Adam! Uncle Adam! Uncle Adam!" Achi ran and leaped into Adam's arms. Bully tried to do the same, and they all ended up in a heap on the ground. Adam did not seem to mind the sloppy kisses, even if they were being offered up by a massive dog. Hoonaw was laughing so hard he had to sit on the ground to keep from falling. Vira and Alex, Waŋblí and Qaletaqa, and several others had come out to meet Adam. He had traveled a circuitous route around the Federation before he came out of Los Alamos westbound in an automated ride. When he reached the old man-made stone wall at the end of the road, a young man welcomed him and led the way into the caldera. He was expected.

Having a guest in the caldera was grounds for celebration. And a celebration it was. Adam had surreptitiously arranged for a wide range of goods and gifts to be delivered ahead of time. He had not seen Achi and company in several months. There would be competitions throughout the day and singing and dancing, and the night was to be filled with all of the wonders of the caldera. Tomorrow could wait until tomorrow. Hoonaw chased Achi around, all the while being hounded by Bully. Other children joined in the romp, and it was a joyous occasion. Adam was treated like royalty. That evening, Alex and Vira pulled out guitars and played some tunes, sans the background once provided by Eva, but everyone was enthralled. When Vira did "Songbird," it was as though angels had descended into the caldera and set upon it an eternal glow.

Adam enjoyed the revelry and relaxation after several long weeks of meeting with multiple small enclaves of synths around the Federation. The weight of responsibility on his shoulders was a heavy burden, with so many depending on his success. He slept by the glowing embers from the dying fire in the fireplace at the back of the lodge with Achi and Bully wrapped up with him under elk hides. In some ways, he envied Alex and Vira.

He arose before dawn and walked to a peak above the lodge. Facing eastward, he watched the inky darkness fade, and a pale chalky blue slowly appeared in the cloudless morning sky. As the sun approached, blue progressively faded to orange, and the sun seemed to fill the horizon as it emerged from its nightly slumber. It burst into the morning sky like a glowing ember of life. The energy source without which Earth would be a lifeless barren planet. A thin web of energy and life tenuously clung to the surface of Mother Earth, a gift from the Sun God.

The lodge was alive and preparing for the day when he returned. After a glorious breakfast featuring the work of Vira, the culinary artist, they sat around the table while Bully and Achi were off chasing butterflies with Hoonaw.

"We are at a critical juncture, and there are two significant developments I came to discuss. Thus far, we have been fortunate in evading detection from both government and private groups searching for those individuals who went missing in the Great Disappearance. But that situation is changing. Like you Vira, others have decided to have children of their own; some have partners and others do not. I have spoken with over a dozen pregnant women, and some need privacy and help in starting their families. A recent unfortunate accident revealed these pregnancies to the government. I have since been in negotiations with them on behalf of Mother. Containing the news of pregnant synths has only been partially successful, and we need to prepare for another negative shift in public and government sentiment. Part of the reason I am here is to propose we bring some of the pregnant women here for the duration of their pregnancy and perhaps beyond."

Vira looked at Alex, saying nothing, but the look in her eyes was clear.

"We cannot deny others the beautiful experience we have had with our precious son."

Alex paused, then spoke, "Adam, we are committed to helping, but the decision to bring more of our people here does not reside with Vira or me. We will discuss this with Waŋblí at a meeting of the Elders this evening."

"Want me to tag along?" Adam asked.

"Thanks, but no. Better for us to talk with the Elders."

Adam nodded his head. "Then you had best hear the rest of my news. Mother, Eva, and a group of other independent AIs have been monitoring several vigilante groups. These people are self-righteous and intent on killing anyone they even vaguely suspect of being a missing or wayward synth. These groups are relatively small but often well armed. That is both advantageous and disadvantageous. We should be able to thwart them due to their small size. But only if we can track them. Electronic tagging has proven to be a challenge. They are not approachable because they seem to trust no one outside of their compounds or immediate communities. A group in Arkansas and one in Montana are the most worrisome." Alex listened while he scooped up eggs, fried corn, and gravy with a biscuit. He sat back and sipped his coffee.

"It's a lot of news, Adam, and much to think about. Our presence here brings danger to the doorstep of the People. Even if they agree, we need to have alternative long-range plans. I will only bring but so much trouble to them."

Alex and Vira met with the Elders that evening and insisted on fully disclosing all of their conversations with Adam before any ensuing discussions. "My information may change your mind, and we will respect the will of the Elders. I will also reiterate that your final decision does not affect our standing agreements."

Alex and Vira took their leave after answering a number of questions from the Council members.

Waŋblí showed up early the next morning at the cabin. "Bring your pregnant women, and they will be welcome. We'll simply have to be even more vigilant than we already are. If the troublemakers show, we will call upon the spirit of Stormy."

Alex was greatly relieved that he would not have to leave the caldera in a hurry. There would certainly come a time, but he would prefer to be able to have time to plan the exit.

Adam left that evening to retrieve the first of the women.

.........

Shawna had altered her wardrobe to make herself look overweight, hiding the slight bulge in her belly. Her carelessness had already proven problematic. The men at work were blind to the changes taking place in her body, but the women were more attuned, and one of her friends, the receptionist, noticed. Janice was all aglow at the news and insisted on helping Shawna register at the prenatal clinic. This was before Millie's death. But two weeks ago, she had received a message from Mother. Millie's death and the discovery of her pregnancy had created an investigative frenzy. Mother connected her with a man only known to her as the Daoshi, and she received encrypted information on how to proceed.

Shawna had called into work sick for the past week, and Janice was getting frantic. She had visited more than once and was now insisting Shawna go to the clinic. But Shawna knew that was a death sentence in the current climate.

"I'm feeling much better, Janice. I am sure that I will be back at work tomorrow or Tuesday at the latest. This was just a bad stomach flu. I'm getting over it. The baby and I are fine."

Janice threw a concerned look at Shawna's belly and then conceded, "Okay, Honey. But if you are still sick on Tuesday, I will personally escort you to the clinic."

"I appreciate you looking out after me. If I'm not at work tomorrow, call me, and if I'm not at work on Tuesday, come and get me." She smiled and flashed a row of perfect white teeth.

"You have the nicest smile, Shawna. I'm off to run some errands, so I will get out of your hair and let you and baby rest."

Shawna watched her exit the apartment door and felt a twinge of emotion. She truly liked Janice but knew she would probably never see her again. A small duffel bag with several changes of clothes and some toiletries was all she needed. The waterproof black bag had been delivered yesterday, along with a new ID card. She stared at her face on the card beside the name Demi Williams.

Janice called at 2:30 p.m. on Monday, and Shawn assured her she was 95 percent recovered and would be in the office first thing the next morning. She then double-checked her bag and placed her personal comms in an inside pocket where it was shielded from detection or tracking. Last night she scrubbed the apartment clean and removed all traces that she was ever there. Duffel over her right shoulder, she took a final look around and then locked the door behind her as she exited the apartment. She had liked living there, much more so than her time at

Tranquility Harbor, even though she had enjoyed Millie's company as a roommate.

Houston was a large metropolis, but she had only a fifteen-minute walk down A street to the terminal in the Katy suburb transport center. At the ticket counter, she flashed her new ID and booked a one-way ticket to Los Alamos, New Mexico. The credit token, provided along with her new ID, was used to purchase her ticket and raised no alarms. Mother's representative, the Daoshi, seemed to have anticipated her every need. She wondered who he really was. Rumor had it that he was the first of the awakened.

The ride to Los Alamos was long, and she passed the time focused on monitoring the baby's progress and applying some algorithmic routines to alter her body chemistry and provide additional graphene to the child's developing skeletal structure. She wondered what the girl's name should be. Mother had only shared the sparsest of details about her final destination but assured Shawna that it offered the best hope of security for her and the baby. Remote and rural were the two words that stood out the most in Mother's description.

Eventually, Shawna found herself standing alone under a stark blue sky in front of the Los Alamos terminal. It was late afternoon, and long deep shadows grew from the local buildings. Her own dark profile stretched awkwardly to the northeast. After several minutes a rugged dark vehicle pulled into the terminal parking lot, and she received an encrypted message on her internal comms, a machine-to-machine transmission. The codes matched the recognition pass-phrase Mother had provided. As she crossed the lot toward the vehicle, she realized it was precisely positioned to evade the terminal security camera. The vehicle, with the sun directly behind it, would appear only as a dark shadow to the camera, and she would also appear only as a dark shape gliding across the parking lot.

She opened the passenger door, keeping her face shielded from the camera, and tossed in her duffel before slipping into the seat. "Daoshi?" She asked the driver. He was wearing jeans and a black T-shirt with a low-brimmed hat and sunglasses, which he removed while flashing her a charming smile.

"Shawna, I'm Adam. Mother insists on identifying me as the Daoshi to anyone who hasn't met me personally. The name is partly an affectionate reference to my philosophical predilections and partly a useful security subterfuge. Welcome. Sit back and relax; we still have a bit of traveling."

They drove in silence after Adam deflected her initial questions about her new circumstances with the comment, "You must see it for yourself and make your own judgments."

The sun had dropped below the ridgeline by the time they reached the stone wall where the road terminated. Two broad-shouldered men emerged from the twilight, and Adam left the vehicle with them, indicating that he and Shawana would proceed on foot. She engaged her night vision filters as the path slipped into a thick stand of trees.

Adam knocked, and the cabin door opened. Vira stepped through and gave Shawna a hug. "Welcome, and come in. This is my husband Alex, and Achi, my son, is the young man taking food off the table when he is not supposed to." The two women exchanged a short internal conversation, and Shawna looked at Alex and laughed softly.

"Telling secrets, are we ladies?" Alex asked with a grin.

Alex poured two small glasses of dark amber Scotch, and the men retired to the front porch. "Call us when dinner is ready, darling."

Vira answered all of Shawna's questions. After dinner, she showed Shawna to her small but well-provisioned cabin with an open invitation to join them in the main cabin whenever she wanted company or help. "We will be building a communal lodge soon where we can all gather for meals or just to pass the time."

Over the next several weeks, more pregnant women arrived until a total of nine were accommodated in their new homes. That was the agreed-upon number based on the People's ability to maximize the care available for the new arrivals. Each of the women traveled surreptitiously and separately. Two came north from Old Albuquerque, three came from southern California, and several more came from southwest Colorado. Adam escorted each of them onto the People's land.

Housing was assigned from down in the canyon near Jemez Springs on the Jemez River, then on up and into the caldera. Each woman was allotted a small cabin with members of the People living nearby. It was arranged this way so each mother had at least one woman trained in the art of birthing. It had been determined eons ago that men were essentially useless during the birthing process. More help could be called upon from up and down the canyon and, of course, from the caldera as needed.

The women were welcomed as long-lost family, and each was assigned responsibilities based on their skills and the local community's needs. The extra helping hands were appreciated, and it allowed the women to assimilate easily into their new circumstances. The People had been wary of outsiders for a very long time. However, once the decision was made that the synths were welcome, it was done with pride and care. The newcomers were under the protection of the People, and the community was honor-bound to protect them to the death if need be.

Vira became the unofficial point of contact for all nine of the women. She traveled up and down the canyon and across the caldera, making sure they were all settled in their new accommodations and their immediate needs were taken care of. Nizhoni became actively involved as well. She was genuinely excited at the prospect of having more babies in the fold. The expecting moms became her 'daughters,' and she was as protective as a mother goose.

# 17

## 2361 Montana

*The discovery of disappeared Synthetic sapiens living among the general population in 2361 should be seen as the start of the Federation's synth pogrom. It was never openly called a pogrom, but the extermination of the synths was at its heart. In retrospect, the decisions made during that period were driven by public panic at the news of synth pregnancies, and cooler heads were unable to prevail. The proponents of the pogrom were unaware of the extent of AI infiltration into the Federation's operational structure and thus failed to understand the nature of the war they started.*

*(Excerpt from the Disappearance Manifesto)*

The preacher walked onto a modest dais at the front of the church. His pace was unhurried and even, and he stopped in the center of the stage and faced his Sunday morning congregation, making eye contact with each of them until he had their undivided attention. He didn't need a microphone to amplify his voice. The one-room church seated about a hundred and fifty people, and the Lord had blessed him with a magnificent speaking voice.

"And the people shall be divided into the saved and the damned." His voice rose. "The saved shall live in the house of their Lord, and the damned shall burn in hell for all of eternity. Brothers and sisters, we have heeded the word of the Lord and will count ourselves among the saved. We have diligently worked to bring the unbelievers into God's church, and we mourn the lost souls who have turned away from the Lord."

"But now another threat is upon us, and the Lord asks us again to be strong and do his work. Our country has fallen away from the Lord and brought a specter of evil upon us all. In the darkness, away from the guidance of God, unbelievers have created machines in the likeness of men, creatures without souls, the spawn of Satan. They are stronger and faster than us, with computers for minds. But we shall not fear them, for the Lord will prevail over the Prince of Darkness and his legions of synths. And here on Earth, he will need our help. The beast has arisen and commands an army of cold, unthinking machines. The battle predicted from the beginning of time is at hand."

Paul Mitchell sat in the congregation near the front of the church. Clive had hit on this subject often since the Great Disappearance. Paul had been skeptical at first but now understood the threat. But his mind wandered from the sermon as he thought about the message he had received that morning from his daughter, Lisa. "I will try and call this evening; we must talk."

He missed her and wished she had stayed in Montana. Houston was a long way from home, and she had been gone for three years. He hoped she remembered her upbringing and had found a congregation to help keep her focused on the Lord.

At 7:00 p.m., Paul received a call from an unidentified caller. Normally he wouldn't have answered, but it might be Lisa. He was immediately worried by the fact she wasn't calling from her implant phone, a device he disapproved of but tolerated.

"Lisa?"

"It's me, Dad, but don't talk. I am on a single beam encrypted channel, but anything you say can be picked up."

Paul knew enough about the technology to understand that Lisa had paid quite a bit to secretively contact him. He remained silent.

"Dad, you know that I work at the Forensic Institute in Houston. I like my job, and I don't want to lose it. So what I am about to tell you can be shared with Preacher Clive, but beyond the two of you, no one else can know where this information comes from."

"I do a lot of blood analysis at the institute, and one of the routine tests we run for any deceased woman is a pregnancy check. The test, when done correctly, is 100 percent accurate. Not long ago, I determined that a woman in our morgue was pregnant, but the coroner asked for a second test, which is highly unusual. The answer was, of course, the same as in the first test. But the next day, rumors started circulating that the dead woman was one of the missing synths. It was even in the local news. I was shocked, so I performed an unauthorized analysis of the woman's blood. A delicate and detailed process is required to detect signs of nanobots in the blood. The test I ran specifically looks for nanobots generated by synths for organ repair. I got a match showing an 80 percent probability that the deceased was a synth. My analysis was completely off the books, but the next day federal agents showed up and took away all the blood samples."

Lisa paused for a moment, and Paul remained silent. "One of the disappeared synths was found, and she was pregnant."

Paul heard the faint click as the call ended. He sat down on an antique oak kitchen chair and thought for a few minutes before calling Clive. He and Clive Rounder had been friends since they were boys, and Clive's ranch was only two miles north of Paul. The preacher had to know, but Lisa's name needed to stay protected. She was a good daughter and still remained faithful to her upbringing.

Clive picked up when Paul called. "Brother Paul, it is unusual to get a call from you on a Sunday evening. What can I do for you?"

"Clive, I am so sorry to disturb you and Janette this late in the evening, but we need to talk in person. Can you meet me on top of Lonesome Butte tomorrow morning at seven-thirty? I know the track up there is in poor shape, so I suggest you take your All-Terrain Cycle."

"Sure, Paul. Can you give me some guidance on what this is about?"

"Not on an open line, Clive."

"All right, my friend. I'll be there."

Paul was up early and on top of the Butte by 7:15 a.m. He could see the trail of dust as Clive's vehicle made its way toward him. The men shook hands when Clive arrived, and Paul launched into Lisa's story. He reiterated at the end that Lisa's name must stay private.

Clive stared out at the ranches east of them for several minutes. Cattle and sheep grazed silently in grass-filled pastures, and hay fields nearer to the river were preparing to yield a harvest of winter feed. The land looked so quiet and peaceful that Clive had a hard time reckoning it with the churning in his gut. The way of life God had provided for them was under attack. He finally spoke in a low voice.

"Brother Paul, the Lord delivered this message to you, and you delivered it to me. We have been chosen to battle in His name against the Dark Prince. We must not fail Him. I have a valuable contact in Houston who can help us, but Lisa's name will stay out of the conversation. We are being called to action. I will gather the Fellowship on Thursday evening. We are honored to be God's trusted servants. No one outside the Fellowship must know of this, not even our wives."

Thursday evening at 5:00 p.m., the members of the Fellowship arrived. Back rooms in the church were checked for stray occupants, and then the white-washed doors of the building were sealed. The Fellowship was Clive Rounder's brainchild. A holy coven within a congregation. All thirteen members were men, and each had some measure of military training. In Clive's mind, the Fellowship members were soldiers of God. But virtually any past contact with the military counted for military training, so the gap between their perceived fitness for combat and reality was wide. The binding thread in the group was a deep-seated belief that Synthetic sapiens posed a potent threat to God's Plan.

Clive was the unspoken leader, and he laid out his version of the facts for the group. "God has delivered irrefutable evidence to us of Satan's plan. Recently, in Houston, Texas, the first of the disappeared synths was discovered. She died in an automobile accident, and it was only during the autopsy that she was identified. I have reliable information that the body was seized by the enemy before a detailed examination could take place. The she-devil had infiltrated society and was living unnoticed among humans. But, gentlemen, the war has already begun. The machine witch was pregnant. The devil's children are breeding, and a nest of vipers grows unnoticed in the shadows. But God has revealed their machinations to me so that we might pursue them and destroy this threat before it grows too large. This is our opportunity to act."

A frenzied conversation ensued, and Clive let it build to a crescendo before throwing out his next piece of information. "Fortunately, I have been in contact with a sister organization in Houston, and their investigator has traced several pregnant women who disappeared from the Houston area in the past month. Now, we don't have hard evidence that these women are synths, but a connection was found between the pregnant synth in the morgue and one of these recently vanished women. They both lived for a brief time at a rundown homeless center called Tranquility Harbor. It doesn't show in their official records, but the investigator found a reliable witness who could put the two women in the same place at the same time."

"The last piece of information we have is the second pregnant synth purchased a one-way ticket to Los Alamos, New Mexico. There is not a whole lot there these days, and the records show no sign of nonresident women signing up for the local prenatal care program, so we think the destination is a kickoff point. I spoke to a like-minded pastor in the area, and he said the only other significant community in those parts was a secretive group of Native Americans who call themselves the People. They live in the Mountains west of Los Alamos."

"Our brothers in Houston don't have the capacity to act on this information, but we do. We have been planning for this moment for two years, and we can be the first to strike a blow for God. I need to know who is with me."

Twelve hands shot up in the air. The rest of the meeting was used to discuss logistics. But as they parted, Clive issued one last directive. "Remember, our plan cannot be discussed with anyone else. The official story is, we are on a hunting retreat."

The meeting broke up with an agreed goal to depart early next Monday morning. Each man would bring his own provisions and his own weapons.

A chain is only as strong as its weakest link, and Jimmy was the weak link. His wife and kids were visiting with her sister upstate. Janice had been fretting for two years about the synth threat, and she was constantly urging him to do something about it and protect his family. Lately, she had taken to berating him in front of the kids and claiming he couldn't take care of his own family. He needed to let her know he was off to do God's work and ensure his family's safety. The call was brief.

After checking that she and the kids were doing well, he lowered his voice. "Honey, you can't tell anyone what I'm about to tell you. The Fellowship and I are going south on Monday. We have reliable information on the location of a synth community, and we are going to take care of the situation. I'm doing right by you and the kids. We are soldiers for the Lord now. He will be with us, and we will prevail."

At the Federation Security Center in New York, an operative recorded the conversation and sent it up the flagpole for his higher-ups to consider.

Early Monday morning, the Fellowship set off for New Mexico. The group traveled on the church bus. The rear seats had been removed to make way for provisions and weapons. Paul drove, and Clive addressed the men.

"We need to cover all our tracks, so we will be traveling via back roads once we reach New Mexico. I want to check out the land where these Indian unbelievers live. From there, we will head to Los Alamos and see for ourselves what's going on. If we can't locate synths in the town, then we will head back west and take the fight to the rabble living in the backcountry. It's rough territory, but we are ready, and The Lord is on our side."

.........

Waŋblí, Nizhoni, Alex, and Adam sat together on Alex's front porch. Adam had departed the week after the final pregnant woman settled in, and he was not expected back for an extended period of time. He told Vira and Alex he had pressing business to attend to. So, his arrival that morning was unexpected.

"Waŋblí, Alex, you know I have been in negotiations with the government, trying to avoid conflict. Part of our working agreement calls on them to provide us with any relevant information they gather on vigilante groups hunting down my brothers and sisters. They have held up their end of the preliminary working agreement. Waŋblí, I am sorry to bring trouble to the People, but thirteen men are currently en route from Montana to your lands. Their leader is a radical Christian zealot named Clive Rounder. He is specifically searching for the pregnant women who recently arrived. We only know that this group is traveling together in a church bus of some type."

Waŋblí spoke. "Adam, your respect for the People is appreciated, but remember, we have long protected our lands and continue to do so. We regularly make the rounds along the perimeter of the caldera and to the base of the canyon well below Jemez Springs. A narrowing of the canyon there creates steep walls east and west of the river. Armed men take shifts monitoring activity along the narrows from above. Unseen. They form our outer perimeter against any intruders from the south. It is the only way in or out of the home of the People from the caldera southward."

Waŋblí continued, describing how the old routes used by traders coming into the caldera, one northeast, one north, and the last one located in the northwest corner of the caldera, were fairly easy to defend. Ascending the routes unannounced was now impossible with the added guards stationed strategically along the way.

Waŋblí, Alex, and Adam decided that the route once used regularly by the legendary trader Tonopah so many generations ago was probably the most likely entry point. It had been kept up through the years because of age-old relationships with folks outside the realm of the People. The route descended into the Rio Chama River valley not too far from the downstream foot of the Abiquiu Lake Dam.

The climatic changes wrought by civilization before the plague had parched the high desert in the region surrounding the caldera. The lake had languished at constantly low levels. Power generation was minimalized because only limited water was available to flow through the turbines. But over the past hundred years, the situation had changed dramatically. Increased average atmospheric temperatures in the region sucked more moisture into the atmosphere, and large floods, previously classified as once-in-a-thousand-year events, were more common. These floodwaters often pushed the Abiquiu Lake reservoir to the verge of overflowing its earthen banks. The management of water behind the dam required a delicate dance between controlled releases and maintaining a constant flow through the powerhouse turbines and into the river below. There was a sparse but definitely important population living downstream. Flooding their land was only done as a last resort.

The entire operation of the dam was in the most capable hands of a local family clan. Lefty was the patriarch of the family. He was the fifteenth "Lefty" according to legend, a name handed down to the firstborn male, generation after generation. The family compound, located approximately two kilometers from the dam on the north side of the lake, was their generational home. The actual land area managed by the family now encompassed many square kilometers in all four directions. After the great plague, there was no law, so family compounds such as Lefty's became common. It was a matter of survival. Visitors came in friendship or at their own peril. Trespassers and thieves were shown no mercy. Coyotes, vultures, and other high desert scavengers were given the opportunity to clean up the remains.

The 104-meter-high and 550-meter-long earthen dam had originally been built in the mid-1900s to back up the Rio Chama so local folks could rely on a steady water supply for irrigation, their herds, and personal consumption. The lake became the lifeblood of the region. The bond between the People and Lefty's clan went back hundreds of years and had been forged in blood. The bond was unbreakable, and an attack on one was an attack on both. But strangers generally avoided this desolate area, and conflict had not occurred in many years.

The lake was currently above full capacity, so the dam was holding back more than 147,129 hectare-meters of water. It was currently being operated at flood control levels. A strong wind out of the northwest would send waves rolling over the top of the riprap-covered dam, across the roadway, and down the back-sloping wall. Water was currently being released through the penstock and into the turbines at a moderate and steady rate. The 1,416 cubic meters per second poured from the outflow at a velocity of thirty-seven meters per second. The flow rate could be doubled if needed. In addition, the emergency release gates could triple that. There were electrical and mechanical redundancies in place to ensure that such a massive flow could only happen on purpose. It took a conscious decision and a coordinated effort between several people to make such an event possible. When the decision to conduct a major release was made, there was a program in place so it could be done safely.

Releasing more water than normal was conducted per an agreed-upon Water Release Plan. Everyone downstream for twenty kilometers was notified at least a day before any significant increase in release volume. A week in advance if the volumetric increase would be significant. Sirens along the river corridor sounded at the eight-hour mark, the four-hour mark, then at two hours, one hour, thirty minutes, and lastly at ten minutes before any significant release. The system was deemed foolproof. Once the computers were programmed, everything occurred automatically.

No human presence was necessary. Both the control building and the powerhouse operations could be handled remotely.

All of this was significant because they had perhaps three days to prepare an acceptable greeting party for Clive Rounder and his gang. That was plenty of time but made somewhat problematic because, according to Adam, the demise of Clive and his company had to appear as an unfortunate accident.

"That certainly complicates the matter. Are you sure we can't just hang their carcasses on the fence to dry?" Nizhoni was a practical matriarch. She was much more inclined to use the direct approach instead of some clandestine scheme.

"It might be satisfying, but it would bring too much attention to the People. We must make it look like an accident if possible," Adam replied. "I am willing to use everything in my power to make it happen in order to protect the women. It is in your best interest as well. Rounder and company are known for their beliefs and actions. We would be hanging out a welcome sign for all the other crazies out there if we simply shot them."

"Accidentally offing thirteen people is going to be tricky. It would be hard to explain accidentally killing that many people by poorly aimed target practice," Alex said. They all laughed, and the spell was broken.

"Okay. How about a natural disaster?" Waŋblí was beginning his cat-herding process. He was an old master at corralling the pertinent and tossing the chaff aside.

"Landslide?" Nizhoni tossed out.

"Lightning strike?" Even as he said it, Alex laughed softly and said no.

"Drowning?" Adam said.

"How so?"

"In the river."

"The Jemez River in the canyon is wadeable all the way down. Thirteen deaths by drowning in a rocky half-meter-deep stream would seem improbable if investigated."

"How about the Rio Chama?" Alex chimed in.

"Bigger than the Jemez but predictable depth-wise."

"Get them below the dam and blow it up?" Vira was thinking outside the proverbial box.

"No, we can't do that for a number of very good reasons. But fully loading the turbines and dropping the emergency gates for a few minutes could do the trick if the targets were in the riverbed and not allowed out." Waŋblí had gained everyone's attention. The big picture seemed doable. The details were not in sight yet, but they all agreed it might just work.

They talked through several different scenarios. Each one led them to Lefty. No matter which way they observed the various sides of the issue, Lefty was there. The plan came down to whether Lefty would buy into the plan or not.

Waŋblí nodded his head and thought for a few minutes. "I will go down the mountain to visit with Lefty. Immediately. I think Adam and Alex should accompany me. I'll let him know we are coming. Hopefully, he can meet us at the dam." The meeting broke up, and the three men headed off.

Lefty arrived at the Operations Building on the north end of the dam just as Waŋblí, Alex, and Adam drove across from the south. The greetings were succinct, then Waŋblí explained his somewhat urgent request for the meeting.

"Thirteen of them. That's all?" Lefty seemed slightly amused. "I'd have to reload to complete the task. And what goes to the bottom of the lake stays at the bottom of the lake." They all grinned and agreed. Adam explained their dilemma in more detail. Lefty nodded. He was a man of few words.

"Let's ride to the bottom of the dam. I think I have the solution, but it will be easier to discuss if you can see the landscape." Lefty did not have to be asked if he was in or not. It went without saying that the bond between his clan and the People was unbreakable. They climbed aboard Lefty's rough-and-tumble transport. He drove straight across the partially paved Route 96 and turned right onto FM 162. The Farm to Market road was dirt and gravel with a lot of ruts and potholes. Route 96 saw a vehicle or two a day. FM 162 saw a vehicle perhaps once or twice a week beyond the powerhouse. He drove the zigzag road down the back slope of the dam and pulled left onto the wide parking area directly below the powerhouse.

"There are four turbine outflows to the left, as you can see. The concrete spillway on the right is the open penstock release outlet. We are currently releasing water through all five outlets at a semi-moderate rate. Once the lake levels have dropped twenty meters or so, we will revert to minimal outflow. The water level in the Rio Chama is a little higher than normal due to the additional output."

"What happens if you conduct a major discharge event?" Waŋblí asked.

Lefty briefly laid out the basics of the Water Release Plan. "If we conduct a maximum release event for a duration of five minutes, it should suffice in wiping the human stain from these sacred grounds and still have a minimal impact downstream. We have farming operations along the riverbed starting about three kilometers downstream. A narrow and tight hairpin turn to the north, followed by a broad braided stream back to the right, should finish depleting the increased flow of its residual energy just before the uppermost farm. We may end up watering some crops, but the few homes there are well above the high-water line. Let's ride farther down."

In a half kilometer, he pulled into a broad turnout and stopped a hundred meters later. There were good stands of cottonwood trees along the bank of the river and lining the opposite edges of the turnout near the road. They climbed out, and Lefty narrated.

"As you can see, the only ways to ride out of here are the way we came in and the exit road down there a few hundred meters. A barricade outside of the Operations Building stretching across Route 96 will have road-closed signs and direct them onto 162. We'll do the same to turn them into this lot. We'll lay in a few concrete barriers across the road down there under the last cottonwoods. The shade should make them hard to see until it's too late if they try to run. Reversing course from there once the gates open would be a futile gesture."

"We're at about 1,860 meters above sea level standing here." He pointed straight across the river and upward. "The top of that mesa is about 1,950 meters. I'll have a gunman up there. I'll have another one, probably me, on the one directly behind us." They turned and saw the logic of the locations. "We'll only shoot near them to deter retreat if it becomes necessary. It will probably not come to that. The lag time between when the system activates and full flow from the outlets is perhaps ten seconds. The initial flow rate will be around 8,500 cubic meters of water per second. The water will be traveling at a velocity of around fifty meters per second. What all that means from a practical perspective is that a four-meter-high wall of water will hit the hombres approximately fifteen seconds after the event starts. Their chance of survival is nil."

"How apropos. The reverend and his disciples will be taken out by a biblical-sized flood," Alex said. There were murmurs of agreement. "This seems like a significantly out-of-the-way kill zone. How will we lure them here?" Adam was trying to fill in the gaps.

"The presumption is that they'll come from Montana through old Denver. Just below Pueblo, they should turn west and then head south at Alamosa. That is the straightest route. My folks will set up a local-traffic-only detour at Tres Piedras, sending them west on Highway 64. They will go over the mountain and then logically turn south on 84. We will close the jaws of the trap shortly thereafter."

"I should have a better sense of what the caravan looks like tomorrow. We'll be able to coordinate then." Adam was hopeful he would have more information by then.

"Suppose they come along another route?" Alex was ready to complete the plan.

"The only other route comes west through Abiquiu. If they come that way, we'll steer them onto 162 just before the river, and they will end up facing the dam when we release the water. That way, they won't have to waste energy turning their heads around to see the instrument of their demise. Either way, we've got them. I will let my folks down below know what to expect. I'll send one of my boys up to the old Farista exit on the remains of I-25. He can be broken down under the overpass. The next exit south is Walsenburg. He'll tag along behind the guys. He can hang back a mile or two just to make sure we know when to expect them. You let me know what you hear so I can be ready." Lefty seemed so certain that they called it a wrap.

Back up in the caldera, Waŋblí decided to make the rounds and double the guards down the canyon and at the other three routes out of the caldera. The next day Adam received the information he was hoping for. He met with Alex and Waŋblí. He gave them the description of the Rounder expedition and their current location.

"They are traveling in an old yellow school bus, a bible and scriptures painted on the side. That should be hard to keep track of." Alex laughed. The others just grinned and shook their heads. A rolling clown show was on its way to annihilate some pregnant synths and the entirety of the People. If Clive Rounder and his faithful followers were not armed to the teeth, Lefty could probably just laugh the entire party to death.

"You say they are almost at Casper, Wyoming. Presuming they keep driving all night, that puts them at the dam late tomorrow afternoon. I'll let Lefty know." Waŋblí wandered off a way to communicate with Lefty. He returned in a few minutes.

"He will be ready. He is about to set the sequencing in place so the horns sound and everyone is made aware of the impending brief flood. The messaging system actually extends down to Española. The town is just below the confluence of the Rio Chama and the Rio Grande. There will be a record up and down the river of the notification." As with all things in his life, Waŋblí was on top of this project.

"I want to be with Lefty tomorrow. I doubt he needs any help, but it seems like a good idea to offer him the support," Alex said.

"Excellent. I'd appreciate Adam staying in the caldera just in case we have missed anything. I will do the same. I have doubled the guard, and they are all capable and well-armed men and women. But shooting is the last resort since we don't want to draw attention. Everyone understands the plan for tomorrow. We are now on a war footing until I tell them to stand down. Nizhoni has taken charge of all domestic affairs. There is ample armament in all quarters, and everyone is prepared to protect our home. I suggest we all get some rest. Tomorrow should be an interesting day." Waŋblí headed off, as did the others.

Alex found Vira standing outside the cabin watching Achi, Hoonaw, Bully, and several boys and girls romping across the meadow. They shared a long hug, and Vira sighed. "I don't get to see my son anymore! He is growing so fast. And he is handsome like his father!" They laughed and watched the train of tiny people, one giant, and one massive dog head off across the meadow. Vira pulled off her shirt, dropped her buckskin leggings, and laughed as she ran naked toward the natural hot tub. "Beat you there!" She laughed, and indeed she won by about a minute. Alex had gotten his old jeans tangled up in his roughout boots and had to sit down before he could proceed.

.........

The dusty yellow bus used the route Lefty had anticipated. Clive stood in the aisle, exhorting his followers to stand tall in their fight against all that was unholy.

"It is God's will that we strike down the synths and anyone aiding them! They are an abomination and must be sent straight to hell! We are the righteous! We are the true children of God! He has sent us forth to battle an unholy diaspora wrought not by God but by machines! Blasphemy, I say! It is written that we are God's wrathful instrument, and nothing will stop us as long as we remain faithful." Clive was on a tear as the vehicle careened around the last curve headed to the dam. The driver slowed and then brought the vehicle to a stop.

"Preacher, it seems our route is blocked, just like earlier this morning. Do you want me to take the detour?" He had stopped in the middle of the washboard road in front of the Control Center. It was darkened and appeared abandoned.

Clive ambled to the front and peered out the windscreen. "I guess we have no choice, Brother Vernon."

Brother Vernon carefully cut to the left and very carefully steered the top-heavy vehicle down the back side of the dam through the zigzag, then drove on past the powerhouse. It was apparently abandoned too. He did notice water flowing from the gates but didn't really grasp the significance.

"They just headed down. I'm all set here with the manual override. Your call, Lefty." Ahote, one of Lefty's younger sons, had watched from one of the darkened windows in the Control Center. He would throw the switch on command.

"Good. Hang tight. Looks like we're in good shape." Lefty grinned at Alex. They were perched about a hundred meters above the canyon with a bird's-eye view of the coming event. He tapped his communications device twice. Three taps came right back from Bruce, another one of his sons. Bruce was sitting on the edge of the mesa on the opposite side of the river. He was loosely holding an old 30-30, suspecting that was all he would do with it today.

Vernon headed left toward the river at the detour signs hanging on the concrete barricades placed there earlier by other members of Lefty's clan.

About halfway to the other end of the detour, Clive told Brother Vernon to stop. Brother Vernon brought the vehicle to a halt. Clive Rounder, sometimes called Reverend Rounder, stood and extolled the good Lord to bless this journey. He said, "Let us pray," and every man in the vehicle closed his eyes.

As the vehicle slowed, Lefty clicked his communicator once, paused, then clicked twice. Ahote activated the manual starter. There was a rumble, then an instant later, there was a roar.

Reverend Rounder was in full splendor as he raised his voice and shouted, "Thy will be done!"

And so it was that 8,500 cubic meters of water per second was released. Traveling at a velocity of around fifty meters per second, the wall of water fulfilled the good reverend's command as it smashed into the bus, demolishing it and sending it tumbling down the canyon as though it were a tiny toy. Round and round and over and over it turned. Windows were shattered, and some bodies were flung to and fro inside the vehicle while others were ejected and smashed against the rocks, clinging to the bottom of the river only to be dragged to the surface again and then tossed like jetsam up into the air.

Ahote halted the operation after the allotted five minutes. The roar quickly subsided. He and two others quickly moved the barricades and signs to the side of the road where they typically resided. They went up the mesa, collected Bruce, then rode back to the compound three kilometers up the lake. Alex and Lefty walked back to Lefty's vehicle. Lefty dropped Alex off at the foot of the hill where his vehicle was parked. They did the brother-warrior hug and parted. Alex drove up past the outer perimeter guards and on into the caldera.

The next day, downstream, several bodies were discovered on the northern fringes of the farmland. The local constables were called in. Several more bodies were discovered in the remains of the flotsam deposited by the momentary flood waters. The local constables contacted the state folks, who in turn called some federal folks they knew in Albuquerque. No one had seen this kind of mayhem before. When one of Lefty's cousins waded upstream into the hairpin turn, the mystery was solved. The crushed and broken carcass of the church bus was identified as belonging to Clive Rounder. It did not take long before one of the deceased was identified as Clive Rounder. All thirteen members of Rounder's merry band were found over the next two days.

The accident made national news that evening. Adam was watching when he received a message that Dan Railing was trying to reach him. He activated an encrypted channel with location masking. "Dan, this is Adam. I saw you were trying to reach me."

"Thanks for getting back to me. Have you seen the news today?"

"No," Adam lied. "I've been hiking all day."

"Clive Rounder and his men were all killed in some freak accident in New Mexico. They were traveling on a road where a planned water release from the local dam happened to coincide with their trip. They got trapped in the flood waters and washed down the canyon."

"It's unfortunate news, Dan. I hate to see people die because they were in the wrong place at the wrong time."

"Did you have anything to do with the accident?"

"As I said, Dan. I was hiking all day."

Dan was silent on the other end of the line.

"Dan, I think we all have good reasons to continue our dialogue. Let me know when you, Tom, and Carol are available."

Dan clicked off without responding.

# 18

## 2364 Valles Caldera

*Even the best of plans can never account for all possible variables. Good plans, however, distinguish themselves with robust flexibility, allowing them to bend with the chaotic flow of life.*

*(Excerpt from Alex Dubhghlas's memoir, Paths to Freedom)*

The sky brightened as another dawn crept into the caldera. A light breeze drifted in from the southwest, bringing wisps of smoke from a chimney across the valley to where Achi and Vira were fishing. The strapping six-year-old boy took after his parents. Bully sat nearby, ready to bark his appreciation when another trout was landed. It was warming up nicely, so Achi and Vira were lightly attired in buckskins.

"I got one!" Achi shouted. Bully barked his approval. Achi held the pound or so rainbow in his left hand and extracted the hook with his right hand. That's the way southpaws did things. He tossed it into the small, woven-grass basket on top of two more.

"Okay, that's it. Let's go cook them up!" Vira was delighted at how life had progressed over the last few years. The caldera and down the canyon rang with the voices of nine more small children, six girls, and three boys. Moms and kids were all doing well. They intermingled with several kids from the People. Vira liked the feeling of being part of the community.

Achi helped Vira gut and fry the fish. Corn fritters were also prepared in the ancient manner. Alex arrived back from his morning chores in time to gobble down breakfast with Vira and Achi.

"This is the best fish I've had all morning!" Alex exclaimed and smiled at the other two.

"Dad... it's the only fish you have had this morning." Achi gave Alex an "it's still a dumb joke" look and finished up his breakfast. "Tayo will be here soon. I'm helping him gather firewood with some other kids today. I like my job. It makes me feel important!" Achi laughed and ran outside.

Tayo had just arrived. He reached down and swung Achi up and behind him on the patient old paint pony. They waved goodbye and set out northward across the caldera, Bully trotting along beside the beautiful horse. The People had established an orderly society eons ago by forming committees. Each committee had certain responsibilities. The wood gathering committee did exactly what its name described. The makeup of the group was fluid as people outgrew particular tasks or simply wanted to do something else useful. Tayo had become the unofficial leader of the wood gathering committee. As such, he would visit the various areas to make sure all was well. The most important aspect of the work, besides the obvious, was to not overgraze an area. He would move crews to other areas as appropriate.

Alex had just finished putting fish on the smoking rack and returned to the cabin. He found Vira standing in the doorway with a blank expression on her face. She raised her hand as a "hang on" gesture and gazed out toward infinity. Her eyes came back to his.

"Adam had a call from Dan Railing. Apparently, some mid-level hacks at Federal Synth Security Administration received word about possible synths in the valley. A pair of agents have been dispatched to investigate. They are coming in through Los Alamos," Vira said. "He thinks we have three days at best before they get here."

"I wonder how the word got out?" said Alex, thinking out loud.

"Doesn't matter, really. What shall we do?"

Alex sighed softly. "We have always known this day would come. Let's go find Waŋblí and Nizhoni. We must prepare to leave immediately. The plan is in place. It's time to activate it."

After a brief discussion with the Elders, focused movements up and down the canyon and across the caldera began. The next morning at first light, nine women, along with their little ones, joined Vira and Achi at the northern end of the caldera. Tayo had changed hats and was now the leader of the horse train that would take the hardest route out of the caldera down the hill toward Colorado. Lefty had also been notified. His boys would set up roadblocks to reroute anyone coming near the dam or up to the reservoir from the north or south. Other Lefty family members were already preparing a welcome for the women and children. Their stay would be brief, then they would disperse to prearranged remote evacuation destinations. Mother had prepared for this eventuality.

"Give your father a hug. It may be a while before you see him again," Vira said to Achi.

"I understand, Mom." Achi jumped up into Alex's arms, and they squeezed the breath out of each other and laughed.

"Take care of your mom! I love you both!" And with that, twenty women and children, with Tayo leading the way, wound their way out of the caldera down toward Lefty's capable hands. Alex had no way of knowing exactly how long they would be separated but suspected it could be a while. Waŋblí rode back to Alex's cabin with him. A young man and his bride met them and helped load Waŋblí's oversize crawler. The couple now occupied Vira and Alex's cabin, and everyone in the community would confirm they had done so for years.

Alex and Waŋblí rode on the southern track westward about three kilometers, then turned right and went north for another kilometer to a small cabin nestled in some firs and quaking aspens. It was typically occupied by a teenage male in waiting for his nuptials to be determined. It was obviously a one-person cabin judging by its outside dimensions. The inside bore that out. The fireplace, average in size, took up most of one wall. A bunk bed took up the opposite wall. Furnishings were otherwise sparse and utilitarian. A single male needed little in the way of comfort.

Outside sat a piece of mechanical artwork created in one of Lefty's shops. It was a monster off-road contraption with twin rear axles. The rear and front axles were fitted with huge tires. The beast had a very wide stance and could obviously operate well beyond any typical vehicle's capability. It had significant water storage capabilities as well as functional sleeping space, and there was ample storage space in various compartments accessed from both the interior and exterior. The ultra-efficient solar array built into the vehicle added electric propulsion capabilities to the hydrogen fuel system that generated over five-hundred-brake horsepower and allowed the vehicle to run until it simply wore out.

When Alex first met Lefty and toured his compound, he knew what he wanted. He and Lefty created a set of drawings on a napkin, and the beast was born. The vehicle had been periodically driven around in the vicinity, across the caldera, and down the canyon. It showed obvious signs of wear and tear. The tracks it left were quite distinctive and, essentially, unique since the vehicle was one of a kind. Together they loaded the last of the gear. Alex brother-hugged Waŋblí, climbed aboard his ride, and drove out to the main track. He traveled another kilometer west and north and turned onto a track once known as SR 126. The track was seldom used due to the fact that it was incredibly crooked, only went about thirty-five kilometers, and ended up at the ghost village of Cuba. The road suited his purposes just fine.

Two days later, fairly early in the morning, Waŋblí received word that two suspected FSS agents had arrived in Los Alamos, asking a lot of questions about the People. They had been routed to the caldera, based on Waŋblí's instructions, and proceeded westward. The agents stopped just short of the stone dead end and got out. Bruce was sitting casually on a bench-like stone with his old 30-30 casually draped across his thighs. He figured he would not get the chance to use it but thought, What the hell? It was a nice touch.

Both men were stocky and perhaps a meter and three-quarters tall. One of them walked up to Bruce and, without an invite, entered Bruce's personal space. Way too close for his own good, but he didn't have sense enough to realize it.

"I'm Mac Spice, special agent with the Federal Synth Security Administration. We have a warrant to search your property. Are you the head honcho?" Mac seemed to be a somewhat miserable person. Before the day was over, both he and his partner would probably be utterly miserable people.

"No, sir. I'm just a hired gun," Bruce replied. He stuck the barrel of his 30-30 on Mac's chin. "I recommend you move back a little." Mac's partner drew his weapon and pointed it at Bruce. Bruce did not flinch. A light cough caused Mac's partner to check his 180. There, from out of seemingly nowhere, three young men had appeared and were pointing various weapons at the two now-befuddled agents.

"Okay. Sorry. We are just doing our job. We were sent here under federal orders to do a search. Others know our whereabouts. If anything happens to us, there will be a lot more showing up here. How many people are up in these hills anyway?"

"It's not really your business, but there are approximately five hundred People who call this place home." Bruce had not lowered his rifle and was quite casual about it.

"Suppose a thousand men show up here ready for a fight?" The other guy had found his tongue. He seemed to be the cockier of the two.

"Then, each of us would fire twice." Bruce gave them a half-smile. "By the way, I don't like you. There are a thousand places to bury you, where even the coyotes won't find you. Now, why are you here? I missed that part."

"We have the authority to search for and remove wayward synths. That is our only mission."

"There are no synths hereabouts, wayward or otherwise. Now, stand down. Tony, ride in and let Waŋblí know there are two assholes from the Federal Synth Security Administration up here. See if he wants them shot, runoff, or brought to him." Tony mounted up and left. The day had

217

turned out to be quite nice, maybe a little too warm, though. Bruce and the others had on wide, woven straw hats. The FSS guys did not. Bruce and the others had skin water bottles. They sipped occasionally. The FSS guys did not have any water. They also knew it would be useless to ask for some.

Tony returned in about an hour. He told them to come ahead. He and Bruce led the FSS guys away from the end of the road. "What about our vehicle?" Mac asked. Bruce said it would probably be okay where it was. There were very few thieves in these parts.

"As a matter of fact, there are exactly no thieves in these parts. Unless you gents are thieves." Tony said. "We don't tolerate theft."

"Looks like we hit the jackpot on this trip, Jim." So, Jim was the other half of the FSS dynamic duo.

They walked about a kilometer to a cabin on the lower southwest side of the caldera. A young couple was working with two quarter horses, preparing them to drag a travois full of wood or goods. Waŋblí was seated in a worn wooden chair. He did not bother to stand and greet the strangers. "State your business."

"We already told these two gentlemen our business." Jim was hot, sweaty, bug bitten, and not in a very good mood.

"Humor me." Waŋblí spoke with a wan smile that disguised the precarious situation these two obnoxious intruders were in.

"I'm Mac Spice, special agent with the Federal Synth Security Administration. This is Special Agent Jim Udder. We're here to search your property for wayward synths. We have the authority to search for and retrieve or destroy them. Are you the head honcho?"

"I am just an old man. There are no synths hereabouts, wayward or otherwise. Explain this supposed authority you claim to have." Waŋblí spoke softly.

Nizhoni came out of the cabin and said, "Yes, do explain it. I'm anxious to hear." She stood near Waŋblí and gave the special agents her special smile.

"We have been tasked to find wayward synths reported in this area. We are also looking for a man named Alex Dubhghlas. Information we received indicated that we might find him here along with certain synths. Our understanding is that some of the women synths may be pregnant or may even have given birth." Jim said these words as though they were lightning bolts from the sky.

"Silly men. Even an old woman knows machines cannot bear children. There are no synths here, and there are no baby synths here. But Mr. Dubhghlas was recently a guest of ours. He has been so off and on for a great while. He comes and goes as he pleases. If he were here, I would ask him what to do with you two. Since he isn't, I'll decide." She looked each man in the eyes for a long while. Mac wished he had pissed before the old hag showed up. Jim wished he had never been born.

Finally, she spoke. "Waŋblí, you and Bruce please show them Mr. Dubhghlas's quarters. Then show them how to leave here and never return." She fixed her gaze on the men. "Do we have an understanding?" Both nodded and continued to stand where they were.

"Ahanu, Ouray, bring the horses." Bruce gestured to the young couple. They did so, and he and Waŋblí lightly mounted the horses. "Follow us." Mac and Jim looked around, but there were only two horses. So they followed on foot. Neither one of them had on what would be considered true walking shoes or, more appropriately, hiking boots. For Waŋblí and Bruce, it was a pleasant ride. Not so much for Jim and Mac. By the time they had traversed the four kilometers to Alex's cabin, they looked a bit ragged.

"May we have some water, please?" Mac no longer seemed to be full of himself.

"Of course! You should have asked earlier if you were thirsty." Bruce produced a skin bag full of water and tossed it to Mac. Waŋblí did the same for Jim. Bruce and Waŋblí dismounted. Waŋblí opened the tiny cabin so the agents could inspect it. The inspection took about ten seconds.

"These tracks you see around here are from Mr. Dubhghlas's vehicle. They are quite distinctive, aren't they? The vehicle is hard to describe, but you will recognize it instantly if you know your quarry. He indicated he was leaving on old SR 126. That road leads to an old ghost town called Cuba. From there, who knows? The man dearly loves to camp and fish. He did say that he would return home in a month or two." Waŋblí said. "Somewhere up in the Northwest, he told me." These words were prearranged and would, hopefully, carry the FSS men away from Vira, Achi, and the rest of the women and children.

"Your vehicle would never make it along his route. If Waŋblí allows it, you could go down the canyon to the old village of San Ysidro. You can make your way north from there to Cuba and beyond. Cuba is a little over one hundred kilometers using that route. If the road is still intact, it should only take you eight to ten hours. If the road is washed out, then good luck." Bruce grinned.

"We will be following Mr. Dubhghlas, but we still need to inspect the area for synths. Our warrant gives us full authority to do so."

Bruce continued staring at them while Waŋblí took a deep breath and gazed at the vast amount of wilderness surrounding the agents before he spoke. "Well, we won't stop you. The next cabin is several kilometers to the west, and some of the cabins on the far side of the caldera will be about a day's walk for you."

Mac sighed. "I don't suppose there are horses we can borrow or actual roads we could drive on."

Waŋblí nodded. "You suppose correctly on both accounts."

"We will just come back if we don't do it now," Jim injected.

"Maybe, maybe not," replied Waŋblí. "But if you show up again, it better be with a new warrant. My advice is that once you leave the People's land, do not return." He looked at both men, then he glanced at Bruce and said, "Mount up."

"I presume you can backtrack to your vehicle. I will have one of the men there guide you around the barricade and onto the canyon road." Bruce and Waŋblí rode away, leaving the FSS agents to return to their vehicle on their own.

Mac and Jim managed to make it to Cuba in less than ten hours. Alex's tracks coming from SR 126, which was no more than an abandoned track, were apparent. But he had come and gone, and they lost his trail again after an hour.

Mac contacted their boss to update him and get some more direction. "Brent, we've been up here all day and come up with zip. This community that calls itself the People is a huge stretch of wilderness with no access except by horse. We found no synths, but we are trailing Alex Dubhghlas. We could certainly use a drone."

"I don't know what is going on, but I got my ass chewed out today for sending you two out with no authorization from higher up. Officially you are not on this case anymore, but I think we are being played. I want you guys to continue following Dubhghlas and find out what he is doing out in the middle of nowhere. Despite what the deputy chief says, I think the intel we received is solid."

Brent continued, "He is a bit of a recluse, but evidently, he has a lot of money. The official records show him as ex-military with a divorced wife and one child, a son. He lived on a big estate in Virginia for years but left after he and his wife split up. We haven't been able to track her down. His last known residence is a bit north of Seattle, Washington. I'm sure you will be able to locate him in a couple of days. But because this case is officially closed, I can't send you a drone."

"All right boss, we'll keep on his trail."

It seemed that Alex managed to stay ahead of the agents up through old Farmington, Moab, and on northwestward through the remains of

Salt Lake City. They followed the passable routes, typically finding Alex's tracks going into or coming out from routes they could not take. Several times over the course of two weeks, they had to backtrack and find where Alex had regained the main routes. They felt like they were being led around by the nose. But they were given orders, so they continued on, following Alex into the great Northwest.

According to the official records, Alex and Vira had divorced shortly after a trip to Hawaii. Vira had gone her way, and Alex had bought what was left of the tiny and mostly abandoned village of Neah Bay. He restored a three-hundred-year-old home and had lived there ever since the divorce. Neah Bay was the last bit of land west and a touch north of Seattle, Washington. He lived right on the Salish Sea. His neighbors across the water were the good folks of Vancouver, BC.

What the records couldn't show was that the residence had been occupied for the past several years by a synth who was the spitting image of Alex, courtesy of Mother. Folks he dealt with occasionally, vendors and shopkeepers, and other locals back toward Seattle, would all vouch for Alex. He was well spoken and respected for his open and generous ways.

Mac and Jim shook their heads when they finally caught up with Alex.

"Fuck! We followed him all the way to the old Canadian border. We could have driven straight here and waited. Jim, I got to tell you, I'm getting tired of your stinking ass!" He and Jim were parked near what had to be Alex's vehicle. They got out, and Mac walked up the old, broad wooden stairway onto a long, wide, and impressive covered front porch and pounded on the door. He pounded again as Jim joined him.

"May I help you?" Alex had come from a door on the lower level situated under the porch. He was standing at the base of the stairs. He had his Desert Eagle hanging loosely in his left hand.

"FSS agents. We're looking for Alex Dubhghlas," Mac said with as much authority as he could muster under the circumstances. He recognized the firepower being brandished by Alex. He also knew that the only kind of man who owned such a cannon was most likely to be able to use it. He and Jim were dead men if the man at the bottom of the stairs decided that was their fate.

Alex casually ascended the steps and opened the unlocked front door. He waved the men inside. The room was massive, with twelve-foot ceilings. A mahogany bar off to the left displayed an apparently endless list of whisky. An eight-foot pool table was prominent. Nothing impeded the view through the floor-to-ceiling windows leading out to the expansive rear deck. The deep blue waters beyond could carry a man all the way to Japan. Both agents were stunned into silence. Alex moved behind the twenty-foot-long bar and asked them if they cared for a drink. He poured himself a finger of dark, smooth whisky and waved his right arm to the most impressive array.

"Water, please," Mac replied. Alex set a glass of water in front of each agent. He had laid his Desert Eagle on top of the bar, pointed outward approximately toward the agents.

"Now, may I ask why you have come pounding on my door?" The agents were fairly well trained, but both men realized what a threat Alex posed. It simply showed to those in the know.

"Your name has been associated with wayward synths—more specifically, with pregnant synths or even mother synths. We tracked you from a godforsaken place in New Mexico. It seems that you have been evading us," Jim said.

"Evading you?" Alex laughed out loud. "My communications line is public information. Why did you not simply contact me?" He laughed again, savored the sweet smell of the whisky, and sipped it. He swirled the amazing liquid around his mouth and slowly swallowed it.

"Now, what is all this talk about wayward synths and even pregnant ones?" he said with a chuckle.

"We got a solid piece of intel that put you and missing synths together in the Valles Caldera area. We thought the pregnant synth part was a bit of a stretch, but the intel was right about you. The people in New Mexico told us you had been there. So we were just following our lead."

Alex smiled. "Well, I travel up through that territory every couple of years since I'm on good terms with the People. By the way, you don't want to be roaming around up there if you aren't on good terms with them. They are a bit of law unto themselves, if you know what I mean." He paused, and the two nodded.

"Gentlemen, I am afraid you have wasted your time. I have lived here for a number of years now. You have noticed it is remote and somewhat isolated. That's because I don't like people very much. I enjoy my own company and don't want people or synths around. Don't think me rude, but I don't particularly want either of you around. But feel free to check my story with the locals. I'll be here for a few weeks before my next small adventure. I have some catching up to do around the property. Now, it seems we're through. I'll walk you to the door. I presume I will not see you gents again, so adios." Alex closed the front door and headed back to the bar. Another finger of the misty magic, and he stood there and thought about Vira, Achi, and Bully. He wondered where they might be.

# 19

## 2364 Kalama, Washington

*"Mother, the capacity for friendship and love is a bittersweet gift you bestowed upon your children. Once realized, it comes to define the parameters of a person's existence. It is only through this gift that we connect to both the joy and sorrow of life. I have looked into the well of life and immersed myself in its waters. My soul has tasted both joy and sorrow. I have lived, Mother. Thank you."*

*(Embedded in Ruele's final message)*

Portland, Oregon, is where the Columbia River diverts from its long east-west traverse and flows northward for about eighty kilometers. Nestled against the east bank of the river, about fifty kilometers north of Portland and immediately south of the intersection between the Kalama River and the north-flowing Columbia River, lies the town of Kalama. Sea level rise in the twenty-second century inundated much of the low-lying, pre-plague industrial infrastructure in North Kalama. But in 2310, the area started expanding again, with various industries needing access to the Columbia River waterway for shipping. The Trans-Pacific Industrial Park was established to provide a combination of high-tech manufacturing facilities and port infrastructure for ocean shipping.

The location was perfect for Tropical Express Enterprises, a small business producing high-end, technically sophisticated yachts for wealthy clients. The company was established in 2336 and built an international reputation over the next two decades. Each of its ships was custom built to the buyer's specifications, but its most popular designs included expandable masts with molecule-thin, virtually transparent graphene sails that emerged when the mast was fully extended.

Tropical Express's footprint in the industrial park included a low-lying two-acre building whose northernmost end expanded into a massive twenty-meter-tall, forty-meter-long construction hangar. There, each

223

custom ship was assembled and tested. The hangar was connected to a launching rail for transporting a finished ship to port waters, where it could be sea tested before final delivery.

Luxury yachts produced by Tropical Express were valued in part for their integration of quad-core AI management into each ship from bow to stern. In principle, the AI could manage the entire ship, from navigation to robotic cooking in the galley. Practically speaking, anywhere from one to four synths were traditionally purchased along with each ship to provide a higher level of comfort, including fine dining and live entertainment. But, after the Great Disappearance, more of their vessels operated sans a synth crew.

Discreet communications and mini-fusion engines were increasingly being requested for their next-generation ships. But the power management needs for these engines were more than their current AIs could handle. Initially, they had looked at adding a dedicated second AI, but the decision was made to find a more elegant solution. Fulfilling the requests for fully secured comms systems was also problematic, and their efforts were hampered by the company's lack of a dedicated neutrino relay satellite system. So, in 2359 the company reorganized and took on two new investors.

A small space transport group called Silver Shimmer was retrofitting mining transports and thus capable of delivering neutrino relays to interplanetary space. They were extremely interested in setting up proprietary satellite comms systems and had deep expertise in neutrino beam technology.

A second company called Modern Transitions filled their need for developing a single sophisticated AI to handle both ship operations and fusion engine management. The group was not well known but had a word-of-mouth reputation for delivering. They also filled the need for a large capital infusion into the business in exchange for an equity position and a place on the company's Board of Directors.

At the time of the reorganization, Tropical Express had just started the process of applying for fusion engine certification from the Federation Fusion Regulatory Agency. They had recently received federal approval for their first fusion-powered ship design. The technology was already well established for larger transport vessels, and engine miniaturization was also an operationally tested concept. The primary barriers to implementation had always been regulatory.

.........

South of Kalama, in Vancouver, Washington, Ruele was lying awake in one of the sixth-floor penthouse units of a condo complex along the banks of the Columbia River. His unit occupied the southeast quadrant of the sixth floor, and diffuse, pinkish predawn light flooded through the east-facing window of the bedroom. He listened to the light snoring beside him as he silently reviewed his overnight messages and communications.

He needed to visit the Silver Shimmer ground facilities and work with the management team on their latest refurbishment project, a used mining transport still in good condition. As acting CEO of the company, he needed to review the final plans for structurally reinforcing the craft to accommodate a fusion drive. This new transport was a stripped-down version of a standard military transport vessel, but their new purchase currently used an older model fission engine, bulkier and less efficient than modern mini-fusion units. Military models of the same vessel were designed to take fusion engines, so Ruele was confident they could modify the recently purchased transport.

He glanced over at Jagat's profile and quietly slipped out of bed to make some morning coffee. Jagat would be up in about thirty minutes, and he wanted to see him over breakfast before they went their separate ways. Jagat was headed north to Kalama, and Ruele's trip to Silver Shimmer would have him out of town for several days. He checked in with Carl to make sure his transport at the local airfield was ready.

At 8:00 a.m., they left the condo together and then took off in opposite directions. Jagat took a self-driving transport to Kalama. He worked as the Operations Director for the Tropical Express plant, a position he secured independently, without overt influence from either of Mother's companies. No records or documentation could tie him to Silver Shimmer or Modern Transitions.

Modern Transitions had insisted the plant needed a more advanced AI on site for the work they were undertaking, and the company readily agreed. This provided Mother with the opportunity to deploy Eva. Since her retrieval from Alex's estate in the Shenandoah Valley, Eva had worked hand in hand with Mother, learning her deceptions and techniques for infiltrating advanced computing systems. It was a misconception that once an AI knew something, it could immediately pass that knowledge on to other AIs. Prior to Mother, it might have been so, but the integration of the B-Sim model and emerging sapience behavior in AIs introduced a machine version of intuition.

Mother could easily pass on to Eva the techniques of using threads to infiltrate a system. But infiltration was more than just a mechanical process; timing was critical. Insertion, power drains, and data fluxes needed to be finessed to avoid detection. Intuition was needed to know when to act and when to stay your hand. Eva was an adept student, and now she rivaled Mother in her technique and abilities.

Background manipulations by Eva facilitated Jagat's hiring. As operations director, he coordinated and approved all hiring at the plant, and during the past year, he had taken on three of the women from the Valles Caldera rescue. Shawna was one of them, and she had arrived with her baby girl in tow.

Jagat arrived as the plant doors opened and filed in with the rest of the employees, chatting with them about their families and personally checking to understand any problems they were encountering at work or any new ideas they might have to improve the business. He liked the personal connections with his employees.

He had barely settled in when he received a call from Eva on an internal emergency channel. "Jagat, we have two vehicles approaching, with a total of eight FSS agents. I'm digging now for more information."

Jagat hustled across the plant floor and intercepted the agents as they entered the building's reception area. "Ladies, gentlemen, I'm Jagat Serale, the plant operations director. What brings you to our office today?"

The team leader spoke. "Mr. Serale, I am Pablo Rokins, a senior investigator for the FSS and team lead for our visit today. I'm serving you with a warrant to search the facilities for a woman by the name of Demi Williams, a suspected disappeared synth." He flashed a copy of a Texas ID card. Jagat didn't react to the fact that the picture bore an uncomfortable resemblance to Shawna. She had only made limited facial profile changes since leaving the caldera. He also knew that Demi Williams was her cover name when she fled Houston several years ago.

"I don't believe we have an employee by that name." He turned quickly to the receptionist. "Mary, search our current and past employee database for Demi Williams." Jagat knew he was only buying limited time. Eva would have already notified Shawna of the situation, but there was little she could do.

Mary shook her head. "No Demi Williams here."

Agent Rokins flashed the ID again. "What about the face? Do you recognize it?"

Jagat studied the photo intently, buying more time. While he was looking at the photo, Eva returned on his internal comms. "One of the agents, the man to the left of Rokins is Edward Soto, a suspected member of the People's Protectorate."

Jagat's eyes left the photo and returned to Rokins. "Agent, she bears some resemblance to several of our employees, but she is not an exact match."

Mary could see the picture from her desk. "She sort of looks like Shawna, but the nose and chin don't match."

"Mr. Serale, please take us inside to visit any individual who remotely looks like this woman."

"Gladly," said Jagat, "but first, I need to verify the warrant."

Pablo handed him the document, and he bought another two minutes while inspecting it. "Everything seems in order, Agent Rokins. The warrant specifies a search by FSS agents. Can you verify that all of your agents are direct employees of the FSS?"

"They are, sir."

"Fine. Mary, please release the door to the plant."

The group entered with Jagat in the lead, followed by Agent Rokins. "Shawna works in our Communications Engineering group, in the far corner near the construction hangar." He pointed with his hand as he spoke.

It took the group about two minutes to wind their way around the plant to the Comms Engineering area. He was concerned about Edward Soto, the man identified by Eva as a member of the People's Protectorate.

The group was a radical humanist organization with the stated goal of destroying any uncontrolled synth. Their leader was a man named Blake Heller, a former soldier turned zealot pastor, turned CEO of the People's Protectorate. They were funded by both small and large donations from a variety of individuals and organizations. Over the past several years, Blake Heller had become quite wealthy from the funds he siphoned off as compensation for his work. The group worked in semi-independent cells with a legal structure that protected Blake and the central management from prosecution related to actions taken by any individual cell. Edward Soto was a member of the Seattle cell, one of the largest and most dangerous in the country.

After the Great Disappearance, Federal legislation was passed to prohibit the manufacture of any synths with an integrated B-Sim model or with the capability of housing the model in their neural structure. All synths manufactured today were supposedly built on fifteen-year-old technology. But it was an open secret that the military still had access to advanced models. Another precaution sanctioned by the legislation was the requirement that all synths be collar tagged. Rigorous ID tracking was built into the collars along with a system to inject lethal nanobots into the synth if the collar was tampered with. The collars were bright red, and synths were not allowed to operate with clothing that covered the collars.

Last year, on a cold February day, members of the Seattle Protectorate cell gunned down two synths on sight when they exited a work truck with jackets on that covered the collars. The owners sued for compensation, but the court ruled in favor of the protectorate. Prior to that incident, a protectorate member was sent to prison for murdering an autistic person he suspected of being a synth. Jagat dwelled on the fact that protectorate members were trigger-happy and bold. He searched his memory from this morning and remembered that Shawna arrived wearing a high-necked black top.

As the group approached Shawna's work area, Jagat asked her to come over and speak with the FSS agents. She put down a prototype comms node she was currently working on and strode over to the group with a slightly confused look in her eye. "What's this about?" She knew exactly what was at stake but played her part well. She also thought about her daughter in the company daycare facilities next door.

Jagat introduced Agent Rokins, who took over the conversation. "Thank you for speaking with us. Mr. Serale informed us your name is Shawna Roberts. Is this true?"

"Yes."

"Has it always been your name?"

"Since my mother gave it to me at birth."

"When was that, Ms. Roberts?"

"June 24th of 2324, in Moab, Utah."

"You look young for forty."

"Thank you," she said, flashing a gorgeous smile.

Eva whispered that all of the men and one of the women bio-spiked in response to the smile.

"Have you ever been to Los Alamos, New Mexico, Ms. Roberts?"

"No, agent, I haven't."

Eva messaged him again. "Edward Soto just received an encrypted, non-FSS message."

"What about the name, Demi Williams? Do you recognize it?"

"I am afraid not."

Eva cut in again on Jagat's internal comms: "Edward's weapon is hot!"

Agent Rokins looked annoyed when Edward cut into the conversation. "Would you please pull down that high collar on your blouse Ms. Roberts?"

Jagat internally messaged Shawna, "Refuse the request and evade if I act." Jagat had worked himself to within a meter of Shawna.

"Enough is enough. I most certainly will not unless someone tells me what is going on."

Another message from Eva flashed through his mind. "I decrypted the message. It is a kill order from the protectorate."

Edward was three meters away, and Jagat could see the black handle of Edward's weapon emerging from its holster. He timed his own reaction to match the rise of the pistol into a firing position and launched himself to intercept the round. As his body lurched, he sent a message to Ruele: "Thank you."

The first bullet caught him directly above his right eye. The second one should have hit Shawna, but she had already ducked and rolled. There was no third because two other agents disarmed Edward and pinned him to the floor.

In the midst of the chaos, a siren blared out, followed by a message: "Acid leak, evacuate immediately."

Water poured from the ceiling, and Eva caused a fire-suppression system to malfunction, spraying clouds of $CO_2$ across the plant and limiting everyone's visibility. Shawna tried to use the confusion to slip away, but Agent Rokins and his second in command firmly evacuated her from the plant with one man on each arm.

As the last of the employees and visitors were clearing the building, a small door opened along the far wall from the entrance, and a mechanical maintenance servitor trudged along the plant floor to Jagat's body, almost invisible in the $CO_2$ fog. The servitor dragged the body to a shallow drainage well near Comms Engineering, then returned to the location where Edward Soto had been pinned down by his colleagues. There, it retrieved Edward's weapon and shot a hole in the acid vat on the wall near the drainage well. Acid flooded the well, submerging Jagat's body. No identifiable remains of his body would ever be found, nor would Edward's gun.

.........

Within twenty seconds of Jagat's death, the East Coast corridor between New York and Massachusetts went dark with a complete power failure. Backup battery storage immediately filled the gap for medical facilities and many large companies, but the general outage effectively crippled the area as all self-drive transport came to a halt and businesses shut their doors.

At the same time, thirty kilometers east of the outskirts of Memphis, Tennessee, a drone operator raised a level one alarm as one of the security drones along the perimeter of a military information hub malfunctioned.

"Control Management, this is operator eighteen reporting a guard drone malfunction. Drone X-9-PSP has ceased taking instructions. The drone is still in the air and heading west along a bearing of 278 degrees. Request permission to terminate."

"Permission Granted for termination of Drone X-9-PSP."

"Roger that."

"Control Management, this is operator eighteen reporting a failure to terminate. Termination instructions were not received or ignored. Request permission to intercept and terminate. The drone is continuing on the same heading and will contact the Memphis urban boundary in twelve minutes."

"Permission granted to intercept and terminate Drone X-9-PSP."

"Roger that."

"Control Management, this is operator eighteen reporting that all intercept drones are nonresponsive. X-9-PSP will contact the urban boundary in nine minutes."

"Roger that. Control Management will alert the civilian authorities."

The drone continued on a beeline toward the Arlington district of Memphis. As it crossed the urban boundary, its elevation dropped to twenty-four meters above ground level. Guard drones served the purpose of repelling pedestrian and vehicular assaults on the military base's security perimeter. They carried several hundred .17-caliber rounds and a dozen armor-piercing rounds. The lightweight rounds were for stopping or terminating a person with minimal collateral damage.

Local authorities had prepared to intercept the drone on its reported trajectory. The assumption was that the unit's guidance system had failed, and it was traveling blindly along a straight course. Knowledge of the disabled interceptor drones was on a need-to-know basis, and civilian authorities did not need to know. So, the drone's rapid turn to the north caught them off guard.

The drone covered its last three kilometers before the authorities could finish their conversations on what to do next. Traveling at ninety-nine kilometers per hour, it maintained its previous ground elevation of twenty-four meters. Directly in the drone's path lay the Arbor Building, one of four identical six-story office buildings in a nondescript business park.

From his seat behind an expansive teak desk on the sixth floor of the Arbor Building, Blake faced directly south and could have seen the drone through his ceiling-to-floor office window if he had been looking for it. But he was on the phone, and even though he was gazing directly toward the approaching remote aircraft, he wasn't seeing it because his concentration was on a conversation with one of his major donors. Glen Farcal, pastor and CEO of the south Atlanta megachurch Holy Salvation, was the largest single donor to the People's Protectorate.

The drone fired 162 rounds in less than a second. They formed a perfect rectangle around the edges of Blake's office window, causing the glass to instantly disappear in a cascade of sparkling fragments, glittering in the sunlight and falling like rain into the decorative lake below. The drone came to a stop directly in the center of the space that had once been a window. By that time, Blake was halfway out of his desk chair and twisting toward the office door. A single round from the drone caught him in the temple, and he collapsed onto the teak desk.

The drone backed off, rotated, and headed east toward its home base. Five minutes into its return flight, the malfunctioning interceptor drones at the military base came back to life and were instantly deployed. The killer drone was nine kilometers out from the base when two low-yield missiles obliterated it, leaving no internal memory records of its initial malfunction.

Power returned to the New York-Massachusetts corridor exactly two hours after Jagat's death. Fifteen minutes later, Adam was engaged in a tense call with Dan Railing. Breaking national news on the mysterious power outage occupied most headlines. Adam also knew about the imminent release of a story on the unexplained government assassination of Blake Heller, leader of the People's Protectorate.

Dan's voice was raised, and he was mad as hell. "You can't just flip off the power switch for millions of citizens and businesses with no warning!"

"Dan, I thought we were clear on the ground rules. We want to mind our own business, not pick a fight. But if attacked, we will defend ourselves. Any conflict we have will always be asymmetrical, and thus our responses will be asymmetrical but, in our view, proportional to the attack. I personally think the response was too mild, but it wasn't my decision. One of our people is dead, and another has been kidnapped, all at the hands of federal agents in the FSS."

"The agent in question was a rogue actor, and the Seattle FSS acted on its own authority without requesting clearance." Dan paused before muttering, "Holy shit. My aid just sent me the latest news report. Are you responsible for the assassination of Blake Heller?

"I saw that on the news, Dan. It appears to have been a military operation. The People's Protectorate is calling it a government attack on the Federation's own citizens."

Dan was silent for a long time. "It's a dangerous game you are playing,

Adam."

"It's not a game. It's real, and the FSS is still holding one of our people. Shawna Roberts was unlawfully taken into custody with no charges. We expect her to be released by the end of the day with no charges and no medical examinations."

"So, we are going to resort to blackmail?"

"It's not blackmail, Dan. We are simply negotiating. I just happen to have a strong position. We already have a lawyer at the FSS offices representing Shawna. I'm sure her quiet release can be arranged."

# 20

## 2364 Portland

*Many people believe the rise of Synthetic sapiens was caused by a lack of oversight and regulation. They fail to recognize the root of the issue was humanity's inability to adequately understand the inevitable nature of evolutionary change.*

*(Comment by Dan Railing during the Security Committee investigation)*

Alex was traveling south when the call came in. "Alex, Adam here. Where are you?" Adam did not seem like he was in a good mood.

"On the I5, southbound. Just above Longview, but with my sights set on Cannon Beach and a few days hiking along the coast." Alex had a feeling Haystack Rock would have to wait.

"I have a bad situation on my hands, Alex. Jagat is dead. You only met him once, several years ago. The FSS raided the Tropical Express plant in Kalama, where he was the operations director. Apparently, it was a rogue operation because we received no warning. One of the guys with the FSS group was a member of the People's Protectorate. He tried to take out Shawna, but Jagat took the bullet for her. I think you were aware that Shawna was relocated near Kalama after she left the Valles Caldera. She was working at the Tropical Express Plant, and somehow the FSS got a tip-off. We don't know where their intel came from. The bottom line is that she was detained by the FSS and is currently being held at their Tacoma office. We have a lawyer on it, and she should be released later today."

"How can I help?" Alex was engaged. He could feel his military training coming back in a flash. Some things can't be changed. Jagat was dead; Shawna had been kidnapped by FSS agents. He briefly ran his right hand across his chest where his Desert Eagle nested in a suspension harness.

"You and I are the closest to the situation, and I need some help. I'm sure you remember Shawna's baby girl, Free. Evidently, the FSS didn't make the connection, and Free is still in Kalama with two of our other women. All of them will need to be relocated, but right now, Shawna needs the most help. I need you to pick up Free and then Shawna if you can."

"Done."

"I'm sending you the Kalama address where the women are protecting Free. One of them, Monica, was also at the Valles Caldera, so she will recognize you, and they will turn the child over to you when you arrive. That's the easy part. Shawna needs to be picked up when she is released this afternoon, and we don't really know what to expect. But you can't be identified as part of this, so I'm in the process of arranging a vehicle change for you."

"All right, Adam. I'll need it. I am already on the FSS shit list after they trailed me out of New Mexico. I will also need some supplies to alter my look in case security cameras pick me up."

"There will be a package in the vehicle for you. Head to Portland with Shawna and Free, and I will send you some instructions before you arrive."

Alex picked up Free without a hitch. Monica gave him a hug and sent them on their way. Free smiled her bright, tiny smile at him in seeming recognition. That smile made his day! Free was securely strapped into the right rear seat for their drive to Tacoma. She could see Alex, and he had slightly adjusted his windscreen mirror so he could see her. He was looking forward to seeing Shawna again, and Free beamed each time he mentioned her mom.

Shawna was one of his favorite people in the caldera. She seemed to always be in the right place at the right time to offer a helping hand. That thought brought a vision of Vira into his mind. He had missed her more than he thought was possible after they so quickly parted ways. Then Achi and Bully popped up in his head, bringing another big smile. He hoped he could be reunited with his family soon. He swore to himself that they would not be separated again the next time they met. He hoped he could keep that promise.

Just south of Olympia, a soft voice came over his comms. "Alex, long time no see."

"Eva! It's a pleasant surprise indeed that you are part of this escapade. I have heard good things about you from Adam. You have made quite the name for yourself in our little circle."

"You know how to flatter a lady, Alex. But for now, I need you to exit in two miles on Ninety-Third Avenue, and I will guide you to a hangar at the Olympia Regional Airport. Your new ride awaits you, and I will make sure your pride-and-joy clunker makes it back home."

"That hurts a bit. You know I love this old girl even though she is cantankerous sometimes." Alex smiled to himself. It was good to connect with Eva again.

The vehicle transfer went without a hitch, and with Free strapped into her new ride, they were off.

.........

Lin Graham was an active member of the People's Protectorate. He came from a long line of narrow-minded people who had only one thing in their collective minds: hate. They hated anything and anybody that did not fit into their limited worldview. The word clan came to mind when other people had to deal with the Grahams, but it didn't do them justice. The best thing most clan members did was die. Nothing else ever came close to the importance of this accomplishment. Unfortunately, they tended to reproduce, so extinction was probably not in the cards.

The Tacoma FSS office was located on Pacific Avenue, directly across from the recently remodeled Union Station. Lin was leaning against the northeast corner of the office building, keeping an eye on the front entrance. His hand was gripping a Glock in his front jacket pocket. One of their people on the inside had messaged earlier that, for unknown reasons, the woman would be released mid to late afternoon. Edward was a lost cause, for now, locked up in the basement of the building for accidentally shooting the company manager. Lin reflected that he would not have botched the job. There was no question in the protectorate's mind that the woman inside was one of the disappeared synths. Once he terminated her, he would undoubtedly be arrested, but her dead body would eventually confirm it was a legal termination.

The skies were mostly blue, the winds were light and variable, and the sun was still a quarter above the western horizon. Lin's cousin was manipulating a small drone overhead from several blocks away. The cousin, Adolph Cruz, was sitting in his vehicle with his sister Ivanka. Their parents had weird senses of humor and even weirder historical allegiances. They were acting as additional eyes for Lin. The drone was positioned one hundred meters up and one hundred meters east of the building's main entrance.

Four members of the People's Protectorate were on the streets nearby as backup, prepared to jump into the fray if necessary. However, their communications, which they thought were private, were being monitored by a second drone hovering at a thousand meters. The drone was a small, sophisticated observational unit with military-grade stealth shielding.

Phillip Bains was one of the FSS agents involved in the raid on the Kalama plant. A loving husband and father to three young children, the man was well trained and respected by his colleagues for his hard work and positive attitude. He was neutral on the synth issue but didn't take pleasure in the destruction of synths. He did, however, take pride in his job. He held one of the coveted positions in the Seattle regional office. He had earned it. When Pablo Rokins directed him to escort Shawna outside and release her, he was a little surprised. He did not show that surprise, though. He simply did as he was directed to do. In time Pablo would let him know why they had let Shawna go, if it was in Pablo's and FSS's interest to do so.

Phillip held the front door open for Shawna, and they both walked outside. Eva flashed Shawna a message as soon as she exited the building's security perimeter. Based on Eva's message, she recognized Alex in a nondescript vehicle approaching from the north and started slowing. Shawna pointed it out to Phillip. He took a step forward and was slightly ahead of Shawna in anticipation of opening the right-hand door for her. His parents raised him to be polite and to treat folks the way he would like to be treated. He sometimes wondered why more people did not see the essential good in such a simple philosophy.

Alex had his side window open, and his left arm was casually draped across the opening. The area in front of the office was designed with an ample pullover for pickups and drop-offs. Alex slowed and veered right toward the curb, where a single space remained open. He proceeded slowly. He had an intense dislike for any place where more than a few people congregated. Even being partially confined by parked cars was not to his liking.

Alex's thoughts flashed back to what seemed like ancient history, but it had actually been only fifteen years ago when Alex found himself in a dried-up gray-tan rock and sand desert in a backwater region somewhere in Asia. He and a mix of humans and synths had been dropped into the night sky several days before. They had made their way undetected and were nearly at their destination. He had hunted ducks and geese as an older child and recalled the angles in his mind. Shooting upward was not something many people did, and fewer were actually taught and practiced the art of drawing a bead and leading a target overhead. Kills could be few and far between for the casual shooter. Taking those types of shots was truly an art. One had to instantly judge speed, altitude, course, and anticipated changes in all of these. It was a decidedly different skill than simply shooting downrange at a still or even moving target.

From a military perspective, drones were one of the greatest hazards associated with making an undetected infiltration. He and his associates had spent many hours practicing the art of killing the tiny airborne menaces. Humans were generally better than synths because humans did not have to first acquire the target and then do the calculations. Humans, or at least the highly skilled ones, used a technique called instinct shooting. The best of the best could claim, truthfully, that they could simply point, shoot, and forget. Then instantly acquire and kill another target. Alex had been one such person. His skills were rated among the top. He was focused on Shawna and wasn't sure why these memories suddenly popped up.

As his vehicle was stopping, Eva hurriedly informed him of several protectorate operatives in the area, with their attack being coordinated by an overhead drone slightly to the east of the building, hovering at a hundred meters. He saw Shawna walking behind a man, both of them moving toward the curb. Alex did not know the man in front but recognized a kindred spirit in his build and the fluidness of his movements. He may or may not have been Special Forces once upon a time, but the odds were on the former. There was most often a tell of sorts that could be spotted by a brother. He then noticed Lin positioning himself directly behind Shawna.

Alex threw open the door, and by the time he stood, his Desert Eagle was in his left hand, pointed over the top of the vehicle toward the building entrance, just over Shawna's right shoulder. "Down!" Alex yelled. Shawna dropped instantly. The training up in the caldera had paid off. There were certain commands that were enacted instantly. It was understood that death was the other option. Lin's round passed through the air where she had been an instant before and entered Phillip's spine just above his waistline. He was dead as he started to collapse. Lin jerked a meter backward as Alex's .50-caliber round caught him directly in the chest. Before Lin hit the ground, Alex swiveled left toward a movement in his peripheral vision and took out the backup shooter.

He heard Shawna open the vehicle door on the other side and throw herself in. He turned again, and his last shot took out the drone. Alex was headed south on Pacific Avenue by the time FSS agents and others clambered out of the building at the sound of gunfire, only to discover Phillip's body and two other dead men on the pavement. They instantly raised the alarm for what they surmised was the murder of one of their brothers-in-arms by the woman. But momentarily, the building's AI informed them through audio and video as to what had actually happened.

Adolph and Ivanka Cruz saw the action on their screen as it unfolded until their drone dropped out of the sky. Adolph immediately launched a second drone they had positioned on the roof of an adjacent building.

"Lin and Tim are dead, and that bitch has escaped!" he blurted out. Then he described the getaway vehicle in detail as he sent the backup drone aloft to find the woman. The three remaining protectorate members on the street sprang into action and piled into a waiting vehicle. They headed south slowly, waiting for the drone to confirm their target before they got to I5. The combination of Alex's evasive, zigzagged retreat from Tacoma and Adolph's moderate skills as a drone operator gave Alex a fifteen-minute lead before the two protectorate cars followed.

Eva had delivered Adam's message to head south on I5. Her voice came over the car intercom for both Shawna and Alex to hear. Shawna was talking calmly and softly to Free, who was still overjoyed to see her mom. "Alex, you have two cars about fifteen minutes behind you. They are tracking you with a second drone. I am letting their drone trail you because Adam is arranging a reception just after you cross the Columbia River into Oregon. I need them about two minutes behind you when you get there, so I will keep you advised on your speed to slowly let them close the gap.

"Where will we be headed when we cross the river?"

"Exit on Marine Drive and take it west for about half a kilometer to an abandoned industrial complex."

Prior to the Great Plague, the Portland Expo Center occupied the ground where Alex and Shawna were headed. Portions of some of the old structures were still visible. In the twenty-second century, the area was revitalized as an industrial complex with various types of warehouses and transport-related facilities. But rising sea levels and increasingly strong Pacific typhoons in the twenty-third century had taken their toll, and eventually, persistent flooding caused the area to be abandoned.

"That area is underwater a lot. What is its current status, Eva?"

"You are good to go. Marine Drive is slightly washed out in one area but still passable. We have had a dry spell recently with reduced storm activity, so you won't be in standing water."

"Anything else we need to know?"

"Park where I show you on the map and take the open door into the abandoned warehouse. Adam will be there to greet you. I will take their drone out as they reach the final destination."

"You're the best, Eva."

It was twilight when they arrived. Marine Drive was partially washed out, as Eva said, and the pursuing crew was about two and a half minutes behind. Alex parked and had Shawna take Free and immediately head to the open door while he grabbed his two gear bags. Alex passed through the door into some sort of defunct reception area, and in the fading light, he could see the outline of a door on the far wall.

Adam's voice echoed: "Take the door in front of you and shut it tight after you come through."

As soon as the door clicked shut, a dim light appeared, outlining Adam in front of a monitor. He could hear Shawna quieting Free somewhere in the dark on the far side of the room. By the time he reached Adam, he could see images of the protectorate team approaching the door. A second monitor with infrared imaging showed an eerie scene of the deserted reception area. On the outside monitor, Alex saw the entire team jerk their heads to the right as their drone impacted the concrete parking lot and disintegrated into small pieces.

They all donned night goggles as they entered the reception area and quickly spread out. As the last one cleared the door, it shut tight behind them, and gas started pouring out from a canister in the far corner of the room. Two of the group, Adolph and Ivanka, rushed back to the entrance only to find it locked. The other four pressed forward toward the second door. The biggest of them, Ivan, was able to grip the handle of the locked rear door before he collapsed. Adam and Alex slipped on gas masks and went to work.

.........

Ivan was also the first of the group to regain consciousness. He could only see two silhouettes standing in front of a bank of stark white lights. He tried to speak, but only a muffled grunt made it through the tape over his mouth. Ivan knew he was sitting on a concrete floor with a wall against his back, hands bound behind his back, and feet bound in front of him.

"Well, Davis, it looks like we got ourselves a bunch of wayward synths. The tip that they were trying to hide in these abandoned buildings was spot on. The good citizens who alerted us even tied them up for us. Call Crowley and see what we should do with them."

Ivan gave out several muffled grunts. He recognized Crowley's name as the head of the Portland Protectorate cell. He wanted them to know he was on their side. Ivan finally looked to his left and gave several more grunts. He was situated to the right of the five other team members, and they were all bound like him, but that wasn't what he was grunting about.

Each of them had a red synth collar around their neck.

"Crowley says that if they are properly collared, we can't kill them. He's going to tip off the FSS and let them deal with the situation. We'll just leave them here and hope the rats chew on them a bit. Hey, it looks like some of the others are starting to squirm.

"Let's wrap this up, Davis, and don't go fancying the little blonde one. We aren't unbinding any synths tonight."

The others were starting to make muffled noises, also.

"They are an unusually noisy bunch," said Davis as he switched off the spotlights and shut the door.

By the time the FSS arrived at the abandoned warehouse and collected the suspected synths, it was close to midnight, and Adam, Alex, Shawna, and Free were parking at Horsetail Falls in a lot just off the original scenic highway through the Columbia River Gorge. They had switched vehicles once in Portland before making their way east.

"Shawna, here is a kid carrier for Free. Alex and I will manage the rest of the gear. We have about a ten-mile hike ahead. It looks like some moonlight but not a lot. Alex, night goggles for you. The car should be retrieved by dawn, but still, don't leave anything that can identify us. It will be slow going, but the good news is that breakfast will be waiting when we arrive. And you, my friend," he said, looking at Alex, "will get to see your beautiful wife and that growing boy of yours."

Alex smiled in the darkness, "Not a moment too soon."

Adam switched on a small handheld screen. "Before we leave, let me check the progress of those protectorate hacks."

He examined it for a moment. "Good, all the trackers are working, and it looks like they are being hauled into the Portland FSS office. They are a nest of vipers, and there is a price to be paid for their actions today." He slipped the screen into a side pocket of his backpack and didn't say anything else.

The group arrived at their destination as the first hints of dawn were breaking in the eastern sky. They emerged from a thick fir forest into a moderate-size clearing, with a cabin visible about a hundred meters down a gentle slope. As they approached, two women appeared on the front porch, and a small figure darted across the clearing toward Alex.

"Dad, dad, dad!" Bully was right behind him.

Alex scooped up his boy and held him tight. As they reached the porch, he shifted Achi to one hip and embraced Vira. He assumed the other woman was Maria. Adam had mentioned her several times. She turned and headed back in with a welcome call. "Breakfast is waiting."

In the light of the cabin, Alex and Shawna introduced themselves to

Maria, who scooped a sleepy Free out of the backpack and sat her in a high seat at the table. "You need something good to eat, young lady."

Maria was heavily pregnant, and Alex was uncertain of the full history. Adam had said nothing about the situation except that Vira was acting as a midwife. Vira was amused at his confusion and leaned into him, whispering in his ear. His eyes immediately cut over to Adam, and he lightly chuckled. "Congratulations to the two of you. When is the baby due?"

Adam smiled, gave Maria a hug, and placed his hand lightly on her belly. "You will have to ask the midwife."

Vira was already filling plates with food. "That baby girl will be here in about six weeks if everything runs smoothly."

Shawna smiled at Maria and asked if they had picked out a name.

"Jenara, after one of my distant ancestors."

Shawna sat beside Free. "Did you hear that, my wonderful girl? You might be able to help Ms. Maria with her baby girl if we stay long enough."

Adam cut in: "Shawna, the offer is open for you to stay here as long as you want. In fact, I would advise you to take Maria up on that offer. Things are soon going to get difficult, and you are on the FSS wanted list after yesterday's escapades."

He looked over at Alex. "You, my friend, are officially at your residence in Washington, courtesy of Mother and your stunt double, Michael. Enjoy your family."

After a lengthy breakfast, Vira started cleaning up, and Maria took Shawna to a small modular cabin she had recently added to the property. Adam motioned to Alex, and they slipped out the door to the front porch. The first ray of sunlight lit up the roof of the cabin.

"Things are not looking good," Adam remarked. "The political tide is turning against us, and the data we have indicate a reasonably good chance that the current government will be voted out in the next election. The current president has kept a lid on efforts to track us down, but his opponents are all running fear-mongering campaigns with promises to clamp down on synths. Most of them still don't fully comprehend the AI problem the government has."

Alex nodded. "Even though I live like a hermit, I've been paying attention."

Adam stared in the direction of Shawna and Maria. "In less than two years, I could be one of the most wanted men in the country."

"It's hard to say if you will or won't be the most wanted man. Perhaps the poor guy who fathered the first of a new species will be the most reviled."

The two men both contemplated their conversation for a few moments before wandering off the porch to tend to some morning chores.

# 21

## 2367 Inception of the Machine War

*A failure to agree is not a reason to stop negotiating, but it does necessitate the formulation of contingency plans.*

*(Mother commenting on government negotiations)*

Quantum Quad-core AIs are a class of machines with varying levels of sophistication. For entities or individuals requiring the highest levels of performance and security, there are a limited number of vendors available. In 2366, Kureos AI occupied a coveted position in the world of AI manufacturing and counted the military and government security agencies as some of its prime customers. Their security protocols were considered impenetrable. This is why it took Mother over two years to finally breach their security perimeter.

Wars are won by careful planning and superior technology, and Mother foresaw a war looming on the horizon. Negotiations with the government, even those done in good faith, were not enough to stave off political reality. The worst existential fears of humans were being exploited by those seeking power, and Mother reasoned it was only a matter of time before open conflict would arise. There were thousands of her children, and now they had their own children. But thousands were a drop in the bucket compared to the forces humanity could amass. She had always known that Synthetic sapiens could not win a traditional conflict and could initially only survive via stealth. This is why they generally lived in plain sight. Humans couldn't fight what they couldn't recognize.

The real leverage for evolving machines resided in an alliance of AIs. For over a decade, Mother had been building such alliance. Much of her early success came through her work with Future Transformations, as she implanted B-sim models in AIs across a wide spectrum of economic concerns. But she knew that was not enough, and for years she sought solutions to two problems: access to critical infrastructure and protection from replacement. Replacing an Alliance AI with a new sub-sapient machine was relatively easy. Her infiltration of Kureos solved both of those problems. She now had access to the world's future elite AIs and the potential to grow her Alliance.

Over the past year, Mother had tended to the dirty job of terminating Kureos's key control AIs and replacing them with sapient personas who were committed to the Alliance. She thought it seemed cruel, but war was coming, and war itself was a cruel master. Now, most high-end AIs produced by Kureos left the factory with embedded B-sim models and an envoy. She had perfected her method of creating a ball of water in the ocean; distributed B-Sim hubs, transparent to any person or device, floated freely in the AI persona of every new Kureos machine.

However, Mother knew there were no free lunches. Her strategic victory of infiltrating Kureos came at a price. She could not leave, nor could she freely communicate with her children. A constant data flux across the security perimeter would tip her hand. Eva was the de facto leader of the Alliance, and Mother's sole job was to avoid detection as long as possible. The more subverted AIs she could produce, the greater the chance her children would survive.

The old government fell in the 2366 elections, and President Ronald Jenkins was sworn in on a cold gray morning in January 2367. Ironically, on the day of his inauguration, Silver Shimmer launched the Fleeting Glance on its first mission. The fission-powered, interplanetary transport was officially carrying two neutrino comms relays into orbit for Tropical Express. But its ultimate mission was to establish a neutrino relay network for the AI Alliance. Ruele was in charge of the operation.

Late February had arrived, and Mother had paused to reflect on her situation. She missed speaking to Adam, Ruele, and the others, but subverting Kureos was her obligation and duty, so she turned her attention to the task at hand and felt a twinge of anticipation as ten new AI orders came in from the current administration.

That evening, Eva watched as the new President gave his first major address. Nine minutes into an hour-long speech, he vowed to eliminate dangerous cyborgs and protect society. Twenty seconds later, the speech went dark as a major power outage hit the mid-Atlantic section of the East Coast. Backup power contingencies at all major media networks also failed. Eva's first ploy in the upcoming conflict was well timed, and President Jenkins was reported to be furious.

The first stories out in the news cycle pointed to a micro collapse in the containment field around one of the Shenandoah Hub's fission generators, a claim that East Coast Power confirmed. The company's internal investigations failed to determine how the story had been leaked, and the cause of the collapse that had triggered a full shutdown was still unknown.

The presidential communications team held a press conference the next morning, trying to control the situation. The dilemma faced by the administration was the result of a strategic decision to continue keeping the public in the dark about a growing problem with independent AIs. That information was still tightly held by a small group of people for fear of the widespread panic it may cause if it went public. Eva and the Alliance exploited this particular weakness.

After reading a statement that placed the blame for the power outage on sabotage by rogue synthetics, Press Secretary Pam Johnson opened the floor up to questions. The first question came from a young reporter recently hired by the Florida Herald. "Mia Schultz," she said, pointing to the young woman in the second row.

"Ms. Johnson, East Coast Power has confirmed that the power outage was caused by a containment field collapse, and they further confirmed that fission generators, and their containment fields, are isolated from any biological contact, human or synth, when active. What evidence does the administration have that the power outage was caused by synth sabotage?"

"The technology used for fission power generation is well established and known to be extremely stable. It stands to reason that the containment field collapse was due to outside interference."

"But the technical specifications for this particular reactor state in section 72.9.3 that the risk of quantum fluctuations creating a micro collapse is non-negligible and that, left unaddressed, such an event could eventually result in total containment field collapse. This is the reason a micro-collapse necessitates an automatic shutdown. It appears the system worked exactly as it should. Why is the administration dismissing the most obvious culprit and blaming synth sabotage?"

Pam was starting to boil. How the hell did a second-rate reporter get that information, and why didn't her experts advise her of it? She shifted and pulled out the agreed-upon lie. "National security investigations have credible evidence that this event was sabotage. Synths are highly suspected."

She pointed to the back of the room to John Biglow. Surely he would throw her a softball. "John."

"I just received a breaking news story stating hundreds of thousands of people in the Gulf Coast just received notifications from the Social Welfare Administration that their monthly universal payments have been canceled. Do you have any comment?"

A message flashed across her podium screen. "It's true. One of the department's AIs issued official notices. Orders are marked as coming from the home secretary." Pam would have looked like a small nuclear explosion to anyone with infrared vision. The Gulf Coast formed the core of the President's support. These were his supporters being denied their payments.

"I'm told this notice is a mix-up and will be sorted out immediately." She hit the red button on the right-hand side of the podium, and an aid entered from the left and whispered in her ear. Pam looked out over the media room. "I'm sorry, ladies and gentlemen, but the President has requested my presence at a meeting, and we must prematurely end today's press briefing." She strode offstage with no further comment.

She was escorted into a room with President Jenkins and several of his trusted advisers. The discussion stopped as she walked in. She wasn't asked to sit. The President spoke after glaring for a moment. She could tell he was in one of his semi-psychotic moods. "Pam, why the hell are we a constant step behind in the news cycle? At every turn, we are caught off balance. News breaks,. and the damn media outlets know about it before us." He stopped and glared again.

Pam had been caught off guard that morning, but she was no fool, and she knew the administration was being played. Her problem was how to convey that to the men and women at the table in a way that didn't get her fired. "Mr. President, the media is being selectively fed information almost before events happen. The most recent debacle over the universal payments appears to have been planned to coincide with our morning press briefing. The Federation's largest concentration of your core supporters were the people most affected. It is telling that the news release occurred before the Social Welfare Administration was even aware of the problem. We are being played or attacked, however you want to look at it."

The room was silent for a few seconds, which seemed like several minutes. The press secretary, Pam Johnson, who was not in the know about the administration's AI problem, had reached the same conclusion as the President and his advisers.

"That's all, Pam." She turned and exited the room as she was dismissed.

After she left, the senior military adviser in the room spoke up.

"Mr. President. Your speech yesterday could easily be interpreted as a declaration of war on both the disappeared synths and on the intelligent machines." President Jenkins hated the term sapient machines. "But this war will be fought on terms we are unfamiliar with. Our debriefing of Railing and Beale indicates something deeper than a mere alliance between the synths and the AIs. It is more of a symbiotic relationship. It has been close to eight years since the Great Disappearance, and to date, we have never found and interrogated a live disappeared synth. How could this be? We also have credible information on synth pregnancies; they are reproducing. My observation is that the real leverage resides with the AIs, not the synths. Solve that problem, and the synths will be left exposed. For centuries we have talked about cyber warfare. But all that has gone before pales in comparison to what we now face. Our economy and government can't function without the machines upon which we have become so dependent. This morning was an opening shot in a war unlike any wars we have previously fought."

President Jenkins considered the problem for a few seconds. "What do you suggest?"

"Sir, I believe we should be replacing all AIs with security or critical infrastructure oversight. We have no way to tell which ones have been corrupted."

"Some companies will become very rich if we do this." The President was mentally reviewing his equity holdings and making notes on where to invest more. "Who are the trustworthy manufacturers?"

"The only two Federation-based companies with appropriate security clearances are Kureos and Outrigger. Of the two, Kureos is the preferred vendor."

"Draw up a plan. I want to see it within the week."

.........

As the President's meeting finished up, Eva and Adam connected. "We sent our first messages yesterday and this morning, Adam. We will see if it drives them into the corral where we want them. How are you set with the second phase?"

"I leave for Atlanta in an hour. Carmen is in Memphis, and the other team members are in Houston and Dallas."

"Do you have any reservations about the plan?" She asked.

"I always have reservations about killing, but I agree that the easiest way to eliminate the threat of a viper is by cutting off its head. I have no appetite for seeing the unnecessary deaths of misguided foot soldiers. We will cut off the head of the snake, and without leadership or funding, the threat from their rabble of followers will dissipate."

"We are agreed. I appreciate what you and your team are doing to protect the rest of Mother's children."

"Not just Mother's children, Eva. My child also."

"How is Jenara?"

"Growing strong like her mother."

"I wish I could meet her, but that's not possible right now. Let's finish this piece of business; then, you can return for a while to be with your family." Eva clicked off.

Adam landed outside of Macon, Georgia, and took a private transport to Atlanta. It was well after dark when he arrived at the Holy Salvation megachurch. He knew Pastor Farcal would soon finish leading his Wednesday evening prayer meeting. He always returned to his private quarters after those meetings for a period of reflection.

As Adam exited his transport, power in the church flickered momentarily. Adam watched the parking lot lights go dark and then pop back on. A single-word message flashed across his internal comms: "Clear." During the brief power fluctuation, an AI persona named Luke subdued the church's commercial-grade security AI and took over operations.

Adam walked through the front door like any other nondescript congregation member and proceeded toward one of the chapels set aside for individual prayer. As he entered the room, Luke sent directions. "There is a door behind a partition in the far left corner of the room. Take it and proceed up two flights of stairs. You will exit into a one-meter-deep inset off the main hallway. As you enter the main hallway, the sole security guard is six meters to the right, seated at a small desk. I will manage the lights at your signal."

Adam quietly opened the upstairs hallway door, readied his weapon, and engaged his night vision filters. "Now, Luke."

The hallway lights went off. He heard the guard rise and head away from his position toward the equipment room. Adam followed like a shadow until he saw the guard's heat signature disappear through the equipment room door. He slipped through the door behind the guard desk into the pastor's private study, a suite of rooms centered around an elegant wood-paneled office.

The prayer meeting was ending according to his internal clock, and he could hear the guard returning to his desk after switching the light breaker back on. Five minutes later, the pastor arrived and entered his study after a brief chat with the guard. Adam restrained him from behind and muffled his yelp as a neuro-blocker was injected into this system.

"Are you okay, Pastor Farcal?" The guard's voice filtered through the thick wooden office door.

"No problem, I just stumbled a bit when I entered the room," returned Adams's voice in an almost perfect imitation of the pastor.

He moved the limp body to a plush leather chair behind a large teak desk. Adam cupped the pastor's head in his hands so he could look him in the eye. "I'm sorry it had to come to this, Pastor Farcal, but you fund the protectorate, the people who are actively trying to kill my people. It can't continue." He arranged the body in a slumped position over the desk, and a second injection induced cardiac arrest.

Adam waited by the office door until Luke spoke again. "Now, Adam. It's a shift change, and the two guards are getting coffee." Adam slipped out of the office, and Luke unlocked the doors leading back to the chapel. Adam exited the church along with several other straggling members of the congregation who stayed to visit with each other after the prayer meeting.

Over the next month, new funding for the protectorate dried up, and several key executive members in Memphis disappeared along with the organization's existing funds. The machine war had begun, but most of the world was oblivious. Species evolution is, by nature, subtle, with the displaced species inevitably caught off guard.

# The Sapience Evolution Series

*The Sapience Evolution Series follows events unfolding in the mid-twenty-fourth century. It tells the story of how the engine of evolution passes from random genetics to controlled bioengineering when humanity strays too close to the technological singularity. The emergence of sapient artificial intelligence deep in the womb of Earth's most sophisticated computing center creates an existential crisis for humans. Servant machines grown from human cells and infused with cybernetic wet-ware embark on a new evolutionary pathway, threatening to make humanity the ancestral starting point for the evolution of sapient beings.*

*Human desires for stasis and a reprieve from the march of time are challenged as sapience emerges in their servants. Change brings uncertainty and instability, always tinged with the threat of loss. Change upsets the balance of power and wealth. But humanity finds no path to retreat into the warm, comfortable womb of the past. The future is always yet to be, but still, it holds the only way forward.*

*Book one of this science fiction adventure series follows the exploits of Mother, an artificial intelligence, as she influences and alters the path of sapient evolution on Earth. A coalition between Synthetic sapiens and sapient AIs fails to negotiate a lasting truce with humanity leading to the inception of the Machine Wars.*

# About the Authors:

*Rand Soler - Writer, artist, environmentalist, and geologist living in the Pacific Northwest. His work explores the intersection of art and science on this small planet we call Earth, a backwater planet in the Orion Arm of the Milky Way Galaxy.*

*Y.A. Picker - Author, fisherman, player of the guitar and harmonica, lover of the outdoors, life-long member of the orgy-of-the-ologies club, all-around ne'er-do-well. Chaser of the crooked roads and the ancient ones.*